Lord James

By the same author:

LES DAMES DE BRIÈRES (t. 1), Albin Michel
  L'ÉTANG DU DIABLE (t. 2), Albin Michel
  LA FILLE DU FEU (t. 3), Albin Michel

LA BOURBONNAISE, Albin Michel

LE CRÉPUSCULE DES ROIS:
  LA ROSE D'ANJOU (t. 1), Albin Michel
  REINES DE CŒUR (t. 2), Albin Michel
  LES LIONNES D'ANGLETERRE (t. 3), Albin Michel

LE GARDIEN DU PHARE, Albin Michel

LE ROMAN D'ALIA, Albin Michel

LES ANNÉES TRIANON, Albin Michel

LE GRAND VIZIR DE LA NUIT, Gallimard

L'ÉPIPHANIE DES DIEUX, Gallimard

L'INFIDÈLE, Gallimard

LE JARDIN DES HENDERSONS, Gallimard

LA MARQUISE DES OMBRES, Olivier Orban

UN AMOUR FOU, Olivier Orban

ROMY, Olivier Orban

LA PISTE DES TURQUOISES, Flammarion

LA POINTE AUX TORTUES, Flammarion

LOLA, Plon

L'INITIÉ, Plon

L'ANGE NOIR, Plon

LE RIVAGE DES ADIEUX, Pygmalion

Lord James

CATHERINE HERMARY-VIEILLE

Luath Press Limited

EDINBURGH

www.luath.co.uk

FT

First published in French 2006
First published in English 2011

ISBN: 978-1-906817-54-1

The publisher acknowledges subsidy from

Scottish
Arts Council

towards the publication of this book.

The paper used in this book is sourced from renewable forestry
and is FSC credited material.

FSC	MIX Paper from responsible sources FSC® C018575

Printed and bound by
MPG Books Ltd., Cornwall

Typeset in 11pt Sabon by
3btype.com

To Sir Alastair and Lady Buchan-Hepburn who so spontaneously gave me their attention and benevolence during the writing of this book. With the expression of my deepest respect and loyal friendship.

And to the memory of James Hepburn, Earl of Bothwell.

Without any hesitation, I would give Scotland, France and England to follow you to the ends of the world in a white petticoat.

MARY STUART TO JAMES HEPBURN

Foreword

Lord James, written in French by Catherine Hermary-Vieille, was first published in Paris in January 2006 by the old and famous publishing house Albin Michel.

Its success was very much due to the author, who is recognised as a brilliant historian in her own right and who considers the Stuart Dynasty to be her favourite period in Scottish history, although her knowledge has a far wider span. She has also written extensively on the Tudors in English history, and in French history has firmly established herself as a leading authority on the 16th to 18th century period. She has lectured for the Quai d'Orsay in many countries, in universities, in hallowed academia, on television, radio, for many societies, and at special historical and literary events and gatherings. She is in great demand as an accomplished speaker on a wide range of subjects. The press, television and radio, and literary organisations frequently request her appearance when she launches a book, or at a special event to which her appearance would add distinction. In the context of her literary prowess and mastery of language and idiom, together with her extensive historical knowledge and detailed research, the media and literary establishment have praised her as a most outstanding author. She has enlightened and given pleasure to readers in seven countries, where her books are published in translation.

Recognising her contribution to literature, France some years ago awarded her the title of Chevalier de la Légion d'honneur, and also the rank of Officier des Arts et des Lettres.

We are now privileged to have her assent and that of her French publisher, Albin Michel, to have her book *Lord James* published in English by Luath Press of Edinburgh.

The reader of *Lord James* will gain unique insight from her research. She shows her intimate knowledge of James Hepburn, the fourth Earl of Bothwell when she describes his early life, his upbringing, his periods spent in France, and his service and loyalty to Marie de Guise when Regent. Ultimately, she reveals his absolute devotion to Mary Stuart Queen of Scots, whom he married, their tragic separation, and finally his cruel death.

Hermary-Vieille's profound knowledge, derived from family and historical archives of France, Scotland, Denmark and Sweden, has added greatly to her perception and understanding of this short but tempestuous period in Scottish and French history. Her detailed knowledge of France, its court life, and the leading families there and in Scotland, with whom Mary Stuart and Bothwell both associated, adds greatly to the interest and veracity of her descriptions, assessments and understanding, so brilliantly conveyed in her own writing and now reflected in the translation she personally has approved.

With her emotional but rational grasp of the actions, forces, disputes, loves, tragedies and evil endeavours, she depicts the successes and failures of leading figures in this period of history. She portrays the events that occurred in the countries where Bothwell lived as a child, student, courtier, soldier, husband of Mary Queen of Scots, for a short time ruler with her, and then finally as prisoner. In *Lord James* she demonstrates a deep knowledge and sensitive awareness of history and factual detail.

The reader will enjoy an evocative and exciting story, but one which accurately traces events. *Lord James* at last brings to parts of this period of Scottish history, all too often treated with repetitive biased similarity, new and intuitive opinions and assessments. Catherine Hermary-Vieille, with her own intelligent analysis, detailed and privileged research, and extensive historical knowledge, challenges some of the old concepts and opinions held. Her conclusions and perception as to where the truth lies surrounding the lives of Bothwell and Mary, from when they first met until their tragic parting at Carberry Hill and ultimately his death in Denmark, are vividly expressed with judgement and credible evidence. This she has gained from historical records and from her own visits to the countries and places, castles, prisons and other sites of significance where either Bothwell or Mary lived or visited.

The French national press and media gave Catherine Hermary-Vieille outstanding reviews and praise for her writing and for the historical portrayal and conclusions at which she arrived in her writing of *Lord James*.

To their praise I am happy and honoured to add my own, as a Hepburn, who is directly linked in ancestry to Lord James... otherwise known as James Hepburn, fourth Earl of Bothwell.

Sir Alastair Buchan-Hepburn, Baronet of Smeaton-Hepburn

I

Dragsholm, Denmark, 16 June 1573

IN ORDER TO FORESTALL any violence eight men escort Lord James to the fortress of Dragsholm. The fresh air galvanises the prisoner, who deprived of physical exercise for the past six years, is struggling even to cross the bridge spanning the moat to walk to the tower, starkly outlined like a rock against the blue sky. A short distance away, the sea shimmers softly in the sunlight and seagulls carried on wind currents soar above the gaily-coloured fishermen's boats.

James, his mind devoid of thoughts, stops on the narrow spiral staircase to catch his breath. Only the command uttered by the governor of the prison who came to meet him remains clear. 'Take the Earl to the pheasant room.' His knowledge of Danish is now sufficient to understand the gist of conversations, and those very words bring back to him memories of his former life and freedom, now sadly shrouded in the darkness of time.

James suddenly finds himself in front of a door and notices its heavy iron lock. Where and when had he seen the like before? Edinburgh Castle! He grits his teeth and again determines that he will try to escape.

He is pushed into a square room with narrow windows through which filters a feeble light revealing a bed, a table, a chair, bare walls and floor and a fireplace. The air is stale and polluted with the odour of faeces and mould.

'My Lord Bothwell is home!' shouts one of the soldiers.

The knowledge of who he is… James Hepburn, Earl of Bothwell, Duke of Orkney, Lord of Shetland, and consort of the Queen of Scots must all be repressed in his mind in order to survive and remain sane. James hears the key turn in the lock. He is quite alone and deprived of his last servant, who stayed behind in Malmö. He had given him his old velvet mules, and in parting the young Dane had kissed his hands saying 'May God protect you, my Lord.'

It seems God no longer has any interest in him.

James hesitantly explores his room. One of the windows overlooks a row of wooden cottages, which conceal the view of the moat and fortifications. On the left he can make out a stretch of the sea and to the right short thick grass with scattered fir trees. The hearth is empty and smells of soot. The mantelpiece is littered with dead and shrivelled flies. James picks one up between his thumb and forefinger and contemplates it at length. Will it now be only Death who sets him free?

He examines the walls and stops. There halfway up and faded with age he sees images of birds painted on the stonework, the reddish breast feathers and rounded eye of a pheasant can clearly be seen. The beating of his heart accelerates. He shivers with cold, but relives in his memory the sight of pheasants in the woods at Hailes, the expanse of moors beyond, the distant hills and the tranquil current of the Tyne flowing past Hailes to its source near Crichton. James shuts his eyes and once again sees the face of his mother, his sister Janet, and Mary, whose lips he kissed at Carberry in front of the traitors' army before parting from her forever. From that moment, he knows she is in the power of his enemies and he can no longer protect her. Savagely he smashes his fist against the wall, which brings back the pain of the old wound inflicted by Jock Elliot's sword, but far crueller to him is the unbearable misery of being unable to be at her side. Worse than his incarceration, hallucinations, and the prospect of a slow death is his inability to fight back against his enemies. Moray, Mary's half-brother, and Lennox, father of her second husband Darnley, have both already been assassinated, John Knox is dead, but other traitors are still alive and wielding power. In his frustration, James punches the walls again. He has no idea how long he has been giving vent to his rage, but a key turns in the lock and a harsh voice growls, 'My Lord, if you behave like a madman you will be taken to the pit.'

Yet James now hears nothing and sees nothing. Slowly the memory of Mary's radiant face and happy smile fades away.

2

Scotland, March 1546

'TRAITOR'S SON!'

The insult stung the young boy. Having slipped past the priest teaching him the rudiments of Latin, English, spelling and grammar, James had left the castle to hunt birds with his slingshot. A cold wind flattened the dry vegetation and whipped up froth where the current flowed round the rocks in the River Tyne. The sky was a uniform slate grey and faded into the horizon, beyond which lay the wild country of the Borders, notorious for the violence of its Reivers, which no Royal Lieutenant or any authority could tame.

'Traitor's son!' the youth repeated.

Standing a few steps away from James, who was both younger and shorter than him, he watched the reaction of the heir to the Earls of Bothwell.

'Bastard!' James blurted out as he stood and faced his opponent.

He felt nothing but contempt for his father, but would never allow his name to be dragged through the mud. Grasping each other the two boys rolled on the ground. James kicked and hit his adversary with feet and fists, then felt his hair being pulled, followed by a violent blow across his face, from which he tasted the salty tang of blood on his lips.

James was quickly on his feet again, his face now swollen and bruised, and he faced his adversary Bob Armstrong, who burst out laughing.

'You are a good fighter Hepburn, but you will never stop anyone here from thinking that your father the Earl of Bothwell is a coward.'

An apothecary urgently summoned to attend James at Hailes Castle applied a poultice of mixed herbs and sheep fat to the nose of his young patient.

'Please don't tell my mother,' pleaded James.

Since her divorce, Agnes Hepburn had been living with her daughter Janet at Morham not far from Edinburgh. Separated from them at the age of eight, the young boy stayed either at Hailes or at Crichton, in the company of a father whose time was taken up mostly with courting the Regent Marie de Guise, at the same time as he was betraying her.

'Your mother soon enough will see it for herself, my Lord – I fear your nose may stay broken.'

James remained silent, but the apothecary reassured him.

'Don't worry, women like to see the marks of a man's courage imprinted on his face. They say that François de Guise, the uncle of our little Queen Mary Stuart, has a scar on his cheek, and the ladies fight over his favours just the same.'

In the vast kitchen, the only warm room at Hailes, the servants, the steward and the old priest who had come to scold his pupil had all gathered round James.

'Broken nose or not you'll be popular with the girls, master James,' the cook commented.

The young boy did not care, but he was concerned at the thought of making his mother cry. Since their separation, he had not ceased rebelling against his father and his preceptor, nor from fighting with the boys in the neighbourhood. At Morham, Agnes Hepburn was worried. From time to time when Patrick, her former husband, requested Janet's presence, she would send her to Hailes, but the little girl, who harboured boundless admiration for her brother, would return to her mother in a vindictive and uncontrollable mood. Eventually it would be necessary to send James away to learn discipline and gain an education, making him worthy of the title and honours he would inherit on his father's death.

In the kitchen at Hailes, the old priest asked what other news there was.

The apothecary, who provided medical care over a large area stretching from Peebles to Haddington, reported items of news which he liked to distil one drop at a time so as better to relish his own importance.

In preparation for that evening's supper, half a dozen chickens and a quarter of mutton were roasting on the spit, and over another fire, a cauldron of soup was simmering. The apothecary thought to himself that if he lingered a little longer while narrating his stories, he might be invited to stay the night at the castle.

'No good news,' he declared in gloomy tones. 'Violence is still raging in the Borders, the English are increasing their attacks with pillage, arson, and cattle rustling, yet they still find allies amongst our own people.'

The cook crossed herself religiously.

'May God forgive them!'

The priest, on the point of mentioning how quick the nobility were to break their trust, decide to keep silent – for was it not true that the Earl of Bothwell, master of this castle, had once sought favour with the English? Now it was rumoured that he was attached to the Regent Marie de Guise, but his financial difficulties might well once more lead him to lend an attentive ear to the siren song of the English.

'The Douglases came back to us,' said the cleric with satisfaction. 'And after spending years in the service of the King of England, are now fighting against him.'

'The English plundered their Scottish estates,' noted the steward bluntly. 'And I believe Archibald Douglas's daughter married that traitor Matthew Lennox with Henry VIII's blessing?'

'Margaret Douglas is the English King's own niece,' the priest remarked. 'She is the daughter of his eldest sister Margaret, our late Queen and a good Catholic.'

The steward frowned. He had recently joined the ranks of those Christians who had rejected papist idolatry, and now secretly attended the preaching of the Calvinists. The arrest of the best among them, George Wishart, had outraged him even more, as the Earl of Bothwell himself had betrayed the saintly man's trust, thereby delivering him into the hands of that vermin Cardinal Beaton in St Andrews Castle.

'The Devil take those liars!' swore the cook.

'What's past is past, and it is to our little Queen that our thoughts must now turn. Despite all his efforts the King of England did not manage to secure her for his son the Prince of Wales, and now he never will.'

'Sooner or later the Regent will send Mary to France to place her under the protection of the Valois and the Guises,' asserted the priest.

The steward shrugged his shoulders. In England, their Queen would have become a confirmed Protestant. What use to the Scots was a puppet whose strings were pulled by Rome?

The night was pitch-black. Besides the crackling of the fire could be heard the barking of a few dogs, and the lowing of cattle brought into the byres built against the castle. Still seated on the kitchen table where the apothecary had placed him, James was deaf to the general conversation, as he mulled over in his mind thoughts hostile to his father. Why had he abandoned his family? Why was he ruining the family fortunes with his extravagance? Why had he betrayed George Wishart? Several times James himself had gone to listen to the old man. His gentleness, conviction, and the depth of his faith had moved him. During his last sermon, Wishart had blessed him, by placing his hands on his head. 'May God protect you Master James,' he had whispered. 'May He grant you the strength and courage to remain loyal to Him and never abandon those to whom one owes loyalty and obedience, which is a sin worse than death.'

Since the previous summer his father had forbidden him to cross the Lammermuir hills, and he missed the long rides over the moors. Too young to fight against the English, he was however mature enough to hate their violent border forays.

His preceptor's voice startled him.

In a severe tone, he said, 'This young man is going to come with me and copy out a hundred times: I will not fight like a common ruffian and above all not with an Armstrong boy.' He sighed. 'And most of the Armstrongs are likely to end up on the gallows!'

A few months earlier, the preceptor had helped one of the Earl's old retainers to set up a ministry near Liddesdale. Finding no church he had expressed his astonishment and received a reply, 'We have no priest here, just Armstrongs and Elliots.'

The serenity of the preacher George Wishart impressed the crowd who had come to witness his execution in the courtyard of St Andrews Castle. The wind was blowing from the north and lifting the last dead leaves, blackened by winter's incessant rain. Guards, together with a multitude of the Archbishop's servants were hurrying along the castle ramparts. Some of his former mistresses who had been lucky enough to be granted the favour of occupying a velvet-cushioned seat joined them. The prelate's current favourite Marion Ogilvy had excused herself, saying that human suffering was abhorrent to her. The arrival of the Cardinal was awaited.

The condemned man was enveloped in a long black cloak and his hands were tied. Motionless and with eyes half-closed, he prayed in a low voice, heedless of the multitude. Tapestries and brightly coloured embroidered silks adorned the castle windows, which overlooked the courtyard and the stake to which he was bound.

Suddenly the rolling sound of drums and clear notes of trumpets heralded the arrival of Beaton, who stepped majestically towards his seat beneath a canopy of crimson velvet. The Cardinal was satisfied that a heretic with dangerous charisma was about to be dispatched for the greater good of the Catholic community. He had seen already how Wishart had spread dissension in the south of the country through his preaching, which he believed to be the voice of the Devil, expressing himself with a false sincerity.

These preachers were a thorn in Beaton's side. In order to be free to fight alongside the Regent Marie de Guise and rescue the Scottish monarchy from the claws of the English, he needed to be rid of them. Money was scarce and traitors numerous. Whom could he count on? Gordon and Huntly in the North, Atholl, Fleming, even the Kerrs and Maxwells in the Borders... the lure of English gold might overcome the keenest devotion and most sensitive honour. Men like George Wishart or John Knox, another fanatic, were undermining Catholic authority and thereby that of the government. He must not allow himself to feel any compassion for them.

'Let the indictment be read,' he commanded in a loud voice.

The list of crimes imputed to Wishart impressed the audience: heresy, schism, sacrilege, incitement to rebel against civil and religious authorities, abuse of trust. Wishart never flinched. The words 'renegade', 'traitor', 'sorceror' seemed not to affect him. Standing bolt upright in the face of an icy wind, he seemed impatient to depart on his great journey as soon as silence prevailed. For a brief moment, his glance met the Cardinal's. 'May God forgive him,' thought the condemned man. He was ready to die for his faith.

Carrying leather pouches and wearing long cloaks of black cloth the two executioners approached the prisoner. In order to speed up the demise of the victim the Cardinal had authorised the placing of gunpowder under his armpits, which when exploding on contact with the flames would blow his body to pieces. Unhurriedly the executioners accomplished their task. Once the bags were in place, Wishart's arms were carefully bound from shoulder to wrist.

The wind lifted his grey beard and ruffled his flat straight hair. Beaton played distractedly with his rings. That very morning he had again received death threats. Most of this intimidation came from agents of Henry VIII who were well known to him: the Earl Marischal, Cassilis, Kirkaldy of Grange, and Leslie, a gang of traitors and ambitious trouble-makers. However, he had the support of the French, and their gold had enabled him to buy himself allies such as the Earls of Argyll and Bothwell, who had betrayed Wishart. Bothwell, 'The Fair Earl' as he was called, due to the delicacy of his features and the harmonious pro-portions of his body, had long been for sale to the highest bidder. Recently he had reaped the rewards, but for how long?

The condemned man was tied to the stake and the bundles of wood soaked in resin were about to be lit. Armed guards pointed their weapons towards the crowd, ready to tame any sedition fomented by the heretics who had come in their multitude to St Andrews to assist their pastor. Yet no one in the audience flinched.

The flames were already high and only the victim's shoulders and face could still be seen. Everyone stood with bated breath. In the midst of the blaze, with the gunpowder attached to his body ready to blow up at any moment, Wishart stared straight at Beaton and in a strong and compelling voice proclaimed, 'He who takes pleasure in my execution will soon be hanged on the very spot where he now stands.'

A moment later, there was the sound of an explosion and a cry of agony, then nothing more was heard except the crackling of flames, the sigh of the wind, and the melancholy cries of seagulls circling over the dungeon.

James pushed away the page on which he was copying a Latin declension. 'I hate Cardinal Beaton,' he declared furiously. 'I hope the Devil is waiting for him in Hell.'

Alarmed, the young boy's preceptor remained silent for a while. Was it possible that Calvinist perversion had penetrated this castle to thus trouble the mind of his pupil?

'No blasphemy James!' he ordered.

He was choked with emotion. That very night he would write to the Earl of Bothwell to inform him of the outrageous views expressed by his son.

'Is it Christian to burn one's brother alive?'

'Wishart had no brothers left,' replied the priest in a trembling voice, 'no friends left. His heresy had cut him off from the Christian community.' The hardness in James's gaze shocked him. Ordinarily courteous and anxious not to cause displeasure, the young boy stood before him with a vindictive light in his dark eyes.

'I despise my father for having given up an innocent man to Cardinal Beaton.'

'Be quiet!' intimated the old priest. 'Or I will have you flogged.'

He realized he would have to be ruthless, perhaps even send his pupil away from an area that had become too violent and troublesome. It was regrettable that at such a young age James had been exposed to the lawlessness of the Borders, the attacks of thieves and miscreants and the destruction by the English of the Abbeys of Melrose, Kelso and Jedburgh. Even if he disapproved of the son's remarks about his father, he still had to recognise that the Earl of Bothwell was not a good example to be followed. His extravagant spending was engendered by vanity, and on two occasions, his sensuality had compromised him in England and caused him to be banished him from Scotland. Alone at Morham the virtuous Lady Agnes was bringing up Janet to the best of her ability, anxious to turn a headstrong child into a woman. The Hepburns were by nature proud, stubborn, and self-willed, and James he feared would be no exception. However, the young boy was loyal and courageous, and his pride made him rely more on himself than on the favours of others. If he were to be sent far from Hailes and Crichton, he would miss him.

James kept his head high in a defiant mood.

'Go to your room,' ordered the old priest, 'and read a few passages from the gospel. I will send for you at supper time.'

The Earl of Bothwell's reply to the preceptor's letter arrived three days later. James was to leave immediately to go to his great-uncle Patrick Hepburn, Bishop of Moray, who resided at Spynie Palace near Elgin on the northern coast of the Earldom of Moray. Learned and good-natured, he wrote, my relative will give James the basis of a good education, and as he grows into adolescence James will find at Spynie a family atmosphere and discipline which I am not in a position to provide.

'Good heavens!' murmured the old priest after he finished reading the letter. He was distressed. Admittedly, the Bishop was reputed to be learned and jovial, but did he not have a string of mistresses and had he not fathered six bastards? To entrust a young boy to such a licentious man was folly. He would write again to the Earl to warn him. Like all his ancestors, his pupil was likely to be of a sensual nature, which needed to be sternly disciplined. What kind of example would he see at Spynie?

3

AT FIRST RESISTING his father's decision to send him away from the family estates, James mounted his horse, a stocky thick-coated animal, and rode all the way to Crichton, galloping most of the way along paths he knew well. Patches of dappled spring sunlight flowed across meadows and moorland and brightened the distant Lammermuir hills.

Flocks of migrating geese were flying in formation across a sparsely cloud-scattered sky. Here and there could be seen columns of smoke, rising from holes cut in the centre of the roofs of peasants' bothies. The moorland tracks of sheep and cattle were familiar to the young boy. He filled his lungs with the scents of spring and of the moorland he loved. He felt free and happy, all resentment and frustration cast aside.

The great mass of the castle built on a hill stood out against the horizon. Crichton was his father's favourite home. Larger and better equipped than Hailes, the vast building dominated the valleys and bogs of the upper reaches of the Tyne, where by night could be heard the screeches, croaks and rustlings of its nocturnal wildlife. At Crichton, Lord Patrick had some fine antique pieces and artefacts that he had brought back from his first exile in Italy; opalescent glasses, busts of gods and goddesses, ancient goblets carved from alabaster and pottery urns on which could be seen traces of bacchanalian scenes.

Leaving Crichton had saddened him. When would be the next time he would see the postern gate and large inner courtyard with the kitchen, two storerooms, well, and enormous reception hall, where as small children he and Janet had loved to play? Spiral staircases led to private rooms, to wooden galleries running along the sides of the walls, and to lookout turrets set with loopholes.

Only a few days after young James Hepburn arrived at Spynie in the Earldom of Moray, the whole diocese was thrown into turmoil. News had just reached them that Cardinal Beaton had been brutally stabbed to death in the middle of the night in St Andrews Castle. While his terrified concubine had fled half-naked, the prelate's blood-spattered body had been dragged to one of the windows overlooking the outer gallery and hung by one foot like a pig freshly bled. The castle had been evacuated immediately, and the murderers, James Kirkaldy of Grange together with his son, Norman Leslie, the Earl Marshall Lord Cassilis and Sir James Melville, all of whom were in league with England, had then occupied it.

A preacher called John Knox, who was a fervent disciple of Calvin, was gaining in popularity and he eagerly spread amongst his flock the news of Beaton's death. Simultaneously the Earl of Lennox whose wife was a niece of Henry VIII, seized Dumbarton Castle, strategically situated on the west coast at the mouth of the River Leven. 'Cardinal Beaton was a good prelate and a great statesman,' the Bishop of Moray sighed with regret. 'Such ordeals suffered by our poor country! Will the Regent Lord Hamilton ever be able to replace such a zealous servant?'

'They say the Queen Dowager bore the Cardinal a very special affection,' insinuated William, a strong lad of some twenty years, who was the eldest of the Bishop's illegitimate children.

The prelate shrugged his shoulders. He had long since made a decision to ignore all gossip and slander.

James listened in silence without condoning the murder, but he was delighted that Beaton had paid for his crime. How could such corrupt men judge a man like Wishart? Philosophically, his great-uncle explained the threat Calvinism represented for Scotland, not only with regard to the Catholic faith, but also to the entire social order. If some noblemen now no longer obeyed the Regent, then the future was bleak. Their Queen little Mary Stuart was not yet four years old and a civil war in Scotland could place her in great danger.

Glorious spring sunlight flooded into the room where the Bishop took his meals surrounded by his chaplains, three of his illegitimate children, James and his preceptors. He intended to provide his children and his great-nephew too with the basis of an excellent education.

Since James was heir to the Earls of Bothwell and offspring of a family counted amongst the noblest in Scotland, he would be sent to Paris as soon as he turned sixteen in order to complete his studies and acquire the courtly manners and bearing of French aristocrats. The Bishop could see immediately that James was gifted with a bright intellect and a strong will. However, he was also quick-tempered, proud, and at times even reckless. Ever since his arrival at Spynie, the boy had kept his distance from his cousins. On several occasions, they had complained of being scorned by the new boy, who seemed to have a grandiose opinion of himself, despite the fact that his father had brought discredit upon the whole family. The Bishop had to act as mediator, as he wished the Hepburns to stay united. Only solidarity among members of the same family would guarantee the future during the very difficult times the country was enduring.

Every morning the boys studied their books. In the afternoons they would ride, train at arms, and occupy their time practising tennis, golf and archery. Already an accomplished rider, James regularly out rode his cousins. He loved to experience the same solitude he had enjoyed around Hailes and Crichton. He missed the familiarity of his own country-side, and he missed his mother and sister, but knew how to hide his sadness by maintaining an inscrutable expression from which his illegitimate cousins could discern nothing. He felt drawn to the seashore near Spynie, where pastures stretched for miles alongside the beach. Flocks of grazing sheep scattered as he passed and in the distance he could hear dogs barking. Riding alone into the wind, he let his imagination run wild. Once he was a grown man he would become everything his father was not and would restore the good name of the Hepburns. Neither Marie de Guise nor the Regent Lord Hamilton could rely on any of the nobles... each one was a potential traitor and James did not know whom he hated most, the English who bought them, or the Scots who let themselves be bought.

Once he reached the shore, he would launch his horse into a full gallop. The sea air invigorated him and he felt stronger and protected from those emotions which all too often overwhelmed him. At nightfall he would return, exhausted and soaked through with sweat and foam. His great-uncle asked him no questions; he undoubtedly loved him, but without telling him so, and James returned his affection. The youngest of his family, his great-uncle although lacking a religious vocation, had coped as best he could with reconciling his faith and his naturally sensual nature.

Each morning before lessons, all the castle's occupants would listen to Mass celebrated by the Bishop. James recited the prayers and hastily mimed the ritual gestures, but he knew his heart no longer belonged to the Catholic Church.

James revealed his convictions in his letters to his sister. In his mind, he saw her slender figure, her long unkempt auburn hair and sweet face with those large eyes showing a hint of rebelliousness. The young girl caused endless trouble to her mother, who sometimes begged James to send his sister a letter of reproof. However, he could never bring himself to write the stern words expected of him. To him Janet was an elf or a fairy, destined to marry a prince and live in a tower lost in the midst of the moors. He would always protect her.

At the end of the year, it was reported that the occupants of St Andrews Castle, the 'Castillians' as they became known, had offered to hand themselves over to the Regent in exchange for a pardon. Hamilton had refused their request and the situation was at a stalemate. Neither faction was sufficiently organised nor well enough armed to mount an attack on the fortress. Unless the French attacked first the English would be certain to intervene. The Bishop continually talked about the possible landing of a French army sent by François I to assist Scotland, his old ally. Henry VIII was now ailing, and if he were to die his son, ten-year-old Edward, would succeed him and his Seymour uncles would seize power. Would they continue the old lion's aggressive policy towards Scotland? Their forceful Protestantism threatened to destabilise their northern neighbour even more by encouraging sedition against the Queen Mother and her French allies. This disturbing news greatly troubled the cheerful Bishop, and the Christmas festivities at Spynie were not as merry as usual. James, who had hoped to join his mother and sister at Morham, was not allowed to do so. Turned into a quagmire by the heavy winter rains the roads had become dangerous and impassable. 'Next summer you will be able to return to the Lothians,' his uncle had promised him.

The landing of French soldiers at Leith in late spring made the political situation even more perilous. Henry VIII was now dead, followed to the grave only a few months later by François I, but their successors proved to be even more belligerent. The Guises had great influence over the new King of France, Henri II, and wanted to hasten to their sister's rescue. The French seized St Andrews Castle, captured and deported the occupants, and sent John Knox who had joined the rebels, to row as a slave in the galleys. Peace seemed at last to have returned.

'I have sad news for you, my son.'

The bishop, trying to spare the boy's feelings, did not know what words to choose. Ashen faced, James listened with apprehension. He was thinking fearfully about his mother, about Janet, and his friends at Hailes and Crichton. New outbreaks of violence in the country prohibited him from travelling and he had remained at Spynie with a heavy heart.

'It's to do with your father.'

As he was speaking, Bishop Hepburn swallowed hard.

'He has been imprisoned again.'

James, feeling a familiar rage rising within him demanded, 'For what reason?'

'By ill fortune his letters to the Governor of Berwick have been intercepted.'

'What? Has he been begging for English money again?' James exclaimed.

'I do not know, my child.'

The distress he saw on his great-nephew's face saddened the Bishop. Over the months, he had become fond of the boy. He showed enthusiasm for those subjects he enjoyed such as mathematics, French, ancient history, and in particular horse training, while remaining impervious to religious education. However the good Bishop did not harass him. He allowed himself great liberties, so did not feel he had the right to lecture others. Women were his soft spot and he could not see an attractive womanly figure or a pretty face without hoping to seduce and possess. This year yet again, despite all his precautions, another child had been born. He would warn his nephew when he became a man and caution him. Although not as handsome as his father, James would certainly grow into a man attractive to women. The Bishop could see that such a man, with those sensual lips, that broken nose and that compelling gaze, sometimes direct and challenging, could not fail to seduce. He well knew that like all Hepburns, when the time came he would not hold back.

'Do not talk to me any more about my father,' James said coldly.

'You owe him respect and obedience,' the Bishop said firmly.

'Obedience perhaps,' James acknowledged.

'A son should never judge his father,' the Bishop insisted. 'Be aware my child that no one in Scotland is safe from criticism these days. In order to survive we must all learn to swim in troubled waters. On the one hand we have the pro-English Protestants and on the other the Catholics allied with France...'

'The Scots have a government,' interrupted James. 'That is whom they must obey.'

'Hamilton is weak,' the Bishop said with regret. 'The Queen Mother's supporters are incapable of agreeing with each other, traitors abound and honest folk remain cautious. Before long, you will see the English army launch a counter-attack against the French. How will we stop them?'

'By fighting them,' James unhesitatingly replied.

The Bishop struggled to suppress a smile. At eleven years old, James already saw himself as a righter of wrongs. Unfortunately, life would teach him some hard lessons.

On the tenth of September, between the sea and the River Esk, the English crushed the Scottish army at Pinkie. Five thousand men were reported dead and fifteen hundred taken prisoner.

The new Duke of Somerset, the eldest of the Seymours, was now in control of the country's key garrisons. There was no cohesion left amongst the Scots and it seemed the whole of society was crumbling. In accordance with Calvin's demands, from now on the prayer books, and Old and New Testaments, would be written and distributed in the English language. The English claimed they had not invaded Scotland as enemies but as liberators.

Spynie and its surroundings remained peaceful. James had celebrated his twelfth birthday, and to earn a little money he had bought several young horses. After breaking in and training them he had resold them at a good profit. Gradually he was getting used to a life of loneliness. Between the responsibilities of his diocese and attention to his mistresses, his great-uncle had little time for James. His cousins were perpetually jealous and never missed an opportunity to ill-treat him. Being a legitimate child he would on the death of his father become Earl of Bothwell, High Admiral of Scotland, Lord of Hailes and Crichton, and would be accepted at court, whilst they being illegitimate and without fortune would lead a mundane and undistinguished life in the Earldom of Moray.

4

Taken by surprise, the servant drops the tray on which there was a bowl of soup, a piece of boiled beef, a couple of smoked herrings and a loaf of bread. He neither saw nor heard the prisoner who pounced on him. Since dawn, James has been working away at the bars of one of the windows. His nails and hands are bleeding and by hammering at the walls with his fists the self-inflicted wounds have reopened. During the night, his mind has been haunted by unbearable images, acute, heartrending, and murderous: Mary's face at Carberry Hill, covered in dust and tears; the face of Moray, the Queen's illegitimate half-brother, whom he would have liked to crush to death; his sister Janet's radiant smile on her wedding day. Today Mary is a prisoner in England, Moray has been assassinated, and Janet has remarried. He wants to travel back in time, escape from this prison and be free...

The Danish servant's lips split open under James' fists. Rolled up in a ball on the floor yelling, he is trying to avoid kicks that bruise his sides. Three guards suddenly appear. James feels a cold gun barrel pressed against his temple and strong arms brutally overpowering him. He is winded. They are twisting his wrists and tying his hands. Where is he, and why is he being manhandled? Standing in front of him the governor of Dragsholm, Francis Lauridson spits out angry words at him. No matter whether they be Dukes or servants, he knows how to bring raving lunatics to heel. The instructions that came from Malmö were that he was free to decide on the means of subduing his prisoner. Now his mind is made up; it is to be the pit, the dungeon. There is nothing like darkness and silence to tame a wild beast.

James is dragged down the stairs of the tower to the ground floor.

To make him walk faster the guards are kicking him and hitting him in the back. His thoughts are confused. What do they want, where are they taking him? His fit of rage subsided, he now feels dreadfully weary.

The open trap door reveals a ladder, and a dark hole, which gives off a nauseating stench of mould. With his bindings severed James descends the rungs one step at a time, one guard before him and one behind; the governor and the rest of the men watch him from above. Then he feels himself pushed, falls onto his knees, hears the sound of the ladder being removed and the opening sealed. A thin ray of light filters through the bars of the trap door. James can just make out a straw mattress and an iron bucket.

How long has he been curled up on this wretched mattress? A terrible anxiety torments him. They are going to let him perish in this hole; never again will he see daylight nor hear the sound of human voices. He is well acquainted with these dungeons; there is one at Crichton, one at Dunbar, and one at Hermitage. They throw dangerous criminals into them until the date of their trial. Yet during the six years he has been the Danish King's prisoner no legal proceedings have been instituted against him. No magistrate has heard his plea, and in France, neither King Charles ix nor the Guises have answered his appeals. Those of his friends who have escaped execution are lying low. From the floor of the dungeon, he hears the sliding of a plank.

'Your meal, my Lord,' someone jeers at him.

He jumps to his feet. Could there be a door, through which he could escape? Feeling his way he reaches the wall. On a board secured to the front of an opening, someone has left a jug of water, a chunk of bread, and a slice of cheese. James remembers that underground dungeons are often double. Like a rabid dog, he has to be fed from the adjacent cell.

No light filters through the trap door. His mouth is dry and icy sweat trickles down his back and dampens his palms. When he wants to take a drink, he is incapable of finding the jug in the dark and returns to lie down. A rumbling sound awakens him. A group of riders is approaching; is it his friends from the Borders, the patrol and the Reivers united in order to rescue him? He sees them galloping at full speed. The horses' hooves are pounding against the hard ground and water splashes up from the streams, sparkling momentarily as they pass on their way. He recognizes Johnnie and Bob, Will and Tom, the Maxwells, Nixons,

Armstrongs, Elliots, and Croziers. He trembles with fever and excitement. Will they find him in the middle of the night? He calls out to them, but the riders continue on their way; he sees the steel helmets and horses' rumps disappearing into the distance. He cries out and a Reiver turns round, but beneath the helmet, there is no face.

5

Spring 1551

'GOD BLESS YOU MY CHILD! If ever you need me I will always be here to welcome you.'

James hugged his great-uncle. Six years earlier, he had arrived at Spynie as a little boy and he was now departing as a grown young man. Over time, he had learned to curb his spiteful outbursts, and the previous summer had even been reunited with his father without experiencing any feelings of displeasure. Together they had discussed his forthcoming trip to France. Patrick Hepburn had promised him reasonable financial help and had given his son the names of Scottish nobles who lived at the court of Henri II as part of the entourage of their young Queen. She was now betrothed to the Dauphin François, and Marie de Guise herself was about to cross the sea to France, to spend a few months at the side of her only daughter, and to visit many members of her extended family.

The French, eager to have the chief of the Hamiltons as an ally, had created him Duke of Châtelherault, with an annual income of twelve thousand pounds. Châtelherault himself was still at the helm of the Regency, but it was commonly known that the Queen Mother was determined to become Regent herself.

The prospect of his journey and of a stay in France which could last four years, the time necessary to obtain a bachelor's degree, had greatly occupied James's last months at Spynie. His great uncle's generosity had enabled him to gather together suitable clothes, and his mother, by using some of her own resources, had managed to complete his wardrobe. Added to this were a few books, some toiletries and a writing case, and all his belongings were in three locked trunks, soon to be loaded aboard a ship bound for Saint-Malo.

James held out a frosty hand to his cousins, and kissed the maid-servants, all of whom had fallen under his charm. Neither old nor young had spared themselves the trouble to please him, but although James was naturally attracted to women, he had held on to his innocence. The example set by his uncle, surrounded by numerous bastard children, did not appeal to him. His uncle had revealed to him in veiled terms the safest way to avoid making a mistress pregnant. In response to his nephew's sarcastic laughter, he had merely given him a mischievous look.

'If I had not taken this advice myself, my son, it is not eight children I would have depending on me now but forty. Chastity is a godsend for some but it is not in the nature of the Hepburns and one must accept this fact with humility.'

As soon as he landed in France James hired a young Breton who wished to go to Paris. He acquired two dappled geldings of nondescript breeding, and arranged for his trunks to be loaded onto the cart with the other passengers' baggage. In Paris, one of his father's friends had booked two rooms for him within the perimeter of the university.

'We are here, my Lord!' exclaimed François the young Breton. The scene viewed by the two riders was of streets of closely built houses, with the spires of parish churches rising up above the River Seine. In the distance, they could just make out the towers of Notre Dame.

The city was teeming with activity and the two young men struggled to push their way through the crowds thronging the many market stalls. They were met by a cacophony of sounds, with friends and families meeting, sellers calling their wares, and animals and children weaving their way amongst the populace who had come to do their shopping. Those on horseback waited patiently, while nobles ordered their servants to clear a way for them. When they reached the Pont-Neuf, they were surprised to find no view of the river, as the four-storied houses on it formed a solid wall. The riverbank they had been advised to follow led to Saint-André des Arts and to the convent of the Grand-Augustins, a dependency of the University of Paris. It was nightfall before they arrived, having lost their way many times.

James was impatient to see his lodgings. In front of the Petit-Pont rose the Rue Saint-Jaques. The young man gave a quick glance at the map given him by his great-uncle. To the left should be the Rue de la Bûcherie, where his accommodation was in the grounds of the university.

Within the space of a few days, James had thoroughly explored his neighbourhood, made friends with other students, and matriculated at the College of Reims. A place had been reserved for him there on the recommendation of Renée de Guise, a sister of the Queen Dowager of Scotland and Abbess of Saint-Pierre des Dames de Reims. He was to study Latin, mathematics, rhetoric and ancient history. A courier from Scotland brought a letter from his mother, telling him that in the absence of Marie de Guise the country remained peaceful, but that due to frequent forced recruitment and constant requisitioning for supplies the French troops were becoming very unpopular. In order to prevent the rise of Calvinism the Church was initiating reforms and starting to print prayer books and bibles in the Scottish tongue. However, admitted Lady Agnes, nothing seemed able to hold back the success currently enjoyed by the preachers of the Reformation. Just as her brother had done, Janet was now also turning to them. Catholicism seemed to be defended only by the elderly, and a few noble families who tended to be isolated on their estates.

'Your father is once again exiled in England,' noted the Lady of Morham at the end of her letter.

With legs outstretched and his face turned towards the sun, James stuffed the letter into a pocket of his breeches. It was a hot summer day and the narrow streets were stinking. Despite all its filth, its numerous thieves and swindlers, the arrogance of its grands seigneurs and all its eccentricities and vices, Paris remained an entrancing city.

One afternoon as he wandered around the Place de Grève, James Hepburn caught sight of his young Queen accompanied by two of her Guise uncles, François the war hero adulated by the crowds, and Charles Cardinal de Lorraine. Tall for her nine years, slim and charming, Mary was dressed in an emerald green riding dress and smiled happily at passers-by. 'Long live the little Queen! Long live our Mary!' they cheered. The young man approached as close as he could to the royal retinue but the little girl never once glanced in his direction.

Fair-haired young Alexander Murray had pale blue eyes and a sunburnt nose. Beneath the shade of a sycamore tree near the Royal College, the two young men were drinking chilled wine served in stoneware pitchers. Professors wearing black gowns, clerics and students came and went. Wagons were collecting refuse left outside houses and women and street urchins busied themselves filling buckets at the communal well.

'Without the French Scotland would be ungovernable,' maintained Alexander. 'The heads of our noble families are constantly plotting, envying each other and coveting each others' possessions. Is it not true your father tried to gain the hand of one of the Tudor princesses, either Mary the religious bigot or the young Elizabeth, in exchange for Hermitage Castle?'

'Let us talk about something else,' interrupted James.

The thought that his father had considered even for one instant handing over Hermitage to the English outraged him. This formidable fortress stood on a wild riverbank in the midst of the moors within reach of the English border, and no other place stirred his emotions more deeply. Once he became Earl of Bothwell, he would become its owner. Alexander swallowed a large gulp of claret. In a few months' time, he would be going back to Scotland and his family castle. There nothing would have changed, while in Paris it seemed as though events and people were caught up in a whirlwind.

'The Earl of Bothwell's ideals are actually not so different from those of his peers: a regular income and a profitable alliance. What are yours?' asked Alexander.

'Mine are obedience to the monarch and a clear conscience. If you find this a little strange, it is because I am more of a conservative than you realise.'

'I know all your weaknesses,' mocked Alexander, 'horses, women, military strategy, good wine...'

'Don't forget Scotland,' James responded with feeling. 'I shall never stop fighting to keep my country independent from England. Seymour's proposal to unite the two countries is a farce. The big fish always swallows the smaller one.'

'Since Elizabeth is considered illegitimate by the Catholics, the Guises could well fancy our little Queen on the English throne if her sister Mary Tudor were to die without an heir,' countered Alexander.

'I hope our Queen will forget this folly. She is a Catholic and Scotland will give her more than enough to contend with,' James commented.

Large clouds were now banking up, harbingers of a storm to come. James signalled to the maidservant and in vain searched the pockets of his doublet.

'I see,' sighed Murray, 'the heir of the powerful Hepburns is yet again destitute. Once more, the humble Murrays are going to be called to the rescue. On what do you squander the funds provided by your father?'

'Women,' James said with a sigh.

Warm raindrops started to fall, and were dripping off the already yellowing sycamore leaves. The damp dust beneath the trees gave off a pungent smell. Dogs ran for cover, their tails between their legs, and a horse whinnied loudly as it pulled a heavy cart loaded high with barrels.

In late autumn, Marie de Guise had to take leave of her daughter to return to Scotland. Edward VI coughed and was feverish, and England was in a state of unrest. If their young King were to die, Mary Tudor would succeed to the English throne and she would show no mercy towards those who had previously humiliated her. Faced with numerous enemies Edward Seymour Duke of Somerset, uncle of the King and English Regent, had been arrested for high treason. Anxiously James followed the news that came from across the Channel.

A diligent student, he now also had a thorough knowledge of the wealthy districts of Paris, which consisted of tall ornate houses with mullioned windows, adorned with capitals, pediments, and pilasters, their carvings of nymphs and fauns inspired by mythology. He was familiar too with the maze of narrow commercial alleys, their reeking network sheltering tanners, metal welders, fat dissolvers, leather dressers, slaughterers and flayers, who set themselves up close to murky waterways. At nightfall weak lanterns lit up the statues of virgins or saints erected near the clusters of thatched dwellings, which housed the large families of the poor.

When he had free time, James liked to go with a few friends to watch the construction work on the Louvre, led by Pierre Lescot. Stone by stone the feudal castle was disappearing and the splendour of the building now being erected dazzled the two young men. Four caryatids were commissioned from Jean Goujon for the great hall at a vast expense, which revealed the opulence of the French Treasury.

James had made a few friends amongst the Lutherans and Calvinists who frequented the university. The Reformation was reaching some 'grands seigneurs' and intellectuals, but the lower classes remained Catholic, hostile to the secret meetings of the Huguenots and outraged by the nocturnal defacement of religious statues. King Henri II kept a firm grasp over the reins of government and there was no question of sedition as in Scotland. At the Pourceaux market outside the city walls, a poor wretch who had been preaching from a Lutheran book in villages in Normandy was burnt alive for heresy. Unlike the death of George Wishart in St Andrews, this execution had not aroused the slightest public reaction. The university was restless, but criticism of the government and bold political ideology were discussed only in taverns over a pitcher of wine rather than in public.

In December 1552, the Scottish nobles who lived in Paris were invited to celebrate the tenth birthday of their Queen, Mary Stuart. The wretched appearance of his horse, together with his lack of resources to buy clothes fit for court and the boorishness of his servant who was incapable of being trained as a page, forced James to stay away from the festivities. Mary had made a brief appearance and with the grace of an accomplished sovereign had addressed a few kindly words to each of them. Despite her young age, she had developed perfect self-confidence combined with great charm, a proud bearing and delightful spontaneity. James heard Alexander's account with a sense of frustration. The young Queen had listened attentively to his impressions as a student and when he mentioned his friend, she had expressed surprise, saying, 'And is the son of the Earl of Bothwell not among us then? In the letters she sends me my mother often speaks of his family.' Taken off guard Alexander had answered that James was ill and had taken to his bed. She had nodded as if saddened by the news and had then walked away laughing, holding the arm of the youngest of her five uncles, the Marquis d'Elbeuf.

'The Guises are watching her closely,' Alexander explained, 'especially the Cardinal, who through his niece is harbouring great ambitions. François the Dauphin is sensitive and shy. The Guises will exert absolute control over him, which causes concern to Queen Catherine de Medicis. Under her soft exterior that woman conceals an iron will.'

James questioned his friend about the Duchesse de Valentinois. The sublime Diane de Poitiers had not taken part in the festivities. It was said she was piqued over the attention bestowed by her royal lover on the spirited Lady Fleming, Mary's Scottish governess and mother of one of her four ladies-in-waiting. At fifty-three years of age, Diane de Poitiers was adored by the King, who was nineteen years younger. In all his palaces, he had combined his initials with hers, and wore only her colours of black and white. Diane, discreet and self-effacing, took great care of the children's education and paid little attention to Catherine de Medicis. Walking one day between the Louvre and the Château des Tournelles, James had caught sight of Diane, elegantly mounted on a snow-white mare. Her mature radiance and the refinement she showed in her clothing and jewellery fascinated him. That is a woman I could love, he thought to himself. His casual conquests suddenly seemed insignificant.

6

1554–1555

ON THE DEATH OF the young King of England, Edward VI, and the accession to the throne of Mary Tudor, the only daughter of Catherine of Aragon, Catholicism was triumphant in England. In Edinburgh, Hamilton, who had been handsomely rewarded, had agreed to renounce the Regency with the promise that he would inherit the crown, should Mary Stuart, the little Queen, die without issue. Marie de Guise had seized power. In favour of appeasement, the new Regent tolerated the sermons of preachers like Willock, Harlaw and above all John Knox, recently returned from the French galleys, whose harsh and accusing language so inflamed his followers. Noblemen such as John Erskine, William Maitland, and the powerful Earl of Argyll were all in open opposition to the Catholic Church. The Regent was satisfied with the marriage of the Queen of England to King Philip II of Spain but what mattered above all to her was to establish a French presence in Scotland.

In France, whether in Paris or at Fontainbleau, new offspring arrived each year to enlarge the royal family, and although still circumspect Catherine de Medicis was in the ascendant. She was now more often to be seen by King Henri II's side, and at court people became more friendly towards her. Cheerful, a good rider and indefatigable in the chase, the Italian lived surrounded by astrologists and magi. Behind the scenes, she was weaving a network of loyalists, often Protestants. Like the Queen, they were enemies of the arrogant and ultra-Catholic Guise clan, who controlled the young Queen of Scots and her sickly fiancé the Dauphin of France. Tall like her uncles, a charmer, and accustomed to having her every wish granted, Mary Stuart spoke in the Scottish language only with the four ladies-in-waiting who had accompanied her from Scotland: Mary Fleming, Mary Beaton, Mary Seton and Mary Livingstone, and she called

France 'son cher pays'. To the Scots she was nothing but a phantom sovereign and a spoilt child who would never consent to reside on her native soil. If the Regent were to die, all eyes would be fixed on her half-brother James, a staunch Protestant. Illegitimate son of James v and Margaret Erskine, this young man was gifted with a lively intelligence and inordinate ambition, together with political finesse, a quality entirely lacking in the Hamiltons, the closest relatives of the Stuarts.

In the summer of 1555, James Hepburn celebrated his twentieth birthday in Paris. Having gained his bachelor's degree he intended to return to Scotland to put himself at the Regent's service. Forgiven yet again by Marie de Guise, his father was appointed Lieutenant of the East Marches. He had returned to Crichton only to discover that all his courtly clothing and jewels had been stolen. Now destitute, 'The Fair Earl' was becoming embittered and blaming everyone but himself for his misfortunes. He now devoted himself to finding marriage prospects for Janet, who in turn begged her brother to intervene in her favour. The titled or wealthy old men her father was considering horrified her. James often thought about his sister. Was she still the tomboy he had left behind three years earlier? Whenever his finances permitted, he would send her a bauble or some fashionable trifle. On the streets of Saint-Denis, la Tabletterie, and la Heaumière the shops displayed embroidered handkerchiefs, fans, gemstone-studded purses, feathers and silk stockings, while jewellers had established themselves on either side of the Pont au Change.

Having dismissed his Breton retainer James had taken on a more resourceful Parisian, who with his velvet hat and colourful doublet could well pass for a page. At the horse market, the young Scot had managed to exchange his earlier mount for an aged but better-bred white-stockinged mare. He had acquired the crafty ways of many impoverished Parisian noblemen, living comfortably on credit as long as it lasted. To his successive mistresses, all of modest means, he remained elusive.

During their fourth year, the Reims College students were granted a certain amount of freedom, which James took advantage of to explore Paris. He had become acquainted with some fellow Scots, mostly exiled Protestants, who never lost an opportunity to criticise the Regent. In their opinion, as with Archbishop Beaton, Marie de Guise would have to be got rid of at some stage. The second object of hate in this little group was the Queen of England, Mary Tudor. Tormented by nervous disorders stemming from her terrible childhood, overly in love with her uncaring husband and a fanatical Catholic, this wretched woman was the target of student sarcasm. The ridicule cast upon her by her phantom pregnancy had so delighted her enemies that even six months later they were still laughing about it.

In England, priests were mocked and ill-treated and in Kent peoples' ears and noses had been cut off. Mary Tudor had retaliated harshly. John Hooper Bishop of Worcester, who remained loyal to the Anglican faith was burnt alive in London, together with several other clerics. Hooper's horrifying and interminable agony had appalled the crowd, who now saw him as a martyr. Everywhere people whispered that King Philip of Spain, with the consent of his wife, was plotting a Protestant 'auto-da-fé'.

In December a party was held at the Louvre to celebrate Mary Stuart's thirteenth birthday, and James was invited to attend. He bought on credit a doublet of iridescent taffeta, breeches of grey silk, and a shirt with a frilled lace-hemmed collar. He was also able to find decent second-hand harness for the horses and an authentic outfit for his page. As it turned out the young Queen of Scots was unwell and never made an appearance, and the Dauphin sullenly greeted a few people but soon made his departure. Catherine de Medicis, who felt no sympathy for her prospective daughter-in-law remained out of sight, and the King was in Fontainbleau with Diane de Poitiers. James could hardly conceal his disappointment. He was tired of Parisian life and for better or worse had decided to return to Scotland before the end of summer.

My child,

Your father is gravely ill, and would surely be pleased to see you again. At forty-three years old, he is worn out by misfortune. He has made us all suffer greatly, and I pray each day for the salvation of his soul.

Sail for Scotland as soon as possible, and go straight to Dumfries, where he has taken to his bed. Your sister Janet refuses to go. She is outraged by the commitment your father has made to marry her without her consent to Robert Lander, a man of a certain age to whom he is indebted.

May God bless you, my son. The joy of seeing you again will be a

*consolation for the trials afflicting the Hepburns, to whom I
remain joined through my children.*

Your mother, Agnes Sinclair, Lady of Morham.

Three days later James had sold off most of his possessions, persuaded
his servant to follow him, obtained safe conducts for both of them, and
set off for Dunkirk. From there they would easily find a ship bound for
Edinburgh. The imminent death of his father affected him more than he
would have believed possible. Past images came back to him. As a child
at Crichton, he remembered riding alongside his father, who would tell
him the names of birds that flew away in front of them, the names of
tracks, of lookout sites, and of woods. He knew by heart the links uniting the various branches of the Hepburns, those of Smeaton, Monkrigg,
Waughton, and Athelstane, all closely knit to the Hepburns of Hailes.
His father was the head of this large family. One day it would be James's
turn to bear this honour and exalt the dignity of their name. Orphaned
in early childhood and adored by women, Patrick had spent his whole
life in a state of self-delusion. Even when back in favour and appointed
Lieutenant of the Marches, he had maintained an air of blind conceit,
which had closed to him the hearts of those who lived in that wild fron-
tier region. How could the Elliots or the Armstrongs respect this elegant
and superficial man with his courtly manners?

Off the coast of Suffolk, the sea was becoming rough. The humiliating fact
was that he who would succeed to the title of High Admiral of Scotland
was prone to seasickness. James was powerless against this affliction, and
he brooded on the many harsh realities to which he would have to adapt.
More than anything, he would suffer from lack of money. His father had
mortgaged a great part of his lands and had neglected the proper main-
tenance of Hailes and Crichton. Of the family jewels, there was nothing
left. He who dreamed of action would have to immerse himself in paper-
work and dismal account books. Afterwards he would offer his services
to Marie de Guise. Under her protection, he hoped to be able to put his
knowledge of military science to good use fighting the English. Perhaps she
would confer on him the title of Lieutenant of the Marches or Captain
of Hermitage Castle. He found it hard imagining himself as the master
of this great fortress, which he had fantasised so much about as a child.

It was a bright sunny day in Edinburgh and James became filled with emotion at once again seeing the stark Scottish hills. He looked with renewed pleasure at the old houses, the cathedral, the castle, and the gracious Palace of Holyrood surrounded by its great park. Although he had come to close his father's eyes, James felt that for himself his return to Scotland was a kind of rebirth.

7

OF THE TWO DAYS passed in the pit James remembers only what he had perceived through his senses: the penetrating cold, the dim light, the humidity and the pain. He recalls his terrible awakening, finding himself chained to a post with his head bandaged. The servant in charge of handing him his meals had confided to him with a snigger that he had tried to smash his skull against the wall. To prevent him reoffending the Governor had decided to have him put in chains. The words are reverberating inside James's head without his full comprehension. Yet it seems to him that he has been endlessly circling round and round this post like a caged beast.

Since the previous day he has remained prostrate, his eyes turned towards the window, watching the racing clouds and seabirds flying past. He drinks straight from the jug placed next to the bed but eats nothing. He desperately tries to understand why he is at Dragsholm. They told him he had been violent and that no one could restrain him during his fits of rage, that he had become insane and the only way to deal with the demented was to tame their spirits. Yet he knows that no matter whether they throw him to the mercy of vermin or beat him to a pulp, he will never give in.

Where is Mary? Is she now a prisoner languishing in some English castle? No news reaches him any more. In Malmö, just before being transferred to Dragsholm, he had heard the news of his mother's death. In her will she had left her estates to Janet, now remarried to John Lord of Caithness, and her money to James's cousin William Hepburn of Gilmerton who has been like a brother to him. The beloved face of the Lady of Morham is fading now. In his despair, James strains to visualise her face as he saw it when last they met, after the battle of Carberry Hill and his separation from Mary.

Dazzled by the bright summer light James closes his eyes. More and more he is letting go of time, losing himself in a haze of oblivion, which draws him in dangerously. It would take so little to dislocate his mind from the past and release himself, so that finally he would be able to sleep peacefully, and dispassionately consume the fish and soup served to him, finding some small pleasure in the pitcher of wine and pint of beer.

James suddenly sees his late father. Death has finally restored peace to the features of this handsome man, who had wasted his life and made such bad use of it. He no longer hates him but only regrets having known him so little and so inadequately. Now James bears his titles and the honours attached to them: Earl of Bothwell, High Admiral of Scotland, Sheriff of the Earldoms of Berwick, Haddington, and Edinburgh, Bailiff of Lauderdale, and Lord of Hailes and Crichton. James repeats the names to himself and searches his memory for the places to which they refer: Hailes and Crichton, the castles where he spent his early childhood before his departure for Spynie: havens of happiness until his parents' divorce, followed by spells of loneliness, adolescent brawls, the taste of freedom and intoxicating sensations of life which flowed through him. In summer the banks of the River Tyne were his favourite haunts. Water cascades over the rounded pebbles of the riverbed, sparkling in the rays of the sun, which filter through the stems of tall grass and highlight pieces of driftwood swept along on the current. Between shadow and light the river loiters, meanders, and ebbs into tiny wavelets on the banks, habitat of myriad frogs and dancing dragonflies with tinted wings. He goes fishing, passes time daydreaming and swims with the sons of local farmers. Hailes is an enchanted abode, Crichton a place full of secrets, whose stark walls conceal a lively inner courtyard, a private haven cut off from the rest of the world. He lurks around the storerooms, helps himself to an oatcake, watches the blacksmith thrusting his sizzling tongs into the red-hot furnace, marvels at the dexterity of maidservants plucking poultry, and ventures on tiptoe into cellars reeking of wine, beer, and moulding fruit. In winter he warms himself at the blazing hearth, hangs around the kitchens where young kitchen hands are busy peeling vegetables and roasting quarters of mutton on the spit. The chef has pancakes cooked on the griddle for him and hands him a mug of hot mulled cider.

Hailes and Crichton… James shuts his eyes so tightly to try to hold on to these memories that he sees moving shapes and fleeting shadows beckoning to him. He opens his eyes immediately. Once upon a time, the walls of his room had been painted; he stares at the evanescent silhouettes of pheasants. Sometimes he can pick out their shapes, their hues, see an eye or a leg, and sometimes he sees nothing but stains and blistering on the flaking wall. The word 'Lauderdale' throbs in his temples. It is the threshold of the Borders, in the Lammermuir Hills; the birthplace of the wind which drove the Reivers by night towards the English border, which carried the sounds of laughter, cries of excitement or pain, and the drumming of horses' hooves in the moonlight.

James does not want to think about the Borders, about the sense of freedom this name brings back, or about its violent ways. Too many memories are torturing him. He rises from his bed and paces round his room. His stiff legs have become painful. He was once an accomplished horseman and soldier. He loved action, taking control and conquering. Today he is pinned down like a falcon whose wings have been clipped. No longer can he gaze on the skies, the damp earth, the heather, the bronze moss, the solid shapes of rocky outcrops and the stark outlines amidst the moors of old border keeps. He staggers round the room as if deaf and blind to the world, trying to delay the moment when he will become a human wreck. If ever he manages to make his escape, he will have to reach France, and convince Charles IX to hasten to Mary's rescue. Does she still think about him? At Carberry, she had promised to stay faithful to him, her hand squeezing his tightly as if she wanted to hold him back a little while longer. He still feels the pressure of her fingers on his palm. She is weeping, she is trying to conceal her fear, he longs to take her in his arms again, but he cannot delay. He needs to mount his horse and head off at a gallop. Is it merely to escape? No, it is to muster an army and put her back on the Scottish throne. Just like in the old days.

8

Late 1556–1557

James observed the Regent closely. Marie de Guise seemed exhausted. This attractive woman, once so susceptible to flattery and courted by his father, although still benevolent and kind, now reveals signs of a suspicious and uncompromising attitude, having had to face up to deceit and disloyalty from some of Scotland's nobility. The young man knew she was fighting to preserve the realm for her daughter Mary Stuart, to which she might never return as Queen. Yet being a Guise, she belonged to a race and family that would never relinquish or desert their rightful heritage.

'Your assistance is very welcome,' continued the Regent as she walked towards the hearth. 'I have great need of someone who will serve me by liaising between the French officers and the Scottish soldiers. The Comte d'Oysel is willing to have you under his command in this role. He is a good strategist and an educated man, and I am sure you will like him. He plans tomorrow to take you to Leith, where our garrison is expecting an English offensive to start at any moment.'

In Edinburgh, the French presence was tolerated with ill will. The efforts the Regent had made to win over the Calvinists, by ordering the release of those who had besieged St Andrews Castle after the murder of Cardinal Beaton, did not make up for the frustration engendered by the nomination of Frenchmen for public appointments which by right were previously held by Scots.

'I am at your service, Madam.'

The perfection of the French spoken by James pleased the Regent. From his mother Lady Agnes the young man had inherited dark brown hair, lightened with tawny highlights from the sun. His brown eyes had a frank and wilful expression, and a narrow moustache of a lighter shade of brown than his hair emphasised his wide mouth and sensual lips. This young man may look like his mother, Marie de Guise thought, but he has inherited the temperament and charm of the Hepburns. She had enjoyed being courted by Patrick. More refined and amusing than his rival the Earl of Lennox, 'The Fair Earl' danced exquisitely and had an attractive mellow voice to which she had always enjoyed listening. However, that favoured suitor had come to believe that he would marry her, so she had had to devise ways to keep him at a distance.

'We will see each other again very soon,' the Regent assured James. 'You must come to the Christmas festivities which we will celebrate at Holyrood in the French fashion.' She paused for a moment, then said to him,

'Please go and see my treasurer. I am no stranger to financial difficulties and can imagine you do have some just now. I have to levy unpopular taxes or beg France to send me funds; the fortifications of Edinburgh will require a thousand men to repair them, and they will have to be paid. I am sure you are also aware that the Queen my daughter is to marry Monseigneur le Dauphin next year, and I shall need sixty thousand pounds for her dowry.'

The Regent's voice had lost its gaiety and James detected a certain amount of anguish in her manner. Taking his leave, he doffed his cap and bowed deeply.

The young man took up his appointment under the French military commander, the Comte d'Oysel. The Scottish alliance with France, which guaranteed the sovereignty of the Stuarts, did not rankle in his mind and he looked forward to testing his theoretical knowledge of military strategy, learned from books in Paris. As soon as he was free he would ride to Crichton, and with his steward's assistance he would check the accounts and look over the mortgage records. By selling some of his land to his Hepburn cousins, he would be able to pay off most of his father's debts and clear the remaining mortgages. Now Lord of Hailes and Crichton, both of them old family castles and homes of his childhood, he wanted to make them more pleasant and comfortable to live in by refurbishing some of the rooms and having fine furniture made for them. If he were to die without issue, they would be left to one of his favourite cousins, William Hepburn, with whom he had shared long summers in bygone days. Together as boys, they had walked along the banks of the River Tyne, often stopping to speak to the villagers, all of whom knew James. They frequently hunted herons, ducks, and other waterfowl, or had their best horses saddled and galloped for miles across the hills.

The clouds in the winter sky obscured the hills, casting a bluish-grey reflection over the moors as he rode through the wind and rain over stunted grass and heather turned brown by the frost. Returning on some dark nights when the waxing or waning moon gave too little light even for the Reivers, he would hear nothing but the whistling of the wind and the thudding of his horse's hooves on the ground. As dawn rose, he would arrive at Crichton exhausted and throw himself on his bed, his head full of limitless exciting possibilities.

When summer weather came to the Borders, violence broke out. Local feuds had existed for generations, but now raiding parties had crossed the border into the Earldom of Northumberland. Responses to these raids had become increasingly brutal against the Scots. Sheep and cattle were driven across the border in both directions, hamlets were burned, women raped and men taken hostage.

The Comte d'Oysel, and the Earl of Huntly, Lieutenant of the Borders, decided to exercise greater vigilance and control. James's knowledge of the border with Northumberland and his personal links with the powerful Borders families made his presence and assistance invaluable. Straightaway he said to them,

'It is no good simply to patrol the boundaries; we need to cross the border into Northumberland. So the English are looting in Scotland! We need to teach them a lesson they will not easily forget, not by stealing their herds and manhandling their women but by fighting the Earl of Northumberland's men on his own lands.'

'Most of our men are in Leith,' objected the Comte d'Oysel. He had learned to appreciate this reckless and loyal young Scot, who in a few years time might prove to be a great Captain of men.

'Our Borderers will suffice, we must send out the call that they are needed. A man fights better when his own interests are at stake, and I know more than one Armstrong, Elliot, or Graham who would gladly don his jack and helmet. Believe me, the thought of penetrating into English territory will instil a rare strength and eagerness in them.'

'Will they obey their Lieutenant?' James was asked. He was doubtful. Huntly was a great Lord of the North, but the Borderers felt no bond of allegiance to him. In this harsh country, only blood ties mattered. Here they barely knew that Marie de Guise, their former King's widow, had become Regent. Edinburgh belonged to another world.

To his dismay, James found only three hundred horsemen at the rallying point. The rumour spread that they were to be led by a foreigner, d'Oysel, and a Highlander had probably put off many of them. Besides, a number of the English Borderers were in one way or another related to the Scots and may well have been negotiating amongst themselves. The Comte turned to James, saying,

'Between us we must come to a decision quickly and not delay.' The weather was hot and humid and midges were plaguing men and horses.

James had reassessed the situation and was elaborating in his mind plans of where and how to cross the border with his three hundred mosstroopers. The harangue he would probably get from his French commander would not shake his determination.

'We are lacking the necessary numbers to succeed.'

In the single room of the cottage they were using as their headquarters, the Earl of Huntly paced back and forth. In order not to attract the attention of the enemy or spies, they had avoided meeting at Hermitage.

'Three hundred mounted horsemen,' James announced calmly.

'Looters!' declared d'Oysel scornfully.

'Tough men and brave!' countered James.

'Criminals, godless and lawless men!'

'There is a code of honour among these Reivers as we call them, which is more rigorous than that at court, Monseigneur.'

The Comte d'Oysel looked hard at James. At twenty the young man showed uncommon tenacity and willpower, but would it be wise to allow the King of France's soldiers to fight alongside these Reivers?

With some relief, James sensed that d'Oysel was slowly coming round to accepting his plan. He badly wanted to lead this raid himself, and so win the admiration of the Reivers and the trust of the Regent. He wanted her to understand that the son of 'The Fair Earl' did not resemble his father.

'I do not need His Majesty's soldiers,' James assured him. 'A well-led force of brave and daring horsemen will strike the enemy harder and more effectively than a regiment of men for whom we would have to arrange quarters and supplies. The Scots, my Lord are men of action; they are impulsive and hate delays and endless discussion of plans. Give them the order to attack and they will obey instantly and fearlessly, but keep them waiting for hours in the sun and rain while plans are made and they will start to desert and return to their homes.'

Huntly, who had been listening intently, cleared his throat,

'Why not trust this young man? And in this action France will not risk losing the life of a single man.' The Comte finally agreed to James's plan.

'Go ahead and win the day. I have a high opinion of you, my Lord Bothwell, which I have no doubt this forthcoming action will uphold and strengthen.'

James had planned the raid down to the last detail. They would cross the border by night with a guide who had a thorough knowledge of the terrain and would lead the men and horses over the treacherous bogs using safe crossing points known to him. Before dawn, they would attack the Earl of Northumberland's men, led by his brother Lord Percy, whilst they were still asleep.

'My congratulations to you, my Lord!' The Regent, smiling took James's hands and held them tightly in her own. The raid had been a complete success. Percy had lost many of his men, without being able to retaliate. Only one Reiver had been wounded, and his comrades had managed to bring him back to Scotland.

'I only performed my duty, Madam.'

Despite her cheerful manner, James sensed the tension within Marie de Guise. Her Protestant nobles had just joined forces to form a Congregation, which had begun to defy her authority. The founding members were the Earls of Argyll, Glencairn, Erskine, Morton, a Douglas, and in particular, James Stuart, an illegitimate son of the late King, her husband. Very soon, this Congregation would make demands and further undermine the influence of the Catholic clergy in the minds of the people.

The Regent invited James to sit with her. September was mild, and the windows of her little reception chamber opened out onto Holyrood park.

'Bring us some wine from the Loire,' she asked a servant. She wanted to discover if the trust she placed in James Hepburn was justified.

'You are a Huguenot, are you not?'

'Indeed, Madam.'

'Would you not consider coming back to the Church of Rome?'

'No, Madam.' The determination that the Regent heard in his voice forbade her to pursue the matter.

'Do you associate with the Lords of the Congregation?'

'Certainly not!'

James was lost for words. He was a Protestant, and would remain so until his last breath, but there was no reason for his religious convictions to affect his loyalty to the Stuarts.

'You are going to be very much alone,' Marie de Guise observed, 'as the Protestant Scottish nobility to which you belong will consider you a traitor and will try to ruin you.'

'I am honoured to have Your Grace's support.'

'That you do have,' the Regent said emphatically. James wondered how long her failing health would enable her to continue her fight to keep her daughter's inheritance secure. Mary would marry in the spring and become Dauphine of France. What would Scotland mean to her then? The Regent's brothers described Mary in each of their letters as a truly charming and virtuous young girl, anxious to please the King and her future husband. Mary had enjoyed a sound education, loved hunting, jewellery, and dancing. She was proud to be a Guise, and soon to become a Valois.

'Being in my service will bring you little glory and much enmity. You will be offered gold to assist you in your struggle to pay off the debts incurred by your father, Lord Patrick, and in return you will be asked to abandon your loyalty to me, who can offer you no such reward.'

James put his glass down abruptly. What was on Marie de Guise's mind?

'Certain ill-advised men, Madam, allow their boats to drift away. As your Lord High Admiral, mine is firmly anchored. A handful of English gold could never entice me to risk my honour and forsake you.' The anger visible on James's face elicited a smile from the Regent. However, he was young and life's temptations could still change him.

'I trust you, James Hepburn,' she assured him. 'How could I not appreciate your loyalty and courage? I have few friends, as you know. The Duke of Châtelherault, my closest relative in Scotland, is a weak man, and his eldest son, young Arran, is unstable and vindictive. The

Lennoxes have betrayed me, as well as some members of the Douglas family. I cannot rely on the Earl of Argyll nor on my stepson James, who aspires to the throne of Scotland in place of Mary. The only support I still have comes from the Lords Huntly, Seton, Livingstone, Fleming, and you, my Lord Bothwell, and the Hepburns.'

'You are omitting many, Madam, who may not openly have declared their loyalty to you but would be ready to take up arms and follow you.'

Looking through the window next to her the Regent seemed to be engrossed in thought as she watched the wind blown clouds race across the sky. The Scots were hard to rule. Quick-tempered and easily offended they were continuously feuding, with each successive generation fermenting old grudges. James VI, her late husband, had been obsessed by those feuds and the unquenchable thirst for revenge.

The Regent expressed her concern to James,

'The friendship and trust I offer you will bring dangers and disappointments. As a member of the Congregation, you would have the support of your peers. With me, you can count only on the friendship of the Queen my daughter. Yet she is far from here, and on my death Scotland will be able to survive only under close French protection. There are those who claim this alliance is treacherous, but I have no army, and no money. How much longer can I hope for Scotland's independence? Queen Mary Tudor is curbing the English Protestants' desire to dominate affairs of State. Alas, Her Majesty will not live long. If Elizabeth the bastard succeeds her then the Lords of the Congregation, no longer hesitant in constraining their desires and aspirations, will seek to govern me.' James was silent. Marie de Guise was right but she was underestimating the public resentment of the French occupation. On the death of the Queen of England, Scotland would be divided into two irreconcilable parties. He knew his loyalty would always belong to the Stuarts.

9

IN EARLY 1558, the pro-French Scottish faction was inflamed by reports that François de Guise, who had become a national hero, had seized Calais. Pushed into war by her husband Philip II of Spain, Mary Tudor had lost the last English possession on French soil, a city that had belonged to England for over two hundred years!

At the beginning of spring James Beaton, Archbishop of Glasgow, along with the Bishops of Ross and Orkney, the Earls of Roth and Cassilis, Lords Fleming and Seton and James Stuart set sail for France in order to represent Scotland at their young Queen's wedding. Aged fifteen and four months, Mary was marrying the Dauphin, also just turned fifteen, with great pomp and ceremony at Notre Dame. Shortly beforehand, Marie de Guise had written to her daughter exhorting her to obey the King of France and her uncles in their every wish, and to ratify the documents they would be submitting to her. These stipulated that the Dauphin of France would become King of Scotland, with the same prerogatives, privileges and rights as Mary, and committing both of them to respect Scottish laws and liberties. Yet what Marie de Guise had concealed from the Scottish delegation was that a secret document would be drafted beforehand, which would render null and void any other ulterior undertaking they might try to introduce. This document specified that should Mary die without issue before her husband, Scotland would belong by right to François, thereby becoming a French province.

The wedding ceremony took place on a large dais erected on the porch of Notre Dame so that the crowd could enjoy looking at the bride and the entire historic spectacle. The bride was dressed in white silk and satin studded with pearls and diamonds. The young woman's enchanting smile had a wonderful effect. People admired her tall stature and slender figure, her graceful gait and her sparkling eyes, and they were distracted from the ashen complexion of François, whose sullen features were even more than usual contorted with shyness and emotion.

Then the terrible news of the deaths of the Lords Roth, Cassilis, Fleming and the Bishop of Orkney was received, all having been poisoned by the meal they had eaten before setting sail from Dieppe. Marie de Guise was extremely upset. Was it an accident or was it murder? Could it be that the four nobles had had word of the documents yielding Scotland to France and had threatened to alert the Edinburgh Parliament? If so, who had taken the decision to poison them?

Caught between her affection for her native country and her attachment to Scotland the Regent was perpetually torn asunder. More and more often, she needed and requested the presence of her friends and tried to minimise the activities of the Lords of the Congregation, who were gaining ground, and now promoted religious freedom and anti-heresy laws. Having been appointed a Member of Parliament, James Hepburn was kept at arm's length by Catholics and Protestants alike. The singular path he had chosen stimulated him. He scorned good advice and ignored warnings. At twenty-two, he felt invincible. Having become the Earl of Bothwell, he had taken on a page, a barber, a master of the robe and a young squire. He needed to maintain his position in society, find a glittering marriage prospect for Janet and keep Crichton and Hailes in good repair. Money trickled through his fingers too quickly and debts returned with the renewed threat of having to remortgage his lands. In the near future, he hoped that Marie de Guise would grant him the revenue of a wealthy abbey. She could not consider him unworthy of it.

At the end of the summer, the Regent conferred on James the Lieutenancy of the Borders and the office of Keeper of Hermitage Castle. He now had the power to raise an army, launch punitive expeditions against looters, and cross the border to bring English rebels to heel, in a region that since childhood had always attracted and fascinated him. He was familiar with each Reiver family and knew most of the Armstrongs, Elliots, Grahams, Nixons, Crosiers and Kerrs by their first names. He was aware of the blood feuds that set Kerrs against Scotts, Scotts against Elliots and Elliots against almost all, as well as their alliances, be they matrimonial or tribal. He commanded a network of information, spies, followers and vassals. Twice a year he would adjudicate in Jedburgh at the trials of prisoners over whom he had the right of life or death, and he would exchange captives with England. This harsh and violent way of life did not in any way frighten him. He never felt happier than at the head of his horsemen galloping across the purple moors at dawn, riding over the hills and through the whins and broom, which scratched the riders' boots and horses' flanks.

With September came flocks of migrating geese crossing the sky in long flight formations, the nights became cooler and blustery gusts of wind came in from the sea. Sometimes in the early mornings James would return to Hermitage, always spellbound by the eerie and forlorn atmosphere of the fortress. The most sinister legends were associated with it, like that of the monstrous Lord Soulis, a giant reputed to be invincible but finally destroyed by a sorcerer who unleashed the river floods to engulf and drown him; or the tales of the lords who were boiled alive; or those of the prisoners who died of starvation in the pit, deprived of air and light. In the corner tower where he had his quarters, James gave little thought to the fate of the hapless prisoners. Worn out, he would take off his riding boots, divest himself of his weapons, and put his clothes to dry. The bed would be warmed for him; the quilt was of goose down, and the sheets of fine linen. He listened to the whistling of the wind and the song of the water of Hermitage and felt a King in his own world.

'So here you are my dear brother, promoted to the rank of Lieutenant of the Borders and Keeper of Hermitage Castle. You took a big gamble taking on those responsibilities. In His clemency God has very conveniently made you deaf and blind.'

Janet's slender face lit up with a mischievous smile. She was overjoyed to see him at Crichton; James seized her by both wrists and feigned to twist them.

'Deaf and blind to what, my lovely sister?'

'To the execution of that old preacher who was roasted alive in St Andrews a few years ago. Have you forgotten how you rebelled when our father handed George Wishart over to Beaton, who burned him bound to a stake? Are you associating with those Members of Parliament who are demanding freedom of conscience?'

'No, not as long as they demand rights which they are refusing to allow the Catholics.'

'You despise the Protestant Lords but you are one of them, Jamie. Do not destroy yourself over a chivalrous ideal which has become out of date.'

The young woman's tone had become sombre. Her brother's isolation amongst the Scottish nobility alarmed her. The Protestants would ostracise him and the Catholics would never consider him as one of theirs. Marie de Guise would not live forever, and when she died, who would hold the reins of power on behalf of the Queen? Most probably James Stuart her half-brother, an intelligent, cold and calculating man, and an inflexible Calvinist who felt no sympathy for the Regent's young protégé. The Hepburns would lose everything, and she, Janet, would have to be content with marrying a lesser provincial lord, who would give her a lacklustre and humdrum existence.

At twenty Janet was slender, vivacious and unruly. Her bright eyes lit up her fine features and suntanned complexion, acquired from an outdoor life as she loved nothing better than to tear across the countryside on horseback. Lady Agnes had not been able to tame her daughter's daring nature and thirst for freedom, and Janet had grown up without any real discipline. Little by little, the wild child had been transformed into a woman who no longer turned up her nose at pretty dresses and dancing.

'How can you talk about outmoded trends when it is a matter of honour?' argued Janet. 'The Congregation is not only an assembly of good Christians but also a political faction aiming for radical changes to our society and greedy for power and wealth. What are their sarcastic comments worth when they talk about lands owned by the Catholic clergy? Do you really think they favour a fair redistribution of those properties among the poor?'

At Crichton where he had come to confer with his steward, life ran smoothly. Edinburgh was a viper's nest of intrigue and James was relieved to get away from it. The Regent had no illusions but possessed great clarity of mind, and remained wary of friends who at any moment might betray her and of enemies who falsely renewed pledges of goodwill. Deprived of a personal life she devoted herself to the limits of her strength, following the path she had chosen after her husband's death: upholding the authority of the Crown, strengthening the old French Alliance and bringing her nobles under control.

Some distance from the castle the Tyne snaked through pastures grazed by flocks of black-faced sheep. The hills rolled away as far as the eye could see, their curved outlines setting off the stark mass of the castle with its solid square tower. Over time, its various owners had added extensive living quarters, built around a central courtyard filled with galleries, shelters and sheds of all kinds. James occupied his father's room, which held moving memories for him. 'The Fair Earl' had harboured ambitions not so different from his own, but in order to achieve them had resorted to means deplored and avoided by James. Packed tightly inside a wooden box he had discovered passionate love letters written to him by women. Yet he was certain his father had never become attached to any one of them. Had James inherited his indifference? Tears, demands and women's foolish hunger for their lover's unconditional love both frightened and exasperated him.

One day a horseman arrived and delivered a small sealed package addressed to him. Opening it, he read:

My Lord,

The news of the death of Her Majesty the Queen Mary Tudor, has just reached me at Holyrood and your prompt return to Edinburgh would be appreciated. Elizabeth's succession to the throne is certainly going to result in the return of Protestantism in England and a surge of unrest at home. I am summoning my Privy Council. Your opinion will be important to me.

Marie de Guise had signed the letter herself and then added three more words: *I await you.*

James rode with all speed in the direction of Edinburgh. The Regent now feared that England was about to change her policy. The Anglo-Spanish alliance had lasted a long while, and Elizabeth would now focus her attention on Scotland, over which she wished to keep considerable influence. She would probably have dealings with the Lords of the Congregation and would support their activities with generous subsidies. There would then follow open rebellion against the Regent and the struggle for power would become remorseless.

'Before extending the hand of friendship, Madam, we need to flex Scotland's muscles with a show of strength. Arguments have all the more force when preceded by a few successful raids. I suggest we make another attack on the Earl of Northumberland and his brother Percy. Let us unleash a small army on the other side of the border and strike quickly and hard!'

'You must act jointly with the French,' Marie de Guise ordered. 'Then we will join forces with Spain and France to ratify a peace treaty, which may it please God is adhered to!'

By the end of the year, James had been victorious in new raids in the Borders, and now his enemies were no longer trying to conceal the hatred they bore him. They asserted young Hepburn was violent, aggressive and cunning. They claimed that the more his influence with the Regent grew, the more emboldened he became, parading down Edinburgh's High Street as though he had become a person of great importance, dressed in fine velvet doublets and suede boots: where did he find the money?

James scorned his ill-wishers. The Regent had given him her full trust; he was in receipt of a pension and was free to enjoy his youth, dine out, fill his cellars with good wine, dress like a gentleman and above all acquire a few horses of fine breeding, which once well-trained could beat Lord Ruthven's, reputed to be the fastest in Scotland. When spring arrived, he would carefully choose his ground and throw down the gauntlet.

IO

JAMES IS IMAGINING HORSES launched into a full gallop, of water splashing round their hooves as they ford shallow streams and about the clouds above which seem to accompany their movements. He sees speed, foam, power and beauty. Without realising it, he is pacing round his room with his eyes closed. He knows exactly how many steps to take and where the obstacles lie. This stark room located in the north-eastern tower defines his space and the limits of his freedom. Time holds him back and carries him forward, overwhelms him and elates him. Those who rob him of his future are powerless to deny him his past. Though every memory is like an open wound, repeatedly he seeks sanctuary within. When he goes back in time, he stops shouting, harming himself or pummelling the door of his cell. He walks in circles or remains prostrated on his bed for hours on end. He is somewhere else, far from Dragsholm and from the world they are inflicting upon him. He is living and reliving the past, leaving moments of happiness intact and distorting broken expectations in order to turn defeats into victories. Painstakingly he tracks down each point of error when he let a good opportunity slip by, and tries to remember every thought and every decision of days gone by. He has led an intense and passionate life, but it was far too short... when exactly did he die? Was it at Carberry? Was it at Strathbogie, the castle belonging to George Gordon, his former brother-in-law and best friend? Was it in Copenhagen when the doors of his first prison, comfortable apartments where he was treated with the greatest consideration, closed behind him? Was it in Malmö, or here at Dragsholm in this bleak godforsaken prison battered by wind and waves?

Today he sees horses and is impressed by their elegance and power.

He is in St Andrews where he has challenged Ruthven. His three race-horses, two white-stockinged full-blooded stallions and a dun gelding are wearing harnesses of buckskin, and he is racing one of the stallions. The ground is dry, the turf brown and withered, the wind raw and the light transparent. His eyes are fixed on the spinney the horses must gallop right round before returning to the finishing line. A rider has caught up with him, wearing Ruthven's colours of red and green. He talks to his stallion to encourage him and urge him on to victory, whispering gentle words he would never say to a woman. His horse gallops like the wind and James is first past the finishing post. He has beaten his rival and feels invincible. Tomorrow he will be in Perth to which the Regent has withdrawn. Young Arran, Hamilton's eldest son has left France, undoubtedly on English advice, to become one of her agents in Scotland. Marie de Guise is not ignorant of this fact. She will give her instructions to her Lieutenant, listen to his advice and invest him with the authority to ratify on her behalf a treaty with Northumberland of non-interference. What she does not yet know is that the real agreement has already been ratified between Elizabeth and the members of the Congregation. Neither does James know. By the time he becomes aware of the collusion between Queen Elizabeth, her all-powerful adviser William Cecil and the Scottish Lords, he has already become an outcast.

His rage returns and swells inside him like a hatred-bearing wave. He recalls the face of James Stuart, The Bastard, and the faces of Lindsay and Kerr of Fawdonside, all traitors in the pay of England. James stops walking, remembering that James Stuart has long since been murdered. The prisoner gives a small chuckle. Gradually Death reaps the strong and the weak, the victors and the vanquished. He knows he will never come out of Dragsholm alive and that this fortress is robbing him of his sanity and strength. Yet he will remain defiant. He was a born fighter and conqueror. At twenty-two years old power lay at his feet. At forty, he is a living-dead whom no sovereign cares to remember, whether from cowardice or ingratitude. James despises Elizabeth and her air of affectation, which conceals a heart of stone and calculated duplicity; he despises Henri III and his spineless subordination to his mother Catherine de Medicis, and he scorns Philip II with his religious bigotry and obsessive need to dominate those around him. He likes to feel alone. He is alone.

II

1559

SNOW WAS FALLING SILENTLY over the moors, covering the bleak ruggedness of the hills with a soft blanket. All was quiet within the slate-roofed stone building. It was more of a fortified keep than a castle and stood stark, square, and unwelcoming, defying the passage of time and the depredations caused both by Reivers and the soldiers sent down from Edinburgh to quell the troubles in the Borders.

Within the curtains surrounding the bed James lay motionless, and beside him slumbered Janet Beaton. As she slept, her face was still beautiful with a touching maturity marked by time and the trials of life. In her thick hair spread out on the pillow, he detected a few strands of grey. He wondered whether he was in love with her. She never dominated him yet he was constantly learning from her and despite the age gap there was no doubt as to their relationship. He was her lover and he possessed this remarkable woman, who was admired yet feared by the local people. Twice widowed, she had of her own accord avenged the murder of her second husband Walter Scott at the hands of one of the Kerrs, lifelong enemies of the Scotts. Leading a force of two hundred Scotts Janet herself had hacked down the door of the Kirk where the killer of her husband, father of her six children, had taken refuge; she had then looked on while Walter's parents stabbed him to death.

Often while gazing at his mistress James was reminded of Diane de Poitiers. Both of them seemed to sail through time with their beauty intact, and he now understood Henri II's continuing infatuation and fascination for a woman nineteen years older than he was. Janet was forty-three and James was twenty-three.

'Stop staring at me in that way,' she murmured, 'I should never have allowed you to sleep in my bed. A woman of my age should only let her young lover see her with her face made up.'

'You don't wear any make-up.'

James propped himself up on his elbow and ran his fingertip down her straight nose and over her voluptuous lips. He should long since have been in the saddle galloping towards Hermitage, but he lacked the heart to leave his mistress and give up the joy he felt in possessing her. She had taught him all the ways of love; he knew how to caress a woman and how to delay his own pleasure in order to increase hers.

Beneath the thick quilt, their two bodies were as one. The words she spoke to him were sometimes gentle and loving, sometimes crude and basic; he was not sure which language aroused him the most.

It had ceased snowing now; the light was dazzling and the sun already high in the sky. Janet lay in bed watching her lover getting dressed. She was much attracted by his muscular physique, the look of uprightness and intelligence in his face, with its bold gaze, generous mouth and broken nose.

James was dressed in knee breeches, a loose linen shirt, and woollen doublet. His boots and cloak were laid out in front of the fire, which he had just rekindled. His sober riding clothes suited him better than the lace-trimmed silk and velvet attire worn at court. Janet was the niece of Cardinal Beaton who had met such a terrible death at St Andrews, and aunt of one of Mary Stuart's ladies-in-waiting, Mary Beaton. She had often been invited by Marie de Guise to Holyrood, but seldom went, and with the passing of the years became less and less inclined to fulfil social obligations. She felt far more at ease with life in the Borders, living in her fortified keep, riding her horse and tending her herds. She preferred the warm hospitality and outspokenness of her tenant farmers to the discourse of lords. When she trotted over the moors, she knew that no man would ever tear her away from this place with its hills and crags, where stark keeps stood like sentinels in the wild countryside.

'Until tomorrow,' she said to him.

'No, I'll see you tonight.'

Janet burst out laughing. 'Young men are quite insatiable,' she declared. In what kind of state would James be to carry out his duties? She had the lambing to take care of, and he had been given the task of signing a truce with the English, who were to be represented by the Earl of Northumberland. The Lords of the Congregation had seized the city of Edinburgh; the Regent had retreated to Perth and was awaiting her Lieutenant.

The lovers prolonged the pleasure of their evening meal, sipping brandy by the fireside with Janet's two spaniels lying at their feet. Both of them treasured these moments spent together but knew they could not last.

'I cannot believe our young Queen would trust her half-brother James Stuart,' Janet remarked.

'The Queen cares little about him! She is the Dauphine of France, worshipped and over-protected by the Guise family, and all she can think about is dancing, dressing in fine clothes, writing poetry or going hunting. I doubt she even remembers much about Scotland and its ancient castles, or its Protestant troublemakers.'

'I hear John Knox is back in Perth,' said Janet, in flat tones.

As a Catholic, she feared this sharp-tongued, violent and uncompromising man who doomed all papists to the fires of eternal damnation. His eloquence fascinated and inspired his audience. Often after one of his sermons, people would stampede into churches, knock down statues of saints, desecrate altars and trample on the Host.

James nodded to her. The Knoxes had been vassals of the Hepburns and the young Earl knew them well. They were ill-mannered and intolerant characters. Though he was not afraid of this death-threatening preacher, he had little respect for him.

'If you don't mind let us not talk about him any more.' James stood up and took Janet into his arms. He loved everything about her; the crows feet which creased the corners of her eyes, the lines etched on her brow, the full slightly drooping breasts, her sensuous curves, her science of love and her boundless generosity. She had turned this young inexperienced man into a skilful lover with the ability to give pleasure to many other women. She knew this yet felt no jealousy.

At Hermitage Castle James found himself once more in the company of soldiers living in spartan conditions. Day after day, he received news of misdeeds committed in the border country, always of the same kind: cattle thefts, acts of violence, houses torched for revenge and bloody settling of scores. He would have his horse saddled, summon a patrol and set off to visit small burghs, which consisted of miserable hovels roofed with thatch or heather. None but heads of families dwelt in stone-built houses, endowed with good chimneys and solid studded oak doors and protected by an iron yett. It was to these that James addressed himself. Their replies tended to be terse and their eyes evasive. They might welcome the protection of a Lieutenant, but the right to revenge was theirs alone. It took the form of a blood feud, which continued for days, months and years, and was passed from father to son, from one cousin to the next.

James had a thorough understanding of these grudges and of the violence that brewed in the dull lives of these poor peasants. The Reivers were looters, but above all else, they were adventurers and intrepid horsemen who were also brutal and cunning adversaries. His task as Lieutenant of the Marches was to punish them and he did not spare any of them. Nevertheless, they respected him.

Sometimes around midday he would arrive to find the village community gathered to watch a cockfight or a fiercely contested game of football. Since it was not uncommon for these to degenerate into pitched battles, he did not linger. Only horseracing held his attention; the skill of the riders and the toughness and stamina of their rough-coated ponies were remarkable. James himself had been able to acquire several horses of quality, purchased in England despite severe restrictions. He knew as well as the Reivers the routes used by rustlers, their hideouts, and the horse dealers who asked no questions. From Hermitage he would have the horses brought to Crichton. There they would be branded with his number before being integrated into his stables.

In spring, James had been forced to leave Hermitage and Janet, and make his way to Perth, where the Regent had become alarmed by the violence engendered by John Knox's inflammatory sermons. The Protestants wanted to take control of the town, destroy churches and prohibit Mass. She was not sure whether to retaliate with force against them, or withdraw to Stirling Castle, which was sufficiently fortified for her to feel safe. James had advised her to go to Stirling, where she could work out the best strategy and prepare a counter-attack. No one would brave the cannons defending the fortress. The court settled into the old castle where Mary had lived as a child before leaving for France. The large buildings consisted of two surrounding walls, lookout towers, guardrooms, arsenal, powder store and food storeroom. It was at Stirling Castle that both James v and his daughter Mary had been crowned, the former at one year old and the latter at nine months. To please two successive French brides James v had undertaken extensive building-works, assisted by architects and masons brought over from France. Marie de Guise remembered how proud he had been showing her round the great hall, the vast kitchens and his own apartments adjacent to those that would become hers. She had preserved unchanged the room she had slept in as a young bride, a spacious chamber with coffered ceilings bordered by a painted fresco of arabesques and decorated with a series of brightly coloured tapestries depicting the life of Jesus. Her bed was enclosed within emerald green curtains, and in front was a long table around which she would gather her friends for informal suppers.

'This is a grave error,' the Earl of Huntly declared. 'This is an act of bravado which will infuriate Queen Elizabeth.'

'My child is the legitimate heir to the English throne,' Marie de Guise retorted. 'From the point of view of the Catholic Church Elizabeth, the daughter of Anne Boleyn, is illegitimate.'

'Who in England cares about the Pope's opinion, Madam? We have no army at our disposal to wage war, and French soldiers will not place our Queen on her cousin's throne. You should not set a challenge without being able to follow it up with action.'

The stout Earl of Huntly was on the verge of apoplexy. The fact that the Guises and Valois had pushed Mary into adding the English Arms to those of Scotland constituted a serious blunder. Everybody knew that Elizabeth, assisted by her all-powerful adviser, William Cecil, was protecting the Lords of the Congregation, and that by making an enemy of her the young Queen was setting fire to her own house out of pure vanity.

'Little by little we are being pushed into a corner,' Huntly continued, 'and French support will never give back to the Catholics the influence they have lost.'

Marie de Guise refrained from further irritating George Huntly, who was chief of the powerful Gordon family and one of the last lords to remain faithful to the Church of Rome. By appropriating the Arms of England, perhaps her daughter had acted prematurely. However, she refused to judge her brothers. There would be no war, merely a frosty exchange of diplomatic notes.

Feeling he had no right to intervene in a matter concerning the Catholic community, James Hepburn stayed silent. Nevertheless, he agreed with Huntly. This business was more serious than mere insolence. Elizabeth, outraged, would continue her financial aid to the Lords of the

Congregation. As far as he was concerned, there was no doubt that James Stuart, the Queen's half-brother, was the bridgehead of English policy in Scotland.

Fresh news had stunned the Scots. During a tournament held in honour of the wedding of his daughter Elizabeth to King Philip II of Spain, widower of Mary Tudor, King Henri II of France had been fatally wounded in the eye. After ten days of terrible agony, he had given up the ghost, making his eldest son François and his daughter-in-law Mary Stuart King and Queen of France. The Guise faction was in the ascendant.

Stirling might have been in mourning, but in Scotland, there was general rejoicing. The fact that Mary was now Queen of France and Scotland would surely deter English intimidation and rein in Protestant opposition.

The effects of this reversal of fortune were immediately apparent. James Stuart's men abandoned Edinburgh to withdraw to Glasgow where English gold still reached them. From there they would plot to retake control of the capital. As for William Cecil, he was inciting a Huguenot, La Renaudie, to foster a Protestant rebellion on French soil. Once he became embroiled in a religious war the sickly François would no longer be a real danger to England.

I2

JAMES WAS AT HAILES and for the last few days had been preparing for his planned attack. It was no good leaving anything to chance or luck; the ambush must be set up to run like clockwork. Those who thought him rash and hotheaded clearly did not know him well. The Comte d'Oysel had been frank with him:

'This mission requires boldness and determination and I believe you are the right man to carry it out.'

'And bear the consequences,' James had replied with some irony. 'It is not as though I lack enemies, and now I am about to acquire some more.'

D'Oysel considered that James deserved to have command of a regiment and had said he would put in a recommendation for him to the King of France, thus he would be able to confer a benefit on his Scottish friend. Bothwell however refused to consider serving any other country than his own.

It was Hallowe'en, that ancient pagan festival which honoured the souls of the departed, and which was known to display unearthly and disturbing manifestations. The mist was so thick that from the window of his bedchamber James could not even see the River Tyne, close though it was. This fog would give him an advantage. That evening he would summon twelve good horsemen, armed only with their dirks. The raid would need to be executed both swiftly and silently.

The little column advanced slowly following sheep tracks across the moors. James was fully aware that on this particular night of the thirty-first of October, his men, who were superstitious, feared supernatural encounters with ghosts, diabolical spirits, will-o'-the wisps or malevolent fairies. He had kept everything as low key as possible. The sole aim of this nocturnal foray was to intercept a package coming from England.

Nothing disturbed the silence except occasional snorting from the horses and the sounds of night birds. With his mind and senses on full alert, James concentrated on his goal; to surprise John Cockburn, seize the consignment of English gold destined for the Lords of the Congregation and flee towards Crichton with all the speed they could muster. It would be a hard two-hour ride across waterlogged pastures, bogs, rain-swollen ditches and through wooded areas. James suddenly signalled his troops to stop. Their horses were blowing and sneezing and he heard a barn owl hooting.

'They are coming. Get ready!'

From afar, carried on the wind, came the muffled sound of horses' hooves. Having set off from the English port of Berwick the escort had made slow but steady progress along the coast and was now heading straight for Edinburgh. In just a few minutes it would pass the exact spot that James had chosen. He gave his signal of a whistle, and his troops set off at a gallop towards the twenty or so horsemen, who had just emerged from a wood and were trotting in their direction. Surprised by the fierce cries uttered by their assailants they stopped and stood as if paralysed. Cockburn was at the head of his men, mounted on a gelding wearing a double saddlebag. Quick as lightning James came up beside him. He loosened the straps that secured the bags and swung them onto the back of his own saddle. Suddenly he saw Cockburn's pistol aimed at him as he shouted at James:

'Thief! traitor!'

With the flat of his sword, James struck his enemy full in the face.

'Enjoy the rest of your trip, gentlemen!' the young Earl cried out, his hands trembling slightly from the mental and physical strain of the moment.

On several occasions during his flight, James had looked round to see whether he was being pursued, but the pastures and stony tracks were deserted. Dawn was breaking, a light haze was rising from the ground and in the farms roosters were starting to crow. The gold he carried was heavy and James had to slow down his horse. In the village of Bolton, he would be able to hire a farm horse and load it with the double saddle-bag. An hour later, he would be in the safe confines of Crichton.

The ambush had turned out to be a complete success. Only Cockburn had attempted to resist. He was a distant cousin of the Hepburns and a stubborn and brave man, but in the darkness of the night, shocked and disorientated, he had been unable to act.

Safely back at Crichton with the bags opened, James saw to his surprise that what lay before him were not English pounds but French crowns. That fox knows how to cover his tracks, he thought. William Cecil was a formidable adversary. Undoubtedly, his network of spies in Scotland would before long relay the bad news to him. Cockburn had been able to identify him and the hounds would soon be on his heels, but he was counting on enough respite to give him time to join Marie de Guise at the Port of Leith, together with his booty. James Stuart, who had just proclaimed the deposition of the Regent, was going to be disappointed.

After forty-eight hours without rest, James fell into a deep sleep. A hand startled him on his shoulder.

'Horsemen are approaching, my Lord,' his servant announced, shaking him. 'They are less than a mile away.'

The young man leapt to his feet, hastily stuffed his nightshirt into his breeches, stuck his bare feet into his boots and grabbed the leather jack reinforced with steel wires, which both troops and Reivers wore as protection. The gold was on the table beside his bed. He snatched the saddle-bag and ran down the stairs.

'Quickly, bridle my horse!' he ordered his servant, who had followed him downstairs.

Moments later riding bareback, he was making for Borthwick Castle where he would find Simon Preston, a trustworthy friend. It would take an hour to get there, galloping all the way, if his horse did not collapse from exhaustion. If his pursuers found Crichton deserted and the gold vanished, would they abandon their search? He could not count on it.

The sound of thudding hooves from the horses launched in his pursuit was getting louder. He drew in his reins, jumped to the ground and freed his horse before hoisting the bags over his shoulder and dashing through the undergrowth towards a small river. Small birds fluttered from the bushes and a rabbit darted away in front. With horror, the young man heard in the distance the sounds of deep baying; his pursuers had put bloodhounds onto his trail. Lower down beneath a canopy of branches, the current flowed and cascaded over large boulders. Stumbling over tree roots and slipping in the mud, the fugitive reached the bank and waded into the river. The water reached halfway up his boots. About a mile upriver, James knew he would find the farm belonging to a Haddington farmer named Sandybed. His feet were hurting from the icy water, the strap binding the saddlebags was cutting into his shoulder and he was bent double under the weight of the gold. At the grass-grown edges of the riverbank thin crusts of ice shimmered in the pale rays of the sun. With great difficulty, James clambered over a fallen tree trunk that lay across the swirling waters. It sounded as though the baying was becoming more distant now. His pursuers were most likely following the current downstream, while he was making his way upstream.

With his strength sapped by exhaustion, the fugitive let his saddlebags drop to the ground. He was on the threshold of a grey stone-built farmhouse, and a tall girl wearing a dress and corselet of brown wool was observing him with bewilderment.

'My Lord Bothwell?' she asked in incredulous tones. On several occasions she had caught sight of the Lord of Hailes, riding through Haddington with his men, or accompanied by his parents. Many Hepburns lived in this area and enjoyed meeting each other socially.

'Open the door quickly, I am being followed!'

Without waiting a moment longer and with a shove of his shoulder James pushed open the door of the kitchen where there was a blazing fire burning in the hearth.

'Run and fetch your master,' he ordered.

He sank onto a stool placed beside the hearth. His feet, numbed by the icy water, were beginning to smart painfully. Having pulled off his boots and stretched his arms and feet towards the flames, he heard a footstep behind him.

'My Lord Bothwell!'

Wearing his nightgown and nightcap Master Sandybed listened unperturbed to the story retailed by his involuntary guest. To shelter a man who had just intercepted 'mail' received by Lord Cockburn in England sounded like trouble, but it was impossible for him to turn away a lord as important as the Earl of Bothwell.

'I am unable to offer you much of a hiding place, my Lord,' he grumbled. 'See for yourself, my barn has no upstairs floor and I just have four horses in my stable. The cellar is only used for storing a few barrels of beer and cannot provide you with a safe shelter.'

'Master Sandybed,' interrupted the maidservant, 'my Lord Bothwell and I are of roughly the same height. If he were clad in a skirt, a shirt and a corselet, he would make a very convincing kitchen maid.'

The farmer shrugged. Since there seemed no other way out of this situation the maidservant's suggestion was as good as any other.

'Hurry up then Bess,' he answered, 'and while you are at it send for Tom so that he may give my Lord Bothwell a shave. A maid with a moustache might arouse suspicions.'

Bess was laughing heartily. Playing her part in this game, the young maidservant had stuffed rags into James's corsage, which now displayed an ample bosom. He was dressed in a skirt of garnet-coloured dimity, a white apron, an ecru woollen shirt, a corselet of cheviot wool, with a pleated bonnet tied under his chin with a ribbon, and he was now unrecognisable. His clean-shaven skin still red from the cold would fool any man who did not observe him too closely.

Peggy, a lanky girl employed to perform thankless chores, had served James a bowl of thick oatmeal porridge onto which she had poured a generous dash of thick cream. With open mouth, she stared at this strange creature who had suddenly emerged from nowhere, and who was now gulping down large spoonfuls of porridge with no regard whatsoever for the ribbons of his pretty bonnet, already spattered with stains.

'Where do you come from?' she ventured to ask.

'From Crichton.'

The girl seemed impressed.

'Do you know Lord Bothwell?'

'A little.'

'They say he married old Lady Scott.'

James was struggling to keep a straight face. The precariousness of his situation, which should have been daunting, was instead causing him amusement. The young man thought about Janet, whom he had not seen for several weeks. During the planning of this mission his mistress had always encouraged him and assured him of her support. At the time, to avoid compromising her and putting her in danger, he had refused to go to her house. He was missing her, but once the gold was in Marie de Guise's possession he would come knocking on her door and would not move from her bed all day long.

The close contact of kitchen life had the effect of making James consider Bess a desirable woman. From flirtation or provocation, she would straighten her hat, tighten her apron strings and continually take him by the hand to lead him to the woodshed, the fruit storeroom or the washhouse. One evening as she was leaning over a cauldron of simmering soup he could not help himself from grabbing her by the waist, and as her giggles sounded like an encouragement he placed his lips on the nape of her neck where her blond curls rested.

'Are you not lonely at night Bessie, all alone in your bed?'

The maidservant burst into peals of laughter. She might have taken pleasure in teasing James, but she was already promised to a young man in Stenton, who owned a handsome herd, and who one day when they were wed, would make her into a highly regarded woman. The whims of lords brought only disillusionment and her feet were fixed too firmly on the ground for her to jeopardise her future.

'Well gorgeous,' she replied, 'if you were a man I would gladly let you have your way even if I had to ask for God's forgiveness. But sleeping with a woman? Fie on you! That is far too great a sin and I will never commit it.'

One morning Master Sandybed strode into the kitchen. Four whole days had elapsed and he was impatient to be rid of his guest. James had decided it was time to leave and was taking great delight at once again being able to dress in his own male clothes, which had been carefully brushed and pressed by Bess.

'The Hepburns will never forget you,' he said to them as he left.

As soon as he got back to Hailes, he would give the order that each year bags of wheat, barley and oats be delivered to Sandybed.

With hands on hips, the farmer watched Bothwell ride away mounted on a horse he had lent him. The nonchalance with which lords risked their lives confounded him. Politics and grand ideas did not fill up granaries, and honour counted for little before an empty plate. Leaving James Hepburn to pursue his pipe dreams, he himself was off to supervise the correct salting of the pigs bled the previous day.

13

'THERE ARE ABOUT five hundred horsemen out there,' announced Sarlebou, d'Oysel's right-hand man. 'I stayed as far away as possible from them, and I don't think they saw me.'

James Hepburn experienced a wave of anxiety.

'I suppose it is too late now to have a horse saddled and take flight.'

'I think it is but we should have nothing to fear here. Our men are ready to keep the assailants at bay for as long as is necessary.'

James was thinking hard. It was raining incessantly and the wood that surrounded the castle would soon become an untenable position for the besiegers. If they came any closer to the fortress, they risked a volley of harquebus shots. In surrounding Borthwick Castle where he had taken refuge, the chief aim of the Lords of the Congregation appeared to be to intimidate him.

'Do you know who is leading this expedition?'

'It is my Lord Arran. He came back from France only a few weeks ago, and is now being handsomely rewarded by William Cecil. For fear of creating a permanent rift with Marie de Guise, his father the Duke of Châtelherault is pretending not to know anything about it. However, we would not need to look very far to find James Stuart at the back of it all.'

'The devil take The Bastard!' exclaimed James. 'Will he always stand in my way?'

He was pacing up and down the great hall, a large chamber whose walls were adorned with torches and hung with tapestries. At any minute, the horsemen would reach the edge of the wood and all he could do was wait. With an angry kick, he splintered one of the logs smouldering in the hearth.

'One of the Lords of the Congregation is requesting a parley,' a servant announced.

James was impatient to face this insolent man who was going to try to justify an act of treason.

He was greatly surprised to find himself facing Patrick Lord Ruthven with whom he enjoyed talking about horses.

'I would have preferred meeting you under different circumstances,' he said harshly. 'Here and now we have nothing to say to one another.'

'Give back the gold you have stolen to its rightful owner, my Lord Bothwell.'

'Traitors' wages?'

'That gold belonged to Cockburn, whom you grievously wounded.'

James's sardonic laughter startled Patrick Ruthven.

'The Cockburn family are my relatives. I know them well enough to be able to call you a liar.'

Ruthven placed his hand onto the pommel of his sword. For as long as he still possessed one ounce of influence this rogue Bothwell would continue to cause them nothing but trouble. Arrogant, provocative and consumed by ambition, he had declared a war against his own kind which was not about to be extinguished.

'If you have come to Borthwick to settle our differences by man-to-man combat, my Lord Ruthven, I am ready.'

Ruthven straightened himself. The blow he was about to deal his enemy would be crueller than the strike of a sword.

'Are you refusing to return the gold?' he said brusquely.

'It belongs by right to the Regent, as does everything else smuggled across our borders.'

James stared at Ruthven contemptuously.

'In Scotland we punish thieves, my Lord Bothwell.'

'In that case you and your friends belong in gaol.'

Ruthven was struggling to contain his exasperation.

'I suggest you climb up on the wall walk, my Lord Bothwell, because before nightfall you will be treated to a delightful spectacle: your family home at Crichton will become a bonfire. What do you say to that?'

While Sarlebou and his escort were galloping towards Leith carrying the English gold, James powerless, had watched the flames rising from his castle. Thrown into a state of panic a few servants had managed to reach Borthwick, and described to their master the sacking of his abode and the destruction of his books and family documents. So the Lords of the Congregation had declared war against him. If that was the case, he resolved to pay them back blow for blow.

Janet Beaton leant over her lover and wrapped her arms around his chest. James had arrived, still distraught over the sacking of Crichton. Fortunately, the fire there had soon been contained, but the furniture had been smashed, curtains ripped, and the few valuable antiques brought back from Italy by his father had been shattered with a sledgehammer. Only his horses, probably through Ruthven's intervention, were spared. James lay back and let Janet caress him. Before resuming his fight he needed some rest and to be soothed.

'You know who your enemies are, Jamie, and you have all the time you want to avenge yourself. Let them sleep, then strike when they believe you have been subdued. You are not in a position just now to do anything against young Arran or James Stuart, and the Regent is powerless to help you. Just bide your time and be patient.'

Outside, large clouds rolled across the sky and brushed against the moors on the horizon.

'In the Borders we learn to be tough,' Janet added. 'Centuries of violence have moulded us in the image of our lands. You and I Jamie, we are two of a kind.'

'Come here,' said James softly.

He badly wanted to hold his mistress's body tightly against his, to smell her fragrance, feel her warmth, and gather up his strength. Before returning to see Marie de Guise, he would stop at Crichton to assess the damage. He would ask his sister to refurnish his ancestral castle and would provide his servants with weapons to enable them to defend themselves in the event of any renewed attack. He had just received the news that he had been declared an 'Enemy of the Congregation,' and young Arran had sent him an abusive letter through which he had skimmed with contempt. James had no illusions about the immediate future. The English were planning to despatch troops to Scotland. There would be war again with its train of death, destruction and pillage; it would turn out to be a conflict that the French, being far from their bases, might not win.

To add glamour to the Christmas festivities Marie de Guise had laid on a banquet followed by a concert, but this year there would be no dancing at Holyrood. An expeditionary force composed of eighteen hundred French and Scottish soldiers was due to set off before dawn for Stirling in order to cut off the road the English would have to follow if they wanted to deliver fresh supplies to the fortress occupied by the Lords of the Congregation. An enemy landing was imminent and a blockade of the Firth of Forth was likely.

As she listened to her favourite musicians, Marie de Guise was trying to recall every aspect of the strategy planned to the last detail by d'Oysel, Sarlebou and Bothwell. Once Stirling had been recaptured, the rebels would have no choice but to withdraw to Glasgow and St Andrews, to which they would be pursued. If she received the aid promised by her brothers, she would be in a position to humble the Lords of the Congregation and temporarily divert English intervention. Marie de Guise speculated that this would at least give her a little respite. She felt at the end of her tether, but she had to keep up appearances so as not to discourage her remaining friends, the Lords Seton, Sempill, and Atholl, as well as the Earl of Bothwell. Trying to ignore the pain gnawing at her legs and distended stomach, every day she would summon the Privy Council, and in addition carry on an active correspondence. Her doctors had diagnosed an oedema caused by a tumour in the womb or ovaries, and had prescribed a light diet and rest. Yet how could she think about herself when Scotland was being consumed by the cancer of Protestantism and was at the mercy of rebels and foreign powers?

The news coming from France was not much better. The young King, her son-in-law, who suffered from delicate health, was complaining of constant migraines and acute earache. Mary lavished care on her sickly husband, but with so frail a consort the likelihood of a pregnancy was remote. Without an heir, the position of the young Queen remained insecure and her influence was always resented by the devious Catherine de Medicis.

Just a few weeks earlier the Regent had received a portrait of her daughter. Drawn by the artist Clouet, the picture depicted an attractive young woman with an oval face and large hazel eyes. It was easy to see that Mary had inherited both the charm of the Stuarts and the authority of the Guises. Yet might the kindness she perceived in her eyes turn out to be a weakness?

'Permit me to take my leave, Madam,' whispered Bothwell. 'In less than three hours from now I have to give the order to depart.'

Roused from her thoughts Marie extended her hand to him, which he raised to his lips. While he led his troops towards Stirling this indomitable woman, her head held high, would remain at Holyrood.

'Go,' she told him, 'and may God be with you.'

With ferocious satisfaction, Bothwell watched while his troops sacked the Hamiltons' castle. Revenge was sweet: Kinneil for Crichton, an eye for an eye. Janet would be pleased. He had been disturbed over the keen sense of sadness he had felt when last taking his leave of her. It was vital not to become too permanently attached to her. He always had to be ready to go and fight, and could not envisage a stable relationship. Their brief encounters were passionate but frustrating, and both suffered as a result.

The vanguard commanded by James had reached Linlithgow. The country-side was desolate in winter and rain was falling relentlessly. He planned to order a halt for the troops to eat and rest. They were ill equipped and badly shod because the treasury was empty, and because money promised by François II had been delayed. They had been wading through mud ever since dawn.

In front of the Palace of Linlithgow where Mary Stuart had been born, the loch looked cold and grey. The peasants who had brought their oxen to drink from its waters raised their heads to watch the passage of the horsemen enveloped in their cloaks. During the past century, they had seen so many armed bands advancing or retreating they seldom questioned their identity. James entered through the imposing east gate and found himself in the large square courtyard, adorned with its majestic fountain. The Queen's apartments had been made ready for him, the very ones in which his young sovereign had been born, an honour bestowed on him by Marie de Guise. He would spend a restful evening at the Palace with d'Oysel and Sarlebou before resuming their march. The soldiers, who would be encamped in the surrounding fields, would gather round large bonfires, and supplies of ale, dried meat and oatcakes would be distrib-uted. Each man carried a blanket, a knife, a tin mug and a woollen hat. Some had included a pipe or flageolet, to accompany the ancient ballads and popular songs, which the soldiers would sing in a rousing chorus in the evenings. They told of war, of lost loves, missing brothers and phantom horsemen galloping across the moors beneath a full moon. James knew them well. They were the soul of Scotland.

While Bothwell, seated between d'Oysel and Sarlebou, was finishing his supper, a mud-spattered messenger forced his way in, his hat and cloak dripping from the rain.

'A message from the Regent,' he said as he handed a sealed sheet of foolscap to James.

It is said there are plans to have you abducted and killed, wrote Marie de Guise. *I order you to leave your command and take refuge at Niddrie Castle with Lord Seton.*

Pacing round in circles in his place of refuge, James received news of the capture of Stirling and its sacking by French troops. Atrocities had been committed on both sides: summary executions, arson and rape. Kirkaldy of Grange's castle had been blown up. With the French troops hot on their heels and having to sleep fully dressed and booted, the Lords of the Congregation had made an orderly retreat to St Andrews. There they now awaited aid from England, while the preacher John Knox increased his inflammatory and vengeful sermons.

In February, James fell ill with quartan fever and dysentery, bouts of which he had suffered since his youth. Powerless to act, he was informed of the arrival of English reinforcements and their entry into Edinburgh. The Regent barricaded herself within the fortress and sent her troops to Leith. Now nothing and no one could hold James back at Niddrie. Without warning Marie de Guise, he called up an escort and had horses saddled. For better or worse, his place was at Leith, which was being besieged.

After a victorious sortie, which succeeded in dislodging the English soldiers entrenched in front of the port, Bothwell predicted the onset of famine. The severely rationed provisions were closely guarded and any thief would be shot on sight. The promised aid from France had not arrived to relieve the besieged, and as the English had blockaded the Firth of Forth, this extinguished any hope of reprovisionment by sea. After the last chickens and sheep had been eaten, donkeys, mules and even the first horses were slaughtered. Soon they would have to make do with dogs, cats, or rats.

Having through ruse or subterfuge managed to cross enemy lines, a messenger would sometimes reach Edinburgh with news of the siege.

The Regent's health was rapidly declining, and she could now barely leave her bed to work for an hour or two. As much as her oedema, it was despair that was killing her. Scotland had become a battlefield on which the French and the English settled their scores. As death approached her, Marie de Guise was beginning to realise that both sides ought to retreat behind their own frontiers, leaving the Scots to solve their own problems and find a modus vivendi. However, any peace treaty would necessitate a strong negotiator, and she retained intact the will to remain at the head of a government representing her daughter, the legitimate Queen.

At Leith d'Oysel and Sarlebou, assisted by the Comte de Martigues and Bothwell, were defending themselves valiantly and had so far succeeded in repelling all attacks, but if they were not soon relieved they would starve. The Regent made up her mind to send Bothwell with all speed to Denmark and then on to France, in order to persuade Frederick II and her own son-in-law to send at least five thousand troops to Scotland. If she herself could assemble an army of three thousand soldiers, Leith would be liberated as well as Edinburgh. Then she would be in a good position to negotiate.

James succeeded in escaping by night from the besieged town and reaching Crichton Castle, from where he sent an urgent message to the Regent: he was ready to go to sea and fulfil his mission. Marie de Guise knew her Lieutenant was crippled with debts, and was having to sell some of his lands. If she could not compensate him, her daughter would do it.

14

THE PIT IS A TOMB in which he is buried alive. In furious desperation, James tries to free himself from the chains shackling him to the post. The iron cuts deeply into his skin. When the pain becomes too intense, he collapses onto the soiled straw which covers the floor and puts his face between his hands. For him the world now no longer exists. He knows not whether the sun is shining, nor if it is raining, nor whether dawn still breaks. In turn, he sleeps and wakes. How many days have gone by? He repeatedly relives in his mind how the warders came and roughly took hold of him to drag him down into this dungeon, and again he feels the humiliation of being at their mercy. How dare they manhandle him thus? Do they not realise he is a prince of Scotland? Once the King of France has ordered his liberation, he will demand that justice be done.

Sometimes in his mind, he very clearly sees old friends and women he has loved. Standing only a few steps away, they seem to watch him with complete detachment. Their eyes are expressionless and show no curiosity, tenderness or hatred. Mary however never comes to visit him. She knows he could not bear the distress of seeing her again without being able to approach and take her in his arms. Even thinking of her fills him with a dreadful sense of loneliness and helplessness. When this feeling of abandonment overwhelms him, he lies prostrate on the ground and falls into a fever, which engulfs him. His mind is delirious and wandering. Twice a day through the trap door they hand him a bowl of cereal soup. He flings the contents onto the floor or against the wall. The fever causes his teeth to chatter and the bouts of dysentery exhaust him. When his gaolers find him motionless and apparently unconscious as if dead, they drag him out of the dungeon and take him back to his room above. There the sudden light blinds him cruelly and the salty air he breathes from behind his prison bars seems to burn his lungs. He sits on his bed, he is willing to eat and drink, he scratches at the old wound on his hand until it draws blood, and stares unendingly at the sky, the sea and the comings and goings of fishing boats. A young Dane who comes to sweep his room once a week tells him that a prisoner has escaped but when caught later hanged himself. James listens to this tale. During his life he has seen many men hanged, but he has never rejoiced in the execution of prisoners. Some were murderers but others had merely stolen a doublet or pair of breeches from their masters.

James clasps his hands around his neck. If he escapes and returns to Scotland they will behead him, and crowds will come to watch him die. He is the same age now as his father when he died of consumption at forty-one years old. James, however, has no son to succeed him. His nephew Francis Stuart will inherit his titles and honours.

In the evening, the shadows stretch out along the shore and the setting sun casts a crimson hue over the meadows where cattle are grazing. Endlessly his mind dwells on Scotland. He tries to dispel the mental haze, which gradually as the months pass clouds his intelligence and suppresses his imagination. Now and then as if by surprise he inhales the pungent fragrance of the moors, hears the swirling current of the Tyne and pictures the summer twilight evenings, when accompanied by his dogs he would walk alongside its banks. He stoops down by the waters edge, cups his hands and quaffs the fresh river water. It is his river, etched deep in his memory, and no one will ever make him forget it. He remembers walking side by side with the Queen following the riverside path. He boldly dares to take her hand in his. She does not withdraw it, but her eyes are questioning and she seems hesitant. The flowing hem of her satin dress catches on twigs and dead leaves. She is now no longer looking at him, but her hand is soft and warm. Were they to fall in love he wonders what the future would hold for them. Mary's grace and beauty are her own and her charm is unique. Her eyes and her smile are unforgettable; he already knows they will enthral him for the rest of his life.

One morning James senses unmistakeable signs of autumn. The sea has turned a cold grey and is topped with foaming crests. The wind is blowing from the east. The long Danish winter is full of gloom, but on stormy nights, the howling wind excites him. He clings to the bars of his cell to avoid being blown away and laughs wildly in the knowledge that he is safe. The cows have disappeared from the pastures, and are replaced by flocks of screaming seagulls. The cottages near the castle seem to take on strange shapes in the mist. Sometimes James is convinced they are transformed into rocky crags. With keen eyes, he searches for ravens, buzzards, sheep and shepherds with their dogs. He listens intently for the noise of pounding hooves, but hears only the ceaseless crashing of the waves and sometimes the voice of a prison warder. He no longer knows whether the wailing he hears comes from his chest or from the wind outside.

15

Denmark and Scotland, 1560

Janet, you are the only one in whom I can confide. You were once my beloved mistress and will forever remain my dearest friend. When we parted, we spoke the words of disappointed lovers, words we do not need to repeat. No resentment or bitterness remains between us, only nostalgia for those hours of intense fulfilment that we shared together.

I am now in Denmark, a friendly country whose inhabitants show themselves to be discreet and obliging. The King granted me two audiences, during which I persuaded him not to abandon Scotland. As soon as the French begin to gather their own fleet, I am certain he will assist by despatching a regiment. Convincing the King of France, François II, and the Guises will be easy, and I will arrive in Paris with a light heart.

In Copenhagen, noble families have given me a cordial reception, and I have befriended Admiral Throndsen, who has a son and seven daughters. The eldest, Anna, has caught my eye. She has black hair and is very bright and vivacious. Having noticed my interest in her the Admiral spoke to me earnestly. My name and title appeal to her family, and they would all favourably consider a union between Anna and me. Her father would give her forty thousand thalers in dowry, a weighty argument when I consider my dire financial straits. However I need to think on it, and certainly do not wish to encumber myself with a woman before my mission in France is completed. It is true I am not wealthy, but the inconvenience of destitution is insignificant to an unattached man. It will be time enough to give them my decision on my way back. However Anna is provoking me, and says she is madly in love. As I am not made of stone, I shall sooner or later make her my mistress, which will make the end of my stay in Copenhagen even

more pleasant. Then I will travel through Germany and Flanders and
hope to be in Paris by August.

My heart still belongs to our beloved Borders, over which reigns
the most attractive woman. Often my thoughts wander back to her...

A Danish merchant ship was bound for Berwick, so the letter would leave
that same evening. More than Janet it was Anna who occupied his mind.
The audacity of this young woman, though subdued in the presence of
her parents, challenged him. He needed to keep a cool head. If he joined
her in her bed without a promise of marriage, he would be betraying the
trust of his hosts, who were already treating him like a son. He needed
to hasten his departure, leaving his ladyfriend full of hope, and who
knows, he might come back to fetch her and her forty thousand thalers
before returning to Scotland.

The young man listlessly stretched his legs and reached for a bottle
of grain alcohol. He must no longer dally in Denmark. The Regent's
strength was rapidly declining, and he needed quickly to provide her
with the joy of knowing that the mission she had entrusted him with had
been successful.

Admiral Throndsen's large mansion echoed with a myriad sounds; the
comings and goings of servants, laughter of children and barking of pet
dogs, all these were manifestations of a family life he had never known.
Even before their divorce, he could not recollect his parents living peacefully side by side. Frequently his father would return to Crichton bringing
with him his friends, vain men who paid no attention to the children of
their hosts. Then 'The Fair Earl' would take off in a whirl, leaving behind
him new debts and a weeping wife.

A faint scratching at the door of his room startled James.

'It's me,' Anna whispered.

In her pretty summer dress of periwinkle blue cloth, with its tightly
laced bodice exposing the provocative roundness of her breasts, the young
woman was irresistible. Although entirely Danish she was endowed with
the sexual attraction possessed by Mediterranean women, to which James
was strongly drawn; an olive complexion, dark eyes and long ebony hair
with auburn highlights from the sun.

'A visit?' he asked softly.

Anna entered the room and closed the door quickly behind her.

'Your servant brought your trunks down from the attic. Would you be thinking of leaving us James?'

By using his Christian name for the first time, she was taking a liberty which excited the young man. This girl was definitely forward!

'You are well aware, Anna, that I have to go to France.'

She stood very close to him. James could smell the heady fragrance of the rose water she had splashed on herself.

'Without me?'

'I am not allowed to take you with me.'

'You are allowed to abduct me, James.'

He put his arms round her then and said,

'But you would lose your honour, my dear.'

'I see no dishonour in love as long as this love is mutual.'

In order to have her at his mercy James was ready to swear that he would die for her. Her young body pressed against his, her perfume, her seductive voice whispering in his ear and the lust he perceived concealed behind a veneer of modesty were fast sweeping away his resolutions and plunging his reason into an abyss from which he had no desire to rescue it.

'Let me prove it to you.'

He had then made love to her hastily and violently and afterwards, assuaged, he had taken her again more gently. Anna had not uttered a single cry or word; she was trembling and holding onto him with all her might like a drowning person clinging on to a raft. As he stroked her slim face, he felt the tears running down her cheeks.

'I hope we have not done wrong,' he whispered.

James felt guilty. Having been welcomed as a friend, he would be leaving having broken the trust the Throndsens had placed in him.

Anna however laid her hand across his mouth and her eyes were shining.

'We made love together James. We are a couple now.'

With great difficulty, the young Scot had persuaded Anna to abandon the idea of absconding during the night. He wanted to approach the Admiral to explain the situation as reasonably as possible; Anna had become his mistress; they wished to live together and possibly marry in Scotland; he respected his daughter and intended to try to make her happy. As for

Anna, she had taken an irrevocable decision and wanted to bind her fate to his. For the time being he wanted nothing more from the Throndsens than their forgiveness and the necessary funds for Anna to survive during their long journey. Once in Scotland he would ensure she was able to live in the style to which she had been born, and he would leave to her the enjoyment of her dowry.

Throndsen had listened to James without saying a word. For some time he and his wife had been anticipating this misfortune which was befalling them. Anna was impulsive and stubborn by nature. She was bored in Copenhagen and the exciting prospect of starting a new life with an attractive man was making her vulnerable.

'I trust you my Lord,' the Admiral declared after a moment of silence, 'and I accept your word of honour that you will not abandon my daughter. You say you will marry her as soon as you are back in Scotland. I have taken note of it and if you fail to keep your word then you will no longer be welcome here.'

James felt disturbed. Entirely on her own, Anna had taken the decision to follow him, and he had given in, while wondering whether he was making an irreparable mistake.

'I would not want to go against a father's will.' he ventured. 'If you forbid Anna to come with me, I will speak to her and attempt to persuade her to comply with your wishes.'

The Throndsens had had a long discussion that same morning. With seven daughters, there were still five to marry off. The prospect that Anna would become a countess appealed to them and they had decided to trust her suitor. If he failed in his pledge, he would not see a farthing of the large sum they had somewhat hastily promised. In reality, Anna's dowry was going to be far less than that, but once he had slipped the ring onto her finger James Hepburn would have to be content with what he received.

While he was settling into a Lübeck inn with Anna, news reached James that Marie de Guise had passed away at Edinburgh Castle on the eleventh of June, surrounded by Lords who for the most part hated her. Nevertheless, she had embraced them all, before begging them in the interests of Scotland to make peace with each other. With the Regent dead, James Stuart was willing to accept a compromise. If the French were to leave

Scotland, he could obtain the withdrawal of English troops and personally lead the government. His proposal was accepted.

On hearing this news, James immediately left Anna and the servant to open the trunks, and with his mind in a state of turmoil, he went outside, wandering aimlessly through the streets. Now that The Bastard had become all-powerful in Scotland, it seemed his own role was over. At just twenty-four years old, with no political future in his country, he was doomed either to withdraw to his estates or to live abroad. His efforts with the King of Denmark and his plans to ignite the interest of the French had come to nought. Added to the fury of knowing James Stuart had triumphed, was the genuine sorrow of not seeing Marie de Guise again. He had loved and admired this brave woman who had devoted herself until her death to Scotland and to her daughter. While Mary Stuart was enjoying herself at Saint-Germain, Fontainebleau or Blois, her mother had exhausted her strength in preserving her realm. Her closest ally Cardinal Beaton had been murdered, the Earl of Lennox, as well as James's own father Patrick Hepburn had betrayed her, but never had she weakened in the upholding of her cause.

Although Protestant, James himself had supported the Regent unconditionally. She alone had the power to keep Scotland independent from England, and he could never accept the possibility of his country being subjugated under foreign rule.

He entered an inn indicated by a lantern and a crude sign depicting a drinker seated in front of a jug. Acrid smoke eddied from the hearth. A few customers were chatting over jugs of beer while a stout waitress stood and smiled as she listened to them. James ordered a carafe of aquavit; alcohol would chase away depression and he would stop thinking about James Stuart or Anna Throndsen. Considering herself his legitimate partner, Anna was watching his every move, giving him advice, even daring to pass judgement on his family or the way he administered his estates. Fiery in bed, as soon as she was dressed she showed that she possessed a cold and calculating head, which caused him endless irritation. Yet it was impossible to abandon her along the way.

After the second glass, James's thoughts became clearer. Instead of pleading for armed resistance, he would present his condolences to the new Queen, Mary Stuart, and gain her trust. If he became her ally, he could request an office and an income in Scotland and would not have to bow before The Bastard. Having emptied the carafe, he felt almost happy. Even if Anna bored him she made a pleasant bed companion, and he was now going straight back to see her. He would somehow find an excuse not to take her to Paris, and would find a place where she could stay while waiting for him. With his pockets now empty he was accepting his mistress's financial aid, certain that with the hoped for reversal of his fortunes he would be able to pay her back. With diplomacy but firmness, he would make the Queen understand that he had become indebted while in her mother's service. She would surely offer him compensation.

In the narrow streets of Lübeck, the air was permeated with the reek of salted fish and cabbage soup. There was a distant rumble of thunder, and intermittent flashes of lightning streaked across the night sky. Walking briskly, James determined that from now on he would make more haste travelling through Germany. In Flanders he would drop off Anna, enabling him to continue his journey alone through the Duchy of Luxembourg and Champagne.

He knew France was enduring hard times and that Protestant unrest there was growing. La Renaudie, an ally of the Prince de Condé, had been hanged together with his friends from the ramparts of Amboise before the very eyes of the young sovereigns. More conspiracies were feared, and the Guises showed no mercy towards the Huguenots. Back at the inn James found Anna waiting for him. Before she had time to reproach him for his lateness, he carried her off to bed.

The Earl of Bothwell's intentions were assisted by luck. In Flanders Anna was reunited with one of her cousins who was pleased to offer them his hospitality. Amidst embraces and caresses from James, the young woman reluctantly agreed to let him go on alone to Paris, while she would remain under the protection of her relatives. The sum granted by Admiral Throndsen to his daughter was already shrinking, but in order to appear at the French Court without demeaning himself, James would need to buy clothes and take on a new servant. Graciously Anna handed over the money he needed, confident in the knowledge that her generosity would bind him to her for ever. All the promises she managed to extract from

James, to write every day, to stay faithful, to announce their forthcoming wedding to his mother, were impossible for him to keep and he knew he would break them.

The young Earl was happy to be back in Paris. He had left that city as a poor student and was returning to be introduced to the Valois Court and to discourse with the Queen of France and Scotland. Far from the Reims College of his youth, he would reside in a lovely building on the corner of the Rue Jean-Tison and the Rue de Bailleul, a short distance from the Louvre. Dating back about a hundred years, the hotel extended at the rear into a small garden, at the end of which stood a barn filled with forage for the horses of the neighbourhood. In the evenings, the air was filled with the scent of freshly harvested hay mingled with the fragrance of mignonette and grenadines. A vine had been trained up the south-facing wall, and bees and wasps buzzed around the ripe bunches of grapes.

James had the use of the ground and first floors. An elderly gentleman, who left his apartments only to report for duty in Catherine de Medicis's service occupied the second floor. The court was due to leave for Saint-Germain any day now and the young Earl would have to make haste to request an audience, which could sometimes take a considerable time to be granted.

James soon explored his new surroundings and was free to reflect at leisure on the situation in which he now found himself. His adventurous nature and the ambitions he nurtured drove him onwards. He had to try to get the Queen to confer on him a post that James Stuart could not call into question, and which would give him some power and influence in the Scottish Parliament. If his ambitions proved to be in vain, he would return to France and gain command of a regiment.

With considerable relief, James received a note summoning him to the Château de Saint-Germain at the end of September. The letter specified that as she had been unwell, Her Majesty the Queen regretted she had been unable earlier to receive her loyal servant, about whom her mother had told her so much. James had a week to spare, during which he procured courtly clothes for himself and a livery for his servant. Once the rent for his lodgings had been paid there was nothing left of the nest egg Anna had given him, and this state of poverty filled him with consternation, although he gave little thought to the young woman waiting for him back in Flanders. He cast an eye with yearning on the pretty women doing their shopping near the Louvre, escorted by their ladies-in-waiting and maidservants. Sometimes one of them would return his glance. If only his lifestyle had matched his titles of nobility, he would not have hesitated to respond to his desires.

16

FOR THE PAST FEW DAYS, the memory of Mary Stuart has been haunting James and breaking his heart. In loving her, he had lost her. Without him, she might have been able to put up with her husband and forgive him. Indeed, she had no longer felt any desire or love for Darnley. Yet do not many women end up resigning themselves to a bad and unsatisfactory marriage? James had seduced, confused and conquered a woman who, her resolve weakened by unhappiness and passion, was prepared to commit folly. He had not attempted to leave her and go to France, neither did she urge him to leave. Both being convinced they were acting in Scotland's best interests, they played into their enemies' hands. The bitter memory of his humiliating defeat at Carberry Hill always returns to him. These thoughts forever torture him. He could have done this, he should have done that... the words plague him and are slowly killing him. He cannot accept being discarded, useless and powerless. Even when in the pit and driven half out of his mind, still his rebellious spirit lives on. A hundred times over, he has killed The Bastard, Maitland, Kirkaldy of Grange, Lennox, and the Earl of Mar with his own hands. Today they are all dead, and he curses them bitterly. Only Morton and Balfour remain, the worst traitors of the lot. His ultimate fancy would be to plunge his dirk into their guts and watch them die slowly. His imagination never tires of it. He drinks straight from the neck of the bottle of wine they bring him twice daily. Soup, salted fish and a round loaf of dark bread accompany this beverage. He had asked for and been granted the favour every week of a small bottle of eau de vie. Having finished half of it, he then falls into a forgetful slumber.

With the passing of the months his body becomes bowed, and

gradually deteriorates. Swollen by oedema, his legs are causing him constant pain. Once upon a time, his body had been strong and muscular. Sleepless nights and drinking binges had no effect on him. From dawn to dusk he would ride in all weathers, and neither the cold, nor the rain, nor the hail could discourage him from his purpose. Few women could resist him. Do they still miss him today? In the early days of his imprisonment, his forced chastity had made him irritable. Even the distant sight of a pretty woman observed from behind his bars, aroused him. Today he has only the memory of arousal, and Mary's body held in his arms is without substance. What were the words he used when he made love to her? He no longer recalls, he only remembers that they shared intense pleasure, and that this sensuality made them dependent on each other. James's thoughts now turn to women only when he has been drinking. The alcohol removes the barriers he has erected to suppress all feelings and nostalgia. Without knowing why, his eyes fill with tears. He remains motionless and prostrate on his bed or else hammers impotently at the wall with his fists, kicking over the table and chair. As long as he remains quiet they forget about him; otherwise they throw him into the pit and tie him up in chains. At night, the same dreams come to torment him. At Crichton, he is walking along beside the Tyne, but when he tries to retrace his steps, he can no longer walk. His body is inert and heavy as lead. He wants to kill himself but lacks a weapon. He is condemned to live. At other times, he is assaulted by savage dogs, which surround him and growl menacingly. He takes a step back and falls from the top of a cliff, a fearless, painless, and endless descent into oblivion.

During periods of lucidity, James makes plans. He needs to escape from Dragsholm, to stow away on a fishing boat and reach a port where he will find a merchant vessel sailing for France. There King Henri will receive him, and he will be able to convince him that ten thousand men should be sufficient to overthrow the Regent Morton, stir up the supporters of the captive Queen and demand her liberation from the English. He is ready to lead this army and take them to victory. He has friends in Scotland, the Hamiltons, the Gordons, and the noble families of the Borders, and despite having been decimated by successive acts of revenge, the Hepburns are still numerous. They will all gather around him. He pictures Mary in the royal Palace of Holyrood to which he has brought her back. He even smells her perfume. In time, they will both forget the suffering and the intolerable injustice which kept them in captivity without any trial.

James also thinks about the King of Denmark, who had been so benevolent towards him when he approached him with a view to obtaining troops, just before his trip to France during which he would meet Mary Stuart for the first time. Frederick liked to drink, and in Copenhagen they had downed a great quantity of wine and spirits in an atmosphere of trust and friendship. Ten years later as a fugitive in Denmark, the King would not even deign to receive him, did not personally respond to his letters, and never got involved in trying to obtain the release of his own cousin Mary from the clutches of Elizabeth. The friendship of Kings now seems nothing but hypocrisy.

James broods over his bitterness. Are there still men who attach importance and priority to honour and loyalty? Are there still nobles in Scotland who feel loyally bound to their sovereign? Carberry Hill was no battle but a most despicable charade. He wishes he had had enough cannons to annihilate all his enemies.

Nightfall is the time he fears most. He feels shrouded and buried alive, and he clings to the bars of his prison. The cottages, the trees, the expanse of sea, all drift away and fade into the shadows. When will he see them again? There is nothing remaining on earth that is not hostile to him. The world disowns him.

17

'I WELCOME YOU, my Lord Bothwell.'

Instantly, James succumbed to the charms of his young Queen. Mary had a persuasive voice and captivating smile. Bending his knee in homage, he placed his lips on the hand she extended towards him.

'Arise Lord Bothwell, and let us walk together in the garden. I have long wanted to meet you, and to be able to talk with you.'

James understood the ways of women well enough to know that Mary was favourably impressed with him. To his amazement, the young Queen seemed very well informed about the religious and political situation in Scotland. However, as her knowledge was theoretical it did not enlighten her much on the reality of the conflicting factions and beliefs now rife in Scotland. The secret ambitions, rivalries, and jealousies of her nobles were still an alien world to her. She placed all her faith in blood ties and felt strongly that her half-brother would always support her: she greatly admired him and never thought of excluding him from a powerful role in Scotland.

After reading the lengthy epistles sent to her by her mother, she understood she could count on the support only of certain families like the Hepburns, but by leaning on those, she would in due course earn the trust of the others. It was necessary for her to tolerate Protestantism, and any going back on that decision would be seriously detrimental to her authority as well as to domestic peace.

James listened to her short speech with a mixture of interest and concern. Living as she did in the most civilized and refined court in Europe, accustomed to her every wish being satisfied, constantly flattered and adored, the Queen would sometimes be hurt and offended by harsh Scottish realism, and the feelings she expressed would not universally curry favour in Edinburgh. France was an absolute monarchy, unlike in Scotland, where the sovereign decided nothing without the endorsement of the Privy Council followed by that of Parliament. The religious tolerance which she advocated, the Earl of Bothwell knew could only be practised by Protestants towards Papists, and he had no illusions about the outcome of this indulgence. Now at the head of the Regency Council, James Stuart would show himself to be merciless against those who did not belong to the Reformation.

The train of Mary's dress was sweeping the fine gravel of the walk along which they were proceeding. Around them, multitudes of gardeners were busy raking paths, trimming hedges and lawns and attending to flower beds. Fallen leaves were already covering the grass where peacocks strutted, showing off their fine plumage, but the autumn weather remained mild.

'I want you to be part of the Regency Council together with my half-brother, and the Duke of Châtelherault, who is one of my relatives, should also be included.'

Leaning on James's arm, Mary frequently stopped to watch a bird, a butterfly, even a cat perched on top of a bench.

'I am at your service, Madam.'

James did not quite know how to inform the Queen of his impecunious state. His need for money was now becoming urgent. He had spent all of Anna's nest egg, and had just written to her asking for another loan. In Paris money slipped all too easily through his fingers, and if he did not promptly receive at least a hundred crowns he would not be able to honour his debts.

'I am in debt to your late mother for her support and kindness, but I now find myself unable to repay it to you,' he ventured finally.

Mary turned around to face him.

'It is I my Lord who am your debtor. The Stuarts are not ungrateful.'

The charm of her smile moved James. It revealed her femininity, combined with an innate sense of seduction and an almost childlike candour.

'I have already given the order to disburse six hundred pounds to you. Moreover, His Majesty the King wishes to appoint you a Gentleman of his Chamber, with the income attached to that office.'

James bowed. As well as having the assurance of being free from all immediate financial worry, he felt exhilarated in the presence of this young woman.

'Thus,' Mary added, in a mischievous tone, 'you will be more often by my side'.

Wherever she was residing, whether at the Louvre, Saint-Germain-en-Laye, or Fontainebleau, James was regularly invited to court. He had long and serious exchanges with François de Guise and his brother the Cardinal of Lorraine. They wished for the formation of a Regency Council in Scotland, on which five Protestants and seven Catholics would sit. In addition to himself, the names of James Stuart, the Earl of Argyll, the Duke of Châtelherault, and the Earl of Morton had been proposed for the Protestant side. Those of George Gordon Earl of Huntly, the Earl of Atholl, the Primate of Scotland John Hamilton, who was the Duke of Châtelherault's brother, and the Lords Seton and Montrose had been proposed for the Catholic side. The Guises had made a strong impression on James. They knew down to the very last detail the terms of the Treaty of Edinburgh ratified between Scotland and England, which stipulated the total withdrawal of English and French troops from Scottish soil and Mary Stuart's renunciation of her immediate rights to the English Crown. The French, the Queen's uncles had assured him, were relieved to be rid of the Scottish burden. France was not spared from religious conflicts either, and following the Amboise conspiracy they were determined to do whatever they could to avoid further rebellion.

The Queen of England, Charles de Guise had noted, *is no fool.*
I trust you heard, my Lord, about the untimely death of Amy
Robsart, the wife of Robert Dudley, Elizabeth's favourite, if not
more, thus leaving her dear Robin conveniently free to remarry.
By banishing him from court until his name was cleared, I have to
admit that Elizabeth acted with discretion.

At the end of October, having gained the Guises trust serving King François II and enjoying the delights of Paris, James received a letter from Anna who was ill in Flanders, begging him to come back. Far from him and from her parents, she was afraid of dying. Despite his new mistresses, James was feeling guilty about neglecting this young woman, who had sacrificed everything to be with him. She was madly in love with him while he felt only affection for her, but this difference of emotion did not give him the right to abandon her. He had made the mistake of abducting the daughter of a gentleman, and would have to bear the consequences.

With a heavy heart, James prepared for his departure. He would collect Anna, find a suitable residence for her in Scotland, then having settled her he would have the freedom to work on the setting up of the Regency Council as recommended by the Guises. He conceded that a gesture of goodwill towards his enemy James Stuart would be necessary. After this he would strive to find a husband for his sister Janet, and as soon as spring arrived he would return to France.

When James announced his imminent departure, Mary's instant response was to say

'Stay, my Lord, you cannot leave. His Majesty the King is not well and I have need of you here.'

To convince James Mary clasped his hand. She appreciated the company of the young Earl, and seeing him had become important to her. Like her uncles, James was virile and charismatic. Though she forbade herself from drawing any comparison, and although she did love him dearly, he made her husband the King seem childlike. The latter's ever frail health caused him to be irritable, often sullen, and demanding. In bed, his expressed desires were yet to be realised, and remained unfulfilled.

In the gardens of the Louvre, flocks of starlings had arrived and pecked busily around on the grass among the falling leaves. The towers of Philippe Auguste stretched their menacing shadows across the flowerbeds, where the violas and autumn daisies were now fast withering.

There was a large hearth in the Queen's elegant morning room, which had walnut panelling on the walls and ceilings picked out in gold. The weary face and anxious expression of the young woman struck James forcibly. Despite all the luxury and attention lavished on her, Mary did not give the impression of being happy. Her previous zest for life seemed restrained and her energy subdued. Between a sickly husband and a hostile mother-in-law, she had gone into a decline.

'I am leaving against my own wishes, Your Grace can be sure of that!' said James, speaking with regret in his voice.

The Queen was wearing lilac water perfume, which filled the room with its fragrance. Constricted by a rigid busk, the slenderness of her waist was emphasised by the fullness of her skirts, which allowed a black velvet-clad foot to appear beneath them. In her face and with her intricately embroidered cloth and ribbons, to James's eyes Mary resembled a young woman dressed for a ball.

Becoming suddenly aware that she held his hand and of the boldness of her earlier impulse, she let it go. In close proximity to her were the four ladies-in-waiting who had left Scotland with her twelve years earlier, and now sat doing their embroidery, Mary Seton, Mary Beaton, Mary Fleming, and Mary Livingstone.

'His Majesty is suffering violent headaches,' she said in a concerned voice, stepping back a pace. 'I am in need of loyal friends, as I have many worries to contend with.'

'I will be back in Paris by the end of winter, Madam.'

Mary forced a smile.

'Bring me my musicians,' she said suddenly, trying to sound cheerful, 'I need some distraction.'

Then turning towards James, 'Since you have to leave me my Lord Bothwell, I insist that you stay with me this evening. You will dine with me. Then you will be free to go whenever you please.'

His belongings packed, James was ready to go. With the money granted by the King of France, he would be able to travel in the style of a gentleman: a servant, a groom, a barber, and a secretary would accompany him. As soon as Anna felt better, they would sail for Edinburgh.

The evening spent with the Queen left him nostalgic. Mary who seemed once again in high spirits, had recited verses by Ronsard, accompanied on the lute by Claude Goudinal, a musician renowned throughout the whole of Europe. Then, pallid and morose as usual the young King had made an appearance. Immediately Mary had rushed to greet him and spontaneously put her arm around his shoulders. With eyes half shut, he had let himself be comforted like a child.

'The Queen informs me you are leaving us, my Lord Bothwell,' François had said, turning to look at him. 'I understand you want to see Scotland again. It is a country of which I am King, but sadly have never seen.'

'Your subjects await you, my Lord.'

François had smiled feebly.

'Travelling exhausts me. Tell me about Scotland, as the Queen remembers little about it.'

'I have not forgotten Stirling,' Mary had interjected, 'and I have a few memories of the Priory of Inchmahome, where my mother sent me for a while to safeguard me from the English. I also remember Dumbarton Castle, from which I sailed to France.'

The servants had placed on the table silver dishes, garnished with candied fruit, dates, figs, and raisins, and silver-plated bowls overflowing with sugared almonds, orange-flower flavoured almond cakes, and quince paste sprinkled with cinnamon. Beside the hearth next to François's greyhounds, the Queen's Maltese terriers lay sleeping.

'Unhappy memories, Madam,' James had replied. 'Come back to Scotland and discover her attractions.'

In his mind, the prospect of a royal progress appealed to him, as it would enable his Queen to learn to love the towns and countryside that he himself loved. The Queen being a bold and accomplished rider, he could take her to the Borders and show her the towns and villages, the panorama of the hills and moors and endless skies, and bring her a taste of freedom she had never before experienced.

Having passed through the gates of Paris, James and his retinue took the road leading northwards. The dreary countryside they passed through matched his mood and added to the bitterness he felt at having to submit to the wishes of a lover he did not cherish. He knew it was Anna's intention that they should get married, but being now graced with Mary's friendship he could hope for a nobler and more meaningful alliance. He was resigned to the fact that Anna would remain his mistress at least in name, until having been continuously left on her own, he hoped she would tire of waiting and return to her own country.

The mild spell was turning the road into a bog, and a dank wind was blowing, sweeping low clouds across the sky. Before his departure, the young man had received a note from the Queen, thanking him again for his services. Adding to the generosity he had already been shown she was promising him the revenues of the Abbeys of Melrose and Haddington, bringing an income that would make it possible for him to maintain his castles and replenish his livestock.

The horses proceeded at a walk. Being in no hurry to reach Flanders,

James was not hastening his pace and tarried at taverns on the way. He had decided to make a detour via Reims to visit Renée de Guise, sister of the late Queen Regent of Scotland, and Prioress of the Abbey of Saint-Pierre des Dames. Together they would remember and talk about this admirable woman whom they had been unable to assist in her final hours in Edinburgh Castle.

It was well into November by the time James crossed the border into Flanders. Here the rain was pouring down onto fields grazed by dairy cows, while flocks of geese frequented the ponds. Having left Paris behind he was now impatient to get back to Scotland as soon as possible, to assess the political situation and act as the Queen's appointed emissary. In his mind, he wondered whether due to The Bastard's personal ambitions, even the legitimacy of the Queen would be questioned, but as he had always done James knew he would remain loyal to his Stuart Queen. He recognized that a country could not survive without the observance of its laws and traditions, but equally he saw that reform was necessary, and in this respect, he was determined to play his part.

18

IT WAS MID-DECEMBER in Ostend, and Anna was taking a walk arm in arm with Bothwell, when a messenger arrived carrying a letter sent by the Queen's Chamberlain: after suffering unbearable pain, François II had died from an abcess on his brain. From being Queen of France Mary had now become Queen Dowager. This allowed Catherine de Medicis much greater power and influence, and at the same time to have more control over the new King Charles IX, who was only ten years old.

This news threw James into a state of deep anxiety. France was no longer able to lay claim to Scotland, and would now distance herself from Scottish affairs. As for Mary, she was oblivious of the difficulties awaiting her. To what future would James now have to reconcile himself? What would the Scottish Queen decide? Already delayed in Flanders with Anna, she was now an even heavier burden on the young Earl's shoulders, but he knew it was essential for him to curb his impatience and try to appear contented. In great haste, he sent his secretary to Paris so that he could keep him informed of any turn of events. If Catherine de Medicis took over the Regency of France, it would be a hard blow for the Guises. Everybody knew the Queen Mother wished for reconciliation with Antoine de Navarre and his brother Condé, who were both Protestants. Although this may have been a wise policy, it would set the Duke of Lorraine's connections against her. Edinburgh must now be in a state of upheaval, and James felt distraught at being kept away when so many opportunities could be opening up for him. Anna did not entertain the slightest suspicions about his frustrations. James began to feel that this young woman, whom he had so admired for her independence and rebellious spirit, was now turning out to be no different from the rest, passionate by nature, but scheming and self-serving. Apart from the pleasure they enjoyed at night, they shared little in common.

By the end of January, James was informed by his secretary of the rumour spreading throughout the French court: Don Carlos, Philip II's son, or young Arran, backed by Scotland to ensure the influence of the Reformation, would come forward as suitors for Mary Stuart's hand.

Anna's health was improving daily and the prospect of their forthcoming departure for Edinburgh raised James's spirits. After establishing Anna in a comfortable house in the Lothians, he would be free to attend to his affairs and would ensure that he received the money promised by the Queen.

When he arrived at Morham James received the warmest welcome.

'Is it true that our Queen is coming back to Scotland?' he was asked straightaway.

Although Lady Agnes had changed little, Janet had grown up and been transformed into an accomplished and elegant young lady. She was now courted by numerous suitors, but ignored them all.

'That is what they say,' James replied.

James Stuart, Mary's half-brother had landed in France to persuade her to rule Scotland herself. The young Earl knew he had taken this step only with the aim of establishing his own authority. Believing her to be ignorant of the realities of the situation in her kingdom, James Stuart hoped she would immediately fall into his clutches. However, Bothwell was determined that he himself would be her chief adviser. The Queen had not forgotten him and he had just received the command of the fortress of Dunbar, an important garrison built on the edge of the sea and defended by a powerful war arsenal. Being the Master of Dunbar and of Hermitage, Lieutenant of the Borders, Governor of the border town of Liddesdale, Lord of Crichton and Hailes, and High Admiral of Scotland, he was now a force to be reckoned with even for James Stuart, a King's illegitimate son.

As they walked slowly side by side, Janet grabbed her brother's arm, whispering excitedly,

'I have a secret to tell you.'

'You are in love, aren't you?' guessed James.

'I think so.'

'And who is the lucky man?' he asked.

Janet was flushed with excitement. As they walked on, flocks of rooks took flight in front of them, their feathers shining in the cold winter light. Scarlet berries gleamed on the holly bushes. The sun was sinking and shadows were lengthening over the outcrops of rock, covered with rust-coloured moss, in the steep fields around them. The beauty of Scotland filled the young Earl with wonder. Although the Ile-de-France and the Val de Loire were attractive regions, they lacked the wild splendour and poetic charm of the Scottish Highlands and Lowlands.

'John Stuart,' Janet whispered, 'the Prior of Coldingham.'

James stopped in his tracks. John was the Queen's youngest half-brother, and King James v's last illegitimate offspring.

'But Lord John is only a child!'

'He is just a year younger than me, my dear brother!' Janet retorted, laughing.

'You must not consider this alliance without obtaining the Queen's consent.' replied James.

However, he now felt a huge sense of satisfaction. Being about to become part of the royal family, Janet would forge solid bonds between the Hepburns and the Stuarts.

'This is why I am so impatient to find out whether our sovereign is coming back!' she exclaimed.

According to the most recent news James had received from Paris, Mary seemed indeed ready to return to her kingdom. At eighteen, the role of Queen Dowager did not tempt her in the least, and she preferred to run her own household rather than submit to the authority of a mother-in-law for whom she felt no affection. Besides, she perhaps might consider Scotland as a temporary base, prior to making a brilliant political match. Although this conjecture appealed to her half-brother James Stuart, it upset most of the members of the nobility.

'They say Arran's marriage proposal was rejected by Elizabeth,' Janet continued, 'and that he is going to address it directly to our Queen.'

'Her Majesty would never consider marrying that devious and narrow-minded creature!'

'What is it to you who she chooses as a husband?' she remarked mischievously. 'Have you perhaps fallen for our Queen's charms?'

George Gordon, fourth Earl of Huntly was pacing up and down his reception hall. His powerful ancestral castle stood on the threshold of the Highlands and controlled a huge area over which the Earl held absolute sway. A moderate Catholic and anxious not to make implacable enemies, Huntly had been striving to remain on civil terms with the Lords of the Congregation.

'Chancellor Cecil cannot refuse our Queen safe conduct through England without the tacit agreement of the Lords of the Congregation!' the Earl declared forcefully. 'Before her cousin has even reached Scotland Elizabeth intends to leave her in no doubt as to who is the dominant ruler.'

Summoned to a meeting at Huntly Castle in the Earldom of Strathbogie, the Earls of Cassilis, Bothwell, Atholl and Montrose had gone over in fine detail events to do with the Queen's imminent return to Scotland. Mary Stuart's decision had been known since May and already the royal castles, neglected for many years, were being renovated. Repeatedly, they had hotly debated the margins of freedom the Lords of the Congregation would grant the Queen, and the stringent limits imposed had exasperated the Catholic Lords.

'At the first sign of weakness she will find herself challenged.'

'Merely making the sign of the cross will become a crime,' Lord Huntly added.

'Knox's arrogance knows no bounds, and before long he will consider his power to be superior to that of the Queen.'

Agitated and flushed, the Earl spoke heatedly and constantly needed to mop his brow. His conciliatory attitude towards James Stuart's friends had proved fruitless, and he had decided to become the leader of the Catholic Opposition.

If he were able to succeed in his efforts to persuade the Queen that he was her most reliable ally, perhaps she would favourably consider a union with his son Lord John Gordon, who had already presented himself as a suitor. Scotland could then come back to the Catholic Church and the Gordons would be in a position of power.

'Her Majesty needs to conform to the wishes of a people who are mainly Protestant.' replied James, annoyed with Huntly's expectations. In his eyes, they were rash and unrealistic, but the strong support of this family would nevertheless be necessary to Mary in the early days of her personal rule. Without this counterweight, The Bastard would meet with no opposition at all and would not hesitate to manipulate his sister for his own interests. Since his return to Scotland James had sensed the hatred his rival bore him, James Stuart being incapable of tolerating a Protestant who was entirely devoted to the legitimate monarchy.

The Earl of Atholl sighed with regret. He was a good Catholic, who did not possess the tempestuous nature of old George Gordon or the passionate spirit of young Hepburn, and he knew that neither of them was fully conscious of how powerful The Bastard had now become. If Huntly or Bothwell attempted to contest his influence, James Stuart would show no mercy towards them.

'Our Queen is due to land at Aberdeen,' Huntly continued. 'She will enter Edinburgh under my protection.'

There was a moment of silence. None of the nobles present could agree to give rein to the one they called the 'Cock o' the North.' Replacing the cunning Stuart with the arrogant Huntly would create a deadly rivalry between those two ambitious men.

The meeting was ending. James had decided not to oppose the Gordons directly and to hasten to find a compromise with the Hamiltons, who had not yet forgiven him for the capture of the English gold. Even though, thanks to the Queen's generosity he had now been freed from his major financial difficulties, he could not afford the permanent protection of an armed guard.

'As High Admiral you will be called to France to organise our Queen's fleet, my Lord Bothwell, and you will be in a position to have fruitful exchanges with her,' Atholl remarked. 'Having no brothers or sisters, nor uncles nor legitimate close relatives in Scotland, Her Majesty will find herself very isolated in Edinburgh. The weight of her Privy Council will therefore be a deciding factor. Let us ensure it is a tolerant one.'

'Who is going to allow James Stuart to wield such power?' retorted Huntly indignantly. 'If Her Majesty trusts him he will be free to weave his web without restraint. As for me my Lords, I do not intend to allow anyone to thwart me. If she rejects the hand I am extending to her, the Queen will soon realize her mistake. Eventually a man must make choices, and if our Queen believes she is landing in a fairytale kingdom, I am afraid she will soon be very much disillusioned.'

George Gordon, son of the Earl of Huntly, had insisted on riding part of the way back with Bothwell. The two young men got along well together and James considered George to be one of his few friends. The lush grass glistened from the rain that had fallen that morning, and a rushing stream flowed between the alders that grew along its banks. From time to time, the riders and their little escort passed through a village and saw a church spire towering above them, or a stone chimney indicating a tavern. Drying in the sun were stacks of peat used to fuel the hearths of the thatched cottages.

'You are very lucky to be going to France,' George said as they were fording a river. 'Here in Scotland the very air reeks of intrigue, and I fear my father and brother John will do nothing to dispel it. Take care of yourself, James; you have enemies!'

'Who in Scotland does not!' retorted James in a mocking tone. 'Most families still brood over ancient grudges whose origins they have long forgotten. I am not the kind of man to ask a favour from anyone.'

'You are too self-confident,' George replied.

'I will have the friendship of the Queen,' replied James. He then fell silent, but he had decided to be on his guard. The blood ties linking Mary to her half-brother James Stuart would he hoped be countered by the trust she placed in Bothwell and his power over the Borders. He did not fear James Stuart, nor did he fear William Maitland, Hamilton's former Secretary of State, who during Marie de Guise's Regency had not been involved in government.

The two young men parted at the Aberdeenshire border. James would head south towards Crichton keeping up a good pace, and make ready for his departure for France. George would return to Strathbogie and the family castle, where various dubious and questionable projects were being planned. He could only hope their foolhardiness would not bring ruin to the Gordons, and that Bothwell's pride would not blind him to the plots being hatched against him by his enemies.

19

JAMES, HORRIFIED, sees his body deteriorating little by little and becoming his own enemy. Lack of activity, dampness, and malnourishment cause his joints to ache and his limbs to swell and give him terrible sensations of breathlessness. Some days he can hardly leave his bed. Employed to shave him every week the barber prescribes bloodlettings, but James refuses. Nothing except freedom can cure him. Already he feels bereft of his sanity, a sick mind in a decrepit body. His life and his freedom have been stolen from him. Never again will he walk through the countryside or ride a horse; never again will he hold a woman in his arms. He is existing in a kind of living death, a living hell.

Confined to his bed with his eyes half-closed, he desperately tries to conjure up his first and last months as a prince. Why did he and the Queen not take refuge in Edinburgh Castle? Why did they leave Dunbar so hastily? He attempts to trace every moment, every snatch of conversation. When the agony of defeat becomes too overwhelming, he shouts and bashes his head against the wall and they drag him down to the pit. There he stops eating and lies in his own faeces. He no longer knows where he is.

It is raining and the nights are getting chilly. James senses winter is approaching. How long has he been at Dragsholm? One year or ten years?

Thinking he was being magnanimous, the King of Denmark has caused him to be buried alive. Since they are refusing to let him go to France, why not let him go back to Scotland and let him be executed? Then before he dies he will reveal the treachery and evil doings of others, and his head will not be the only one to roll. Often he pictures himself talking from the height of the gallows. He lists facts, discloses names;

what he saw and heard remains clear in his mind. The fact that he is powerless to reveal it all chokes him. It is a dark night and it is snowing. An abscess has surfaced on his right leg and the pain has become unbearable. Four men hold him down on his bed while the barber makes an incision and dresses the wound. Why do they want to prolong his existence? What monstrous sense of charity urges his gaolers to keep him alive when he wishes to die? He knows he counts for nothing any more. To the world James Hepburn, Earl of Bothwell and Duke of Orkney, no longer exists. He is the survivor of a past era, which everyone prefers to forget.

One night it is blowing a gale. Sitting on his bed James relives his escape from Scotland, in which fear and excitement are intermingled. He has managed to give his pursuers the slip, and is now free to rally to her cause those who remain loyal to Mary Stuart. The Kings of Sweden, Denmark, Spain, and France will muster their troops. Soon he will land in Scotland at the head of a powerful army and will crush the traitors. As yet he is still unaware that an ill wind will cast him onto the Norwegian coast and that Frederick II will refuse to see him. James Stuart and Maitland have triumphed. The Scots believed the traitors' lies, and followed them as sheep follow their shepherd. Peace has returned they say. What peace? A series of plots and murders, exiles, imprisonments, forced submission, merciless oppression in the Borders, and hasty settling of old scores.

James is aware that after the Saint Bartholomew Day massacre France abandoned any idea of sending troops to Scotland, and Mary lost her last remaining friends. Where is she? From now on, the wall separating James from his wife is insurmountable. Since his transfer from Malmö, no news reaches him any more. Yet he knows that she still lives. The scandal of a Queen's execution would have reached even the walls of Dragsholm.

If Mary needs to remarry in order to re-ascend her throne, he is prepared to sign a decree of divorce. He is now indifferent to everything, and after a few more months have passed, the physical and mental distress he endures will finally have gained the better of him.

20

AFTER THE PERIOD OF seclusion imposed by etiquette on royal widows, Mary Stuart vacated her apartments to take refuge with the Guises at Joinville within the confines of Champagne. This was a period of reflection, of preparing for her forthcoming departure for Scotland, and surrounding herself with those who were going to escort her to Edinburgh. Three of her uncles had already announced their intention to accompany her, as well as a great many of her faithful supporters who had served her since her youth, whether nobles, prelates, poets, or musicians. Most of her servants would also accompany her on her journey.

Each day her uncle, the Cardinal de Lorraine, summoned her to his study to brief her on her future responsibilities. With some dismay, Mary read her mother's long epistles, in which she revealed the enormous difficulties she had faced. Every time he considered it necessary, her uncle would interrupt her reading to emphasise a name or comment on a situation. Day after day, the young Queen was assimilating the current state of affairs in Scotland. As a Catholic, she would be isolated and would only be able to practise her religion discreetly and in private. Perceived as a Frenchwoman, she would arouse mistrust, which only a policy that was unequivocally Scottish would appease. Her uncles had vehemently rejected the Earl of Huntly's proposal; the young Queen could not make her entry into Edinburgh escorted only by Catholics. This challenge to the Lords of the Congregation would be unwise and inappropriate. From the outset, the Scottish Catholics should be made aware they would enjoy no special favours.

Mary dreaded the prospect of the isolation into which she was likely to be immersed, and confessed that she thought her only consolation would be the affection of her half-brother James Stuart, who a few days previously had come to visit her at Joinville. The Cardinal de Lorraine abstained from passing on to his niece the considerable doubts he entertained about the latter's intentions. During the early days of Mary's rule, The Bastard would indeed be indispensable, but little by little, she would find out his true nature.

The names of the nobles noted by Marie de Guise as being trustworthy were very few, but the late Regent had stressed that her daughter could entirely rely on those she had named. Mary was delighted to see James Hepburn listed amongst them. Her thoughts had often turned to him, and to the immediate feeling of harmony she felt between them which had brought them closer. Some people hinted to her that the Earl of Bothwell was a proud and violent man, but what she herself had discovered was his charm without affectation, his complete outspokenness, and an impetuousness that matched her own. Although unconventional, his striking looks were unforgettable. His full lips, broken nose and dark, almost black, eyes suggested sensuality, but also an aura of authority to which she was susceptible. The young man was expected at Joinville any day now, and Mary was careful not to show any sign of the joy she felt at the prospect of this reunion.

Neglecting the ancient fortified castle which stood sentinel on the hill above, Duke Claude de Guise had built an elegant Italianate palace on lower ground close to a bend in the River Marne. Surrounded by water and capped with three domes, the new edifice, known as the Château du Grand Jardin, was a show of ostentation in keeping with its owner's prestige, and the young Queen could rediscover there the pleasures and refinements which a royal palace provided. On Claude de Guise's death, this great palace had passed to his widow Antoinette de Bourbon, who loved nothing better than to surround herself with her numerous children and grandchildren. United with her uncles, aunts and cousins, Mary Stuart was in her element, enjoying a mutual tender affection, which she felt sad at having soon to forgo.

James arrived at Joinville and was immediately dazzled by the splendour of the great chateau and the luxury of its furnishings and décor. The Guises had gathered together a collection of the rarest tapestries, velvet curtains, gold threaded damask, delicately embroidered silks, Turkish carpets and gold and silver vessels. Forty musicians were permanently in residence for the entertainment of their hosts, and the size of its domestic staff was so great that it was impossible to go anywhere without encountering a servant, a majordomo, a washerwoman, a seamstress, or a chambermaid.

Passing the large reception room on the ground floor, James was taken to the first floor where the guest bedrooms and apartments of the masters of the house were located. Everything about the quarters that had been set aside for his use delighted the young Scot. Hard-backed chairs were upholstered with embossed leather, and comfortable armchairs covered in gold-trimmed crimson velvet. Hanging on the walls were painted wooden cartouches depicting flowers, fruit, and familiar or exotic animal heads. Spread on the floors were rugs and carpets in harmonious colours, altogether demonstrating a degree of sophistication he had never previously experienced.

While his two servants were unpacking his trunk, James went outside to take a walk in the park. Rainy weather had delayed his journey between Paris and Joinville, and to save the Queen from waiting he had been obliged to curtail his stopovers. This stay, James was convinced, would determine his future relationship with Mary Stuart. On numerous occasions, he had pondered over George Gordon's warning. It was true his enemies outnumbered his friends, and that without the Queen's trust and backing his situation might become precarious. A Protestant in the service of a Catholic monarch and a nobleman who had always refused English gold could be considered a black sheep in Scotland. Moreover, his stubbornness and lack of flexibility would not make things easier for him.

In the garden, which was enclosed within turreted walls, gardeners were busy with rakes and shears. A multitude of flowerbeds succeeded one another, each planted with an individual species of flower, and all of which, viewed from the windows of the chateau, giving the impression of a giant bouquet. Labyrinths, leafy bowers and arcades led to the orchard located in the southern section of the park, and James headed in that direction. Groups of gentlemen and ladies-in-waiting were taking a walk with their small pet dogs, which raced up and down the paths and flushed little birds from amongst the bushes. The air was full of butterflies and the humming of bees gathering nectar from the flowers. The sight of the orchard roused James from his daydream. Trees unfamiliar to him were trained against the south-facing wall, while others less exotic were planted alongside an irrigation canal or grouped around pools filled by cascading water. On a bench sheltered within an arbour sat three ladies conversing together.

'You have come to see us at Joinville, my Lord Bothwell!'

James instantly recognized the teasing voice of Mary Fleming, nicknamed 'La Flamina' because of her red hair and liveliness. She was one of the four Marys who were childhood friends and ladies-in-waiting to Mary Stuart.

As he approached with a smile one of the women looked up and with surprise he recognized the Queen, who suddenly and without quite knowing why appeared flustered and lost for words.

Bending his knee to the ground, James kissed her hand extended towards him.

La Flamina broke the silence:

'If you don't change out of those dusty travelling clothes, my Lord, you will make a sorry sight at the dinner which the Duke is giving this evening in your honour.'

The Queen, who had regained her composure, stood up and responded,

'My friends are never unseemly. Give me your arm, my Lord Bothwell, and let us walk a bit. '

The apple and peach trees were shedding their last blossoms, and the grass was still wet from recent showers.

'So you have come to arrange my departure. I would have preferred to have been allowed to travel up through England, but since my dear cousin Elizabeth seems little inclined to provide me with safe conduct, I shall have to set sail directly for Scotland and place myself in the hands of my High Admiral.'

'I am only taking care of Your Majesty's retinue, who will travel aboard one of the King of France's galleys.'

'A significant retinue my Lord, as I intend to take to Edinburgh everything I hold dear.'

Conscious of the superficiality of their discourse, they both stayed silent for a while. Just beside them, a stone gargoyle was spouting a slender stream of water, which disappeared into the irrigation pool.

'May I again present my sincere condolences to Your Majesty?' James finally managed to say, despising his own awkwardness.

The young woman nodded in acceptance. Her brief marriage to François had brought her more sorrow than joy.

'My friends did not forget me and a great many came to console me. In Paris I received Lord Darnley, my Aunt Margaret's son, and here a few days ago my half-brother James Stuart. I feel more at peace now and am ready to return to the country of which I have little memory. I trust you will help me to adjust?'

Mary hated the state of confusion she felt in James's presence. She dropped his arm, stopped, and turned to face him:

'We will talk about all this together with my uncles, my Lord. I do not wish to hold you back.'

Mary Fleming and Mary Beaton had caught up with her. James bowed and turned to go. He was disappointed by such a short and superficial exchange, and regretted having to take his leave so hastily from a woman whose company he very much enjoyed.

'The remarriage of the Queen is the subject on all our lips, my Lord,' La Flamina announced. 'They are talking about Don Carlos, in spite of vehement opposition from Catherine de Medicis, who refuses to contemplate the prestige of her own daughter the Queen of Spain being sullied by our beautiful sovereign. The names of some of the Hapsburg princes are still on the list too, but Queen Elizabeth will not hear of them.'

'And what are Her Majesty's wishes?' James asked.

'She is saying nothing but I think her sights are more set on Don Carlos.'

'Is Scotland not enough for her?'

'I am afraid not. Our Queen's designs for the future are more ambitious, in particular as far as England is concerned.'

La Flamina had asked for James to be woken early so that he could accompany her on her daily ride. Side by side their horses proceeded at a walk, their flanks almost touching. In discussing the Queen's remarriage, the young woman astutely realised the ambiguity of a situation that could prove detrimental to her Queen. As long as the threat of a foreign king on the Scottish throne remained, Mary would be accepted only superficially.

All around them, the countryside unfolded with broad pastures, the dark tones of the forests where the Guises enjoyed hunting expeditions and the lazy meanderings of the River Marne with its rushy overgrown banks.

James felt worried. As soon as she arrived in Scotland, the Queen would have to set out to win the hearts and minds of her subjects. Her youth and charm were important assets, but they alone would not suffice to gain the support of all her subjects.

'James Stuart will probably keep a close watch on the subject of his sister's remarriage. A husband with too much influence could be an obstacle to his ambitions for power,' commented James guardedly.

La Flamina glanced at him with raised eyebrows. The green linen dress she wore emphasized the colours of her flaming hair and tawny eyes. She had inherited the beauty of her mother Lady Fleming, who had seduced King Henri II and to whom she had borne a son.

'Indeed,' she agreed. 'James Stuart would be in favour of one of his friends, a Scottish nobleman such as young Arran, becoming a prospective husband for the Queen. He is good-looking and is one of Mary's cousins, but is known to be weak and somewhat eccentric. As far as The Bastard and his ambitions are concerned, it would be an ideal match.'

'Her Majesty cannot possibly marry one who is a traitor!'

The thought of Mary sharing a bed with the son of the Duke of Châtelherault incensed James. Arran had fed abundantly from the French trough before turning to the English manna. Moreover, he would never ever forgive him for the ransacking of Crichton.

'That said, my Lord,' Mary Fleming joked, 'the wind has so often changed in Scotland that weathercocks have become disorientated and do not know which way to turn!'

'Scotland cannot be ruled by France, England, or any other foreign power. Every one of us has to agree about this. Without such neutrality, we will sink back into a state of civil war and despair.'

James remembered Henry VIII's 'rough wooing', during which he had tried to impose the betrothal of his only son to Mary Stuart. Arson, pillage, rape, and carnage had devastated the southern regions following Marie de Guise's refusal.

Scotland had suffered too much to be thrown once again to the wolves.

Mary Fleming's horse, suddenly frightened by the flight of a pair of turtledoves, shied violently. James quickly grabbed her reins, but the young woman, remaining firm in the saddle, gave him a taunting look:

'You are an accomplished knight, my Lord! If I were Queen of Scots, it is perhaps you whom I would choose to wed! '

They trotted back to Joinville while the sun rising in the sky heralded a warm day, and cast a golden glow over the pastures and amber reflections in the water.

Although he tried to suppress his thoughts, James's mind repeatedly returned to the question of the Queen's marriage. If whoever was to become her husband intended to use his power and authority, that would be the end for The Bastard, and equally for himself. He would then become but a mere adviser, a courtier, and a pawn amongst many others.

The preparations for Mary Stuart's departure were coming to an end. After leaving Joinville, the young Queen had planned a stop in Reims, where she would meet her aunt Renée de Guise, Prioress of the Abbey of Saint-Pierre des Dames. Bothwell would remain part of her retinue until they reached the capital of Champagne. He would then proceed to Paris and Calais in order to make ready the fleet that would escort the royal galleys. The catalogue of the first consignments had astounded the High Admiral. Besides an extraordinary quantity of furniture, carpets, tapestries, and hangings, Mary was taking with her a good part of her stables, including twenty valuable horses, her dogs, monkeys and song-birds. She was also taking her crockery, an extensive wardrobe, mattresses, curtains, counterpanes and great quantities of linen, her library, and supplies for her cooks, bakers, confectioners and roasters to enable them to serve the Queen's favourite dishes as soon as she arrived in Scotland. A cargo of this size would require at least two heavy tonnage vessels, and meticulous loading for which he would be responsible.

James had had the opportunity to have a private conversation with the Queen and her uncles, excepting the Cardinal of Lorraine who had been held up at court. Surrounded by her family, Mary did not show the embarrassment she frequently displayed when alone with James. He too felt more relaxed. Whatever happened, the harmony of their relationship must not be jeopardised.

On the eve of the Queen's departure with her large retinue the Dowager Duchess, Antoinette de Bourbon, threw a grand ball in honour of her granddaughter. The great hall looked splendid, bedecked with banks of flowering shrubs and adorned with ribbons. The Guises had no reason to be envious of the luxury displayed by the Valois, and James understood Catherine de Medicis's wariness concerning them. Handsome, brilliant and popular, the members of this family spread their influence far and wide. Eventually the ambitions of one side and manoeuvres of the other would clash violently, fuelled by the Prince de Condé, the brother of the King, and Antoine de Navarre. Being back in favour after the Amboise rebellion, this Protestant prince of royal blood had sworn to bring the Guises down, and from being only political, the conflict had now become religious. France was on the brink of sinking into the same intolerance which was afflicting Scotland.

The flutes, viols, guitars, spinets and rebecs began playing a volte. Lacking experience in the kind of dancing practised at the court, James kept a low profile. The elegance of both ladies and gentlemen dazzled James, and gave him the incentive to bring the same glamour to his own family. Under his gaze, gemstones glittered, gold glistened, moiré and damask shimmered and pearls sparkled. Within the movements of the dances, shades of rose, blue, emerald and brown intermingled as if reflected in a play of mirrors. James saw the Queen smiling and laughing with her young uncle the Marquis d'Elbeuf. With their tall stature and haughty demeanour, the Guises dominated their supporters. It was easy to understand why they were suspected of coveting power; however, the death of François II and the snubbing of their young niece had been a hard blow for them. Although Catherine de Medicis was still making an effort to be gracious towards them, from now on they were dependant on the influence of the Montmorencys, as well as on that of the Bourbons.

'It is a shame to see such a handsome gentleman without a lady on his arm.'

Mary Fleming's cheerful face and impudent voice lifted James's spirits. 'Come and dance.'

Without waiting for his reply, La Flamina grabbed the young Earl's hand and dragged him off with her.

'I am not much of an expert!'

'What does it matter? Ladies only have eyes for their dancing partner and pay little attention to the movement of his feet.'

With the rotation of partners during the course of the dance, James had moved from Mary Fleming to Louise de Brézé, wife of the Duc d'Aumale.

'I did not know you were such a good dancer, my Lord Bothwell.'

Mary Stuart was standing in front of him, her back slightly arched as befitted the volte, with a mocking smile on her lips.

'Slap my hand if you do not want to stand out from everyone else.'

A fragrance of iris and violet wafted from the Queen's bodice.

'Scotland will love you, Madam,' James whispered.

'I am not there yet.'

'Did the French not adore their sovereign?'

'I am that no longer.'

Mary's voice showed no tinge of nostalgia. At eighteen years old, perhaps out of a love of adventure, this young woman had taken a difficult decision, and as a Guise she was ready to follow it through.

Their palms were touching now, and they stood so close to each other that James could feel Mary's breath against his face. Something less straightforward than lust was unsettling him, perhaps the thought that such an attractive woman could never be his.

21

THE SAFE CONDUCT granted by Queen Elizabeth allowing Mary and her retinue to travel through England on her way to Scotland had not arrived in France by the thirteenth of August, so the young Queen made up her mind to sail directly to Leith. Two royal galleys were awaiting her at Calais, and the vessels, loaded with her baggage, were ready to cast off. The High Admiral of Scotland had personally overseen the loading of the valuable cargo. The horses would be taken aboard a few hours before the time of departure along with the pets, except for two of the Queen's favourite dogs who would travel with their mistress.

After the lesser fleet had weighed anchor James would stay behind in Calais in case some delayed cartloads turned up, then he would board a merchant vessel. His friend Lord Eglinton would command the two escort vessels, while Monsieur de Meullan was in charge of the royal galleys carrying the Guises who were to accompany the Queen, the ladies-in-waiting, the pages, the Comte de Damville, youngest son of the Constable de Montmorency, the poets Brantôme and Chastelard and numerous other gentlemen.

James had not seen Mary again privately. Caught up in a whirlwind of festivities given in her honour, monopolized by her family and courted by all, she gave the impression of living in another world. Who knew what her thoughts were, hidden behind those eyes which sparkled with joy, and what passions lay behind that engaging smile?

The thick mist shrouding Calais meant that it was barely possible to distinguish the quays where the galleys were berthed, one bearing the standard of France with the Fleur de Lys, and the other with the Lion Rampant of Scotland. With the harvest finished and straw stacked for winter, farmers were busy ploughing their fields of stubble. Plumes of acrid smoke blended with the mist and emphasized the oppressive atmosphere. A curious crowd of onlookers had come to stare at the galleys and two escort vessels, which teemed with sailors and cabin boys. The galley slaves, who had been under lock and key since the day before in the former English gaol, awaited orders for boarding. Mary Stuart had requested Monsieur de Meullan that none of them should be whipped for the duration of the journey, a request that had baffled the members of the crew. What kind of Queen would a woman with such delicate feelings make?

On the morning of the fourteenth of August, the vanguard of the royal cortege entered Calais and headed for the port. The mist was unrelenting, and onlookers and passers-by saw nothing but fleeting ghostly shadows, quickly swallowed up by the fog that became even more dense along the shore.

The clarion notes of trumpets finally announced the arrival of the Queen, accompanied by her four uncles, Louis Cardinal de Sens, Charles Cardinal de Lorraine, Claude Duc d'Aumale, and René Marquis d'Elbeuf, all of them mounted on splendid horses. Feeble rays of sunlight were attempting to pierce the mist and the sea was calm and grey.

High on the bridge of one of the galleys, holding his plumed hat in his hand, Monsieur de Meullan was waiting patiently. James watched the Queen dismount and then approach him. With erect bearing and looking rather pale, Mary wore a headdress of fine lawn, resplendent with a criss-cross pattern of pearls, and she seemed to be summoning all her strength to conceal her evident distress. James observed her intently. Behind the delightful smile, graceful gestures and kind words, he thought he perceived a wilful, undoubtedly brave and passionate young woman. He believed that he and she possessed similar qualities of character. He felt an irresistible urge to return to his responsibilities and affairs of state in Scotland as soon as possible. Back in the Scottish Borders in the midst of the countryside he cherished, things would surely fall into place. The Queen would marry a noble prince and provide Scotland with a future king. As for James himself, he would loyally serve her, and having rid himself of the unfortunate Anna, he would then be free to wed a young woman of suitable rank.

The news of Mary Stuart's safe landing at Leith reached Calais five days later. Unfortunately, the English had boarded one of the escorting ships for inspection. As it had been in the vicinity of their coast, they had impounded it and confiscated its cargo, which included the royal horses. Lord Eglinton was negotiating and was hopeful of being allowed to return to sea, but there was no certainty.

Now sadly deprived of a glorious cavalcade, Mary Stuart entered Edinburgh through the mist, mounted together with her retinue on common ill-bred horses, hastily requisitioned for the royal party. However, her people had given her a rousing welcome, and once installed at the Palace of Holyrood she had placed herself in the hands of her half-brother James Stuart to whom she wished to refuse nothing.

The vexation James felt on receiving this news was exacerbated by a letter he had been handed two days before his departure for Scotland, on which he recognised Anna Throndsen's handwriting. Residing in the Lothians, she was burning with impatience to see her 'dear heart' again. She intimated to him that she was bored of living in the countryside, and when they were married she would prefer to live in Edinburgh. To James these neatly written words gave a bitter taste. Would he be saddled with the burden of Anna for the rest of his life? Admittedly, he had benefited from her money, and she had agreed to sell a few pieces of her jewellery in order to help him, but the young Dane's generosity was her means of attempting to control him, as if gratitude and love went hand in hand. It seemed she was a poor judge of character as far as the hearts of men were concerned.

Impatiently he stuffed the letter into a pocket of his breeches. Between a mistress he could not rid himself of and the devious manoeuvres of James Stuart, who had wasted no time in establishing himself at his half-sister's side, he found plenty of material to fuel his foul mood. However, there was nothing he could do for the time being, and he headed for the nearest tavern to order a bottle of gin.

Two parallel streets crossed Edinburgh from the Palace of Holyrood; the High Street, which beyond the city wall turned into the Canongate, and the Cowgate, bordered with gardens and vegetable plots. Clean and full of life these two arteries were linked by Blackfriars Wynd and a number of narrow, dark and fetid closes, which were wisely avoided after dusk by passers-by.

When James arrived in Edinburgh, the city was bustling with frenetic activity. The presence of the French retinue had attracted a multitude of street pedlars, dealers, crooks and schemers looking for adventure. All manner of riff-raff mingled with the artisans, burghers, apprentices and housewives going about their usual business. The arrival of their sovereign had altogether changed the city's atmosphere and given it a new lease of life. Finding himself at the Netherbow Port, which gave access through the city walls intersecting the High Street and Canongate, James encountered William Maitland, who gave him a very cold greeting. The young Earl harboured no illusions about Maitland and did not underestimate him. Intelligent, ambitious and cunning, he was setting out to make himself indispensable to the Queen. The Hamiltons, followed to a lesser extent by Marie de Guise, had trusted him in the past by taking him on as Chancellor, then as Treasurer and Comptroller. A keen proponent of union between Scotland and England, William Maitland turned to James Stuart as a matter of course. In reality, Mary Stuart's Privy Council would remain the same as the one that had ruled Scotland since the death of the Regent.

William Hepburn, the cousin who had put James up in his lodgings in the Cowgate, had a dinner prepared in his honour, and the table was lavishly spread with delectable dishes; cow's liver fried with onions, joints of roast mutton, quails, pheasants and partridges, a large salmon garnished in a sauce and boiled sheep's head. Ale flowed in abundance together with French and German wine, and the guests' faces soon became flushed in the heat of a warm September evening. While servants sliced the meat and carved the poultry, gentlemen divested themselves of their doublets and ladies fanned themselves to keep cool. From the still lively Cowgate came sounds of barking and whinnying, the creaking of cartwheels and the cries of street hawkers.

'Maitland is gaining power and influence every day that passes,' commented old Ormiston. 'Our young sovereign shares his wish to see Scotland at peace and on good terms with England. I sincerely believe them to be on the same intellectual level, if not in religious harmony.'

'I see him more in league with The Bastard,' remarked James coldly, 'as both of them are ready to impose their political convictions by force.'

Daylight was now fading. Soon the lanterns that sparsely illuminated the two streets would be lit and the night watchman would begin his rounds, which lasted until the early hours of the morning.

'The Queen will suffer Maitland better than she will suffer John Knox,' mocked William Hepburn. 'You are probably unaware, my dear cousin, that about ten days ago Knox had an exchange with our sovereign. She did her best to keep her composure until our saintly man hurled these words at her, 'I have rescued many souls and will continue to do so. The Scots will live under the authority of their legitimate sovereign as Paul the Apostle accepted to live under the authority of Nero.'

The guests burst out laughing. Knox was well respected, but he was also feared for his vengeful temperament, and no one wished to attract the fiery preacher's wrath.

'Did Her Majesty answer him back?' James asked.

'She retorted in regal tones, "I wish to defend the Church of Rome, which I hold as the only true Church of God".'

'A mistake...' muttered the young Earl.

Mary seemed far away at that precise moment. Would he find at Holyrood the same young woman who had so unsettled him in France?

As soon as she had arrived in Edinburgh Mary had taken to her bed. The doctors were talking about quartan fever, but everybody knew that the real cause of her indisposition was the sorrow she felt at leaving France combined with anxiety at having to adapt to a new country. Besides, the negotiations initiated with Philip II of Spain with a view to marriage with the Infante Don Carlos were making no headway.

'Who is the person that never makes a mistake?' William replied, helping himself to a pint of ale. 'The stream of French courtiers over-running the city are already an irritant to the Scottish nobility. Fickle and impudent by nature, these French have something to say about every-thing and their retorts leave our most learned men tongue-tied. Amongst them is a certain Brantome whose sharp wit is such that you never know whether he is deriding you or complimenting you!'

'They are only here temporarily. Amongst our Queen's uncles, only the Marquis d'Elbeuf intends to stay on until winter. He is a cheerful fellow and I appreciate his friendship,' James remarked.

After clearing the table, the servants brought in the dessert, consisting of fruit tartlets, plum and raisin puddings soaked in brandy and ginger-flavoured orange peel.

The street was now deserted. A light breeze blew in through the window, which opened out onto the garden. In the countryside that stretched beyond the city, bonfires lit by shepherds glowed in the distance.

'Here you are at last my Lord Bothwell!'

Mary extended both her hands to James. The young man found her changed. Wearing a dress of light turtledove silk layered with embroidered tulle, a hairnet encrusted with pearls, and entwined with gold ribbons, the sovereign stood in her audience chamber surrounded by her four Marys.

As James was about to bend his knee to the ground in homage, Mary stopped him.

'You are my friend from France are you not?' The young Earl sensed the emotion in Mary's voice. It was obvious she felt acute homesickness for the country where she had passed most of her youth.

'Come,' she said, 'the members of my Council are waiting for us to join them. From now on I intend to honour all my responsibilities as Queen.'

Mary took his arm in a spontaneous gesture as she had done in France, but there was no trace of the light exuberance he had felt in her at that time. The Queen stood stiffly, dignified and slightly distant in her manner. Seated round a long table covered with a fringed velvet cloth, Bothwell was reunited reluctantly with those who had been his enemies during the Regency of Marie de Guise. They were smiling at him now but they still filled him with the same feelings of revulsion as before.

'My Lord's place is assuredly in the Borders,' Maitland said to James. 'No one is in a better position to enforce Your Grace's authority there.'

The issue of unrest in the Borders had come up during the course of the discussion. Spontaneously the Queen had proposed to send her Lieutenant down there.

The young Earl was torn. To return to his beloved Borders would be a happy prospect. Nowhere else did he feel so at home as in that barren, wild and windswept area. However, that mission would mean distancing himself from the court, which served his enemies' purposes. Mary was young, trusting and easily influenced. In his absence, all of them, except George Gordon, would surreptitiously seek to discredit him.

'I insist Lord James remains a member of my Privy Council,' the Queen demanded.

Her eyes were on Bothwell, and James read a kind of resignation in her expression. He could see she was now not fooled by the intentions of her half-brother, nor by those of William Maitland, nor the Duke of Argyll, but was admitting her powerlessness to countermand them.

Maitland had resumed his post as Secretary of State, while the Duke of Châtelherault and his son young Arran were retaining their positions as privileged counsellors. In reality, the ultra-Protestant faction dominated, and among the moderates James could rely only on the support of the Earl Marischal and the Catholic Lords, themselves divided by family quarrels.

Seated at the end of the table, The Bastard maintained a stern countenance and cold expression. James knew him to be his worst enemy, and he was a man who never put a step forward without first having tested the ground. The proposal to distance him promptly from Edinburgh was most likely to have come from him. Next to Stuart sat James Douglas, Earl of Morton, head of the powerful Douglas family during the minority of his nephew, with his fiery red hair and beard. Anxious not to get too involved on one side or the other, his role was to play the part of the indispensable middleman.

Suddenly Arran's shrill voice startled James…

'I would like, Madam, to defend my rights over Melrose Abbey, which I am told Your Grace intends to confer on my Lord Bothwell.' Indeed it was true that the Queen had committed herself to granting James the revenues of Melrose, and he was not about to let this gift slip through his fingers.

The question had been hotly debated, and James on several occasions had needed to control himself to avoid grabbing Arran by the collar of his doublet. Worried and embarrassed, the Queen did not know what to say. Finally, Maitland had managed to defuse the situation by getting them very reluctantly to agree to a temporary sharing arrangement.

James was determined to set off the next day for the Borders. In Edinburgh, he might at any moment lose his sangfroid and commit some hotheaded action which could result in dire consequences. The Queen had sorely disappointed him. Was she trying to please everybody?

At the end of the table, James Stuart remained silent and expressionless, during the session he had not uttered a single word.

As the members of her Council were dispersing, Mary held Bothwell back for a moment.

'We will see each other again in the middle of October, my Lord, as I want you to attend my Councils. My knowledge of my nobles' ways and customs is lacking and I admit I am shocked by their harsh behaviour.'

'The French are no angels, Madam,' replied James, 'but they hide their feelings better than we do.'

Mary remained silent for a while, and then she declared suddenly, 'Let us talk about something dear to my heart. I hear my half-brother John, Prior of Coldingham, is in love with your sister Janet. I am favourable to a marriage, which would bring us closer. John is my favourite brother. I trust you are aware of that, are you not?'

James sighed to himself. He could see that this young woman was proficient in the art of manipulating men!

'Your Majesty's approval is an honour for the Hepburns. I do believe Janet is very much in love too.'

'Well let us marry them without further delay!' Mary exclaimed. 'I am in such need of a happy occasion to celebrate.'

22

THE SOUND OF RAIN falling on the slates is echoing through James's brain. Each drop seems to slip away like times long past, times of his childhood in the Lothians, his adolescent years at Spynie, his years as a student in Paris, his periods of exile, his rise to supreme authority in the land, his marriage to the Queen. Then everything seems to darken and fall apart. He is at a dead end and there is no future for him. What meaning does life hold for him? Hardly had he held power and honour in his grasp when they were snatched away. He was betrayed, crushed and imprisoned, and never given the slightest opportunity to defend himself. What does the word 'power' mean? James tries to define it. He has owned large estates and ruled over Scotland... yet for such a brief time. At Holyrood, he slept in Darnley's bed, and in the bed of the King of Scots. The Queen loved him and she bore his children.

Twins, his secretary had written. Her Majesty is shattered by the premature births and by the humiliating act of abdication, which her halfbrother has forced her to sign. James received this letter, secretly sent to Spynie where his uncle has given him shelter. Two stillborn sons; two unfulfilled lives. Another failure.

The rain is drumming on the roof. James holds his head between his hands and plugs his ears. He hears the endless parleying on Carberry Hill battlefield while weapons and cannons stay silent. Why did he ever agree to negotiate with traitors? He had sensed the trap... Mary had not. He remembers how they held hands tightly, their lips joined, before he had set out alone with his mind raging on his long ride to Dunbar. He should have attacked Morton and stuck his dirk into his guts before dying too, weapon in hand. They stole his honour, his manhood and his life. To find out who he really is he needs to relive everything, but always a piece of the puzzle eludes him. He loses himself in the details, strays and sinks into a state of despair.

James is parched. He rises from his bed and swallows tepid water from the flagon. Why is he now incapable of standing upright? He stoops a little as he walks, and his swollen legs torture him.

The wind arrives to banish the rain. James hates those gusts of wind. It was they that drove his ship towards Norway. He still hears the creaking of the shrouds, the yards and the hull of the *Pelican*, and the flapping of her torn sails; he feels the biting cold and the stinging salty air. The captain is yelling orders while James sits hunched up on deck overwhelmed with seasickness. Nevertheless, hope is not dead within him; not yet anyway. He sees again the greenish breakers, the *Pelican* catching them sideways on and gliding at astonishing speed. The ship has only one mast left; the other one was brought down by his pursuers' cannons. Which pursuers? James knows there is a large pack of them in pursuit. The whole of Scotland! He laughs. Who would hunt him down in Dragsholm now, this fortress that stands on the edge of the world?

James is doubled up with agony. He feels he is suffocating and struggles to the window in order to inhale the wind, but the pain persists and feels as though it is tearing him apart. His body has become repulsive to him, with muscles and genitals now useless. When he falls asleep, his dreams are of horses, who lead him to endless free, wide-open, spaces.

It has been a long time since they last took him down into the bowels of the dungeon. Now he neither speaks nor screams, and no longer tries to harm himself. His body and his soul are barely alive. It is now many years since his agony began.

James is waiting for his mother and sister. One of these days, they will come to see him and comfort him. Often he looks out for them, and spends hours at a time staring out at the stretches of sea visible between the fir trees, until eventually the light blinds him. Then he forgets them and his mind turns to the polished gleam of armour in the sunshine. He was once a warrior. Did the English themselves not say he was the best general in Scotland? Why then at Carberry Hill did he not order his men to fire their cannons and command his Borderers to charge the enemy?

James pictures himself returning victorious to Holyrood. He is weeping now. Tears relieve his suffering a little... so very little...

23

THE MOMENT OF departure had arrived. The Cardinal de Guise and the Duc d'Aumale boarded a ship for France, leaving behind only their youngest brother, twenty-five-year-old René Marquis d'Elbeuf. Brantôme, Damville, and their followers were also leaving Scotland. To Mary, her country had now become an inescapable reality.

In Liddesdale, close to the English border, Bothwell was kept informed of everything taking place in Edinburgh. The Queen had decided to make a short trip to the North without asking him to join the nobles who would be escorting her; James Stuart, the Earls of Argyll and Huntly, and her uncle Elbeuf. Burning in his mind was the certainty that a coterie had been set up against him.

In the Borders, the Elliots were once more feuding with the Croziers, who were themselves exacting their own revenge against the Armstrongs. Allies of the Elliots, the Scotts were at odds with the Kerrs, while everybody was in league when it came to crossing the border by night to rustle English cattle. Besides making punitive raids, James organised negotiations in order to calm tempers and initiate dialogues between families. Sometimes Janet came to visit him at Hermitage Castle and they had long talks together. His former mistress did not at all approve of his behaviour towards Anna. James, she insisted, should arrange for her to return to Denmark, so that she could rebuild her life. However, he refused to add this worry to those already sapping his spirits. He saw Anna from time to time, and the young woman seemed content with that.

'One day she will hate you as much as she now loves you,' Janet predicted. 'Women can turn against you in a flash and never look back.'

'Don't you love me any more, then?' he said, teasing her. Janet stroked his hair and kissed the edge of his lips.

'You are quite unforgettable, Jamie!'

Her sister Lady Margaret Reres, lady-in-waiting to Mary Stuart, kept Janet informed of the course of events at court. Maitland was on his way to London, entrusted with the mission of negotiating amendments to the Treaty of Edinburgh with Queen Elizabeth. The royal progress was proceeding to plan. The Queen had visited Linlithgow, the place of her birth, followed by Stirling Castle where at less than a year old she had been crowned. On the fourteenth of September, the Protestants had caused a commotion in order to prevent Mass being sung in the chapel of the castle. A few priests had been roughly treated, and to try to restore order Mary had resolved to listen to a brief Low Mass. In Perth, the Queen had once again been harassed. Not accustomed to being contradicted or upset, she had lost her composure for the first time since her return to Scotland. Words of outrage had been followed on her part by floods of tears, which according to whoever reported the event, had been greeted with either compassion or sarcasm.

Lady Reres, always of a cheerful disposition, was trying to narrate the brighter side of the journey, but her letter betrayed her disenchantment and fears about the future. In St Andrews, a priest had been murdered, thus dashing hopes harboured by the Queen for possible harmony between Catholics and Protestants. The constant altercations between James Stuart and the Earl of Huntly were undermining the morale of the travellers. In retaliation to the Calvinist inflexibility of The Bastard, Huntly had decided to hold Mass in every single parish of his enormous territory, including the Earldom of Moray, which he administered, and which James Stuart hoped to obtain from his sister. Those two, Lady Reres warned, will one day draw their swords and go for each other's throats; everyone there was certain of it.

James often went riding over the hills around Hermitage, escorted only by a few patrolmen. He needed solitude and the rugged beauty of the moors to ponder over his future. The weather was temperamental. Sometimes the wind blew in strong gusts, sometimes it drizzled from morning until night, and sometimes a thick mist shrouded the hills and stifled all sounds. Wrapped in his rough riding cloak, James was slowly coming to realise he should at all costs hasten his return to Edinburgh in order to stop The Bastard from weaving his web, in which the Queen was already becoming entangled. Order now prevailed in the Borders and there was nothing to keep him there any longer.

Moreover, his sister Janet was bombarding him with letters. She and John Stuart wanted to get married as soon as possible and Janet had chosen the old castle of Crichton for the ceremony. All of the nobility would attend together with the Queen, and major building alterations as well as embellishment works were urgently required. Janet was jubilant; Mary had made her a gift of tussore silk and broche satin for a wedding dress, which three tailors were busy making at Morham. In one of her missives to James, she had written: I am going to tell you a secret, which you must swear to keep on pain of your eternal salvation. John is already my husband, and this is why we need a public ceremony to unite us as quickly as possible. Janet had underlined the word secret three times. By return, James had replied that she was crazy but that he forgave her, and that he had chosen a date in early January for the wedding.

With the establishment of Calvinism, Christmas festivities lost their former gaiety. Profane dances and songs were banned, as were the last traces of pagan celebrations of the winter solstice. Before returning to court James's conscience forced him to spend a few days with Anna. In addition to the comfortable house in which he had settled her, she enjoyed the services of a cook, a scullion, a gardener and two maidservants. The ladies of the neighbourhood had been slow in warming to the young woman, but her discreet behaviour, good manners and assiduous attendance at church had finally dissipated their misgivings and curiosity had won them over. They now visited her from time to time.

Anna however was bored. Separated from her family and far from her own country, she lived only for her lover, for his short letters and all too rare visits. Eventually she was certain that, moved by the love she bestowed on him, he would marry her. With all her heart she wished for a pregnancy which would sway his decision, but he always remained in full control of himself, even at the climax of pleasure, thus depriving her of this weapon.

To celebrate the forthcoming Christmas festivities Anna had decorated her house with fir and holly branches, and bowls of scented greenery, cloves and nutmeg. Fresh sheets had been placed on the bed and there was an abundant supply of firewood in the woodshed. A pair of slippers and a belt she had embroidered herself awaited the young Earl, who was taking his time arriving.

In the first hours of their reunion, James was once again seduced by his mistress's beauty. Her raven hair flowed down her back, her skin had a velvety texture, and her body was curved to perfection. Yet despite her sensuality, Anna lacked true charm, and James could not look at her without remembering the captivating smile and eyes of Mary Stuart.

Anna held him tightly in her arms, covered his face with kisses, and with eyes closed he let her have her way. Soon he would be overcome with desire and would carry her off to bed, disrobe her, and unbraid her hair. Lying close against him, she represented nothing more than a deliciously warm body, offered to him uninhibitedly.

Afterwards while Anna slept, James poured himself a glass of wine. In two days time he would stop at Morham to greet his mother and sister and would then ride on to Edinburgh. Was the Queen angry with him for not attending the Requiem Mass held in honour of the first anniversary of the death of the King of France? Despite their friendship, Mary knew James never attended Catholic services.

It was cosy by the fireside. With his body satiated, James sank into an armchair and stretched his legs towards the firedogs. He thought about Crichton. Builders had already started work there, and soon a horde of decorators, florists, perfumers and cooks would move in. To settle those considerable expenses he had mortgaged some land and sold a house. However, as the Queen would be attending Janet's wedding celebrations, he needed to receive her with pomp and allow the Hepburns their moment of shining splendour. Mary would sleep on the second floor, in the bedroom once used by his mother before her divorce. For his sovereign's wellbeing, James had ordered a special bed, had curtains embroidered and bought a carpet, an unprecedented luxury at the castle.

The Earl allowed the warmth generated by the fire to envelop him. There would be a banquet, a ball, concerts and mounted games. During the three days of celebrations, he would be the master, and James Stuart, Maitland, Morton and Argyll would all have to bow to him.

Anna was sleeping peacefully. James had abstained from mentioning Janet's wedding. The Queen's attendance forbade the presence of a mistress, and by the time Anna heard about it he would be in Edinburgh at a safe distance from her recriminations. It had been a long time since the young Earl had been blessed with such felicity. His future looked full of promise. By resuming his place at court, he could defend himself against those who were slandering him. He would attempt a peace offering with The Bastard and with the Hamiltons. Those hard feelings were costing him dearly. In Edinburgh, he could not go out without an escort for fear of the Duke of Châtelherault's henchmen or those of his son, the Earl of Arran. Paying for his bodyguards and their equipment had given rise to significant expenses, and with the matter of Melrose Abbey remaining unsettled, he was lacking the funds on which he relied.

Anna's tears when he left made James feel uncomfortable. As he was mounting his horse, she suddenly produced a young Skye terrier, his favourite breed, from underneath her shawl, and handed it to him.

'That way,' she said, with sadness in her voice, 'a little of me is going with you.' He went back to her and held her tightly in his arms. Maybe he should marry her after all, start a family, lead a peaceful life between court and his castles and estates, and give his family the happiness that he and his sister Janet had never known. Yet a powerful force kept driving him onwards. He was twenty-six years old, possessed of an impetuous nature, an unshakable faith in his future and a taste for pleasure and action. Enthralled, he loved to read and re-read the works of the great strategists of antiquity, and to study old maps and battle plans. He was not yet ready to lead the existence of a country gentleman. If he chose such a destiny now, he would only bring unhappiness on himself and on those near and dear to him.

Despite the shortness of the days, the skies often laden with dark clouds, and the dank cold weather, court life in Edinburgh was full of cheer. The gaiety displayed by John Stuart, the youngest of the Queen's half-brothers, the Marquis d'Elbeuf and George Gordon contrasted with the solemnity of the other lords and encouraged the Queen to put her own worries on one side. Effortlessly James Hepburn had joined those happy companions, and they passed their time with hawking, endless games of cards and dice, wild gallops through the surrounding country and concerts and balls that all helped to soften the harshness of winter. With the presence of the French, jokes were crude, and gossip was abrasive and often cruel. They made a mockery of young Arran and his secret mistress Alison, a young woman of easy virtue whose favours had been shared by several gentle-men, including the Marquis d'Elbeuf. As it happened, the elderly husband of Arran's lady friend had previously been married to one of James's grandmothers, so he had decided to devise a nocturnal foray destined to mortify Arran, a strait-laced young man who prided himself on his scrup-ulous and untainted morality. With great hilarity John Stuart, Rene de Guise, and James had concocted their scheme. On the pretext of greeting his grandfather-in-law, James would knock on Craig's door and the three friends would then take advantage of the accommodating old man's hos-pitality to force open Alison's door and surprise her lover. At this time of year, Edinburgh's streets remained busy until late in the night. Friends enjoyed visiting each other, tarrying in taverns, lingering at a rotisserie, listening to some charlatan, or watching a fire-eater or torch juggler.

Well wrapped in their capes and wearing broad-brimmed hats to avoid recognition, the friends stopped at a tavern, delighted by the prank they were about to play. Young Arran's retreat would be particularly gratifying for James, who had not forgotten his old grudges.

The air was biting cold, and to left and right of the residential street of the Cowgate the houses presented sombre facades. The sudden yowling cries of stray cats broke the silence as they fought amongst the piles of refuse rotting in the gutters, into which at ten o'clock each morning the inhabitants were permitted to jettison their waste water. Having warmed themselves up with a few drams of whisky, John Stuart, Elbeuf and James headed straight for the Craigs' house. All seemed peaceful and no candle was lit. A bleary-eyed servant took several minutes to open the door. Craig and his wife were sleeping. He had received no instructions and begged the gentlemen to come back the next day at a more civilized hour.

'The bird has flown the nest,' Elbeuf remarked in French. 'Let us be patient. I have a feeling luck will be more on our side tomorrow.'

Drizzle made the following night feel colder still, but to their great sat-isfaction the three young men had spotted a light in Alison's bedroom. They had a brief consultation. To knock on the door would give Arran time to flee through the window, which gave access to a lean-to built against the house. It was better to break the door down and rush up the stairs.

The setback of the previous day had only served to whet their appetites and add spice to the prank.

At the third shoulder bash administered by James the door gave way and the trio surged up the staircase. Despite their precautions, the steps creaked under their feet, and halfway up the stairs the three friends heard the sounds of running footsteps above them, followed by a sudden cry. Suddenly the light filtering from beneath Alison's door disappeared.

The door was not locked, and immediately the young men saw the unmade bed, the window ajar and heard the woman's screams. Two servants in their nightshirts barged into the room, while a third rushed downstairs to fetch the night watch.

'It will not be easy to bring Elbeuf and John Stuart before a tribunal,' the Duke of Châtelherault admitted. 'Let us make James Hepburn suffer. He has always been a thorn in the side of our family.'

His eldest son hung his head in shame. His precipitous flight from Alison Craig's house had terrified him, and his weak nerves had thrown him into a state of mental confusion.

'We will ask the Queen for an audience.'

'The Queen is protecting Bothwell,' stammered Arran.

'It is time someone opened her eyes for her. If she refuses to give us justice, I will gather together as many men as necessary to avenge you without having recourse to the law.'

Hamilton was at last satisfied to be able to show Mary Stuart that he could be unyielding. On numerous occasions in the past he had been incapable of keeping the word he had given to her mother Marie de Guise, and the acknowledgement of his own weakness humiliated him. Being instrumental in the banishment of the Earl of Bothwell would give him back a good opinion of himself.

Besides, the Queen did not take many political decisions herself and was happy to leave the reins of government to her half-brother James Stuart. As long as she was a widow, the Hamiltons would remain her closest relatives and successors. However, rumours of a potential marriage were spreading, and strong as his position might be, Hamilton dreaded the presence of a prince consort. Philip II had finally announced that his son the Infante Don Carlos was incapable of marrying, and Catherine de Medicis would not consider the union of her son Charles IX to one who had been his sister-in-law. Those who remained on the list were a few Italian or German princes who presented no threat at all, together with the Queen of England's candidate, her favourite, Robert Dudley.

Pensively the old Duke observed his eldest son, who bore a sly and self-conscious expression. For some time he had gravely suspected that Arran might have inherited the instability of his mother, who with every year that passed was lapsing a little more into insanity. Regardless of his younger brother's qualities, Arran was heir to the Duke's titles and pretender to the throne of Scotland.

Mary was waiting for James Hepburn with a mixture of pleasure and reluctance. As a friend, he reassured her, but as a man, he managed to unsettle her, even if she refused to admit it to herself. The qualities of sensuality, authority and vitality which emanated from him, could seduce even the most frigid woman, and she was aware that Mary Livingstone, among many other women, was eager to seek his company. His reputation as a ladies' man upset her.

On the previous day, the Duke of Châtelherault had importuned her with a narrative about the indiscretions committed by her half-brother John, her uncle Rene de Guise, and the Earl of Bothwell. She felt no sympathy for young Arran, and had it not been for the aggrieved expression of the head of the Hamiltons, Mary would have found the young men's prank rather amusing. The thought of bony Arran decamping in his nightshirt through the window of the Craigs' house was very entertaining. However, she would have to be ruthless. Neither kith nor kin of the Queen could with impunity break a door down in the middle of the night and run riot in the house of an honest man. That morning she had lectured her uncle Rene and her half-brother John. She would now have to speak to James more harshly.

The young Earl was pacing up and down the Queen's outer chamber. He was ready to acknowledge his mistakes, while playing down their impact, and to promise to try to make amends to the Hamilton family. The Queen would forgive him. Anxious to love and be loved, Mary did not possess the toughness needed by a head of state. Deeply sensitive by nature, she was impervious to schemes and lies, which both Elizabeth of England and Catherine de Medicis used without any qualms.

Mary had allowed James to express himself without interruption. She seemed weary and anxious. Outside, a westerly wind was blowing large clouds towards the sea. Mary Stuart's outer chamber was adorned with tapestries, silverware, and ornate furniture brought over from France. However, it retained a slightly forlorn atmosphere, as if the objects surrounding the young woman failed to blend with the plain beauty of their setting. Two curly-coated Maltese terriers were lying at their mistress's feet. A little distance away stood Mary Beaton and Mary Livingstone.

'My cousins are demanding that you be punished,' the Queen said anxiously.

'They hate me, Madam,' replied James

'I don't see you making much of an effort to secure their favours, my Lord'.

Mary was disconcerted and exasperated by the incessant rivalries between the great Scottish families.

'Even my friends cannot act in my realm with impunity. You must withdraw to Crichton to organise your sister's wedding. You know how much I look forward to attending it.'

The sadness in the Queen's eyes disturbed Bothwell as if he were a chance witness to some incongruity.

'May I venture to ask whether Your Majesty is making the decision to banish me in order to oblige the Duke of Châtelherault?'

Mary attempted a smile. She wanted to forget all this bickering and enjoy a brief moment of harmony and peace.

'Do not use such formal words, my Lord. I am only requesting a short absence from you.'

'I will leave Edinburgh tomorrow.'

The Queen extended her hands, which he held between his. Beneath her skin he felt a certain agitation, probably generated by the difficult situation in which she found herself. Her half-brother James was coveting a title and harassing her over the revenue of the important Earldom of Moray; the Gordons were plotting their revenge against the Ogilvies; Elizabeth was delaying their meeting and was sending contradictory letters, no doubt dictated by her Secretary of State William Cecil. James was well acquainted with the blissful and worry-free life which had blessed Mary's childhood in France, her adolescence and her brief life as married woman and Queen. She had been but a spectator of the clashes between opposing Catholics and Huguenots. Now aged twenty, the burden of the small realm of Scotland weighed very heavily indeed on her shoulders.

24

CRISP AND SUNNY weather ushered in the celebrations. The old castle had not witnessed such activity for decades. The inner courtyard bustled with the comings and goings of numerous traders, servants and grooms, together with a few farmers, who had come to catch a glimpse of their Queen. The heads of the most powerful families in Scotland, united for once, were all present to celebrate Janet's wedding. The sister of the master of the house was marrying John Stuart, Prior of Coldingham, a fair-haired and genial young man, who among the illegitimate sons of the late King James v seemed the least driven by political ambitions. A banquet and an evening of lavish entertainment would follow the religious ceremony in the collegiate church. After copious tears and reproaches, Anna had resigned herself to not being invited. It was a matter of propriety rather than his own volition, James had assured her, which had dictated this decision. This latest rebuff he hoped would finally quench the last flames of her seemingly inextinguishable passion for him. However, he was angry with himself at his weakness in continuing to desire her from time to time.

After settling into the apartments which James had made ready for her, Mary asked to be shown round the castle. Night was falling, and at dawn the following day they would set up the banquet table, put benches round the lists where the contests were to take place and position the Queen's canopied chair and those chairs destined for the newly-weds. The fabric of the dress worn by Janet, a gift from the Queen, was of heavy ivory satin, set off against cream tussore silk embroidered in gold thread. The bride-to-be had opted for a simple and elegant shape; a close-fitting Spanish style bodice, softened by a ruff of floating lace framing her face. The dress had a hoop skirt widened at the base, and to emphasise her slim waist, a braid tapered towards her lower abdomen. A lawn head-dress would be secured to her forehead by golden straps bejewelled with pearls. With her delicate features and beautiful complexion Janet would make a lovely bride, and James, who the next day would combine the roles of both father and brother, was feeling quite emotional.

Leaning on her host's arm the Queen proceeded into the large reception hall, through the windows of which the setting sun had cast a sudden reddish gleam of light. Continuing on through James's apartments and the tower which had been the first building erected by Chancellor Crichton at the beginning of the fifteenth century, she lingered awhile walking along the wall, looking out over the Tyne and the stretch of rolling countryside which in winter was a patchwork of browns and muted greens. In the distance in the gathering dusk a blanket of mist was unfurling, gradually obscuring the landscape and giving rein to wild flights of imagination. James felt her hand on his forearm, and inhaled the lilac fragrance, regularly sent to the Queen by a French parfumier. In the frosty air, the young Queen's breath turned to vapour and she seemed relaxed and happy.

'When you were living here as a young boy, I was at Stirling,' she whispered, almost to herself, 'so little distance separated us, yet I knew nothing of your existence.'

'But your subjects knew you well, Madam. Every Sunday I prayed for you.'

'In a Catholic church?'

'Indeed, Madam. I converted to Protestantism later on.'

Mary smiled. It was easy to see that nothing could disturb or displease her at that moment.

To entertain the Queen during her first night at Crichton, James had brought in musicians, sent for a famous conjurer from England who had performed at Elizabeth's court, and invited a singer who was familiar with ancient Border ballads, battle verses and love poems that had been passed on from generation to generation.

The fire was crackling in the huge fireplace. Outside in the winter night all was silent except for the soughing of the wind blowing over the tower. It chased heavy banks of clouds across the night sky, which obscured the stars. With her chin resting in the hollow of her hand, Mary listened intently to the ballads. James gazed at her gently rounded forehead, the sharp profile of her nose, the curve of her lips and the softness of her chin. Every now and then, the Queen would close her eyes as if to suppress emotions roused by those songs speaking of love and of death. Sometime in the future James knew he would find occasion to take her down to the Borders, and the two of them would ride across the russet moors beneath a granite sky. They would inhale the scent of peat bogs and be surrounded by heather-clad hills with tumbled masses of ancient rocks. They would follow Reivers' paths through narrow glens and gorges where no herdsmen ventured, where stunted bushes clung to the hillsides against the storms that had bent and twisted them.

Glorious sunshine greeted the day of the wedding. The brief Calvinist nuptials were followed by a splendid banquet. Ten peacocks had been skinned and roasted before being wrapped again in their skins with their spectacular plumage. Swans had been prepared in the same way, but served with their wings outspread. Roast geese, capons, partridges, young wild boar and venison were also served, with side dishes of apples, pears, plums and dried figs, steamed salmon resting on beds of aromatic herbs, various pies and a selection of vegetables. After that came the desserts: tarts, candied fruit, oranges and tangerines, crystallized ginger, roasted pineapple and marzipan figurines. The abundant flow of wine from Arbois and Anjou encouraged the guests to relax and made for lively conversation. The groom's friends ventured a few ribald stories, which he took in good heart. Seated between her half-brother John and her host, the Queen laughed heartily. As if by magic, nobody seemed at odds with each other any more. The Hamiltons were chatting with The Bastard, Huntly was conversing happily with Argyll and William Maitland for once addressed James in a friendly manner.

'See, Madam,' said the young Earl, 'how good-natured your subjects are.'

Wine had brought a glow to the Queen's cheeks. Away from the pomp and royal decorum of the court, she was just a young woman enjoying herself, there to see her favourite brother being married. Only a few days earlier at the Palace of Holyrood she had celebrated her own twentieth birthday.

The musicians played the familiar tunes to which she had so often danced at Saint Germain, Blois and Amboise, places in France where she had spent the best days of her youth with others of her own age, surrounded by a host of servants, jesters, dwarfs and performing animals whose tricks made her weep with laughter. In France in the royal castles, every room was endowed with wall hangings of tapestry and carpets on the floor, and every bedroom had a full-length mirror. Ladies dressed in bright colours and gentlemen wore clothing made of precious fabrics set off with feathers in many colours.

'Are you some kind of magician?' she asked in teasing tones.

James burst out laughing. So she had got wind of the legend that he lured women with witchcraft learned in France.

'We are all blessed with a few assets, Madam. It is up to us to put them to good use.'

'And what are yours, my Lord?'

'The ability to adapt to whatever is expected of me.'

Mary feigned a smile. The Earl of Bothwell's love affairs made her feel uncomfortable and by the same token aroused her curiosity. She was aware that near Morham where Lady Agnes resided lived a young Danish woman who had left her country and her family for him. Tales also abounded about his long liaison with Janet Scott of Buccleuch. This woman, who could have been his mother, had loved him passionately and still maintained a close relationship with him.

After the banquet, the guests made their way towards the lists where the games were about to take place. They consisted of glove or ring jousting, during which the riders tried to outdo each other in dexterity, to pick up at full gallop a lady's glove placed on the ground, or use their dirks to sever the rope at the end of which dangled a ring. To conclude the afternoon James had organised a horse race. The men who were due to take part were Robert Stuart, one of the young groom's half-brothers, Lord Ruthven, George Huntly, John Fleming, brother of the Queen's pretty lady-in-waiting, William Hepburn and René de Guise, Marquis d'Elbeuf. White silk rosettes were fastened to the harnesses and the horses' tails were braided with gold ribbons. The sun was already low in the sky and the hills were becoming veiled in a bluish haze. Wrapped in warm cloaks the spectators took their seats on benches, with the Queen on her crimson velvet upholstered chair. Huddling close to each other, the newly married couple shared a wide cape lined with red squirrel fur.

The horses charged off at full gallop, and the silk rosettes, torn from the harnesses, were strewn over the yellowed grass and clung to the broom and juniper bushes. Mary caught sight of Bothwell leaning forward on his horse, urging it on and straining to put distance between himself and René de Guise. To this man winning means everything, she mused.

That evening there was a concert followed by a ball. A French poet recited sonnets, sextains and rondeaux, accompanied by viol and flute players. Glowing logs smouldered in the hearth and the candles were burning low. Soon it would be time for the bridal bedding with all the traditional pleasantries. Mary suddenly felt a tinge of melancholy. At the age of twenty, she was alone with neither husband nor lover, surrounded by ambitious men who lay in wait for her slightest mistake or weakness in order to take advantage of her. Would she ever see her beloved France again, with the golden banks of the Loire, the enchanting gardens of the royal palaces, and her uncles' chateau at Joinville where her much-loved grandmother was growing old, and where they had all enjoyed masked balls, fireworks displays and water jousting? Would she ever be wooed again?

Sitting beside her the young Earl of Bothwell was resting folded hands in his lap. They had danced together once, a Scottish dance during which the partners never touched. The loud music of the bagpipes and fifes prevented all conversation, but several times their eyes had met. Did they share the same feelings? She was not sure. Whatever the situation she would have to find a husband without delay and build a barrier between them.

The following morning James escorted the Queen and her retinue all the way to Borthwick Castle. He had been unable to spend much time alone with Mary and was disconcerted by the ambivalence of her attitude towards him. Was she protecting him from the hostility of her half-brother James Stuart or Secretary of State William Maitland? As he kissed her hand to bid her farewell the Queen's thumb brushed against his skin; then she leaned towards him.

'Hurry back to Edinburgh, my Lord.' she said quietly in French, and in French he whispered:

'I am at your service, Madam.'

Her small kid-gloved hand had lingered briefly in his.

25

AFTER SPENDING TWO months in Edinburgh during which time he was unable to venture out in the streets without an escort of armed body-guards, James Hepburn was keen to make peace with the Hamiltons. It seemed that the only available intermediary was John Knox, and James had decided to arrange a meeting as soon as possible. He knew the preacher could not ignore him. Several generations of Knoxes had been vassals of the Hepburns and had fought under their banner; however, he was aware the old man had a wily and spiteful nature; also, James had been bored by his lengthy sermons, and hence did not regularly attend the Kirk.

Finally one morning he received the eagerly awaited answer to his request. Knox would see him in his office that same evening.

Anxiously James waited for the appointed time of the meeting. The peace he would seek to obtain that day with the Hamiltons after years of hostility was in accord with the wishes of the Queen, who was deeply disheartened by family feuds. Once more James had bowed to pressure. Since his sister Janet's wedding, he had been leading a less riotous life. René de Guise had returned to France and John Stuart had married and settled down. Of his convivial companions, there remained only George Gordon and his cousin William, both of whom had returned to their estates; Gordon to Strathbogie and William to Gilmerton in the Lothians. With-out elaborating on his misgivings, George had confided to James that he was very worried about his father the Earl of Huntly. The Queen had just offered the Earldom of Moray to The Bastard. The Gordons had admin-istered this region for many years hitherto, and such a unilateral decision had deeply offended and upset the old Earl; now his faith in the Queen had been sorely shaken. James Stuart was ambitious and power seeking, and there was no doubt that Mary was afraid of him.

'Beware of James Stuart,' George Gordon had warned him when he left Edinburgh. 'He always goes for his objective one step at a time, and nothing will deflect him from his ultimate goal. He is quite prepared to strike down and remove, one by one, each and every obstacle that hinders his progress. He hates both the Protestant Hepburns and the Catholic Gordons.'

'The Queen is on our side,' James had insisted, but George had smiled ruefully;

'Her Majesty is incapable of standing up to her half-brother. Be careful, my friend.'

On his way to John Knox's house James recalled George's warning. It was undeniable that James Stuart now exerted immense influence over his sister. Mary was changing. She seemed to be becoming tougher and to be stifling the spontaneity that had so charmed those closest to her. He had noticed that her great warmth of friendship towards him was followed by long periods when she barely spoke to him. The young man was under the impression that she now no longer placed unlimited trust in him. Once he had become reconciled with the Hamiltons, he would confront The Bastard and demand an explanation.

John Knox listened without interruption to the Earl of Bothwell. The old preacher was greatly relishing this moment, when the head of the family to which his own had always been in fealty had come to request his help.

'I am prepared to help you,' he said in gentle tones, 'but before making peace with the Hamiltons, my son, you need to come closer to God. I seldom see you at St Giles on Sundays.'

James lowered his gaze to convey an appearance of humility.

'I will be at St Giles next Sunday.'

'Good, my Lord. God has been very generous with some of his children, and in return is looking for them to serve as examples for their brothers. If the Lord bestows upon me the grace to be able to resolve the differences which have come between the Hepburns and the Hamiltons then I will ask both parties to listen to God's Word and give thanks.'

Knox lightly stroked his beard, which reached right down to his girdle. The candlelight made his haggard face appear even hollower, and although his thoughts may have seemed otherworldly, beneath his bushy eyebrows his small eyes had a very worldly expression.

'In order to put an end to your wretched quarrel,' he continued after a silence, 'you need to go back to its source. That gold you stole from John Cockburn a few years ago.'

'I was merely obeying the orders of the Regent who ruled this country,' James protested. 'The crowns I took possession of came from England, and were being delivered to the Hamiltons to enable them to fuel the rebellion.'

The old preacher looked at him with raised eyebrows. He did not intend to get dragged onto political ground.

'Although I did nothing more than my duty,' James added, 'I suffered great loss as a result with the sacking of Crichton Castle.'

'The consequences of violence,' sighed Knox. 'There is also the matter of your unworthy conduct towards Master Craig and his wife, which was aimed at compromising young Arran's honour.'

'Since when does a man who sleeps with a husband's wife have the right to talk about honour? I am sure you are aware that the spouse in question was once married to my own grandmother.'

In the hearth the flames danced and hissed, reflecting shafts of golden light onto the polished floor and the plain dark oak furniture. As if trying to brush aside those unclean details, Knox made a wide sweeping gesture with his hand.

'The licentiousness indulged in by the Papists should be alien to good Calvinists, my Lord Bothwell. But what is done is done, and let us now look to the future. I shall first visit the Duke of Châtelherault, followed by a visit to his son young Arran, and I shall ask him to welcome you as a friend. Rest assured my son, I will use all my influence to pacify them and tip the scales in your favour.'

James, holding his velvet cap in his hand, bowed to Knox. He was not too sure how to comport himself in the presence of this man who seemed to him like a gaunt spectre. Without a sound a maidservant brought in a tray, bearing tall glasses filled with a golden wine. Knox offered one to James then raised his own.

'Let us drink to the glory of God,' he commanded.

Arran hugged James closely to him.

'All is forgotten,' he whispered. There was a haggard expression on the young man's sallow face, which made James feel uncomfortable.

'Let us spend the whole day together,' he continued. 'We will eat together then let us go hunting. Tomorrow I shall take you to call on my father in order to seal our friendship.'

The swift and happy conclusion of Knox's intervention had delighted James, though it also filled him with a slight sense of foreboding. Nevertheless, he chose to ignore it in order to move on, bury the hatchet and so turn Hamilton into his ally. A meeting with the Duke had been arranged for the next day and he had sent word to James expressing his profound satisfaction at the prospect of receiving him. Having asked to be woken early James retired to bed that night in excellent spirits. The arrangement was that Arran would come to collect him early next morning, and the young Earl wanted to look his best before presenting himself before the head of the Hamiltons. After all had been settled James would request an audience with the Queen to let her know that her wishes had been obeyed. Mary was going through a period of melancholy; from her father, as well as from her grandfather James IV, she had inherited these sudden bouts of depression which confined her to her apartments, lost in thoughts that filled her eyes with tears. Soon her love of life would again prevail and banish her sadness.

The news coming from France was far from comforting. The atmosphere between Huguenots and Catholics remained very tense, several murders in various provinces had been committed, and persistent enmity between towns spread more discord in the country. Catherine de Medicis was trying to promote a policy of appeasement, but the Guises, unchallenged champions of Catholicism, opposed all religious tolerance and perceived every Huguenot to be a potential enemy of the realm.

Now deeply entangled in their own dissensions, the French were fast losing interest in Scotland, thus leaving England as the sole conceivable ally of her northern neighbour.

James placed himself in the hands of his barber, who gave him a close shave and trimmed his moustache with fine scissors. Then he dressed himself in his finest clothes; a ruffle shirt, a plum velvet doublet with close-fitting sleeves as dictated by fashion, soft knee breeches and suede boots. A weak sun was rising above the horizon, steeping the rocks in a pale mauve-tinted light.

In his home, Kinneil Castle near Edinburgh, the old Duke of Châtelherault was waiting for James. His son the Earl of Arran had turned up suddenly the previous evening in a state of agitation after his day spent with Bothwell, and he seemed overflowing with enthusiasm for his new friend. The Duke was alarmed over the change and deterioration in his eldest son's mental health. Would he become a wretched lunatic like his mother, who survived locked up in her apartments under the close supervision of her servants. Added to this worry was the provocation from his lifelong enemy Matthew Lennox. From his domicile in England, whence he had fled for refuge many years earlier having betrayed Scotland, he was now plotting to marry off the eldest of his sons, Lord Darnley, to his cousin Mary Stuart. Lennox, having himself married Margaret, daughter of the Earl of Angus, widow of King James IV, and the eldest of the Tudors, was now looking to see his son on the throne of Scotland.

The old Duke welcomed James warmly. The sight of his own son standing next to the son of 'The Fair Earl' who had been his contemporary filled him with a feeling of sadness. Whilst James cut a virile figure, whose expression showed intelligence, honesty, and single-mindedness, young Arran was pallid of countenance, with a sly and vacillating look on his face.

Hamilton had ordered refreshments, including bottles of vintage Bordeaux wine, to be brought straight to his own bedchamber where there was a fire burning in the hearth. The two windows looked out onto the park, where bare-branched weeping willow trees overlooked the slate-grey waters of the lake.

'I am so happy the dispute between us has at last been laid to rest,' declared Hamilton cheerfully. 'I know you had your reasons, my Lord, for relieving us of that gold, and we had our reasons for considering it ours. All that is past history now and I will do my best to reconcile you with John Cockburn your former victim. All is now forgotten.'

Young Arran was standing beside his father with a slightly vacuous smile on his lips. He was happy to count Hepburn as his friend. Being a lover of women and of good wine, Bothwell would be able to show him how to live life to the full and relieve the boredom from which he suffered. His feelings of anxiety would be dispelled by Bothwell's confidence, and together they would enjoy great adventures.

'Her Majesty the Queen trusts you,' the Duke said, as he poured wine for his guest. 'As her loyal subjects we would all like her to find a consort. Has she perhaps informed you of her intentions?'

'I know that the Queen has consulted Elizabeth.'

Hamilton stayed silent. He could not bring himself to confide so soon in a man who only a few days earlier had been an enemy. However, he was haunted by this latest threat of a match with Darnley.

'Mary Stuart, my cousin, has rejected me,' Arran complained in his high-pitched voice. 'It is unthinkable that she would prefer a Lennox to a Hamilton.'

James listened to his host in silence. He was wondering what might be asked of him in exchange for this reconciliation. Was it to talk Mary into agreeing to marry his poor demented son?

'Let us drink to our new alliance,' the Duke said. 'The Hepburn family united to ours, this is indeed a happy occasion!'

'If Her Majesty were to die childless,' young Arran spoke out suddenly, 'our family would come to power and we would not forget you.'

'Who would want a throne resting on the tomb of such a charming princess,' the Duke replied immediately. 'We all wish the Stuarts many healthy children. A toast to the Queen's health!'

James raised his glass in his turn. While he trusted Hamilton completely, he was at the same time baffled by his son's strange behaviour. As soon as he brought up the subject of his family's rights of succession Arran's voice had taken on a perfidious tone.

'Let us all attend the service together this Sunday,' Hamilton suggested. 'John Knox, to whom we owe our reconciliation, will appreciate that.'

James promised to do so. The end of his enmity was well worth two hours of sermonising.

'Calm yourself, my Lord, I beg of you.'

John Knox was beside himself. While he was working on his sermon, Arran had stormed in unannounced. Dishevelled and wide-eyed, the latter had gabbled an incoherent story centring on the Queen's abduction as planned by Bothwell and himself. However, he, Arran, could not bring himself to accomplish such a misdeed, and he had come to seek advice. He was pacing up and down wringing his hands, and from time to time he would laugh hysterically and dab at his eyes with a handkerchief.

'Such treachery seems inconceivable to me,' John Knox whispered to himself.

However, he was told that the Earl of Bothwell had once again become the talk of Edinburgh. On his way to the Borders, he claimed to have been shot at by Cockburn's son, whom he had then taken prisoner and led to Berwick before releasing him.

The old preacher did not know what to make of this tale.

Then with jerky delivery, Arran unravelled his fantasy. He was crying unashamedly, speaking of ghastly treachery, of the forthcoming murder of James Stuart and of a flight to Dumbarton from where he and Bothwell would run their dictatorship.

'We will rule over Scotland, he and I!' the wretched man finally exclaimed.

John Knox remained speechless for only a moment.

'Nobody, my Lord, can coerce you to follow the terrible conspiracy you have expounded to me.'

'Bothwell will compel me by witchcraft,' he whined.

Then as if animated by an irresistible impulse, he left the room, ran down the small staircase and slammed the door behind him.

I implore Your Grace on my bended knees to pay no attention to the accusations or confessions of my wretched son. Having myself locked him up in his room, he managed to escape my surveillance and to send to Your Majesty two letters whose contents I fear to surmise. This morning he fled from Kinneil by tying together his bed linen and blankets, and I do not know where he has found refuge. I beg Your Majesty not to give any credit to the words contained in the two notes, and not to receive my unfortunate son if he appears at Falkland.

My cousin Gavin Hamilton, the bearer of this message, will be better able to explain than these few words can, in what sorry state my son James finds himself. After accusing the Earl of Bothwell of the most execrable villainy, he pointed his finger at me, his own father. Judge such insanity for yourself...

At Falkland James Stuart felt triumphant. Having been accused by a member of the Hamilton family of high treason, Bothwell was in a dangerous predicament. Upon reading the letters from her young cousin, one sent from Edinburgh and the other from Kinneil, the Queen, at first stunned, had become greatly agitated. Her half-brother had immediately taken advantage of her vulnerability, thus leaving her no alternative. Why defend Bothwell? Was he above the law? For quite some time James Stuart had been warning her about this young adventurer who was willing to risk anything in order to fulfil his ambitions. Arran might be feeble-minded but this kind of plot could never have been conjured up out of thin air. Mary had not refuted any of his arguments but she had refused to make accusations. Yet her half-brother knew she would not have the courage to support Bothwell against all opposition, and therefore she would allow his imprisonment. Hepburn was an attractive man, and known to be a lover of women, while Mary was lonely and vulnerable. He should be put out of action as soon as possible and preferably for a lengthy period. The young Earl was expected at Falkland Palace at any moment. Having only just returned from the Borders, he was totally unaware of the accusations made against him by young Arran, and would have no time to prepare his defence.

The Queen declared she was unwell and retired to her chamber. She felt like hiding herself away and disappearing. Her half-brother was harassing her, and Maitland's eloquent silence had revived her fears and her hatred of violence. Memories came flooding back to her of the men hung from the battlements of Amboise, and the bodies of executed victims exposed to her view and to the public at street corners and beside path-ways. Her fervent desire for peace and harmony was turning out to be mere wishful thinking, and in her despair, her habitual ailments returned to afflict her body: a stitch, stomach pains, and uncontrollable vomiting. If, contrary to her half-brother's advice, she spared Hepburn, how far would her indulgence towards him stretch? Perhaps it was preferable not to see him for a while and to suppress the feelings of happiness she felt in his presence. Even the English Ambassador Randolph, who had been invited to Falkland, had continually insinuated that Bothwell was danger-ous, and a potential traitor like his father. The hounds were in pursuit.

'Her Majesty has issued us with orders to arrest you and Gavin Hamilton.'

Bothwell was dumbstruck. On the eve of the day of his arrival at court, Gavin Hamilton had informed him of the two letters, of the accusations contained within them, and of the insanity of young Arran, whom the Queen had just summoned to Falkland. At first James had not taken it seriously. There had been a reconciliation with the Hamiltons and he had left Kinneil a few days earlier in a climate of reciprocal cordiality. Why would Arran, crazy though he was, concoct such absurd tales of plots and abduction? Jealousy perhaps, Gavin had suggested.

'Don't forget, my Lord, that young Arran aspired to the Queen's hand, and that she favours you above him.'

Bothwell had shrugged his shoulders and demanded to see Mary, but the audience had been refused.

Tension mounted as the day progressed. Having arrived at Falkland a few hours earlier Arran had reiterated his accusations but had eventually exonerated his father from all complicity: James, he asserted, was the sole instigator of a plot aiming to seize power. Livid, James defended himself strenuously. He was enormously vexed by Mary's absence and infuriated by The Bastard's cold irony.

'As is my right by law I demand a legal inquiry!' he insisted finally. 'Institute an investigation, my Lord. Find my accomplices; make them talk. I am eager to hear their statements. But until the date of my trial, I demand to be set free!'

James Stuart's grey eyes expressed no emotion.

'The Queen's orders are that you be incarcerated.'

'I wish to see Her Majesty. If she personally orders my imprisonment then I will obey.'

Surrounded by her Privy Council Mary remained silent. She had passed a sleepless night and felt nauseous. Nevertheless, her honour compelled her to shirk her responsibilities no longer. Young Arran's letters had just been read. The English Ambassador had reported his conversation with the accuser, who after recanting had just backtracked again. There had indeed been a plot and Arran was ready to accept his punishment.

'When will the legal trial take place, Madam?' Bothwell asked coldly.

'We will think about it, my Lord. In the mean time you will go to St Andrews Castle, where together with my cousin Lord Arran you will remain in custody under surveillance until further notice.'

Mary was biting her lip, and knotting and un-knotting her hands. James read the pleading in her eyes and kept silent.

26

FROM ST ANDREWS James had been taken to Edinburgh Castle, and for the past three months he had been staring out at the unseasonably wet weather from behind the windows of his room which overlooked the rocky promontory. The Queen had not replied to his numerous requests for a trial. Even more than he deplored his sovereign's weakness, James despised The Bastard's triumph, and he wondered against whom he would next launch his attacks now that he and the Hamiltons had been put out of action. Would it be the Gordons that powerful Catholic family from the North? It was said that John, brother of his friend George, was aspiring to be a suitor for the Queen's hand and this rumour must have infuriated James Stuart.

James had no complaint to make regarding the conditions of his incarceration. He had two servants at his disposal and he was free to communicate with the outside world. He regularly received news from the court. Mary Stuart was finally to meet her cousin, either in York or in Nottingham, and they said she was delighted at the prospect of this audience, which she had long been hoping for. In the Borders, James Stuart was repressing violence with even greater violence. For want of gallows, they had tied together the hands and feet of Reivers and drowned them in the River Jed. This appropriation of what he considered his own domain by his worst enemy, filled the prisoner's heart with rage and instilled within him a fierce determination to escape if no trial was forthcoming. In an adjacent apartment was young Arran, haggard with jaundice and wasting away. Gavin Hamilton had been set free.

James's mother had informed him that Anna was considering going back to Denmark, and the thought of this cheered him up a little. With her lover now imprisoned, the young woman could go home with her head held high. Why would she marry a man who had become discredited? She was not a woman who made light of the future, and she would be able to claim to all and sundry that she had rejected him. James still held a soft spot in his heart for Anna, who had forsaken everything to follow him. In Flanders she had without any hesitation handed over to him the nest egg that her father had given her, and she had always supported him, waited for him, and welcomed him back. Now, just like the Queen, Anna, who had proclaimed her undying love for him, had become cool towards him. James felt cynical; there could be no guarantee of constancy by any man or woman.

The continuous rain was distressing James. The crops would be ruined and the farmers unable to pay their dues. Deprived of half the revenues from Melrose Abbey he found himself once again in grave financial difficulties. For months, Hailes had been in need of urgent repairs. At Crichton, adjacent buildings, wood stores, laundry rooms and salting rooms threatened to collapse. Around fifty servants depended on him for their subsistence. Entirely engrossed now in serving the interests of her half-brother to whom she was about to grant the wealthy Earldom of Moray, the Queen appeared to give no more thought to him whom she had once called her most faithful friend.

One July morning, the servant whom James had despatched with a message returned in a state of agitation. The Queen of England had cancelled her meeting with their sovereign under the pretext that this would be tantamount to condoning the acts of violence committed by the Guises against the Huguenots. Mary Stuart was exceedingly vexed, and since she was prevented from crossing the borders of her little realm she had decided to spend the summer travelling through its regions.

In early August, there came a succession of astonishing news from Edinburgh. Accompanied by a handful of his friends, John Gordon, son of the Earl of Huntly, had crossed swords in the High Street with Lord Ogilvie and some of his relatives. Ogilvie had been seriously wounded and his family were crying out for revenge. Gordon had taken refuge with his father at Strathbogie, but Mary had ordered Huntly to deliver his son into the hands of justice. Already thoroughly disgusted over having to yield up the Earldom of Moray, the Gordons had retaliated by raising an army.

When, on the twenty-seventh of August, the Countess of Huntly threw herself at Mary's feet imploring a pardon for her son, James Stuart who had now become the Earl of Moray, silenced her. He was now finally in possession of the weapon he needed in order to exterminate the Gordons.

Astounded, James followed the news that his servants or his friends brought him. Mary now stood on very perilous ground. If she lost the support of the Gordons, who were the most powerful Catholics in Scotland, she ran the risk of becoming completely isolated without necessarily being able to count on the sympathy of the Protestants. Once again, the young Earl wrote to the Queen stressing the iniquity of his incarceration and the absence of any inquiry or legal proceedings. Six days later he received a note from her: *Do what you can; I am powerless to help you.*

My Lord,
This evening, put on some sturdy clothes and soft leather boots.
On the way down, you will follow me and I shall guide you.

James Porterfield, one of the fortress commander's servants, had come to see Bothwell a few days earlier to organise his escape. His master would hear and see nothing, he assured him, and they could take their time. James Porterfield was an experienced climber and Bothwell was a bold and daring young man. The enterprise had every chance of succeeding. However, one false move, one rockslide, or one missed grip, would result in a possibly fatal fall. James was ready by nightfall. The rain had ceased two days previously and Porterfield was pleased with the excellent conditions which would ease their descent. A new crescent moon cast its feeble rays onto the rocky cliff, appearing to soften the harshness of the steep rock face with its crevices and lessen the overhangs.

'This way, my Lord, grasp the rock just above your left shoulder,' his guide pointed out calmly.

Intent but relaxed, James was progressing well in his descent. He felt in control of his movements, and his muscles, well developed from constant physical exercise, gave his limbs perfect control. Every now and then a stone would break loose and plunge into the void below.

As soon as his feet reached solid ground, James gazed back up at the fortress towering above him, looking apparently impregnable.

'Don't thank me, my Lord. You helped me with your courage as much as I helped you with my advice. May God come to your rescue,' Porterfield said simply, in answer to James's expressions of gratitude.

Just a short distance away James knew that he would find his cousin William Hepburn with a ready-saddled horse. He would gallop all the way to Morham to greet his mother and say goodbye to Anna before hiding away at Crichton. From there he would reflect on his next move. An extension to such arbitrary imprisonment seemed very unlikely. Either he would not be troubled again or he would stand a fair trial at which he was certain he would be acquitted.

James savoured the intense joy of being free, despite the scenes of devastation caused by the rains. Oats and barley would not ripen and wheat was rotting in the fields. The lush rolling pastures were covered with thick tufts of rough grass interspersed with stagnant puddles of water. Urging his horse to a gallop, he leapt across burns that cascaded between mossy rocks, and raced along muddy tracks. At his rapid approach, crows and jackdaws took flight and sheep ran scattering in all directions. With renewed pleasure, he inhaled the scents of the wet earth and the wild herbs and vegetation. He wondered how he could possibly have spent four long months locked up, existing without the feel of the wind on his face or the warmth of the sun or the firmness of a horse's flanks between his thighs.

The sun was already high in the sky when he entered the courtyard of his mother's small castle. A stable boy ran to meet him, a servant bade him welcome, and dogs jumped up to greet him. Behind Lady Agnes stood Anna, with a frozen expression on her face.

'When is your ship sailing?'

After the meal, James and Anna had managed to find time alone together. He had followed her into the room that she occupied at Morham, where the compassionate Lady Agnes had the kindness to receive her from time to time. Anna's hair was dressed in a braid and reached down to her waist. She was dressed in a plain cream coloured bonnet and a flared skirt of yellow cotton. Her blouse had a pleated collar, and laced over it was a plain bodice, which enhanced her bust and the slenderness of her waist. However, when James tried to take her in his arms she pushed him away. The young man took a step back. Little accustomed to being rejected, he was disconcerted.

'It is you of your own accord who have taken the decision to leave me,' he said flatly.

'Really?' Anna's sarcastic tone intensified his displeasure.

'I never asked for a separation. You have everything you need to live here, including the presence of my mother.'

'I have a lover who only deigns to visit me in order to satisfy his lust, who never writes me a letter, and who refuses to show himself in my company in Edinburgh as though I were a common prostitute!'

Bothwell did not utter a sound.

'And finally when in despair I decide to go back to Denmark, you say nothing to try to hold me back.'

'Tomorrow I may be forced to go into exile.'

Suddenly Anna placed her face between her hands and burst into tears. Her beautiful love story and exhilarating adventure had come to a sad end. Back in Denmark, she would turn away any suitor, and all because of some ungrateful man, a hypocrite who she could not get out of her mind. For fear of further infuriating Anna or of adding to her despair James did not dare say anything to comfort her. Anna raised her head, and her eyes were still full of tears. She gazed intently at her lover as if she were trying to commit his features to her memory forever.

'Come here,' Bothwell whispered. 'Let us not part like this.'

He took Anna's hand and drew her towards him, and while she rested her cheek against his shoulder with her arms wrapped around him, his thoughts were of Mary Stuart turning away from him.

Since James had arrived back at Crichton, the steward had done nothing but give him bad news: sheep had died of the staggers, there had been a failed harvest, the farm rents were not coming in and the torrential rains had shown up leaks in the roofs. The young Earl was calm and practical. They could manage by just replacing a few slates, and by forcing the farmers to hand over cattle in lieu of grain. Summer was coming to an end, but if the weather stayed fair for just a week or two longer, late haymaking would be possible. In reality James was too tense and anxious to concentrate on such matters. Any day now, he was expecting a message from the Queen. Sometimes he trusted that she would forgive him, but at other times he grew impatient waiting for an inquiry or legal process to begin.

Moreover, the sadness in Anna's eyes when he left Morham continued to haunt him.

When no messenger appeared at Crichton James's anxiety increased twofold. The news of his spectacular escape was at the centre of every conversation in Edinburgh but the Queen kept an ominous silence. It was probably best for him to withdraw to Hermitage. There protected by his Borderers, he would be ready to defy the Earl of Moray by shutting himself away for as long as necessary in his impregnable fortress.

James left Crichton at dawn accompanied by three servants. Having not given any previous warning of his impending arrival, he would find the castle's supplies depleted, with no comforts of any kind. However, he would get things organised, gather his adherents together, and send to Hailes for some furniture.

The young Earl felt strong twinges of emotion at the sight of Hermitage, standing magnificently alone in the midst of the moors. There were many legends connected to this grim fortress, but in its own right the dark building took the imagination back to a lost realm of witches, giants and beings endowed with supernatural powers. Despite the atrocities which had been committed there in bygone times, he felt protected and at peace with himself.

Wide-eyed, the few guards there watched their Lieutenant as he rode through the gates of the enclosing walls. Hermitage was empty and the stately rooms unfurnished. The two maidservants busied themselves preparing basic meals consisting mainly of oatmeal porridge and some vegetables. The salting rooms, smoking rooms and cellars were bare; there were only a few barrels of ale and but two jars of lard. As soon as his presence there became known, many others would turn up and all would need to be accommodated, fed and watered. However, James was not worrying over such trivial matters. For the time being, alone in his fortress, he felt like a king. He was not afraid to sleep on a straw mat and if need be he could drink water from the well. He strode rapidly towards the outhouses and climbed the narrow spiral staircase leading to the wall walk. All around him the hills stretched out, clothed in heather, bleached grass and moss. Chased by windswept clouds a dappled light played over the moors, lending an amazing intensity to the varying shades of purple, green, and brown. The little river of Hermitage wound its way between banks overgrown with bushes and small trees.

In just a few weeks time the arrival of autumn would signal the return of the Reivers. Once again, the echoing sounds of pounding hooves and fierce laughter would be heard, and at night scattered bonfires would light up the night with the flickering flames drawn out by the harsh wind from the hills.

Suddenly James stopped and stared. Beyond the river he had spotted a small closely grouped herd approaching the fortress in a peaceful manner. It was headed by a horseman riding slowly, accompanied by two large dogs.

'God save us, Janet!' Bothwell exclaimed.

He descended rapidly to the courtyard, ordered the portcullis to be raised, and strode across the drawbridge. He could now clearly see his former mistress with her two red-coated Irish setters at her side, followed by a group of ten oxen and a small flock of sheep, herded by Tempest, her favourite sheepdog.

'I caught sight of you this morning, making for Hermitage as if the Devil himself was after you, and I just thought you might be in need of some provisions.'

James hugged Janet. His bitter parting with Anna made him appreciate even more the quality of love and thoughtfulness shown by this serene and mature woman.

'There is a cart following on behind with a few bags of rye and oat flour,' Janet added cheerfully. 'My Lord and Master will not now starve to death!' She dismounted and with a maternal gesture took James's arm.

The fire was roaring in the kitchen hearth, which was positioned in the large tower facing the river. Betty, one of the two maidservants, had put water on to boil and fetched a pot of heather honey from a store cupboard. From one of the spacious pockets of her riding dress Janet had produced a bag of oatmeal.

'We will have to make do without cream in our porridge my love, as beggars cannot be choosers.'

Leaning on the long oak table, Janet and James discussed the events and happenings of the past few months.

'The Earl of Moray is a shrewd politician,' Janet remarked, while finishing her bowl of porridge. 'He has managed to build up a network of English supporters, and in Elizabeth's eyes he is better suited to governing Scotland than his Catholic half-sister.'

'The Queen knows how to rule,' James countered, 'Mary is not as pliant as she appears and I believe she is capable of rebelling against any person who tries to restrain her.'

'May God awaken this impulse in her, Jamie. Moray will never leave you in peace until you have gone back to prison or crossed the sea.'

George Gordon made a sudden appearance at Hermitage one evening. Exhausted by the haste of his ride from Edinburgh, he had come to beg James to send reinforcements to his father at Strathbogie. For two weeks, the young Earl had been waiting for a reply to the letter he had sent to the Queen, and the uncertainty was tormenting him. If Janet was right, James should consider leaving Scotland to seek refuge in France and he dreaded this eventuality. The influence he had over Mary and his friendship with her would be ruined by a long absence, and lack of money would make his life in exile difficult. For the time being he could take no initiative. Infuriating Moray further by sending Borderers to the aid of the Earl of Huntly would only rebound on him. George Gordon did not insist, but James could see that he was very alarmed about the situation in the North, which was so tense that a confrontation between the Gordons and the Royal army seemed inevitable.

October was drawing to a close. Despite the long rides on horseback, which physically tired him out, serenity eluded James. No news had reached him from Strathbogie, and from this silence he feared the worst. Finally one morning, three of his Hepburn cousins from Smeaton arrived at Hermitage, looking sombre. There had been a battle at Corrichie, between the forces of the Earl of Huntly and those of the Queen. During the fighting the Earl had fallen from his horse, struck down by a fit of apoplexy, and despite the bravery of his sons, his army had disbanded. John and George Gordon had been taken prisoner, stripped of their titles and honours and their property forfeited. John was going to stand trial. After the Hamiltons and the Hepburns, it was the Gordons' turn to be crushed and humiliated.

John Gordon was beheaded in Aberdeen before the very eyes of the Queen, who, horrified, had fainted. George was still in prison. For James, the possibility of returning to Edinburgh was inconceivable. There, forgotten by all, he might rot for years. He would have to go into exile.

A merchant ship was leaving Leith in December bound for St Malo. Taking two of his servants, James had decided to go to Paris where he would try to secure a position at the court of Charles IX. In his absence, members of the Hepburn family would approach the Queen to beg for a pardon. Mary kept her feelings to herself and no one knew what she thought of the injustice committed against her Lieutenant.

His trunks were ready to go when at last a letter arrived from the Queen. James walked to the banks of the Hermitage River through drizzling rain, which had been falling since the previous day. He needed to be alone to avoid inquisitive glances and unspoken questions. The westerly wind was blowing in his face, carrying the scent of wet grass and peat from the moors, and the colour of the water reflected the greyness of the sky. His feet sank into the damp moss and mud. The atmosphere was quiet and almost surreal.

The events of the past few months have been a source of sorrow for me, in particular your imprisonment and the death of Sir John Gordon. My responsibilities as Queen may force me in my mind to act in a manner that is alien to my heart. I have never doubted your innocence, but the accusations made by my cousin could not be ignored just because I did not believe them.

I have been informed of your forthcoming departure for France.

Although I envy you that you are soon to be in Paris, and I will do my best to secure a position for you there, I shall regret your absence. In losing you, I lose much.

Before sailing, if you can, please visit Lady Janet, your sister, at Coldingham; I intend to spend the last days of the year there. Your presence, even though brief, would be the most welcome present to me.

Do not harbour any hostility towards me, my Lord. As God is my witness, I have never decided anything that was unfavourable to you. Even sovereigns sometimes have to submit to resolutions that are hurtful to them.

The fine rain was dampening the sheet of paper and causing the ink to run. Standing motionless on the opposite bank, a heron was seeking its prey. Although the Queen's weakness irritated him, James could not bring himself to feel resentment for the woman herself. He knew that she was a stranger to political intrigue and that she was alone and vulnerable.

27

ONE ACT OF betrayal had followed another. What a fool he had been to trust some men's word of honour.

James rests his head against the damp wall of his room. He has a fever and has been shivering for several days, and he has suffered another haemorrhage. The outside world is losing all sense of reality. Alone now he is left with his pitifully weakened body, his consuming obsessions and the ghosts of the past that haunt him. He had made a fatal error in believing Morton and Balfour, and he had fallen headlong into the trap they had laid for him.

James is delirious, and is now under the impression that he has only lived life to the full for the brief period of two years, a ridiculously short time to justify an existence. He has had everything in life he desired and now has lost it all. Since early childhood, he has been entranced by knightly legends, but now he sees himself as having failed their code of honour. He has been unable to protect his deeply beloved wife, he has ruined the reputation of the Hepburns, and he has lost them all their titles and their lands. He likens it to an all-consuming fire that turns everything to ashes. Has Mary forgotten him? He would sacrifice anything to receive a letter from her, but does she care? Who wants him now? Does even the Devil want him? It is more than nine years since Mary and he parted. James sees again the scene at Carberry Hill with Mary's tears streaming down her face already soiled with perspiration and dust, and he tastes again the salty tears on her lips. She wraps her arms around him and he whispers to her; 'Soon we will be together again, in just a few weeks, a few months at most, be brave!' Then he adds a little louder,

'I beg you my dearest love, to remain faithful to me.' Now their bodies part... the distance grows between them... just one last glance...

James sees Mary's face again, with her light brown almond-shaped eyes beneath slightly heavy eyelids. They are the eyes of the Stuarts; he is husband to one who is a daughter, granddaughter, and great-grand-daughter of kings. The Stuarts and Scotland are intertwined throughout its history; James too has a long and noble Scottish ancestry of which he is rightly proud.

At Dragsholm, winter seems to last for ever. Where is Mary? Do they treat her with the respect she deserves? Do they comfort her? One day perhaps some sovereign will help her to regain her throne, but will his body be broken and worn out by that time, and thus no longer able to stand at her side?

In Copenhagen, they had told him that after their separation she had shorn off all her hair and now only wore a wig, and that she either kept silent or else burst into tears at the mere mention of his name. In those days, he was still receiving letters from her. In short, stilted sentences Mary had assured him of her undying love, and promised she would wait for him until death should part them.

James thinks again about all the letters that Mary wrote to him, which he hid in the silver casket, and he remembers her poems. His ene-mies, men of dishonour, had read them, but they remained for him the most beautiful and passionate letters a man could receive.

James tries to remember the sentences, but his memory is failing; 'Into your hands I place the safekeeping of my young son James, my honour and my life.' With difficulty, he struggles with the meaning of those words Mary had written. Each one is now a dagger that pierces his flesh. If those letters had still been in his possession perhaps he might have had something to live for. Now he has nothing left to remind him of her, no jewellery, no handkerchief, no lock of hair. Only on his finger, he still wears the wedding ring that his warders had not the nerve to try to take from him.

Everything is grey... the sky, the earth, the sea. Around him it is dark and damp, with water dripping down the walls. Through the narrow window, he discerns wooden hovels and clumps of rushes withered by the salt sea winds. 'Without hesitation, I would give up Scotland, France and England to follow you to the end of the world, wearing my white petticoat.' Mary is speaking to him, but he has to make a tremendous effort to try to understand her. They should indeed have fled to the ends of the earth together with their offspring she was carrying... twin boys, his sons.

James hears a noise. They have just opened the hatch to serve him his meal as though he were a wild beast. He no longer has contact with his fellow humans. Sometimes he eats and sometimes he hurls the plate against the wall; but the flask of spirits, he finishes down to the last drop and asks for more, begs for more. After he has drunk it, he collapses onto his straw mat. Now he no longer sees Mary, or his mother, or his sister Janet. His suffering ceases.

The candle casts strange shadows onto the ceiling. He tries to decipher their meaning. Why does death not glide in among all these shadowy ghosts? James is waiting for death, looking out for her, lest she should leave without him.

James's teeth are chattering and he can barely move his hands, which are crippled with rheumatism. He should have fled when he was in Bergen or in Copenhagen.

He was so certain then that he would soon be freed and would be able to make his way to France.

To stop himself from screaming he buries his face in the straw of his vermin-infested pillow. One cry and he will again be thrown into the pit, which he could not bear. The rusty shackles have bruised his ankles and wrists, and the sores that will not heal have become infected. Like a dog, he licks at them to clean them or else pours spirit onto the open wounds. The stinging pain reminds him that he is still alive.

Throughout the evening the storm rages. He loves the whistling sound of the wind and the mournful cries of the seagulls. He loves to watch the great banks of clouds being swept across the sky towards the end of the world, that place where he will be reunited with Mary, wearing her white petticoat, and with a ribbon in her hair.

Finding his way in the dark James feels with his fingers along the wall but there is no door; he has been walled in alive. Mary is waiting for him but he is unable reach her.

The candle is burnt out and James hears only the scampering of mice and the distant crashing of waves onto the shore. He lies motionless and ceases thinking of anything, letting his mind go blank.

28

THE CAPTAIN HAD given the order to reef in the sails, which had been torn in the strong gusts of wind, and had taken the helm himself. Through the mist the passengers had sighted land, but were unable to gauge the distance.

'Holy Island!' exclaimed the watchman suddenly.

There was a general sigh of relief from the passengers. The island was located south of Berwick, not far from the Scottish border. The ship would be able to drop anchor in the little port for repairs.

'At low tide,' one of the passengers explained, 'you can walk to the mainland, but you have to be careful, as the causeway floods rapidly with the incoming tide.'

The travellers, who had been battered in the rough seas and soaked to the skin, took refuge in the fishermen's dwellings that surrounded the port. The quays were cluttered with rush cages and fishing nets, and reeked of fish and brine.

'Perhaps this delay is a portent that I should go to see the Queen at Coldingham,' Bothwell said to himself.

He had sufficient time to do so as it would take several days to bail out the water from the hold, repair the rigging and dry out the baggage before re-embarking, and Coldingham was a five hour walk from there.

James chose Willie, the youngest of his servants, to accompany him. He was a strong good-natured boy who was not afraid of a long walk. The wind had moderated now and the two men, striding along muddy and waterlogged paths still saturated from the rain, made good progress. A light mist drifted seawards from the line of jagged rocks on the coast, which was lapped by the surf at high tide. Down on the shore barelegged children collected seashells.

The Scottish border was close to the English town of Berwick. North of the River Tweed, James knew the countryside well. He was familiar with every path, short cut and ford, and especially the treacherous bogs in which men and cattle ran the risk of being mired. The two men would reach Coldingham before nightfall.

'The Queen has gone hawking,' announced Janet, leading her brother into her bedchamber. 'You can wash, get changed and have something to eat; you will see her at dinner this evening. Her surprise at seeing you will be to your advantage and you will soon know whether your presence pleases or vexes her.'

James gave Janet a brotherly hug. Though married to the Queen's half-brother and now pregnant with her first child, his sister still exhibited the frankness, cheerful spontaneity and taste for free expression, which in the old days had made her such an untamed spirit. Even the silk and velvet fabrics in which she now dressed could not banish that familiar vision of Janet running barefoot in her cotton shift across the moors.

When James entered the great hall, he found Mary Stuart warming herself beside the hearth, making light conversation with her half-brother John and her ladies-in-waiting. Darkness had fallen and the light from the tall candelabra cast soft-tinted hues over the saffron velvet of her dress and over her auburn hair, on which was pinned a gold-embroidered cap.

'Madam, we have a visitor,' announced Janet with a cheerful smile.

The Queen turned round and as her eyes met James's she blushed deeply.

The hunt that day had been disappointing. Mary's favourite gerfalcon had killed only two ducks and a heron, and John's goshawks had caught three rabbits and a pigeon. The following morning they again set forth, with Janet and her husband leading the way. They were followed by the ladies and gentlemen who made up the Queen's retinue, and behind them the falconers and dog handlers with their pointers and water spaniels. The Queen and Bothwell brought up the rear. There was a light breeze, and low clouds were moving slowly across the grey skies. Mary's lilac scent mingled with the pungent smell of the horses and the fine salty sea mist. Below them by the shore low cliffs bordered a sandy cove, where sea-gulls searched for morsels amongst the seaweed and debris washed in by the tides.

'We have always been frank and open with each other, Madam,' the young Earl said. 'At risk of offending you I have to admit I am confused by your recent attitude towards me. You know that I am ruined and about to be exiled, all because of lies so outrageous that even a child would not believe them.'

'I never wished nor ordered your fall into disgrace, nor did I ever believe that tale of treason.'

'Yet you let me rot in gaol for months, and never deigned to reply to my petitions.'

As they rode along the path the pebbles rolled under the horses' hooves; a faint quarter moon could be seen rising above the horizon.

'As Queen I have above all else to consider my own interests, which are those of my country. It is my duty.'

'Is getting rid of me beneficial to Scotland, Madam?'

The tone of James's voice was harsh and aggressive. Mary felt she was discovering a side of this man she did not wish to know.

'I am also the legitimate heir to the throne of England, my Lord Bothwell, as you must be aware. In order for my cousin Queen Elizabeth to choose me as her successor it is imperative that I maintain the friendliest relations with her. My brother the Earl of Moray and my Secretary of State Maitland are working towards fostering a close alliance with England. How can you expect them to support your attachment to France?'

'I thought you shared my sentiments about this.'

'I am Queen of Scots.'

'And friend of England, so that you may gain another throne? Have you forgotten Flodden, Madam, where your grandfather and mine perished? Or the devastation caused by the English when King Henry VIII wanted to betroth you to his son the Prince of Wales? With my own eyes, I saw Scotsmen's throats being slit, their houses burned down and their daughters raped. Despite this, you would have me grovel like a dog, Madam, before them? Scotland may be a small country but she is a proud nation whose soul is not for sale.'

Mary sat up very tall in her saddle. Not since her childhood had anyone dared to lecture her.

'You are forgetting to whom you are speaking, my Lord!'

She wanted to put this man in his place even though at the same time she was delighted with his patriotism and sense of friendship. Both of them felt unhappy and unable to disentangle the confusion over what their feelings really were for each other, and for a while they rode on in silence, while their two horses tossed their manes and pranced with excitement.

'I approve of the firm way in which my half-brother James governs but I do not like his aggressive manner,' declared Mary suddenly. 'The Stuarts do not like those who resist them, and you have constantly been at odds with the Lords of the Congregation and have criticised their policies.'

'My Lord Moray and I have different goals, and are indeed of a very different nature.'

'But just as he is, you are also my friend, are you not?'

The note of anxiousness in her voice touched James. How could he bear resentment against his young Queen, who had to learn the hard way how to rule her people? The time would come when she would see very clearly who her real friends were.

'I am ready to die for your cause, Madam.'

Unhesitatingly Mary put her hand into James's outstretched hand and for a while they rode on, their fingers entwined.

The hour of departure had arrived. John and Janet put two of their horses at James's disposal, which servants would bring back to Coldingham. James was preoccupied with his thoughts. How long would it be before he was allowed back into Scotland? The Queen had promised she would do all she could to shorten his exile, but he had few illusions and knew that Moray would always have the last word. Janet had given her brother some pieces of gold bullion, which would enable him to find lodgings in Paris while waiting for a position at the Valois Court. Mary had written to her uncles to request their protection for him.

The ship lay at anchor, and was making ready to leave in the morning. Sandy Durham and Gabriel Sempill were awaiting their master at a humble inn on the far side of the bay, and they had been joined by James Porterfield, who had decided to link his fate with that of the man whom he had helped to escape from Edinburgh Castle. The Earl arrived to join them, desolate in the face of his forthcoming separation from his family and from the Queen. He was also very concerned about the possibility of hostile action against him by the English. Ambassador Randolph had numerous spies in the area and must have been warned of his impromptu landing on Holy Island. It would be sweet revenge for him to get his own back and make the Earl of Bothwell pay for having captured the English gold all those years ago and for his unfriendly attitude towards England.

When night came, the young Earl barricaded his door and kept his pistols beside him. On the other side of the partition wall, his servants snored as they slept. Was it possible that one of them would betray him for a handful of crowns?

Suddenly with a crash, the door gave way under the impact of men's shoulders. Before he even had time to leap to his feet James was roughly assaulted and overpowered.

'No need to put up a fight, my Lord,' growled a man with a Northumbrian accent.

Without the benefit of his friendship with the Earl of Northumberland and his brother Lord Percy, both of them Borderers like himself, James would not have got off as lightly as he did. Imprisoned at Berwick, he had immediately sent a message to his friends asking to be set free. The Earl of Northumberland had replied with compassion, securing for him a release on parole followed by house arrest in his castle at Alnwick. On receiving this news, the Queen of Scots had protested and threatened to intervene. Moray and Maitland were surprised by this sudden renewal of affection, and agreed that Bothwell was more dangerous than they had previously thought.

After being held in Northumberland for several months, James was escorted to London and imprisoned in the Tower. Released again on parole at the request of Mary Stuart, he had returned to Alnwick Castle to await the renewal of his safe conduct to France. Not having received it he had returned to London, where Queen Elizabeth had granted him a brief audience. Bedecked in extravagant jewels, with her hair curled and her face powdered, the young Queen had feigned ignorance. What grievance could she possibly have against the Earl of Bothwell, a friend of her very dear cousin Mary? England did not detain gentlemen against their will, and James would soon be free to go wherever he pleased.

Elizabeth liked men and appreciated them for their own particular qualities. For a few moments she had contemplated him, a faint smile on her lips, then with an abrupt wave of her fan had indicated the interview was over. Beside her stood Robert Dudley who she called her beloved Robin, and who bore the self-important air of an untouchable favourite.

After this audience, James's wait was still far from over. In the brief letters that she sent him during his interminable custody in England, Mary carefully avoided expressing her true feelings. She told him of the execution of the poet Chastelard; on two occasions he had hidden in her room at night, and for her honour's sake, she had been left with no alternative but to have him killed. Once only had she allowed a hint of emotion in her letters.

You are my rock, she wrote. *If I feel threatened or too isolated, my heart tells me that I will always be able to lean on you. Did you not assure me at Coldingham that you would be prepared to die for me? You are the first to have said such words to me, and rest assured, I will never forget them.*

Finally, in September the precious documents reached the Earl, and with them some letters addressed to Catherine de Medicis. James was free to sail for France, but the twenty months spent in England against his will had affected the young man deeply. While he had been languishing in Northumberland, events of considerable importance had taken place. In France, Mary's uncle François de Guise had been murdered by a young Protestant Poltrot de Méré, thus depriving Mary of her most powerful protector. In England the Earl of Lennox, husband of Henry VIII's niece and father of two sons, had been allowed to return to Scotland from whence he had been banished for treason at the time of the Hamilton Regency. Queen Elizabeth had asked Mary Stuart, 'her beloved sister,' to give a warm welcome to her repentant relative and to restore to him his lands, titles and honours. The rumour that his eldest son Henry Lord Darnley, a handsome eighteen-year-old nobleman, would soon follow him to Scotland vexed James. What intrigue was the Queen of England planning? Was it Mary's marriage to this harmless adolescent cousin, in order to obtain increased control over Scotland's fate?

29

Paris, 1565

ON HIS RETURN to Paris, the Earl of Bothwell was reunited with familiar faces and resumed a leisurely lifestyle, which frustrated him in his urge for action, and soon became hard to bear. He also felt the widespread tension in the city; despite Catherine de Medicis' efforts to preserve the peace, religious intolerance and strife was on the increase. The young King Charles IX, together with his brothers, the Queen Mother and most of the French Court, had left Paris to go on a tour through France and were presently in Avignon, capital of the Venaissin region, which belonged to the Holy See.

Before leaving England, James had written to Anna Throndsen asking her for financial aid. Her immediate response had been to send him a small coin with the words: 'in full settlement.' He had now banished all thoughts of Anna from his mind. News from the Borders came to him by way of his sister Janet. The bitter feud between the Scotts and the Elliots had been revived; the Scotts had raided the small township of Liddesdale, and the Elliots had ransacked the villages inhabited by dependants of the Scotts. The Elliots had offered the fortress of Hermitage to the English in order to gain their assistance, an offer which Lord Scrope the English Lieutenant of the Borders had declined. James had been shaken at the thought that his beloved fortress might fall into English hands. Why did destiny always seem to be persecuting him? He felt that everything seemed to be against him, including the absence of his friend the Marquis d'Elbeuf René de Guise, who as Admiral of the Royal Galleys was in Provence to welcome the King.

Now his only pleasure was the presence of a young Frenchman who had just entered his service. He was a replacement for Sandy Pringle who had suddenly and without warning left to return to Scotland. He had christened the young man French Paris to distinguish him from another Paris, a Scotsman who had served him in Edinburgh. French Paris was a resolute carefree fellow, and something of a comedian. His real name was Nicolas Hubert and he lost no time in encouraging his master to frequent the more disreputable districts in the city, where they could at little cost make love, eat and drink their fill.

The month of February was bitterly cold. James received news that Lennox's son Lord Darnley had arrived in Edinburgh due to the safe conduct granted by Queen Elizabeth, and that Mary Stuart had immediately received him at Wemyss Castle in Fife. Some days previously, James had received a letter from the Queen promising him the command of the Scottish Guard in Paris, a lucrative position that would help him out of his financial predicament.

The wildest rumours were now spreading in Paris. It was said that with the assistance of their German brothers large numbers of Huguenots were on their way back to the capital, and that at the instigation of the King of Spain, backed by the Pope, the Duke of Savoy was on the verge of launching an attack on Geneva.

In the deserted Louvre without any feeling of enthusiasm, James took command of the Scottish Guard, now in a depleted state as many men had left to escort the King and his retinue down to the Garonne.

One March evening the young Earl walked back to his lodgings and was surprised to find a messenger waiting for him wearing the livery of Mary Stuart's uncle the Cardinal de Lorraine.

'Monseigneur has asked me to wait for your reply,' the man said.

James hastily unfolded the sheet of paper.

Being aware of the friendship you have always shown the house of Guise, we are begging you to leave for Edinburgh without delay in order to persuade our niece, the Queen of Scots, not to marry the Earl of Lennox's son. The Guises view this proposed alliance as a means to weaken the Queen of Scots by placing her under the influence of her cousin the Queen of England...

'Tell Monsieur le Cardinal that I will do as he asks,' James replied to the messenger.

The joy James felt at returning to his own country was short-lived. Immediately on being informed of his arrival, Moray revived the legal action taken against him after his escape from Edinburgh Castle. James was now in danger of being arrested at any moment.

After ousting the Elliots from Hermitage Castle, the young Earl once again took refuge there. He made contact with Janet Beaton, who begged him to go back to France as quickly as possible. The Queen, she assured him, would not pay any attention to her uncle's warning as she was infatuated with young Darnley and determined to take him for her husband, despite Moray's opposition.

James asked Janet to stay the night with him. He felt lost and uncertain and needed her comforting presence and her ability to soothe and calm him. What would become of him? And what did the future hold for him?

By morning, he had made up his mind. It was not worth putting himself in danger for the dynastic interests of Mary Stuart. He would go back to France.

'Come with me,' he asked Janet.

She shook her head, laughing.

'Paris is no place for a woman of my age. What would I do without my horse, my moors, and my herds? It would take less than two weeks before we started fighting like cat and dog, Jamie. Since you have to live in Paris, you should make the most of it. Get yourself a pretty mistress; they say French women are witty and uninhibited.'

James was exhausted by so much travelling, and not looking forward to arriving back in France. To eke out his finances he had kept only two servants, French Paris, who had been promoted to the position of page, and Gabriel Sempill. Spring had arrived and Paris had recovered some of its gaiety. The scent of the lilacs which bloomed in abundance in the gardens reminded him constantly of Mary Stuart, who was now about to marry again and belong physically to another man. He had never pictured himself as her lover, but in a manner of speaking he had thought of her as being his. From now on there would be no more titillating confusion between them. Would Mary put him out of her mind and forget all about him? For James everything seemed to be falling apart. News had just come that John Stuart, his brother-in-law, had suddenly and unexpectedly died, leaving Janet a widow alone with a young son. He keenly felt the loss of

John who had been his only ally within the royal family. John and Janet's wedding celebrations had been the happiest moments of his life.

'Could it be that we are related, my Lord?'

James looked over his shoulder and saw a young woman smiling at him.

'I am Eléonore de Crissey. I have been told you own property of that name in Scotland.'

'Crichton, Madam. If only one or two letters in the spelling of your name had been different then we might indeed have been cousins, which would have filled me with delight.'

The young woman was of a similar age to him and had a slim figure and a pretty face.

The evening reception given by Jean d'Aubigny, uncle of Lord Darnley and a long-term resident in France, was drawing to a close. There had been copious toasts in honour of the future royal couple, after which the guests had listened to a concert of flutes, viols and drums, and now they were enjoying some appetisers before taking their leave. It was a balmy night and Parisians were lingering in the streets. Through the open windows the sound of people laughing and calling to each other could be heard, as well as the noise of drunken revellers emerging from their drinking dens. In the Seigneur d'Aubigny's salon voices were raised, and sounds of laughter blended with the general sounds of conversation.

'My husband is with Monsieur de Lansac in Angoulême,' Eléonore explained, before James had even had time to ask her any questions. 'The court is due to visit our fortified château in the autumn.'

James appreciated the forwardness of French women. In a short space of time, he had found out from this charming person that her husband was absent and that she was a Huguenot.

'They say the Queen Mother is negotiating the marriage of her daughter Princess Margot with Prince Henri de Navarre. This seems to open the door to many more unions between Catholics and Reformists. As for myself I approve of tolerance in matters of the heart,' James said to her.

'Women acquired that quality a long time ago, Monsieur,' answered Eléonore.

James took her hand and brought it to his lips.

'May I walk with you?'

Eléonore had put up only a small show of resistance. He had visited her the following day, accompanied her on a walk the day after, and three days later had slipped into her bed. This young woman who had so quickly seduced James was elegant, cultured and knowledgeable in the field of love. She had entered his life at just the right time to help him chase away his ghosts, his regrets and worries over the past and his fear of the future. Being well connected to all matters of importance in Paris she took him along with her to one party after another and seemed very happy to show off her dashing Scottish lover, with his broken nose and sensual features, who was said to be close to Mary Stuart. The romance of Mary's marriage moved those who remembered the pretty young Queen of France with her exquisite smile. From among all the princes of Europe, she had chosen Darnley, this beardless young boy with his delicate features and refined elegance who loved to dance, drink, compose rhymes and play the lute... the perfect man in fact, mocked Eléonore. James perceived the contempt and sarcasm hidden behind the accolade and it made him feel sorry for Mary. Little by little, he got into the habit of spending the entire night at his mistress's house. He would leave at dawn to walk back to his apartment where he would find French Paris and Gabriel Sempill still fast asleep. The young woman left a sweet fragrance of mignonette on his skin, which reminded him of Mary's perfume. James enjoyed his walks in the fresh early morning air through the streets of Paris. Market gardeners pushed their wares in handcarts, night watchmen kicked the drunks who sprawled in the gutter out of the way, and here and there he heard cocks crowing. His sleepless nights made the young Earl feel slightly intoxicated, and the events of the past were losing their importance for him. He rejoiced in the fact that he was loved, that the air smelt good, and that women looked beautiful in the first light of a Parisian morning. What did it matter if Darnley and Moray contemplated each other with malice, or if the Queen had taken David Rizzio, an Italian, as her close adviser and personal secretary? Rizzio had arrived with the Comte de Moretta, the Ambassador of Savoy, and due to his talents as a singer had first been taken on as chorister, before gaining Mary's trust and eventually her friendship. As soon as his son had been proclaimed King Henry, Lennox considered himself all-powerful in the country that years earlier he had so despicably betrayed. Moray and the Hamiltons were in league with William Cecil and were plotting against the royal couple. Darnley had taken to excessive drinking in the local taverns, while Rizzio was engaged in court intrigues.

As he walked through the narrow streets bordering the gardens, James sometimes laughed hysterically. The decaying political situation in Scotland, his exile and his poverty, had all become meaningless now. The only things that mattered to him were making love, feeling the warmth of the sun, eating, drinking and sleeping.

Every day Eléonore sent him two or three letters, which he eagerly answered. Her words of love brought sheer pleasure to him. Sometimes she came to visit him in broad daylight, wearing a mask. As they went upstairs French Paris and Gabriel gazed at them with knowing smiles. James would draw the curtains, the bed would swallow them up, and in the heat of passion they swore eternal love to each other.

In August a Scottish merchant arrived in Paris and informed the Earl of Bothwell that the Earl of Moray had taken up arms against the Queen of Scots; he had just been outlawed and his lands and property confiscated. George Gordon's titles and honours had been restored and he had regained possession of his family estates. James's friend had now become Earl of Huntly and was once again a powerful Lord.

As soon as he had taken leave of his compatriot, James felt a burning desire for action. Paris suddenly seemed like a prison and Eléonore a mistress just like any other. In rapid strides, the young Earl walked along the Seine, over the Pont au Change, through the Ile de la Cité, continuing up the river towards the Petit Châtelet. The weather was oppressive, the air close and humid, and James felt extremely tense. Who would take over command of the royal army? Kirkcaldy of Grange who was considered a tactician of genius was among the rebel ranks. Then there was Lennox, who was incapable of leading soldiers to victory, the King who was not yet nineteen and had no military experience, and his friend Huntly who had no taste for the art of warfare. At last, he would be able to satisfy his desire for vengeance instead of stagnating in Paris, which had currently been deserted by the court.

When he reached the front of the Tower of Nesle James turned back. The collar of his shirt and the back of his unbuttoned cotton doublet were getting wet from large almost lukewarm raindrops. The Queen had no right to treat him in such a manner. He had risked and lost everything for her then she had discarded him like an old rag. Why had she pretended to appreciate his services? Why the smiles, the flattery and flirtatiousness, which at the time had seemed so spontaneous?

The sky was ink-black, and strong gusts blew away the litter piled high on the quays. A dappled horse trotted past ridden by an elegant gentleman, splashing dirty water onto his breeches. James's thoughts went back in time to the scent of the moors after rain and to the banks of the Tyne where wild flowers bloomed in the summer. He would seek out the first drinking den he came to and consume a bottle of spirits, then he would make love to Eléonore and fall asleep at dawn, his hopes dashed.

'You had only been gone three minutes Monsieur le Comte, when an urgent note was left for you,' announced French Paris with evident lack of enthusiasm. 'If you had not walked so fast, I would have tried to catch up with you.'

James felt like giving his page a good kicking, but only the day before he had disciplined him for insolence with such severity that he still felt guilty about it.

Angrily he snatched the sealed letter and broke the wax.

Your silence leads me to believe that my first letter never reached you, Mary wrote in her pretty italic writing. *The King and I are in great need of your assistance. Hurry back to Edinburgh and be careful not to fall into the hands of your enemies who are now mine too...*

'By the blood of Christ!' Bothwell exclaimed.

A wave of joy washed over him.

'Hurry up; fetch my horses and get them harnessed; get Gabriel to prepare supplies for the journey; pack my belongings into trunks and give them to Mr Maxwell, an Edinburgh merchant, who will load them onto the next ship leaving for Scotland. You will find him at the Hotel de la Couronne in Ave Maria Street, which is adjacent to the Provost's house. Sell my chain and my gold belt buckle; I trust you to get as much for it as you can, then come back here without delay. We are leaving for Edinburgh at dawn tomorrow.'

Before putting together his documents and drawing up an itinerary, he would write to Eléonore. She was the only one in Paris whom he would miss.

30

NEWLY ARRIVED AT HOLYROOD, James was getting accustomed to this extraordinary reversal of fortune. In order to evade the English he had returned through Flanders, and had narrowly avoided capture when the small merchant vessel on which he had embarked with French Paris and Gabriel had been in danger of being intercepted, but had escaped thanks to a timely pall of fog. After landing at Eyemouth, the young Earl had galloped all the way to Holyrood where the young royal couple were staying. Having been ushered into their presence James beheld at Mary's side a tall, fair-haired and slightly effeminate-looking young man, with well-balanced features and graceful manners. Henry Darnley gave him a warm welcome, and expressed the joy he felt at meeting a man whom the Queen had so often praised. He assured Bothwell that they were in great need of his military expertise in order to crush Moray's rebellion, and he was ready to entrust him with part of the army, while the Earl of Lennox would remain in overall command. In order to lessen James's disappointment Mary immediately announced that he would be reinstated as Lieutenant of the Borders and Sheriff of Liddesdale and Edinburgh; he would also be allocated an apartment at the Palace.

The next day he had another opportunity to meet the Queen as she returned from the chapel accompanied by Mary Fleming. The beautiful La Flamina, who had always been his ally, spontaneously stepped aside, leaving him alone to escort Mary back to her apartments. At first the two of them were rendered speechless with emotion, and then, conscious of the little time available to them, the Queen was the first to break the silence.

'I have missed you,' she confessed.

'If my fate has caused you sorrow Madam, then the prejudice I have suffered will seem less unfair.'

Mary smiled without making any reply. James sensed she was searching for words which were neither over-familiar nor indifferent.

'Many things have happened since we last saw each saw each other, my Lord,' she said, not looking at him. 'We have both changed now, you and I. My brother's betrayal was a most painful blow to me and I don't know whether I can ever forgive him.'

'Let us first crush this rebellion, Madam, and force the Earl of Moray to realise that it is you alone who wields the power.'

James suspected that Mary had not been able to banish the remnant of affection she still felt for her half-brother whom she had always previously considered to be her protector. Nevertheless, if the Queen had any good sense she would have to be ruthless towards him.

'The King does not like my half-brother,' said Mary. 'They have detested each other since the very first day they met.'

'His Majesty the King and the Earl of Moray seem to be very contrasting characters.'

'Lord Darnley has little taste for politics.'

Mary stopped walking, and the smile she gave James seemed tinged with sadness.

'He prefers to take part in activities for people of his own age, such as dancing, music and dining in the company of his friends. But he is ready to follow me to war.'

James felt ill at ease with conversations in which reason was swayed by sentiment.

'You chose to marry the man you considered most worthy of making you happy and ruling by your side, Madam. There are many who envy Lord Darnley and I am sure he fully appreciates the love you bear him.'

'Who knows?' Mary whispered.

They walked on again in silence. They had almost reached the Palace, where they would be in the presence of guards and courtiers.

'Did you hate me when you were in Paris?' Mary asked suddenly.

James felt even more awkward. What did she want to hear?

'Even if I wanted to, Your Majesty is well aware that I could not.'

The military campaign was swift and unprecedented. James had galloped all the way to the Borders to gather his troops and had returned immediately to Edinburgh, followed by his horsemen. Knowing that the Royal regiments were in hot pursuit Moray had managed to elude them, clearly trying to avoid an armed confrontation until the Earl of Argyll's forces had had time to catch up with his own soldiers. However, Lennox's army had made it impossible for their forces to link up, and James Stuart had been compelled to retreat to Carlisle, south of the border, where he would not be allowed to stay without an express request for asylum and protection from the Queen of England.

The troops commanded by Bothwell had left Edinburgh to march south towards Dumfries and the English border. Darnley, wearing silver-gilt armour and with scented gloves, paraded at their head, followed closely by Mary wearing a breastplate and with pistols on her saddle-bow. James brought up the rear, together with Huntly and the loyal Earl of Atholl. The horses' hooves clattered on the frozen ground and as they passed through the villages peasants came out of their houses and waved their bonnets, wishing the royal couple a long and happy life. Mary rewarded their greetings with a smile and a wave but Darnley rode on without responding. He watched his nobles studying maps and from time to time gave them unsolicited advice, which they ignored. Even his presence there made them feel uncomfortable. The Queen did her best to liven up the evening meal of which they all partook together. James could sense how tense and preoccupied she was and how distraught at having to fight a brother to whom she had given unconditional love. She showed not the slightest embarrassment in the presence of her soldiers, and took pleasure in riding at their head. She never complained of fatigue and put up with the discomfort of their rest breaks without demur. She treated the King with tenderness and often spoke with him, giving him the chance to shine in conversation. However, Darnley, full of his own self-importance, made no effort to reply.

James Stuart's rebellion had failed. He and his friends had for the time being given up any idea of returning to Scotland. He had accepted the calculated coldness shown towards them by Elizabeth, who felt trapped between the friendship she had previously borne them and the impropriety of expressing it openly.

'You must declare the Earl of Moray a traitor, Madam,' Bothwell insisted, 'and immediately confiscate his property and his estates. You have to show that you are uncompromising.'

'I will have him declared a rebel and outlawed at the Mercat Cross in Edinburgh,' Mary promised. 'Keep close watch on your frontiers my Lord Bothwell, to prevent my brother from sending or receiving any messages.'

Standing just behind the Queen David Rizzio smiled with an air of complicity. Having given his unconditional support to her marriage with Darnley, he was now enjoying the fruits of his efforts. The King treated him as a close friend, played tennis with him and even shared his bed on those nights that he went drinking. Mary was fond of the Italian, with his bright intelligence, the finesse of his political views, his exuberance and his musical talents. More and more often, she drew him into her circle of friends to which James also belonged. The group of young people would gather in the evenings in the Queen's small inner chamber, which adjoined her bedchamber. Mary had recently become pregnant, but she did not show the bloom of a woman carrying her first child. James did not want to try to understand the reason for her air of sadness; his mind was too much occupied with troubles in the Borders, and he was negotiating with the Elliots, who had previously supported Moray but now wanted to make amends. Darnley spent most of his time drinking to excess or sulking. It was obvious that the Royal marriage was in trouble but the young Earl did not feel qualified to try to disentangle the tortuous strands of the lovers' quarrels. He had not had a mistress since his return from France and was enjoying the feeling of freedom and uncomplicated emotions.

Darnley agreed to attend Christmas Mass. Nobody quite knew whether he was a Catholic like his mother the Countess of Lennox, whom Elizabeth, fearing her influence over her indecisive son, kept locked up in the Tower of London, or whether he was indifferent to religion. During the early days of his marriage, the young Earl had sat in boredom through John Knox's interminable sermons. However he had long since shunned them and put all his energy into repeated demands to be awarded the Crown Matrimonial, which would have made him the sole and legitimate sovereign should Mary die before him. Yet whether out of foresight or from disillusionment Mary steadfastly refused her consent.

James had arranged to spend the Christmas celebrations at Crichton with his mother, his sister and his nephew little Francis, left fatherless by the premature death of John Stuart. It had been only two years ago that he had arrived at Coldingham after a five hour walk, leaving at Holy Island the ship which would take him to France. At that time, the Queen had had complete faith in her half-brother. What feelings did she have for him now? James concluded from her brief allusions that despite his betrayal she still missed his presence and advice. Moreover, the English and French Ambassadors, Throckmorton and Paul de Foix, were pressing for a pardon, a move to which Darnley was vigorously opposed.

After the festivities were over James spent a week at Hermitage before returning to Edinburgh. The Queen had taken to her bed with a cold and Darnley was away hunting at Falkland. Too few members of the Privy Council were available for a sitting. There seemed to be a still eeriness about the old Palace of Holyrood. A freezing fog was rising from the icy ground, coating the windowpanes and stifling all sounds, and James sensed some ominous hidden danger in this muffled silence.

One morning the Queen summoned the young Earl to her chamber. She was feeling better and wished to resume her normal activities as soon as possible. She was seated beside the fire and James saw she was looking pale but serene.

'Sit down, my Lord,' she said immediately. 'We need to talk.'

Carefully Mary inserted a needle into her canvas, which depicted the outline of a fruit tree.

'I thought about you during my illness,' she murmured, with her eyes lowered.

Sitting not far from her, her four Marys were silently occupied with their needlework.

'Should I feel honoured, flattered, or frightened, Madam?'

The young woman smiled faintly as she drew the silk thread through the canvas.

Suddenly she turned to look at him.

'It is not good for a man to live on his own. Therefore I wish you to get married as soon as possible to a lady whom I hold in high esteem.'

Mary had rapidly reeled off the sentence, as though to take a weight off her mind. Shocked, James did not reply.

'A marriage is necessary for all sorts of reasons,' she continued. 'You know most of them and perhaps you can guess at the others. Yesterday

I approached George Gordon about the possibility of a union between you and his sister Jean. He shares my opinion, and indeed seemed very enthusiastic about the idea.'

'Jean!' exclaimed James. 'But they say she is very attached to Lord Alexander Ogilvie.'

James remembered a slim young woman with a slightly elongated face and large brown eyes. He was not against an alliance with the Gordons. Coming from an ancient family and the owner of vast estates restored to the family after the royal pardon, George would provide his sister with an ample dowry.

'The Earl of Huntly refuses even to consider Lord Ogilvie. On the other hand, he thinks a great deal of you.'

Mary returned to her needlework. She seemed so engrossed in her work that James did not dare ask her any more questions. As it happened, he had been thinking for a while about getting married. He needed to find himself a wife and provide the Hepburns with heirs, and he could not dream of a better alliance than with the Gordons. Besides, George was his closest friend.

'A marriage,' the Queen whispered suddenly, 'is a door which excludes other women. You will have to forego mistresses, or indeed even thinking about anyone else.'

Mary suddenly blushed.

'It is not always possible to control ones thoughts, Madam.'

Again, he felt drawn towards this woman, from whom he had also learned to distance himself. Was she insinuating that there was still a place for him in her heart?

'You will have to do this none the less.'

Suddenly as if she was trying to extricate herself from an embarrassing situation, the Queen stuck her needle into the canvas and stood up.

'Lady Jean will be in Edinburgh next week. The marriage will be celebrated here at Holyrood at the end of February.'

'In less than a month, Madam?'

'Why wait? You are going to be thirty-one and Lady Jean is twenty. You are too old for endless courting.'

'It helps to get to know one another.'

Mary turned round, with a stern expression on her face.

'Men and women take part in all sorts of lies and deceptions in order to please one another. By marrying quickly at least you will not suffer from false expectations.'

Jean was trying to be friendly, having no doubt received a lecture from her brother, but James could imagine the reservations and even dislike she must feel in marrying a man she did not love. In order to try to win her over he was prepared to do something that was difficult for him; to try to please her and enter the intricate maze of emotions in which he risked being entangled and losing his way.

Since he had been living at court he had often missed those times of hardship and comradeship during the war against the English when he had slept between Sarlebou and d'Oysel on the bare ground, even the occasion when under siege and starving, they had feasted on a rat caught in the waters of Leith.

Later in Paris, James had met up again with Sarlebou. He had left the army and was living on a modest pension but was still jovial and ready to entertain his guest in style. As for d'Oysel, he had retired to his estates near Nantes and seldom showed himself at court.

Mary seemed very absorbed in preparations for the coming celebrations. They were all paid for out of her privy purse and included such items as the bride's dress, made of blue and silver brocaded satin, which was to be worn under a sapphire blue velvet coat hemmed with sable and lined with white satin. A French artist had been sent for and was expected at any moment, commissioned with painting miniatures of the bridal couple. Rizzio had been made responsible for the musicians and for the masque, which would follow the wedding banquet. The wedding festivities would last for five days.

Every morning James went to visit his betrothed and also her brother George, Earl of Huntly. Jean gradually started to bestow some attention on James. She was bright and vivacious and had evidently decided to make the best of a union she could not avoid. However, James could not tell whether deep in her heart Jean still hankered longingly after her lost love.

The nuptial contract was about to be signed. Jean would bring a large dowry. It would release from debt virtually all of James's estates, which had been heavily mortgaged. On his part, the young man would give his wife the title of Countess, legal possession of Crichton for her lifetime, and the protection of the Queen of Scots. James's great-grandfather had been married to Jean's great-grandmother, and the Dowager Countess of Huntly, who was a staunch Catholic, insisted on a papal dispensation. Thus, married according to Protestant rites but with the Holy Father's benediction, the newly-weds would be indissolubly united.

'I am sure you will be happy,' insisted Mary, who was seated next to Bothwell at the banqueting table.

James thought he detected a note of anxiety in the Queen's voice, as if the happiness she wished for him was at the same time painful to her. Once again, Darnley had disappeared a few days previously to join his merrymaking friends. However, as he wished to honour the Earls of Bothwell and Huntly, he had promised to return in time for the marriage ceremony. James looked towards Mary and then at Jean who was sitting opposite him. Compared to the Queen Jean's expression seemed cold and austere. Nevertheless, he must not let himself draw comparisons.

'If you still have affection for me, Madam, then I shall indeed be happy.'

James looked at the Queen's hand and at her slender be-ringed fingers as she rested them on the table. Several times, he had held that hand in his own and had enjoyed the sensation of feeling her skin in contact with his.

After the masque came the mummeries, followed by a ball and a concert, and on the next day ring and glove races and jousting, in which the bridegroom took part, mounted on a spirited Barb stallion, which he mastered with panache. The festivities were brought to an end with one final ball. As he twirled round during a dance, he suddenly felt the Queen's hand in his own. He was now desperate to retire with Jean to the castle which Lord Seton had made available for their honeymoon, and to flee those deep wells of emotion in which he felt he was being submerged. Jean kept a fixed smile on her lips and gave him no inkling of what she was feeling.

Jean lay in James's arms without moving and he caressed her gently so as not to alarm her. She might be giving herself to him but he was tormented by doubt whether she was doing so of her own free will. As he placed his hand on her shapely breasts and on her softly rounded belly, he wondered whether her thoughts were of Ogilvie. With her hair let down and her eyes closed, she was as beautiful and as still as a statue and James was lost for words.

'Do you desire me?' he asked eventually.

'I belong to you, James.'

The young Earl stopped caressing Jean's stomach.

'I have never forced myself on a woman and unless you freely consent to offer yourself to me I will not touch you.'

He turned away from her, rolled onto his back and folded his arms behind his neck. Flickers of candlelight danced among the shadows and onto the vermilion bed canopy. Up until then he had always let women seduce him and he was disconcerted now to find the situation reversed. Jean lay beside him without stirring. Perhaps she felt as awkward as he did, beset by feelings of embarrassment, which neither of them knew how to dispel. Suddenly James rose and put on his knee breeches, his shirt and his slippers.

'I will let you sleep; we will see each other tomorrow morning.'

He went to the door; the young woman did not call him back.

However, on the eve of their return to Edinburgh as he was about to bid her goodnight, Jean looked down at the floor.

'Come tonight,' she whispered, 'I will be waiting for you.'

The candle was burning low but James was not asleep. Gently he had made love to a wife who despite her apparent abandon remained emotionally distant. However she had kissed him, held him close and tried hard to behave like a lover, and James had resigned himself not to ask any more of her. She was his wife and she would be the mother of his children. As for the passionate physical love he craved, he would seek another partner.

In Edinburgh, the Privy Council was in turmoil. It was claimed that the Queen was about to nominate the Italian David Rizzio as Chancellor, and the Scottish nobility was outraged. What exactly were the ambitions of this sly little man? Where would his intentions lead him? Into the Queen's bed?

Up until now James had shown a benevolent attitude towards Mary's personal secretary, but he now started to shun his company. Only Darnley continued to give the Italian proof of his affection, which was even more surprising since he showed no sympathy towards most of Mary's close friends.

Moray, who was still kicking his heels in England and brooding over his defeat, wrote to friends and enemies alike to ask for an early pardon before the next session of Parliament, when his goods and estates were due to be sequestered. Even James had received a message from him requesting a truce. He wrote that he was aware of the trust that the Queen placed in her Lieutenant of the Borders, adding that a friendly intervention on his part would be much appreciated. Moray also congratulated him on his marriage to Jean Gordon, a beautiful and virtuous young person held in high esteem by all. On reading this short letter, the young Earl could not help but smile. This cunning fox was using the velvet glove approach in order to deceive his prey. However, in the interests of Scotland he would not refuse to extend a cautious hand to him.

James's relationship with Jean was cordial but she obviously had no taste for physical love and he reduced the frequency of their lovemaking. George, who was not blind to the couple's difficulties, tried to reassure his brother-in-law: Jean was stubborn and proud, things would get better with time, and he knew how attached she was to her young husband. James doubted it.

The King suddenly reappeared at Holyrood. He was present at the Privy Council but not by the side of the Queen, who had now entered the fifth month of her pregnancy. He dined with the Lords Ruthven, Lindsay, Morton, and Secretary of State Maitland until late into the night. Curiously, in a palace where normally everything was public knowledge, the discussions, in which the Queen never took part, remained secret. Mary's friends gathered round her during the day, and in the evenings she enjoyed playing cards with Rizzio, who, like her, suffered from insomnia. The Italian amused her, he knew better than anyone how to bring out the comical side of a situation and he was an excellent mimic. He had become aware of the hostility shown towards him by some of Mary's friends, but took little notice of it. His only real enemy, Moray, had been banished from the kingdom, and in three weeks time an order of Parliament would take from him all his worldly goods.

'He may be in exile, but he is certainly not harmless,' commented James as he returned from a game of tennis with Rizzio. 'Moray has the ear of William Cecil, who has great influence in Scotland. If Her Majesty had the courage she should make sure he is banished permanently.'

The Italian mopped his brow with a handkerchief handed to him by a servant. He exerted enough influence over the Queen to ensure that James Stuart would not cross over the border in a hurry.

'The Queen is not sufficiently wary of her half-brother,' the little man asserted, adding, 'I believe she is more suspicious of the King, but I take a different view of him. Lord Darnley does make mistakes but they are the follies of youth.'

James did not wish to pursue this conversation any further. He did not particularly dislike Rizzio but he was not a friend of his. He feared treachery from him and did not at all approve of his influence over Mary.

In their Holyrood apartment, which consisted of a chamber, an ante-chamber and two recesses, Jean sat reading. The light from the candela-brum placed at her side gave her hair a reddish glow and accentuated the length of her nose and the roundness of her lips. If she had wanted him, James could have loved her and been faithful to her, but not once since their marriage had she really given herself to him. Submitting to his desire was all she could offer and gradually his desire was dwindling. Already James had cast an eye on one of her maidservants, Bessie Crawford, who was in charge of the sewing. Brown-haired and flirta-tious she had left him in no doubt that she fancied him. When the occa-sion presented itself, he would take her as a temporary and no doubt exciting mistress.

Jean looked up from her book and gave her husband a faint smile. She was bored at Holyrood.

'I shall leave tomorrow for Crichton,' she said, in a non-committal tone. 'The farms need inspecting before the spring sowing. I want to buy lambs and sell some cattle too as we are overstocked for the available pastureland.'

French Paris helped James take off his sweat-soaked shirt, exposing a well-muscled chest with a downy covering of dark blond hair.

'When are you coming back?'

Jean shrugged her shoulders.

'I don't know. In a few days, a few weeks possibly. You can come and join me there if you like.'

James felt he would like to grab his wife by the shoulders and give her a good shaking to get some reaction from her. But after all what did it matter? As soon as she had gone, he would go and look for Bessie Crawford.

3 I

'JAMES, I BELIEVE you know that tonight the Queen is dining with Rizzio, the Countess of Argyll, Lord Erskine and her equerry Anthony Standen. Since you and I are both on our own let us spend the evening together.'

George Gordon's proposal was very welcome since James did not much relish the thought of staying at home by himself. His brother-in-law's company, which he always enjoyed, would restore his good mood, which had been spoilt by the news that Moray was now in regular correspondence with those of his friends who had remained in Scotland. As long as Parliament had not declared the dispossession of his goods and estates The Bastard's power would remain a very real threat, but Mary was trying to play this down either through being blind to the dangers or from fear of confronting him.

To add to his worries his sister had announced she intended to marry the Lord of Caithness as her second husband. He was a man with whom the Hepburn family had little in common, but Janet was so stubborn that any remark aimed at dissuading her would only result in making her even more determined. However, James had managed to persuade her to defer a final decision until the end of summer.

In order not to be disturbed by the inconvenience of people coming and going James and his brother-in-law had their dinner served in a quiet room, which overlooked the royal menagerie where several lions were kept. Located opposite Mary Stuart's apartments and the entrance to Holyrood Palace, the salon was an ideal setting for those courtiers who wished to play games of cards or dice, or simply converse in peace.

French Paris had placed on the table a bottle of whisky from the

Highlands, a spirit very highly prized, and a carafe of claret. The fire crackling in the hearth and the heavy curtains, which had been drawn together, imparted a feeling of intimacy to the sparsely furnished room.

'I encountered Rizzio a little while ago,' George remarked as he helped himself to a drink. 'He was dressed so elegantly that the King of France himself could not outdo him! One of these days he will carry a sword and we shall have to call him your Lordship!'

James burst out laughing; the little Italian was indeed becoming more and more arrogant. Mary had taken a great liking to him, and was inclined to adopt too familiar an attitude towards him. It was true he was a gifted adviser and convivial friend, but she believed the modesty of his origins would protect her from gossip. Even the jealous Darnley favoured him, and only that morning they had happily played tennis together.

'The peacock's parade may come to an abrupt end,' remarked Bothwell mockingly. 'Rizzio has enemies who have sworn to ruin him.'

Without saying a word, George slid two fingers across his throat.

'They also say the Earl of Lennox is concocting some evil plot to coerce the Queen into granting his son the Crown Matrimonial,' continued Bothwell.

The door opened and French Paris entered bearing dishes of food which he deposited on the oak table with its carved legs; mutton kidney pie fragrant with the aroma of cloves and cumin, a pair of roast pigeons stuffed with pistachios and dried figs, a dish of barley, and vegetables seasoned with thyme, sage, and rosemary. James with a wave dismissed his servant.

'I spoke to Maitland last night,' he said gravely. 'He tried to persuade me to intervene in favour of Moray, for the greater good of all, as he expressed it. Seeing that I doubted the good sense of his request, he added that one way or another James Stuart would undoubtedly return to Scotland and resume a prominent position on the Council. He assured me it is better to be with him than against him.'

'That is probably true,' replied George, who ignoring finer manners tore into the pigeon breast with his teeth while the grease ran down his chin.

'But why would The Bastard come back into favour when Parliament is about to forfeit all his possessions?' queried James.

George wiped his mouth with a corner of the tablecloth.

'He shouldn't unless by some reversal of fortune his presence becomes indispensable. I went to see Ruthven this morning, and for a man who claims to be at death's door he seemed extremely agitated. Lindsay took my place at his bedside and I thought he looked even more devious than he usually does. He was accompanied by one of your countrymen from the Borders whom I don't care for much, Andrew Kerr of Fawdonside.'

'He is certainly a bird of ill-omen,' admitted James, helping himself to a glass of whisky. 'The Kerrs are either fine lords or they are brigands, with nothing in between.'

'So what were Lindsay and Kerr doing at Ruthven's house?' insisted Huntly.

James, who was finishing his pie, merely shrugged his shoulders. The Palace was a nest of intrigue, which he tried to avoid as much as possible. His periods of exile and imprisonment had had the effect of making him long for a quiet life. Thanks to Jean's dowry, his estates were now mortgage-free and his farmers brought him regular supplies of grain and livestock. He had even been able to buy a couple of promising yearlings. The Queen had now taken rightful place in his heart as an attractive woman who would always be a part of his life but would never belong to him. Had it not been for Jean's coldness and the uneasiness he felt after his affair with Bessie Crawford, he would have considered himself a happy man.

French Paris had just brought in dishes of walnuts, hazelnuts and almonds, when they were alerted by loud noises of shouting and stampeding feet.

'Go and find out what is happening,' James ordered his servant.

Moments later the young man returned, his cheeks flushed.

'My Lord, there are soldiers everywhere, blocking the exits with their halberds.'

James and George heard the sound of voices yelling orders and doors slamming.

'By the Blood of Christ!' Bothwell exclaimed, 'Something serious is taking place in the Queen's apartments!'

A large number of soldiers were stamping around outside the door of Mary Stuart's antechamber and their disarray suggested they had no leader. Two crossed pikes barred James's progress.

'Nobody goes through!'

The young man was about to shove them aside with his shoulder when George Douglas, Morton's half-brother burst into the antechamber. They heard distinct sounds of wailing and screaming.

'Leave quickly my Lord Bothwell, your life depends upon it!'

'Where is the Queen?' snarled James.

'With Lady Argyll. Go away!'

James drew his sword.

'Do as you are told, my Lord,' George Gordon pleaded, in a voice that trembled as he tried to keep his composure. 'If they assassinate us, what will become of Her Majesty? My mother is here,' he added in a low voice, 'I shall write her a note to let her know we are fleeing the Palace, and that we await the Queen's orders.'

George hastily scribbled a few words on a sheet of paper which he handed to French Paris, then with Bothwell's assistance, they locked and barricaded the room in which only a few minutes earlier they had been dining. James opened the windows. It was a cold night and the sky was clear and starry.

'It is not into the jaws of a wolf but into the jaws of lions that we are about to cast ourselves,' he tried to jest. 'Let us hope their bellies are as full as ours!'

From the first floor, all they could see were a few bushes and the rocky outcrop on which the big cats enjoyed lazing in the sun. However, in winter they barely ventured from the shed built for them at the far end of their enclosure.

'By the Grace of God,' exclaimed Bothwell as he leapt over the casement.

The courtyard was teeming with a motley crowd who had all rushed there on hearing the news. The alarm bell was tolling and a few scattered torches cast menacing shadows against the stone towers erected by James V.

The stables were deserted and James and his brother-in-law saddled their horses without hindrance. Before dawn, they would reach Lord Seton's castle from where Huntly had indicated to his mother they would be awaiting news and orders.

The night seemed to last forever, and at Seton the two young men remained on tenterhooks. Why had Lady Huntly not replied immediately to their urgent message?

The sun was already high in the sky when a horseman galloped into the courtyard. James raced headlong down the stairs and seized the horse's bridle. He was consumed by anxiety.

'Is Her Majesty still alive?' he asked in an expressionless voice. The page nodded.

'The Queen has been taken prisoner, my Lord.'

In simple but crude language, the messenger related how Darnley had burst into the little dining room in which the Queen was having supper. The King was followed closely by Lord Ruthven wearing helmet and armour, Andrew Kerr of Fawdonside, Lindsay, George Douglas, Patrick Bellenden, Thomas Scott and Henry Yair. All the conspirators crowded into the tiny room, their dirks in their hands. Had it not been for the foresight of Lady Argyll who had grabbed a torch before the table was overturned, the only source of light would have come from the fire in the hearth. Rizzio, who had become their prey, fell down at Mary's feet and clung to her dress.

'Justizia, justizia, Regina mia, salve me, salve la mia vita!' he cried.

Darnley put his arms round Mary to prevent her from taking any action while George Douglas, grabbing the King's dirk, was the first to strike Rizzio. Then they all set upon him. Prying open each of the Italian's fingers, which clutched the Queen's skirt, they dragged him covered in blood and screaming with terror, into the antechamber. From behind the closed door and in the presence of the other guests who were rendered speechless with horror, Mary listened to the murder of her Secretary and to his heart-rending and pleading cries. Ruthven re-emerged into the tiny room looking grey and exhausted. He collapsed into a chair, asked for a drink, and in the same breath accused Mary of favouring a foreigner over her own lords and neglecting her husband. Darnley concurred with him, saying his wife no longer came to see him in his bedchamber, and that he was jealous and frustrated.

Like a spoilt child, the King listed his grievances: he wanted the Crown Matrimonial but this was denied him; he wanted the company of his wife but she spent her evenings with Rizzio or with other friends. He was the King yet was hardly ever asked for his opinion...

Bothwell was beside himself with rage.

'Darnley must be tried for treason at once!'

'Lord Darnley is our King,' Lord Seton reminded him simply.

The page continued his narrative. Realising her husband was involved in the murder the Queen had confronted him.

'You traitor,' she said in an icy voice, 'you son of a traitor! This is what you had in mind for one whom you called a friend!'

She sent Anthony Standen to find out what had happened to her Secretary. In a moment he returned saying Rizzio was dead. It was afterwards confirmed that he had been stabbed fifty four times. As if to leave his signature to the crime, Darnley's dirk had remained plunged in the body of the little Piedmontese man. The page knew nothing more. Lady Huntly had received the note written by her son, and it was she who had sent him. Her Majesty's friends would have to wait until she had been able to confer with the Queen.

The two days that followed seemed interminable to both men. Silent and in a grim mood James shunned all company and went riding alone through the surrounding countryside. He was trying to find answers to the many questions that plagued him. Who was the instigator of the plot? Darnley, Morton, or even Moray?

The King and The Bastard both had strong motives to hold the Queen at their mercy, the former to exact the Crown Matrimonial from her, and the latter to regain the political influence he had lost and recover his estates before Parliament ratified their forfeiture. Rizzio was a mere scapegoat, a sacrificial victim. Who would believe for an instant that he had behaved inappropriately with the Queen? It was inconceivable that Mary Stuart, daughter of Marie de Guise would compromise herself with an Italian musician. The Queen was spontaneous, trusting, and in need of affection, and those qualities so remarkable in a sovereign were being sullied by scoundrels.

Finally, on the evening of the second day another messenger arrived. That night, he told them the Queen would try to escape from Holyrood where she was being held prisoner. She asked that Lord Bothwell should have a few horses saddled, and to assemble a well-armed escort to accompany her to Dunbar Castle. If all went according to Her Majesty's plans, the fugitives including the King, Lord Erskine, Anthony Standen and a maidservant would be at Seton before break of dawn.

32

'MADAM,' WHISPERED JAMES who was riding next to Mary, 'how is it possible that His Majesty is here with us?'

'I convinced him that my enemies were his enemies too. The King puts me in great danger by bending to any will stronger than his own.'

Riding pillion behind Arthur Erskine the Queen had reached Seton after midnight, and without pausing for a rest had insisted on setting out immediately for Dunbar.

As dawn broke the little troop saw in front of them the walls of the imposing fortress, clinging to the rocks that towered over the Firth of Forth. During their journey, Darnley had ridden on ahead, paying no attention to the other fugitives.

As soon as they reached the postern leading into the inner courtyard, Mary brightened up.

'Now let me cook you all some eggs for breakfast!' she cheerfully announced.

Some soldiers had arrived before them and had lit a fire in the great hearth in one of the kitchens. A cauldron of barley soup was already heating up.

Ignoring her fatigue Mary asked for an apron to be tied round her waist, which accentuated the swelling roundness of her stomach. Loosened from her cap her curls framed her face and cascaded onto her shoulders. For some time James watched her as she stood before the hearth with flushed cheeks, engrossed in stirring the eggs with a long wooden spoon. The tip of her white petticoat was showing beneath her skirt of thick crimson velvet. Was this the same woman, who had been threatened, maltreated and held prisoner? She had listened to the screams of her friend being put to death then had escaped in the middle of the night from her own palace. He felt as if he was discovering a different person, enterprising, combative, and as close to him as a sister.

Spontaneously the Queen sat herself beside James at the large kitchen table, which was scarred with grooves and stained with marks of blood and grease.

Having devoured some slices of buttered bread Darnley, evidently annoyed at the presence of the others, had disappeared.

Without showing any trace of emotion, Mary related the traumatic moments she had lived through. She told them how as a prisoner in her own room she had feigned illness. The King had come to visit her, and without wasting time, she had striven to persuade him that the conspirators were playing a double game. She told him they had taken advantage of his inexperience to exploit him before then getting rid of him, and they were now both in great danger. Believing her, the King asked the conspirators to relieve the guard, promising not to leave his wife's bedside as her alarming condition portended a possible miscarriage. Morton and Lindsay agreed to dismiss the troops. Left without surveillance they were able to escape through the kitchens.

'And my Lord Moray?' George Seton asked. 'They say he is back in Scotland and that he visited Your Majesty.'

'If my brother had arrived in Edinburgh three days earlier, Rizzio would still be alive.'

The Queen's eyes were brimming with her emotions, and James refrained from intervening. It was obvious Mary did not wish to question the providential return of the man she had banished for treason. In her state of despair, Moray represented the political and moral stability she craved. Doubtless it would only be at a later date that the timeliness of his return would appear strange to her.

'Has my Lord Moray been informed of your escape?' he asked.

'Nobody knows yet.'

James nodded. Mary was not revealing her innermost thoughts. How far had she trusted her half-brother? Did she suspect he had seen Darnley again and made him promises? Who was playing which game? And who was being fooled?

His shoulder brushed against the Queen who suddenly seemed exhausted.

'I am cold,' she whispered.

He removed the cloak from his shoulders and placed it round her. At that moment he became certain he was the only one who could defend and protect her.

'I am going to take a rest,' Mary said. 'After that I shall write to the King of France, the Queen of England, and my uncle the Cardinal de Lorraine, to inform them of what I have just been subjected to. We will meet again later, my Lords.'

The companions rose.

'Permit me to escort you, Madam,' said Bothwell. 'Then I will go down to the Borders to muster as many men as possible. You will return to Edinburgh only at the head of an army.'

Close behind them followed Margaret Carwood, the maidservant who had fled Edinburgh with the Queen. James felt constrained. He had so much to say and so little time…

'I feel very weary,' Mary suddenly admitted. 'Please give me your arm.'

Again James felt the pressure of her body against his, and again the same emotion and embarrassing pleasure enveloped him.

'When Andrew Kerr pointed his pistol against my stomach,' Mary confessed, 'I was afraid for my child!'

By way of reply, James placed his hand over hers while she held his arm.

'The King has now become a stranger to me,' the young woman continued. 'The qualities I thought I saw in him do not exist.'

The servant who was carrying the torches stopped in front of one of the doors.

Mary let go of Bothwell's arm. For a while she looked intently at the young Earl.

'You are my only friend, my Lord,' she said.

James took a step back. For a brief moment, he had been tempted to take the Queen into his arms.

After her triumphant entry into Edinburgh at the head of an army recruited in the Borders by James, the Queen went back to her normal life. With all her heart she wished Moray and Argyll should be reconciled with Huntly and Bothwell. James accepted the meeting and shook hands reluctantly with men he continued to view as traitors, in particular

Moray, whom he considered to be the instigator of the murder of Rizzio in connivance with the Douglases. He believed that Darnley, who was a Douglas himself through his maternal grandfather, had foolishly allowed himself to be swayed. The King's cowardice, his self-importance, his power to harm and the contempt he showed for the interests of the Queen of Scotland and her unborn child made him in James's eyes a despicable character. Although his treachery deserved to be punished as much as the other miscreants, only his cronies had been sent into exile. Darnley continued to parade at Holyrood, to hunt, drink to excess, haunt brothels and insult his servants. The Queen bolted the door of her bedchamber, and seemed to have resigned herself to the situation. However, James knew the Guises forgot nothing.

Being a Member of Parliament and a Privy Councillor, the young Earl did his best to spend time with his wife in Edinburgh when his duties in the Borders did not keep him away. Undoubtedly suspecting that her husband was turning away from her, Jean was trying to be a little more obliging towards him, but when he held her in his arms James still sensed a degree of restraint, which hurt him. Besides, he was getting bored with Bessie and her unimaginative sensuality. The Queen filled his thoughts. Estranged from her young husband, tormented by the imminent birth of her first child and haunted by the horrible memory of Rizzio's murder, she performed her duties and presented a resolute and serene front through which he nevertheless perceived her suffering. Mary was leaning on him more and more and they were often alone when discussing affairs of state.

After the dismissal of the English Ambassador Randolph due to his indiscretion and malicious remarks, Mary had adopted the attitude of Sovereign rather than friend towards his successor, Elizabeth's new envoy Henry Killingrew. Using as much persuasion as possible James was encouraging her to curb her spontaneous nature in order to avoid being exploited.

During the warm month of May, Mary took to walking arm in arm with him in the gardens of Holyrood. Being eight months pregnant, she walked in measured steps and welcomed frequent rests on a bench. James sat beside her while her ladies-in-waiting settled on the lawn as best they could.

'I plan soon to draw up a will.'

The Queen read the astonishment on the faces of those surrounding her. The mallow and hyacinth flowerbeds and the sweet peas climbing up the trellis of the bower were bathed in bright sunlight. Beyond them stretched the forest where her father James V had gone hunting, just as she also had done in the company of her young husband. The hilltops stood out against the sky in patches of soft green and in the dazzling light the rocky mounds of Arthur's Seat seemed almost to lean against the castle.

'No woman can be certain of surviving childbirth,' the Queen continued, 'I no more than any other. I wish for my personal things to go to those who love me and who have served me well. Once this will is drawn up, I will retire to Edinburgh Castle where my child will be safe. If I were to die I know my friends will protect him and serve him as their legitimate monarch.'

Mary liked to talk about France with James, who had spent several years there and shared her love of that country. Regret at having left behind the land of her happy youth was gnawing away at her. In Blois, Fontainebleau, Saint-Germain-en-Laye and Chambord she remembered how everyone had excelled at enjoying the pleasures of life, at conversing with wit, dancing with talent and bearing their troubles with grace. She would never forget her royal entry into Chenonceau. She and François II had arrived at nightfall. The château had been illuminated with hundreds of torches and barely had they crossed over the arm of the river when the sky was set alight by fireworks, and the roar of thirty cannons resounded. Along the great avenue strewn with leaves, bunches of violets and gillyflowers the crowd had gathered, each one holding a small branch. Acclamations echoed from all directions: Long live the King! Long live the Queen! Beside the fountains where water gushed out from the stone jaws of lions, two chestnut trees, their branches laid bare by winter, had been decorated with little windmills and fireworks, which were set alight as the sovereigns passed by... Mary, her eyes shining, never tired of describing the splendours of Chenonceau. James knew she continued to suffer from having, when only eighteen years old, witnessed the death of her husband. She had had to bear her mother-in-law's hostility, and to come to terms with the end of a dream. Adjusting to life in Scotland had not been easy. The suspicious natures of the Scottish nobles and their incessant quarrels had mortified her. In Darnley she believed she had found a true gentleman of the type so appreciated at the Valois Court: handsome, elegant, clever with verse and an accomplished musician. However, that brilliant exterior concealed an empty spirit, a cowardly character and despicable ambitions. At the age of twenty-four, she found herself alone. During her conversations with James, which they conducted in French, Mary sometimes forgot her station as sovereign and revealed her tastes, enthusiasms and dislikes, but then suddenly realising she was speaking with too much intimacy would abruptly change the subject. James realised however that a very strong bond now united them, and this perturbed him. Behaving in a coquettish and seductive manner one day, Mary would the next day become cool and distant, speaking as a Queen who demanded obedience.

'Her Majesty has suffered greatly but she has borne a healthy child. It is a boy.'

Jean, who had attended Mary during her protracted labour, seemed exhausted. Had she even given him a smile or held his hand James would have taken her into his arms. But she had turned from him and was already walking away with her mother the Countess of Argyll. For a while, James watched her tall slim figure as she retreated into the distance. If he could not win her love, he did not want her. She would remain his wife but would no longer be his lover. He had never grovelled to anyone. The sudden feeling of relief and freedom he experienced filled him with a sense of exhilaration.

'The Queen is asking for you,' Mary Fleming whispered beside him. 'She wants all her friends to be present when the King comes to embrace his child.'

33

Summer, 1566

MARY STUART HAD TAKEN a month to recover from her delivery. Like the other lords, the Earl of Bothwell went to her bedside every day. One morning towards the end of July, Mary held him back. Now out of bed and dressed she seemed to be coming back to life.

'Can you keep a secret?' she asked.

He smiled.

'Do you believe I am given to idle gossip, Madam?'

Mary, who was looking out of the window, suddenly turned round. In the summer light, her hair took on an auburn radiance and her smile an almost childlike charm.

'I want to leave for Alloa discreetly tomorrow at dawn. I need you to get two boats ready for me. I do not want the King to follow me.'

James gave a nod, however this order surprised him. Having barely recovered from her ordeal the Queen was running away from the capital in order to visit John Erskine, the Earl of Mar, an austere elderly Lord who aspired to command Edinburgh Castle and to be the young Prince's guardian, a charge that had always been entrusted to the Erskines.

'I need solitude,' Mary continued, as though she understood James's silent questioning. 'At Alloa I will effect a reconciliation with Maitland, because his services are very valuable to me and I will only associate with those who are dear to me. I have had more than enough of plots, treachery and hypocrites. I want to live for today. We will hold a meeting in Alloa and when it is over I will ask my friends to stay behind.'

'Will I have the privilege to be among them, Madam?'

James was looking intently at the Queen's face as he talked to her. Mary smiled. She had put on a slightly condescending smile, which reminded him of the French women he had met in Paris in Eléonore's entourage; only the very young had been taken in by it.

'Would I be telling you my secret if I did not consider you to be a friend?'

At the far end of the room, loyal Margaret Carwood was winding a hank of green silk, which shone with an emerald sheen in the oblique shafts of sunlight.

The waters of the Firth of Forth sparkled in the bright afternoon sun. Seated in the bow of the boat taking him to Alloa, James was trying to collect his thoughts. During the days when he had been busy preparing the vessels that would transport the Queen and her small retinue and putting together a crew who were competent and discreet, he had not had time to reflect upon his brief conversation with Mary. Now sitting idle, lulled by a light swell and caressed by the sun's rays, James dared to think the unthinkable. Up until then, despite their complicity and the pleasure they derived from each other's company, he had never considered the Queen as a potential lover.

James stared at the small foam-crested waves below the stern while seagulls swooped around the boat.

Was it his reputation as a ladies man which appealed to Mary or was it his temperament, his commitment, and his faith in a strong and independent Scotland? Did she wish to have him as her bed companion or was she merely prepared to share his political opinions? And what about himself, did he desire her? Physically to possess his sovereign was an indulgence of vanity no man could refuse, but to be devoted to her and love her in the shadows was another matter. Both of them were married. Where would an affair lead them? 'Why torture myself with questions I will not need to answer?' he said to himself. 'Mary is alone; she has been betrayed by her half-brother, by her husband, and by her Secretary of State; the Queen of England treats her shamefully, her nobles torment her incessantly, she has just given birth, and she is exhausted. She treats me as her loyal friend and confidant, what could be more natural?'

The Firth was getting narrower and there was a clear view of the steep banks where the hills dropped away. Luxuriant thickets at the edge of the water contrasted with the grey rocks and wide barren stretches of land where only moss, fern and heather grew. A chill came down with the setting sun and James buttoned up his doublet of Dutch cloth. In what mood would the Queen be when he saw her again at Alloa? He knew that Darnley, furious at learning of his wife's secret departure had leapt on his horse to go to her. He had barely arrived when she had given him two hours to be gone. The rift between the spouses now seemed irreconcilable and the King's few friends were distancing themselves from him. The only ones who remained faithful were his merrymaking friends, young people for whom reckless bravado took the place of an ordered life.

French Paris and Gabriel Sempill had already brought his bags up onto the deck. The Firth was taking on a pinkish glow in the evening light and in the near distance stood the solid square tower of Alloa crowned with its four corbelled turrets. At this hour Bothwell thought the Earl of Mar and his guests were probably listening to music or partaking of a light meal. Mar would be likely to give him a cool reception. He was the brother of Margaret Erskine, The Bastard's mother, but he had taken a strong aversion to his own kin and despite several formal reconciliations, the Earl of Moray and he barely tolerated each other. The Queen however, was at home at all her nobles' houses and was free to invite whomever she chose to accompany her.

'At last here is my dear Earl of Bothwell.'

Mary extended her hand for him to kiss and with a light mocking laugh she went back to rejoin the Earl and Countess of Mar and the Countesses of Argyll and Moray. The young man received the impression that no one was pleased to see him arrive.

'Her Majesty is feeling better,' whispered George Gordon, 'and tomorrow I am leaving to go back to Strathbogie. The Queen went hunting and even danced last night. The scandal caused by her repudiation of the King seems not to affect her in the slightest. No one dares mention Darnley's name in front of her.'

James had pulled himself together and felt more at ease. He was offered a glass of wine, which he drank with pleasure. Sitting in the sun during the boat crossing had deepened his suntan. When compared with those pale gentlemen with their carefully trimmed beards he could have been mistaken for a freebooter or a highwayman.

'Tomorrow we are all going hunting,' announced Mary, 'and the Earl of Moray may be joining us… '

James frowned. Why did Mary insist on subjecting him to her half-brother's company?

'The Queen wishes that Maitland, Moray and you should form some sort of triumvirate. Maitland was here the day before yesterday and made a good impression on her when he took his leave,' whispered Huntly in his ear.

James burst out laughing. Was Mary sweetening him up to make him become part of her Utopia? Did she not know that Moray was jealous of her and that Maitland would never be deflected from following his own path? Did she not suspect that her beloved half-brother was even now in active correspondence with Rizzio's murderers?

He slept badly that night. What was the cause of his frustration? The Queen wanted his co-operation and she trusted him. What folly could have had crossed his mind? But if she was just playing with his feelings, she was making a mistake. He would never be like those gallants who composed verses for her at Chenonceau, and sighed when she passed by in the corridors of the Louvre.

It was the end of summer and nature was already clothing herself in shades of red and gold. At dusk, the mist rose and floated in ethereal blankets above the meadows.

The Queen, together with those she had selected to join her on the hunt, had left Edinburgh early in the morning. They had ridden past Penicuik and Eddleston and were approaching Lord Tweedale's Neidpath Castle, a great tower that stood above the Tweed, where they would stop for the night. The following morning they would ride on to Traquair where they would go hunting in the Royal deer forest. Since his sojourn at Alloa James had seen the Queen every day without ever finding himself alone with her. Mary had once again become distant towards him. A few days earlier, she had escorted her newborn son to Stirling and left him in the hands of the Earl of Mar. Already the little Prince was being separated from her, and from now on, she would only ever see him from time to time. Darnley rarely appeared, and when by chance the spouses did meet, their exchanges were stormy.

James had been preparing to ride to Liddesdale and Hermitage when he heard the Queen was organising a hunting party near Peebles and was requesting his presence, as well as that of the Earl of Moray, Mary

Fleming and Mary Beaton. Since giving birth, Mary constantly seemed to be seeking out travel and entertainment. No sooner had she arrived at Holyrood than she would use any excuse to depart again.

James was surprised at this request. Her hunting parties seemed to be reserved for her current group of close friends, and the Queen had not invited James since the beginning of August. Should he give in to this whim of hers or head for the Borders as he had intended?

Riding beside Moray, who remained taciturn and unforthcoming, James was thinking about his sister, who was preoccupied over her forthcoming marriage. His own union with Jean was disintegrating. One evening he had finally lost his temper with her: the memory of Ogilvie she kept locked in her heart stood like a ghost between them and he could no longer tolerate this situation, which he found degrading. He was no man to share, not even with a shadow. Jean protested: how dare he lecture her? Did he think she did not know about his affair with Bessie Crawford, a mere sewing maid? Did he think she did not suffer from his jealousy, his pride and his fits of temper? Several days had elapsed before they spoke to each other again, this time with a polite, calm and indifferent tone. The outbursts and reproaches had finally ended. From now on, they would cultivate a courteous and platonic way of living together.

Setting out from Traquair for the day's hunting, the riders arrived at the banks of the River Tweed. The skies were grey, a gentle breeze was blowing, and a brace of wild duck burst suddenly from the rushes at the water's edge and took flight. With water rising over their stirrups, the riders raised their legs above the current as they forded the river. On reaching the opposite bank, almost immediately a group of three roe deer, a buck and two does, leapt out of the bushes, quickly scattering in different directions. The deerhounds strained excitedly on their leashes. In a few moments a blast on the horn would signal the start of the chase, and the hounds would be unleashed on the trail of the buck. The dense undergrowth and steep rocky slopes near the river favoured the escape of the quarry, but the hounds were onto the scent straightaway and running fast, followed as best they could by the huntsmen on their horses, who had to plunge through the bushes, dodge between rocks and leap over fallen tree trunks. Bothwell boldly galloped on ahead, closely followed by Lord Traquair, Lord Tweedale the Master of Neidpath, and the Queen. Clad like a man, booted and spurred, and with her hair gathered up beneath a deep feathered beret, Mary cut an elegant figure riding her horse astride, galloping and leaping obstacles in her path, and leaving her two ladies-in-waiting far behind. Her tight knee breeches and fitted doublet showed off her legs, the slenderness of her waist and curve of her bosom. She was well aware that this outfit suited her and attracted the attention of men; since her youth, she had worn it on many occasions to go hunting, and sometimes even to roam the streets incognito.

In the past weeks summer heat had dried up many burns, but recent rains had raised the water level again, causing a rushing spate that flowed swiftly between large rocks and narrow strips of gravel. Following the fresh scent, the hunt had covered some distance across the hills before hounds finally brought their quarry to bay against a rock face beside the burn. Cornered and with flanks heaving, the buck stopped and turned to face the hounds. A little further back Mary and James checked their horses and stood side by side, watching.

'Now for the kill!' cried Mary with excitement. The boldest hounds had already gone in to attack, while the others circled round baying. At first the buck fended them off valiantly with its antlers, but after a few minutes it was brought to its knees, and the Artois hounds, trying to avoid the slashing antlers, were going for its throat.

'Quickly! Finish that animal off!' demanded Mary, turning to James.

Hunting had always fascinated her. It seemed to bring out a violent side in her, which disconcerted James. She who hated blood and suffering felt a sensuous frisson at the scene of the kill.

James leapt from his saddle, drew his dirk and slit the throat of the buck, wiping his blade against the animal's fur.

On their way back to Edinburgh, the Hays, who were close friends of Mary's, had again invited them to break their journey at Neidpath Castle. That evening after they had been entertained with a concert, the Queen expressed a wish to dance, and the chairs, benches and table which occupied the centre of the reception hall were pushed back to make room. The old castle had never been modernised and had none of the sophistication favoured by the Queen. Its walls were bare and its floors of stone, its beams were plain and unadorned with frescoes, and there were no carved reliefs to give its ample fireplaces Italian artistry. However, the thick walls and narrow windows, which had made this fortified tower a safe haven, still gave a feeling of security.

'You are without a partner, my Lord Bothwell. Come and dance with me.'

Mary extended a hand to James, which he could not refuse to take. Once more, a mixture of desire and caution overcame him.

'Why choose me?' he whispered as their fingers linked. 'I am probably the clumsiest dancer in this entourage.'

'But to me you are unique.'

James was moved by her husky voice and almost anxious tone. He could not, should not, remain indifferent.

'Am I to understand you are singling me out from the men surrounding you?'

Their bodies were very close. James had to hold his dance partner round the waist. He tightened his grip, but already the movements of the dance were drawing them apart.

'Take it as you wish, my Lord. They say at court you are very perceptive.'

'They say a lot of things about me, which are not always true.'

'I know you well; I have been observing you for the past two years.' James smiled.

'Except when I am in prison or exiled by your orders, Madam.'

'Even when you are punished unfairly I find you to be loyal and brave.'

'And when I am free?'

'A difficult man and a charmer.'

Mary clapped her hands as the dance required, and the dancers turned their backs on each other.

'Men try to please women they desire, and whose love they hope to conquer.'

James bit his lip. What he had just said could warrant his dismissal.

'Who doesn't want to love?' Mary whispered. 'And who doesn't hope to be loved?'

34

THE SIGHT OF A dark-haired girl in the courtyard reminds James of Anna Throndsen. He curses her. It is entirely because of her that he is locked up and treated like an animal. In his nightmares she appears to him as a witch who has come to destroy him, turn him to dust or change him into a rat. When his hazy memory clears, he remembers his arrival at Bergen in Norway and his first meeting with Erik Rosencrantz, on whom his fate depended and that of the hundred and forty men accompanying him. At that time he had been certain he would soon be free to return to France.

The legal action instituted by Anna had struck him like a bolt of lightning. He likens her to a bird of prey bringing down its quarry and tearing it apart. She wants her money back, the money she gave him when they were still in love…

He huddles in a corner of his room with his arms wrapped around his swollen and painful knees. James shuts his eyes and pictures Anna's mane of thick black flowing hair on her pillow. Anna tosses her head from side to side like a demented creature, saying, repeating, screaming; I love you! I love you! Then she suddenly sits up, looking cold, stern and accusing: Give me back the money that you stole from me! Thief! she screams.

Last week nobody came to shave him. Already his beard peppered with white hair is swallowing up his face. He is dirty; his clothing is of coarse fabric, spattered with stains. For a long while James stays there motionless, curled up like a mummy or a dead foetus. But Anna refuses to go away and leave him. She wants to humiliate him over and over again. You have had your revenge now, he groans. What more do you want? Leave me alone! Perhaps before she goes she will insist he has to admit to having loved her. But no, he has never loved anyone but Janet Beaton and Mary Stuart, both of them exceptional women. He looks up and shouts at her: Go away, go away!

Suddenly he recalls the buck whose throat he had cut before Mary's eyes during a hunt at Neidpath. The hounds tear at the buck's neck with their teeth, dipping their muzzles into the bleeding wound. The buck is dead, and at this moment, he envies it.

The oatmeal porridge is cold and the fish stinks but today, trying to keep warm wrapped in his blanket, James is eating the food and thirstily swallowing the beer, which leaves traces of froth on his moustache. When he has emptied the bowl, he licks it then hurls it against the wall. He walks over to the window and shakes the bars vigorously. Why do they not break? Why do they continue to deny him his freedom? Ever since he loyally served Marie de Guise they have hated him, spied on him and sought to bring him down. They are all suspicious of him, of his loyalty to the crown and of his ambitions. 'Yet what about you, my Lords,' he shouts, 'did not you yourselves seek for power, honours and wealth, even more than I did?' He visualises them gathered round him, those hypocrites with their false smiles, cunning ways and treacherous friendships... they and their English accomplices had long ago sworn to bring about his ruin. As James is about to turn away from the window he hears the sound of a plaintive tune. Down in the courtyard a scullion is playing on a reed pipe to a plump young woman with a self-satisfied smile on her face. So life goes on without him, the merry-go-round of men and love. Suddenly he has a vision of his father dressed in a fine linen shirt with lace-trimmed collar, black satin bejewelled doublet embroidered with purple thistles, and velvet cap that accentuates his fine features and the perfumed fairness of his moustache. Patrick 'The Fair Earl' jests with Marie de Guise, whom he wishes to seduce and wed. He bows, dances, sings, plays the viol and the flute. The notes fade into the distance... the Regent walks away. His father's smile freezes...

Does he take after this man he so despises? Did they not share the same ambition to marry a powerful woman who would assure them the highest position amongst the Scottish nobility? Both men divorced their wives in order to make their dream come true. James recalls his mother's bitter tears and Jean's false tears. It mattered not whether the suffering was genuine or feigned, everything and everyone had to give way.

In his anger, James smashes his fist against the wall. No there is definitely no comparison with his father. He loved Mary and he fulfilled his ambitions. For a while, he became the most powerful man in Scotland.

James collapses onto the ground in a corner of the room. Sometimes he stays there for hours without moving. When he finally tries to get up his knees give way and he has to drag himself to his bed. There he lies curled up, his body cold and racked with pain. He remembers how during the period of his parents' divorce he had slept with his knees pulled up against his chest; because he was scared, because he could feel the pain suffered by his mother and because of his need to feel loved.

Sometimes James feels as if he is travelling back in time to the days of his childhood. He is at the mercy of those who dominate him. He eats when they put food in front of him, and if he misbehaves, they lock him up in a black hole, which swallows him up.

He has always wanted to lead the life of a warrior, to be a general leading his troops. He was made for the open air, for long rides on horseback, for bivouacs in the countryside. James remembers how he had built up a library at Crichton and had often bought books. He was fascinated by works teaching the art of warfare, how to choose the terrain and how to manoeuvre the cavalry, artillery, and infantry. At Carberry he had been so sure of his victory yet he had lost everything. Why had he not given the order to attack in the morning? Why had he agreed to accept those meaningless parleys? Why had he not forced Morton to single combat, man to man, hatred to hatred?

James spits on the ground in disgust. What he would most like is to see is Morton climbing up onto the scaffold, to see the blow of the axe and the blood spurting from his neck. He sneers at this vision and then pictures himself slitting the throat of a buck.

35

TRANSFIXED, MARY KEPT her eyes on Bothwell. She had been about to fall asleep but jumped up startled when she heard the creak of the door opening. The feeble glow of the candlelight illuminated the Earl's silhouette and part of his face.

He took a few steps forward into the room. Tomorrow they would be back at Holyrood and once again the Queen would be surrounded by pages servants and maids, and it would be impossible for him to see her alone without an invitation.

The previous day as they walked alongside the moat they had talked together, and Mary had rested her head on his shoulder, her eyes sparkling with happiness. For a long time they had been aware of their mutual attraction. Now the Queen seemed to have let her guard down and to be yielding to him. Why hesitate any longer? He could not bear the thought of endless courtship. Tender looks, kisses and sweet nothings were all very well as long as they did not go on forever.

James now approached Mary and without a single word passing between them, he took her in his arms. Her lips parted under his and she was trembling. He drew her towards the bed, pushed her back on to it and lifted up her long gown. Mary closed her eyes. Her hasty breathing and her passivity convinced him, that she was offering herself to him. When he lay on top of her, she let out a little muffled sound, her hands pulling him towards her yet at the same time pushing him back. He tried to kiss her again but she turned her face away.

James did not ask himself any more questions. He was holding the Queen tightly against him, inhaling the fragrance of her skin and feeling her breath on him, and he was about to make love to her when she suddenly pushed him back with such force that it startled him.

'Get out immediately, or I shall call my guards!' she ordered him in an icy tone.

> *Since it is my misfortune to have caused your displeasure, I am taking my leave from court. Thus, Your Highness will no longer be inconvenienced by my presence. I am and remain forever your humble and obedient servant.*
>
> *James Hepburn, Earl of Bothwell*

James folded the letter angrily, sealed it and handed it to French Paris.

'As soon as I have left take this note to the Queen. I will wait for you at Hailes.'

Since they had returned from Neidpath, the young Frenchman had been horrified at his master's foul mood. On the previous day, just because he had spilt a little wine on the tablecloth while pouring him a drink, the Earl had threatened to break his back with his stick. Then he had had words with Secretary of State Maitland, who was just back in favour, and had very nearly got into a fight with Lord Maxwell. Even his most loyal friend David Chalmers, who had followed him to France after his English exile, was keeping out of his way. Had it not been for the friendship of his brother-in-law George Gordon, Mary Fleming and Lady Reres, sister of Janet Beaton, at court he would have been treated like a leper.

French Paris sighed to himself. With such dull company, life at Hailes was going to be very tedious. However, on his good days, James Hepburn could be jovial, generous, charming and attentive, and the young Frenchman had decided to put up with him.

After his servant had left, James put his head between his hands. He hated himself for having acted so frivolously and he cursed the Queen for provoking him and leading him on before then rejecting him. Why tease a man she did not want? Did she think he was a puppet whose strings she could pull at her will? At night, the memory of their brief embrace haunted him. More than anything in the world he wanted to become the lover of this woman who had dismissed him like a mere servant.

His horses were waiting in the stables. He would only take five servants with him and would stay at Hailes for a while. In his despair, the castle of his early childhood seemed the only possible refuge until he returned to Hermitage.

When they had been at Neidpath, the Queen had accepted with enthusiasm his proposal that she should accompany him to the Borders. In October, she was to hold a Justice Tribunal at Jedburgh and spend some time in the Borders area. He had described to her at length the region that he was so attached to, with its hills and moors, the beauty of its skies and the play of light and shadows over the landscape, and the Queen had listened with rapt attention.

James clenched his teeth in chagrin. What good did it do to torment himself? Mary was fickle and capricious. He had believed he knew her but he had been mistaken. After some time had passed, he would be able to see her again, in the role of a good courtier and loyal servant. But in the meantime all he wanted to do was to put distance between them; put out of his mind the sight of Mary's body on the cream satin counterpane, her hands drawing him towards her, her breathing and her flowing auburn lilac-scented hair.

It was some time since the young Earl had last stayed at Hailes, and he was able to find peace and calm in the old castle and the beauty of the surrounding countryside. The Tyne flowed and cascaded over its bed of pebbles and boulders, and the sunlight that filtered through the yellow autumn leaves of the willows played on the water where clouds of small long-legged spiders skimmed the surface.

In late afternoon, James would wander along the banks of the river, returning along shepherds' paths through the fields. The hills on the horizon were tinged with blue, and near to the castle clumps of hazel trees hung their nut-laden branches low over the footpaths. He plucked some nuts in passing and crushed them between his teeth, savouring their milky kernels.

Some days James would set off at dawn to ride through the country-side. He knew every part of his estates intimately and passed through villages populated by peasants who worked for the Hepburns, whose young men would be called to arms by them in case of war. Late hay crops were being cut, cereals harvested and peas gathered. Behind rush-thatched cottages, long drooping leaves of beet and rhubarb could be seen growing in the vegetable gardens. James thought of Edinburgh and wondered whether life at court was not some kind of poison. However, the image of Mary lying on the counterpane with her long slim legs and gently curving stomach obsessed him.

In two weeks time he would be back in the Borders, to try yet again to force hardened rebels into submission and to punish cattle rustlers. They were rough, wild and brave characters, whom he would haul in chains to Jedburgh, where Mary Stuart would pass sentence on them. How could a Queen who lived amongst silk and satin possibly understand the Reivers, or the force that impelled them to gallop by night across the moors in their quest for ill-gotten gains? Mounted on their stocky horses these men felt free and all-powerful. In short, they were standing up for themselves, they were their own masters and nothing would stop them, neither the troops launched on their trail, nor the Lieutenant of the Marches, nor even the prospect of death. When the wind blew around Hermitage James felt as though they were surrounding him and taunting him. Would he dare emerge from his fortress to confront them?

Sometimes he would go down to the kitchen at Hailes, where as a child he had so often loved to seek refuge. The conversation of the maid-servants and the appetising aroma of the simple dishes they were preparing helped him to divest himself of the refinement of Holyrood and blunt the memory of Mary.

One morning he received a letter from David Chalmers, who was still in Edinburgh. He told him Darnley had left Holyrood to go to his father and complain about the bad treatment inflicted on him by his wife. It was said that several violent quarrels had broken out between the two sovereigns. The Queen was irritable and morose and nothing or nobody seemed able to raise her spirits. Lady Reres, who owned a house in the Canongate adjacent to that of Chalmers, had claimed that Mary wished to separate from Darnley and obtain a divorce or an annulment, but that the risk of seeing her son labelled a bastard filled her with horror. Her ladies-in-waiting had been instructed not to admit the King to her apartments and the door leading to the stairwell linking the spouses' bed-chambers had been padlocked.

As he folded up the letter, James shrugged his shoulders. What did he care about court gossip?

On his way to Hermitage, the Earl stopped at Morham to greet his mother.

Living in the serenity of her castle Lady Agnes was approaching a peaceful old age. Janet and her son Francis Stuart often came to visit her. His sister seemed happy in her new marriage but her former carefree spirit had died with John. She attended court seldom now, and only on occasions when the Queen asked for her.

James tried not to upset his mother with his melancholy mood; he did his best to entertain her and kept his horse to the steady pace of her mare when they went riding together. The peaceful rhythm of the days they spent together and their gentle monotony helped to appease his bitter feelings. In the evenings the young village girls with their longhaired cattle dogs brought the black and red cows into the byres, the grooms led the horses to the drinking trough, and the servants' children played in the courtyard. James wondered to himself whether he would ever be able to live the quiet existence of a country gentleman, occupying himself with his harvests, trying out new seeds, improving the breeding of his herds and attending the Kirk each Sunday to listen to the sermon. He knew that kind of life would soon become unbearable to him. If he could no longer go to court, he would return to exile in France and enrol in King Charles IX's army, in which he would be able to pursue a distinguished career.

On the eve of his departure for Hermitage, Lady Agnes kept him back after supper.

For a while the Earl admired the dexterity of her fingers as she wove lace with a small spindle. The pale candlelight blended with the golden glow of the fire.

'I know, Jamie,' gently began the châtelaine of Morham, 'that you and your wife are not happy together. I experienced the ruin of my own marriage. Love, my son, is a trap into which only young people fall. When you got married did you want to live a romantic idyll or did you want to raise a family together with a young woman of the noblest birth, and have a son who would inherit the name of your ancestors and a daughter who would look after you when you are old and sick?'

James stiffened. Even his mother whom he cherished did not have the right to judge him nor even advise him. Ever since the Queen had dismissed him, Jean's coldness repelled him even more than before.

'Your wife was given to you by the Queen and the Earl of Huntly. It is up to you to conquer her heart and make her love you. I fear your parents' discord has given you misguided ideas about conjugal relationships. Happy marriages require much effort. I would like you to try to court Lady Jean so that she will grow fond of you and become a fulfilled mother.'

Agnes Sinclair looked up from her work and observed her son. James, looking cold and withdrawn kept his eyes lowered and did not answer. Suddenly the sound of footsteps on the staircase made them both look towards the door. A young man entered.

'A message for Lord Bothwell.'

The seal bore no sign of an initial or coat-of-arms.

My Lord,

I was hoping that my own willpower and courage would overcome the war I have been waging against myself. Today I am admitting defeat. This letter is very hard for me to write, but it would be lack of courage on my part to try to repress it. I accept the consequences of this failure and surrender to you.

Treat me well for my fate is from now on linked with yours.

When he returned to Edinburgh James found a note from Lady Reres at his home. The following day the Queen would come in the late afternoon to visit her. Sir David Chalmers, her next-door neighbour would expect James at the same time. The two gardens communicated with each other via a door that would be left unlocked.

The lawyer David Chalmers greeted his old friend with a worried expression. Although he and Lady Reres were the only ones privy to the secret, nevertheless he could not help feeling somewhat anxious. There were a great number of malicious people at court and gossip spread rapidly. Despite the complete devotion of Mary Stuart's lady-in-waiting and his own friendship with James Hepburn, the slightest indiscretion or blunder could have disastrous consequences. However, he knew the Earl of Bothwell well enough to realise that neither adventure nor danger frightened him. Impulsive, audacious, and ambitious, he would see this liaison as the fulfilment of his desires as well as the gratification of his pride. A Hepburn in the Queen's bed, was this not the privilege for which his family had for so long aspired? Patrick 'The Fair Earl' had made a fool of himself in order to try to seduce Marie de Guise and he had divorced his wife with no regard for the consequences. Moreover, before him had not his great-great-grandfather been the lover of Marie de Gueldres, wife of James II?

Having walked to Chalmers' house, James did not utter a word and his friend respected his silence. In order to avoid being recognised, he had enveloped himself in a riding cloak and wore a broad-brimmed hat. It was drizzling, and in late afternoon the Canongate was still sufficiently busy for a pedestrian to pass unnoticed. When David had gone over each detail of the meeting with Lady Reres, she assured him that the Queen would have only a much-reduced escort, consisting of a page, a lady-in-waiting and a maid. James was to wait for her in the chamber, which she would make ready. Mary Fleming would remain at Holyrood and would send a message at once if the slightest unforeseen event required the Queen's presence.

'Her Majesty deserves to be happy, think about that,' said David Chalmers quietly, placing his hand on his friend's shoulder.

'So much emotion is overwhelming,' the young Earl whispered.

'To a woman it is the most fragile and precious gift.'

Still wrapped in each other's arms, they were resting on the bed with the curtains drawn around them. The desire to make love had been all-consuming. Speaking in French, Mary cried out, 'James, make love to me now.' He had helped her to disrobe, then gently lifted her up and carried her to the bed. He enclosed her in his arms, and their bodies joined in a passionate embrace. Mary had whispered in wonder in James's ear, 'We fit so well together, so wonderfully well... ' Her words excited James even more, as he felt her body rise and fall in the rhythm of love. She gasped in joy and pleasure, and at the same time he found his own desires fulfilled. Afterwards they lay quiet in each other's arms in an ecstasy of love consummated. But in a little while James again felt Mary roused and wanting to feel his power within her.

'I need you James,' she whispered. 'We are meant for each other.' As he felt her body quiver with pleasure, he too felt the release of passion surge from him. He knew then that he had found the true love of his life and that he would die for her. He looked into her eyes and vowed to her,

'My darling, I am yours for ever in my heart, mind and body. Destiny has brought us together, and no one must ever part us now.' As he held her closely to him, Mary said in French,

'My dearest love, we have a unique bond of love between us which we must protect and cherish.' She held his face between her hands and gave him a deep and passionate kiss. Then laying her head back on the pillow and looking into his eyes, she whispered,

'I am yours and will be true to you always. We have been blessed with this gift of great love and desire for one another, and now we are joined together in an eternal and unbreakable union.' This was a turning point, and a critical moment, which would change the course of their lives.

James inhaled the fragrance of her floral scent, and with his lips he caressed the warm skin on the back of her neck. Never had he imagined the Queen's body could be so perfect, her skin so white and soft and her hair so silky and sensuous to the touch. Had either the Dauphin or Darnley fully appreciated such a woman? From now on Mary was his, and no other man would ever lay a hand on her.

Tears were streaming down Mary's cheeks. Giving in to her passion for the Earl of Bothwell, she had sinned by breaking the rigid rules of her upbringing; she had damaged her pride and modesty and had infringed Christian laws. She now felt as naked and vulnerable as a little child, yet whatever the future held, nothing would now make her turn back. Far from humiliating her, what she had just dared to do was a source of pride to her. She was starting out on a new life with the intensity and freedom of love and desire.

36

'WE WILL BE TOGETHER again at Jedburgh in ten days time!' Bothwell promised. 'Do not worry, His Majesty the King is in Glasgow and will not torment you again.'

The ridiculous scene that had occurred in the middle of her Council session had upset Mary so much it had made her physically sick and unable to touch any food until the following day. For the past few days, everyone at court had been appalled by Darnley's behaviour. He now addressed the Queen only in an unpleasant and sometimes offensive manner. He was drinking even more heavily than usual and was frequently intoxicated by the middle of the day. During the last session of the Privy Council, he had stood up and threatened to leave Scotland, where he complained he was being treated like a nonentity. He had friends abroad, he had blurted out, who were disturbed by the policies pursued by the Queen of Scots and by her lukewarm attitude to the Catholic faith. Ignoring the protests of the French Ambassador Philibert du Croc, Darnley continued with his diatribe: 'Scotland is at the mercy of miscreants like Moray and Maitland who are trying to influence the Queen against me and undermine my authority in her mind.' Immediately Mary's half-brother had demanded that he should explain himself. What exactly were Darnley's grievances against him? He wanted facts. Under the Earl of Moray's icy glare the young King became disconcerted and started stammering, while at the other end of the table his father the Earl of Lennox looked ashen-faced, but refrained from intervening and thus making a bad situation worse. Huntly, Atholl, Argyll and Bothwell were dumbfounded and looked at each other questioningly. They all felt Darnley was behaving like a spoilt child and that the slightest word or contrary point of view might cause him to lose control and fly into a blind rage. Maitland who was normally very self-controlled took part in the altercation... What was the King doing, and what had he already undertaken in the interests of Scotland? He did not participate in government, had no interest in matters of State, did not preside at any Justice Tribunals, nor did he even confer privately with any of the Privy Councillors. However, although he was rarely seen at the Council or in Parliament, he was often to be seen setting off magnificently dressed on his way to go hawking, hunting or some other form of recreation. As Secretary of State, Maitland knew that Darnley was corresponding with foreign powers, Spain in particular, posing as a defender of Catholicism; he who on numerous occasions had given proof of his indifference to religion. Mary, who could feel the altercation was moving onto dangerous ground, stood up and intervened:

'My Lord,' she asked, in a ringing voice, 'what is it you are blaming me for?' Darnley turned round to face his wife and once more was disconcerted by her commanding presence. His face turned red and he stammered 'Nothing, Madam.'

Mary sat down again. A deadly silence filled the room, and after what seemed to all an interminable moment, the Earl of Lennox rose and made his way to the door.

'The King and I have nothing more to say or do here,' he declared in an arrogant voice. Darnley followed his father, but incapable of making an honourable exit he turned back towards the Queen. Like a child who has been chastised he exclaimed, 'Farewell Madam, it will be a good while before you see me again!'

As he trotted south with his escort, James was trying to chase from his mind the memories of the previous day, of those all too brief hours spent at Lady Reres' house. All trace of awkwardness between him and the Queen had vanished, Mary's daring sensuality had surprised and enthralled him. Together their bodies had melded together in absolute rapture and he had taken immense pride in giving such pleasure as a lover to his sovereign.

The closer the horsemen approached to Liddesdale, the wilder the countryside became. Prosperous villages were replaced by poor hamlets, fine castles by plain four-storied keeps and lush pastures by barren moorland. In this landscape, there were no woodlands and few trees.

As the massive shape of Hermitage loomed up in the distance, James spurred his horse into a gallop. From now on, he would be fulfilling his role as Lieutenant of the Marches and would show the Elliots, Grahams, Kerrs and Scotts that he had come to restore order. Either by consent or by force he would make them obey the laws of the kingdom; he would imprison the rebels and take them to Jedburgh where their Queen would judge them at a Tribunal.

Following his orders, his servants had furnished his chamber austerely with a bed, two chairs, a trunk and a table. While undertaking his duties as Lieutenant James lived like a soldier among his troops, who camped in the courtyard of the castle. To avoid spreading disorder amongst his men, no woman was allowed to reside at Hermitage, where life proceeded according to strict rules. Before dusk, James went for a walk across the moor, where black-faced sheep grazed on the tussocks of grass and the ground was damp and boggy. Clouds drifted in from the west, casting moving shadows across the hills, and a light mist hovered over the low ground. James knew the name of every inhabitant of this wild land. He was well versed in the blood ties, lineage and peculiarities of every family. He knew for instance that the Kerrs were left-handed, the Armstrongs red-haired and the Elliots thin-lipped and square jawed. All of them were taciturn by nature and James found it hard to get any names or information out of them. For them their own justice was preferable to royal justice.

'Some Armstrongs had a fight with the Elliots last night, my Lord. One man was killed and many were wounded.'

James buckled his belt, girded on his baldric, and put on thick leather boots with the spurs already attached. He would be at Hollows Tower, den of the Armstrongs, in less than an hour and hoped to dislodge Old Johnnie. This old Reiver had been arrested and sentenced numerous times yet had always succeeded in avoiding the gallows and returning home to continue his misdeeds. However, he was brave, obstinate and tough and James bore him a certain admiration.

With fifty mosstroopers following him, James set off at a brisk trot. The day was chilly and a light mist covered the hills.

'Look over there, Lieutenant!'

With Hollows Tower already in view, a patroller pointed out two horsemen fleeing at full gallop.

'Armstrong's spies have done a good job,' James remarked, 'we will only catch small fry today.'

With their hands tied and feet roped to the stirrups, eight Armstrongs increased the ranks of the little troop on its return journey to Hermitage.

Old Johnnie had bolted with his brother, leaving his eldest son in charge of the ancestral home, where being only eight in number against fifty they were forced to surrender. James would lock them up in Hermitage prison before having them taken to Jedburgh under close guard.

For a long while James remained standing, looking out from one of the narrow windows of his room. The full moon cast a surreal glow over the hills. He could hear the sound of swirling water coming from the nearby river. The peaceful look of the countryside soothed him and distracted his thoughts from the violent ways of many of its inhabitants. He decided that one way or another Darnley would be kept at a distance, and after spending some time under surveillance in one of the royal castles he would probably leave Scotland to join his mother and younger brother in England. In this eventuality James felt he could count on the support of a number of nobles, including the entire Hamilton family who were sworn enemies of the Lennoxes; on the Douglases who would never forgive the treason of their relative the King following Rizzio's murder; on Moray who unaware of James's liaison with the Queen, thought he would once more be able to regain all his authority; on Maitland who was appalled by the King's incompetence, and on the Balfours, a wealthy and influential family of lawyers with whom he was on friendly terms and who were ambitious to acquire property and honours. James sighed. He felt like writing to Mary but he would not do so. Since childhood she had been accustomed to receiving compliments and expecting from others the proof of affection she herself barely took the trouble to express to others. Now she would have to learn to be more thoughtful and considerate in her outlook and responses.

In order to track down and seize Jock o' the Park, a hardened troublemaker, intrepid Reiver and head of the Elliot family, James would be followed by his entire company of mosstroopers. The Elliots ruled supreme around Liddesdale and the old reprobate would probably receive the support of a great number of his kith and kin. Once Jock o' the Park had been captured and incarcerated at Hermitage, all that remained for him to do was to inspect the border country one last time before heading back to Jedburgh to join the Queen. James was jubilant. An hour earlier as he was finishing a bowl of oatmeal porridge and some biscuits, a porter had handed him a letter from Mary, which said, 'I am yours body and soul.' Although the letter was unsigned, he recognised the Queen's distinctive handwriting with its firm strokes and flourishes. He had hesitated before setting light to the letter in the candle flame. That evening he would write to her.

James's escort waited patiently outside the fortress as he descended the spiral staircase that linked his apartments to the great hall. The weather was clear and dry and a thin layer of white frost lay over the mossy ground, bleached grass and patches of bare brown earth outside the castle. James walked out into the open air, and the bright glare made him blink. At that particular moment, his future seemed radiant and he felt invincible. Johnnie Armstrong might have been lucky enough to escape but Jock o' the Park would not and James was determined to arrest him at all costs.

All was quiet in the vicinity of the tower. Only a few chickens, dogs and goats betrayed the presence of the inhabitants who must have seen them approaching from a long way off. It would be easy to break the door down and lay siege to the dwelling but James doubted the fox was in his den. If they had set off on some nocturnal pillaging foray, Jock and his sons might perhaps not make an appearance at all and he would have to send his troopers on their trail.

'Listen.' From far away came the distant thunder of hooves pounding the frozen ground.

'About ten horses, my Lord,' the young trooper estimated. 'They are coming towards us.'

James expressed his satisfaction with an oath and gave the signal to his men to move. The Elliots, unaware of their danger, were about to throw themselves into the trap he had laid for them.

Spurred on by his rider, James's English stallion was gaining ground. A few hundred yards ahead of him Jock o' the Park was fleeing at the gallop, whipping his horse and digging his spurs into its flanks while chunks of earth and loose stones scattered under its hooves. Leaving his mosstroopers to pursue Jock's accomplices, James had dashed after their leader. His horse was catching up with Jock's and he could almost reach out to him. Jock was stockily built, and wore a steel-reinforced leather jack and close-fitting helmet.

'Stop!' ordered James.

Jock looked round and seeing his pursuer very close he savagely hauled on the reins, causing his horse to rear. He leapt to the ground and ran straight ahead to the shelter of a pile of rocks.

'Give yourself up Jock,' James shouted, 'or I'll shoot!'

He pulled out a pistol from the cast-iron saddletree and aimed at the fugitive's legs. Jock collapsed heavily.

James dismounted and grasped hold of a cord wrapped round the pommel of his saddle. He intended to tie the Reiver's hands together and take him to Hermitage, where he would receive medical attention.

He barely had time to jump back. Jock had risen up and unsheathed his sword.

'Did you think you could catch me that easily, Lieutenant?' he sneered.

His first stroke hit James's side, who, ignoring the searing pain, drew his dirk and waited. Instinctively he stopped the Reiver's sword from striking him full in the face by shielding it with his hand, then with blood streaming down his arm he plunged his weapon under his enemy's ribs into the exposed spot where the jack offered no protection. Jock grunted and raised his sword again, striking his adversary on the head before he collapsed with fingers clenched over his wound. James tried to walk a few steps. A short distance away his horse was grazing on the rough grass. He grasped hold of the saddle and tried to cling to it but lost consciousness.

In haste, the mosstroopers gathered branches to make a litter to take their Lieutenant back to Hermitage. They had found him lying face down and apparently lifeless, and believing him to be dead had stood there shocked and indecisive until one of the troopers, more persevering than the others, had turned the body over and noticed their leader was still breathing.

Harnessed to the magnificent English stallion the litter bounced over the track, shaking the inert body. The Earl's deathly pale complexion and the blood he was losing profusely left little hope to his men, who rode in silence. When they reached Hermitage, the troop was astounded to find the portcullis lowered. Who had instructed this and for what reason? The sun was going down and a cold wind blew across the moors.

'We are the masters here!'

Two Armstrongs had appeared at one of the windows of James's apartment on the first floor of the kitchen tower, and the men conferred with each other. During their absence, the prisoners had succeeded in taking control of the fortress. If the Lieutenant was not given urgent medical treatment there was little hope he would survive the night.

'We want to negotiate!' exclaimed a trooper. The talks lasted almost half an hour and dusk had already fallen when they finished. Still lying on the litter James remained unconscious, shaken by a few spasms and with his eyes shut. Eventually the eight Armstrongs left the fortress with cries of joy. Their freedom in exchange for a place they could not hope to hold for long seemed like an excellent bargain to them.

The apothecary finished cleaning, probing and bandaging the wounds. James had still not regained consciousness. The blow he had received to his temple was not violent enough to fracture his skull, but the palm of his left hand was slashed to the bone, and the wound in his right side was deep.

'Make all haste to Jedburgh,' the steward of the fortress ordered a trooper, 'and tell Her Majesty the Queen that the Lieutenant is hovering between life and death.'

It was late into the night when the messenger reached the house where the Queen was staying. Man and horse were exhausted, having many times floundered and struggled through mosses and peat bogs rendered invisible in the dark.

'Her Majesty and her retinue are sleeping,' a guard declared at once. 'Come back tomorrow.'

'Tell the Queen that the Earl of Bothwell is more dead than alive,' the messenger exclaimed. 'He has been sorely wounded by Jock o' the Park.'

Now relieved of his mission, he would be able to go down to the kitchens, have something to eat and fall asleep by the fire.

Without delay the commander of the guard went to see Lord Seton, head of the Queen's household. The news seemed serious enough for him to risk waking him up.

'The Earl of Bothwell has been killed by Jock Elliot,' he said simply. 'A trooper from Hermitage has just brought me the news.'

37

WITH GREAT DIFFICULTY James half-opened his eyes.

'God be praised,' a servant sitting by his bed exclaimed. Several others then approached his bedside.

'Can you hear me, my Lord?' asked the steward.

Two troopers and a stricken-looking French Paris stood behind him. James managed to nod.

'You were wounded six days ago,' the steward told him. 'We all feared for your life.'

The Earl tried to collect his thoughts. The memory of Jock o' the Park, their fight and his wounds came back to his mind.

'Six days,' he whispered. That same day he should have been on his way to Jedburgh with his prisoners.

'And the Queen?' the wounded man enunciated with difficulty.

'When she was given the news you were dead Her Majesty showed great distress. She has since been informed you have regained consciousness, and is enquiring daily about your health.'

James let his head drop back onto the pillow and asked French Paris to come closer.

'Send a message to Her Majesty and tell her that in two weeks at the most I will be in Jedburgh. Let me sign the letter.'

It was a rainy morning and as it was dark in the room, the candles remained lit. Red-hot coals glowed in the hearth, reflecting their light onto the cold flagstones, which sweated with humidity. The oak chest was blackened from smoke and the four chairs were devoid of cushions to alleviate their discomfort.

When he awoke, James managed to swallow a few spoonfuls of

boiled chicken and drink a glass of wine. The sharpest pain came from his left hand, which had been expertly bandaged. He could not imagine how he could have let himself be caught off-guard by Jock.

The hours passed. He fell asleep, woke and asked for a drink, and demanded that fresh candles be placed by his bedside.

'I have got something that is going to raise your spirits, my Lord,' French Paris whispered in his ear. 'I have a letter for you.' The Frenchman had recovered his usual smile and cheerful voice. James propped himself up on his good arm. He was suffering from a headache and his throat felt dry.

His servant handed him a letter bearing a seal.

'From Her Majesty the Queen,' he announced.

For a long time James held the letter without opening it. Until his physical pain and his anger towards the Elliots had subsided, he had barely been able to bring himself to think about Mary. Now confined to his bed and feeling isolated, he felt unable to compete with Mary's ardour. He felt weak and vulnerable and hated being in such a state of incapacity.

You were so sorely wounded, my sweet love, I have known no happiness, and I must shut myself away to weep for you. Losing you would have devastated me. Without the strength of your presence, I would be plunged again into my former state of anguish and sorrow. Be certain that I cannot live without you, which I shall prove to you by coming to visit you in two days time. I am aware that it would be impossible for me to stay at Hermitage, so I will return that same day. Far from discouraging me, the prospect of this long ride is increasing my impatience to see you again. I will ask Lord Moray and a few other nobles to accompany me. Time weighs heavy with me, but my love for you lightens my heart...

James took a deep breath. The touching frankness with which the Queen confided her feelings for him both delighted and moved him. Mary would have to ride a round trip of nearly sixty miles just to see him for an all too brief visit. It was a long ride which even a hardened horseman would consider exhausting. Once again, he was astounded by the courage and sheer determination of this young woman. He wondered how a Queen who possessed such moral fibre could allow herself to be dominated by a man like Moray, whose ambition and insensitivity were plain to see? How could she have been attracted to an immature, pretentious and deceitful individual like Darnley? The only way James could make sense of this behaviour was that it was caused by her isolation and great need of affection.

He committed the letter to the flames of the candles placed beside his bed. Once consumed all that remained were ashes. He wondered if in future he should conserve any letters from his Queen.

James had arranged to have a double rank of troopers mounted in front of Hermitage to welcome Mary. They had been instructed to be beardless and to wear freshly laundered shirts beneath their leather jacks. He had asked to be propped into a sitting position, and had donned an indoor robe of thick brown wool lined with fur. In the vast kitchens, the cooks and scullions had been busy since dawn preparing a meal for their Queen's visit. Barrels of beer had been drawn up from the cellar and jugs filled with water from the well.

It was almost noon when James heard the sound of horses neighing and the muffled noise of an approaching cavalcade. This was followed by a fanfare of trumpets and the furious barking of his dogs. All within Hermitage now rushed to greet the Queen.

The Earl could not control his emotions. Was it the thought of the presence of the Queen at his bedside or the fact that he was her lover that thrilled him most?

From the open door of his bedchamber he heard the sound of footsteps, the rustle of a skirt against the stone steps and the echo of a female voice.

'You upset your Queen, my Lord Bothwell, by leading her to believe you were abandoning her!'

When James tried to straighten himself a little more Mary laid her hand on his right arm to prevent him from doing so. With a smile she said,

'It is up to the sovereign, my Lord, to bow before those who are wounded in her service.'

The Earl of Moray had taken his place next to the Queen. His inquisitive and puzzled glance did not go unnoticed by James who wondered if Moray really believed that he and the Queen would be naïve enough to reveal a mutual attraction. Mary had been wise to let Moray escort her. Did his mere presence not bear witness to the innocence of her undertaking?

In light-hearted tones Mary told James about her installation at Jedburgh and the preparations for the various Justice Tribunals which she personally attended.

Behind this discussion, her glance and slightest smile conveyed a meaning to which James responded with joy. This silent complicity was as sensuous as the most loving embrace.

Preceded by French Paris, servants brought simple dishes of food from the Hermitage kitchens.

'It is a pleasure to see you Nicholas!' the Queen exclaimed in French, 'You are a good lad! I will soon be asking permission of the Earl of Bothwell to take you into my service.'

James gave a slight smile.

'French Paris is yours Madam, as are all of those who are present.'

After they had eaten, Moray briefly referred to topics recently debated by the Privy Council. In France, the religious peace so fervently advocated by Catherine de Medicis was being abused on all sides, and King Charles IX had been forced to take refuge in Meaux. This state of unrest had strengthened the Scots in their resolve to see their country become a Protestant State under the protection of their sovereign. James approved, but maintained that Scottish Catholics should be allowed to practise their religion without being attacked or even threatened.

'There is no possibility of going back,' Moray interjected dryly, 'and we will do everything we can to prevent trouble caused by those who would plot with the Papists.'

Although Darnley was on everyone's minds, no one dared utter his name.

The Queen accepted the dishes of food offered to her together with a glass of wine. The sky was turning dark with clouds that presaged rain, when Moray said,

'Madam, we need to think about leaving.'

When her half-brother left the bedside to fetch Mary's cloak, she leant over the wounded man and whispered,

'I cannot bear to be so close to you, yet not be able to embrace you.'

Two days later James heard the Queen had fallen ill. On her way back to Jedburgh, they had been delayed by rain, and being mired in a bog her horse had thrown her to the ground. On her return to Jedburgh, tired, chilled and wet through she had nevertheless written him a letter, which he had received only hours before news was brought of her serious illness. The Queen was vomiting blood and had fainted several times, before taking to her bed and losing consciousness. It was thought she was dying, and a priest had been sent for to administer the last rites.

'Go at once to Jedburgh,' James ordered French Paris, 'and seek the latest news from Mary Fleming.'

He was steadily gaining strength, and now could even walk a little leaning on the shoulder of a servant. As soon as the apothecary deemed it time to replace his thick bandages with lighter ones he would ride to Jedburgh himself. James wondered what kind of message fate could be sending him and Mary. Within a few days of each other both had come close to death.

'Just speak French,' James said to French Paris in an irritated voice, 'I can't understand a word of your Scots.'

He was sitting by the fireside wrapped in a warm coat. His wounds had not become infected and the apothecary was now confident he would live.

'Her Majesty has not yet regained consciousness,' French Paris told him solemnly. 'When her body is not shaken from head to toe by convulsions, she lies inert on her bed. Lady Fleming attributes this illness to the Queen's distress at being married to a man such as Darnley and to the terrible torment caused by the prospect of her future. When by chance Her Majesty does regain her senses, she wishes for death. If I may give you my opinion my Lord, the Queen is dying of anxiety and sorrow.'

'This cannot be possible!' cried James.

He instantly tried to rise but fell back into his chair in excruciating pain.

'Lady Fleming also surmises Her Majesty has suffered deep disquiet from recent worries which have added to her misery. Fearing the Queen, her friend, may have lost the will to live, she requests your presence as soon as you are fit to travel. They will despatch a litter shortly to bring you to Jedburgh.

James swallowed down a draught of whisky that had been placed beside him... Mary was dying and he was unable to be by her side. He stared into the flames of the fire. If the Queen were to die, his life would then have little meaning. Lady Fleming had said Mary was in torment about the future. Why was she torturing herself like this? Admittedly, even after she had obtained a divorce from Darnley they would have to wait and be patient and trust each other. He would remove Moray and Maitland from power and would seek support from the Earl of Huntly and the Hamiltons, who would be only too happy to be rid of the Lennoxes, and thus become closer to the Queen. Mary had no reason to be alarmed; he felt confident he would be able to subdue his enemies, and, together with the Queen, govern Scotland. As soon as he reached Jedburgh, she would be sure to recover.

38

SAVED FROM NEAR DEATH thanks to the dedicated medical care provided by Monsieur Arnault, her French doctor, Mary was beginning to recover when James reached Jedburgh.

'We are starting a new life, you and I,' she said in a soft voice, 'I shall gain strength from now on.'

They smiled at each other; she from her bed looking pale and drawn and he with his head, chest and hand still bound in strips of linen.

The Privy Council had gathered in the Queen's chamber in order to plan the next royal progress in the Borders. Bothwell confirmed he would be fit to ride by the tenth of November at the latest. He was surprised by the friendly attitude shown by Moray and Maitland. Both seemed to have given up their antagonism towards him. However, the Earl remained on his guard.

The unexpected arrival of Darnley, who had come to enquire about his wife, suddenly threw everything into turmoil. The King by his mere presence, caused unease and discord in their previously harmonious gathering. The magnificent harness of Darnley's horses and ostentatious clothes worn by him and his friends looked totally out of place in the Borders town of Jedburgh. The Queen became distant and curt in her responses to him and it was feared a quarrel might break out at any moment. Strangely enough, the King contrived to maintain a jovial front, but this only succeeded in increasing Mary's irritation.

Two days later Darnley announced he was leaving Jedburgh for Stirling.

Far from being idle, he asserted he was diligently promoting Scotland's interests with influential allies. On the morning of his departure the French Ambassador, Philibert du Croc, had a long conversation with him, which left him disquieted.

As soon as Darnley had made his departure, the Queen became pre-occupied with her forthcoming ten day progress through the Borders, which would be accompanied by the Earl of Bothwell and would end at Craigmillar Castle near Edinburgh. Even now when she had recovered well and was in a serene frame of mind, the Queen looked a shadow of her former self. The Earl was impatient for Mary to be well enough to travel and for them to be able at last to enjoy some intimacy. Seeing each other constantly without being alone for one minute was putting a strain on both of them.

When they reached the town of Kelso where the River Teviot joins the Tweed, the little court scattered to look at the ruins of what a few years earlier had been a prosperous Abbey. Under orders from King Henry VIII, while Mary was still a child, the Earl of Hertford had ransacked it and the ruins had been abandoned. After several nights of frost, the sky had clouded over and the weather had become milder. James took Mary's arm and as they walked between the moss-covered gravestones where a few sheep were grazing, and he quietly said to her,

'Tomorrow I want to show you a place nearby which I have loved since I was a child and where we could be alone together for an hour or two.'

'Yes, I should like that,' whispered Mary. 'We can take Margaret Carwood and French Paris with us part of the way and meet them again on the way back.'

Proceeding at a walk the two horses followed the path leading up the hill. Down below them the Tweed Valley was bathed in a light that made the water in the river shimmer while the midday sun cast a golden glow on the leaves still clinging to the branches of the willow trees lining the banks. Mary was now becoming more relaxed and at ease. Until the moment they were ready to go she had feared something might happen to delay them, but fortunately nothing had occurred, and she was able to set out in the company of her Lieutenant, together with their two servants, whom they left at the bottom of the hill to await their return. They rode their horses up the narrow stony track that rose steeply towards the sky-line. For a while, both of them seemed lost in thought.

'Looking to our future we have a long road ahead of us,' said Bothwell, 'we must go forward bravely and never look back.'

Riding beside him, Mary took hold of her lover's wounded hand, still wrapped in a thin strip of linen.

'I am not afraid of the future,' she answered

'You will need courage and strength of mind. Be yourself and do not fear unpopularity.'

The Queen looked down. She was not accustomed to receiving such advice, and even though it came from her lover, it displeased her. James sensed the reason for her lack of response.

'I am speaking freely from the heart, Mary, as a man to the woman he loves, and not as a subject seeking to please his Queen. You are a good person, but under difficult political circumstances it is sometimes necessary to silence one's heart and let reason rule one's head.'

'As long as Lord Darnley remains by my side I feel I can no longer shoulder my responsibilities,' replied Mary.

She was aware that together with his father, the King was constantly plotting against her. Being still denied the Crown Matrimonial he intended to seize it by force, oust Mary and take over power in the name of their child. Although hardly a fervent Catholic, he was building up alliances with the King of Spain and the Pope. He hoped to obtain their support by luring them with the prospect of his eagerness to re-establish the true faith in Scotland.

James, replying to her concern, said;

'Your Privy Council will be meeting at Craigmillar in a few days time and will find an acceptable way to get rid of the King.'

As the horses struggled up the steep slope, loose pebbles rolled from under the horses' hooves. Here and there on either side, stunted pines plunged their roots into invisible crevices in the moss-grown rocks, and clumps of thistles and wild herbs were withering.

The riders reached the summit of the hill. From here as far as the eye could see the Tweed Valley unfurled in a patchwork of pastures and square plots of cultivated land bordered by stone walls. The lovers stood for a while contemplating the scenery and absorbing the peace around them.

'Moray and Maitland need to be reined in,' James continued. 'They have never wished you well.'

Mary gave a sigh. At that precise moment, she did not want to speak about government but about herself.

'Do you truly love me?' she asked.

The riders dismounted. James knew Mary was waiting for reassurance and words of love.

'My life belongs to you,' he whispered, 'never doubt it.'

He wrapped his arm round her waist and drew her to him. Dressed in her boyish clothes she looked like a young man.

'I am not here to tie you down,' he continued,' but to enable you to be at peace with yourself and be a great Queen.'

Mary leaned her head towards James and he kissed her on her lips. She was crying now. Tenderly he caressed her cheeks and mouth, while high above them a sparrowhawk hovered in the almost cloudless sky.

'I love you,' he whispered.

He was touched anew by the radiant charm of Mary's smile. This beautiful young woman was better suited to seduction and attracting love than to ruling a country. Protected and flattered since childhood she had suddenly been thrown unprepared into an alien and brutal world, whose laws and customs were foreign to her and in which she had done her best to survive.

From the top of the hill, James and Mary watched small clouds drifting from the south-west and casting light shadows over the valley and the River Tweed while the breeze carried the scent of bonfires and fallen leaves.

'We will be able to spend one night together at Craigmillar,' Mary assured him. 'It has been too long since we last lay with our arms around each other.'

As they reached Craigmillar Castle, the last stop on her journey, Mary felt both relieved and anxious. The decision she had to make would lead to serious consequences. James had reiterated that he would tolerate no changes to the objectives he had set: Darnley should be got out of the way and his staunchest enemies should not be free to take justice into their own hands.

Less than one hour's ride on horseback from Edinburgh, the fortress of Craigmillar towered above a pastoral valley with woods and hills sloping down towards the sea. Mary loved this castle, which did not possess the wild beauty of Tantallon, perched on its cliffs overlooking the sea, nor Dumbarton, defended by a steep circular rock face, but lent itself to a happy social life and peaceful entertainment. It was there she had chosen to meet the most influential members of her nobility to decide jointly on her future: a separation from the King.

Since their experiences in the Borders James had tormented himself over the Queen's ability to hold her ground. Although she had been buffeted by her few years of rule she nevertheless retained many of the same illusions as before.

The Earls of Moray, Argyll, Huntly and Secretary of State Maitland had just arrived at Craigmillar. All five of them were going to assess the troublesome situation in which Darnley had placed the Queen and seek an honourable solution for her.

Although very close to his brother-in-law, Bothwell had not breathed a word of his liaison to George. As if she sensed something was amiss, Jean was being more forthcoming. She had sent him a few letters from Crichton in which for the first time her words were affectionate towards him. With time, she claimed, his qualities as a husband were becoming evident and she was impatient to see him again. God willing they would grow fonder of each other and would build a real family. James read these letters with sadness in his heart. It was now too late to consider a happy union. It was no longer Jean, but the Queen who occupied his thoughts, and their divorce was inevitable.

For over two hours Moray, Argyll, Huntly and Secretary Maitland weighed up with Bothwell the possible options. Although the Queen had insisted she would tolerate no decision prejudicial to her honour, her resolve to remove the King remained unchanged. To arrest him for treason seemed to be the best solution. After being divested of his titles and honours, Darnley could be tried and sentenced, and the verdict allowed no other alternative: arrest and surveillance in a fortress or exile. There was still the possibility that upon being arrested the King would try to defend himself, and that an over-zealous reaction might inflict a mortal wound on him. No one could be held responsible for such an unforeseen turn of events.

As dusk fell, a unanimous agreement was reached. The lords sat gathered round the table and the shifting flood of light from the torches accentuated Moray's black beard, Argyll's sharp features and Bothwell's watchful and distrustful gaze. The motive for Darnley's arrest was indisputable: no sovereign could form alliances with foreign powers against his own country. Moreover, Moray and Maitland had proof of the King's correspondence with the Pope and Philip II of Spain. Besides, Darnley had a few ships at his disposal ready to weigh anchor in order to join his allies if he thought fit. When questioned about this, the young sovereign had made a pitiful effort to deny it.

Entrenched in his fief of Glasgow, his father the Earl of Lennox no longer participated in political life. There was however no doubt he was the instigator of the decisions made by his son. Darnley was too frivolous and inconsistent to devise such twisted manoeuvres on his own.

Their decision taken, the lords remained silent for a while, each lost in his own thoughts. Moray and his brother-in-law Argyll saw boundless territory opening up before them; Huntly the reinstatement of his clan's power in the north of the country; Maitland a closer collaboration with England leading to profitable agreements for Scotland, and Bothwell the elimination of a bad King, a despicable man and a rival. All without even consulting each other intended to obtain the Queen's pardon for the Douglases, who had been in exile since the murder of Rizzio, Darnley having betrayed them. Their revenge would be released on the young sovereign as soon as he returned to Scotland. At nineteen years of age, his fate was sealed.

39

JAMES WAKES WITH A START. Despite the biting cold, he is sweating. The letters... why did he not destroy them? Out of vanity? To use them as a weapon in case he needed to defend himself? Moray and Maitland seized them in order to dishonour Mary. That had been his unintentional and fatal gift to them.

The prisoner searches his memory and tries to recall the incriminating words. Were they even there? Mary expressed her love passionately, as well as her jealousy. Jean... James remembers the coldness in Jean's eyes, her reluctant body and her tears too when he announced his wish to divorce her, as well as her reproaches, bitter and aggressive words. Mary's words are soothing, pleading and questioning. He hears her voice but cannot understand what she is saying. He begs her to come to him and fall into his arms. He feels his way around the room, his legs give way under him and he drops to his knees. A memory haunts him... the failure of a life that used to be so full of promise. Everything he fought for and succeeded in achieving slips from his grasp.

Dawn is about to break and the grey early morning lights up the white walls of Dragsholm. Why does the King of Denmark not hand him over to the Scots? Dying on the scaffold in the centre of Edinburgh would be a moral victory. In a muted voice James repeats over and over the words he would utter before lowering his head onto the block; precise words of accusation which might perhaps open the door of Mary Stuart's prison. Who wished for Darnley's death? Who executed the King and why?

Perched on a gutter an owl hoots. A few servants in charge of rekindling the fires walk across the courtyard with a load of firewood and there are dogs barking.

James believes that three events were indelibly engraved on his life: his parents' divorce, his marriage to the Queen, and his defeat at Carberry Hill. After that, in thrall to uncontrollable forces he sank into darkness. He was like an animal trapped in quicksand, suffocating little by little.

On his knees James drags himself to his bed. He is waiting for the bowl of boiled oatmeal and the flask of spirit. Then he will either sleep or unleash the self-destructive forces lurking within him.

The sun does not rise. A mixture of sleet and snow falls from a slate grey sky. The only thing James now wishes for is to rest in Scotland at home at Crichton, in the cemetery of the old Kirk where his sister was married. May the Danes not keep his remains in a country that brought him nothing but misfortune, dishonour and the slow disintegration of his body and soul. His only weapon is his resistance. Chained to a stake he has managed to survive the pit with its darkness, cold and filth. As a Hepburn he will never surrender.

Today he will not rise from his bed of straw. His legs and knees are causing him agony. He will not get up to watch the falling snow nor stare at the seagulls gliding over the small stretch of grey sea. Instead, he will close his eyes and allow himself to be transported back to the past; his triumphs, frustrations, despair and the curse that marked his destiny. Everything he touched turned to decay or ashes. Carried on the wind, a fragrance takes him back to Paris. He never learned how fully to appreciate the refinement and culture which life in France offered to the grands seigneurs. His thoughts always remained in Scotland.

James whispers the name 'Eléonore'. He recalls the lively expression, the exquisitely shaped mouth and the perfect breasts. He was attached to this free and desirable woman and he left her without any promise of return. Scotland called him back. He has no idea what happened to his friends and his mistresses. He is dead to them and they are dead to him; his memory buried them in oblivion. Only Mary lives on. She had demanded that he burn her letters. The letters… why do they haunt him? What is he trying to find, explain, and forgive himself for? For an adulterous liaison? For the confusion of feelings which linked his love to his ambitions? Admittedly, he loved Mary partly because she was a Queen and partly because this powerful woman surrendered herself to him. She loved him for who he was, for his strength of character and his sensuality. She sent him long passionate letters and he replied only with brief notes, which she destroyed. Today he wants to tell her that even if he was not skilled in the art of writing love letters, he did truly love her. However, it is too late now.

40

AT STIRLING CASTLE, standards and banners were waving in the wind. The stables had been re-equipped, the kitchens refurbished, the woodwork waxed, the marble pillars and hallways polished and the chapel had been adorned with tapestries brought over from Edinburgh. Hundreds of candles and mountains of firewood had been purchased for the comfort of the guests, and the larders and sculleries were overflowing with eggs, poultry, mutton and both sea and river fish. Casks of Burgundy and Bordeaux wine were arriving from France, and in addition, a mixture of rare spices, butter, boxes of marzipan, candied fruit, sugared almonds, jams and sugarcoated rose and violet petals. Arriving at the ports of Leith and Dumbarton, processions of princes, prelates, ambassadors and grands seigneurs from the principal kingdoms of Europe travelled to Stirling along pot-holed roads, overtaking troops of harquebusiers and halberdiers sent from Edinburgh to ensure the safety of the Queen's guests.

Ignoring Bothwell's advice Mary had insisted on a Catholic christening. Her son would inherit the religion of his forebears, and if he were to become King of England he would restore freedom to the English Catholics. Nothing would change the young woman's mind.

James and Jean had arrived at Stirling and had settled into apartments close to the Queen's own. Darnley had promised to attend his son's christening but no one trusted his word anymore.

'Lord Darnley is capable of disappearing before the ceremony just to annoy me, unless his servants find him lying in a drunken stupor on his bed. You, my Lord Bothwell, will be at my side to welcome the guests and will make a better host than the King.'

Cuddling close to James, Mary was giving free rein to her joy. Her child's lavish christening was her way of rebelling against her constantly curbed freedom, her lack of money and her isolation in Scotland. Queen Elizabeth of England had accepted an invitation to be godmother to the little Prince and had appointed the Earl of Bedford to represent her. Charles IX was to be the godfather. The Comtes de Brienne and Moretta as well as a number of representatives of the highest English nobility were expected shortly in Edinburgh.

James hardly dared express his satisfaction. Only a few months earlier, the honour that Mary, now in Darnley's absence, had bestowed upon him to stand at her side, would have been given to the Earl of Moray. Now James had irrevocably supplanted him. The position he had come to occupy in Scotland would finally enable him to keep at a distance those who had betrayed their country.

James could not think of Scotland either in the present or in the foreseeable future, as a nation living under the narrow political and economic dependency of England.

Softly James caressed Mary's auburn hair. She was now giving herself to him without restraint. He was her lover but also her friend, adviser and defender. Since the death of her father-in-law King Henri II of France and her separation from the Guises, Mary had been existing in complete moral and emotional isolation. She was naturally spontaneous, yet carefully had to weigh up every word she spoke; she was generous by nature but was forced to restrain her spending. Moreover, neither of her two husbands had been able to fulfil her physical needs. The temperament of the Stuarts and the passionate nature of the Guises had soon turned her into a demanding lover, who combined the directness of the Scots with the refined sensuality of the French. Teaching the art of love to his Queen was a task that James accomplished with ardour.

James gently advised her, 'I will be beside you if the King chooses not to show his face. However, for the sake of your honour my dearest one, you should give him no choice. His absence could start to create and spread rumours against us, which would do us harm and would question our relationship in the eyes of many.'

Mary closed her eyes. How could she ever have been in love with such a despicable character as Darnley? His contemptible little intrigues might turn out to be dangerous. What promises had he made to the Spaniards, the Pope, or even the French? The hostility of Catherine de Medicis towards her former daughter-in-law remained unaltered, and as Queen Mother she might well pressurise Darnley into entrusting her with the Catholic upbringing of little James at the French Court in exchange for a long regency. If the Lords of the Congregation were prepared to sell Scotland to England, the Lennoxes would gladly hand Mary over to the highest bidder.

'The King wants me out of the way,' Mary reflected, 'He has been humiliated by his own mistakes which are the consequence of his stubbornness and cowardice, and he is now trying to prove to me he is still a force to be reckoned with in the Kingdom. If I am not the first to strike it is I who will be the one to be eliminated.'

'We will act as planned,' James asserted.

'And what about us, Jamie?'

'We must be patient. Only political motives can be put forward as justification for your separation from the King. You must not give your enemies any pretext or weapon to use against us.'

The fanfare of trumpets, the skirl of bagpipes and the rolling of drums heralded the solemn procession making its way to the chapel at Stirling Castle. As the Queen had feared, Darnley, knowing he was hated and despised, was hiding away in his apartments and refusing to attend the festivities. None of the guests had dared openly express surprise about the King's absence but all understood that this amounted to a declaration of war between Mary and her spouse.

The memories Mary had of festivities held at the Valois Court had given her the incentive to opt for pomp and ceremony with no expense spared. Some of her silverware had been melted down and she had had sumptuous clothes made for the representatives of the noblest Scottish families. For the man she loved she had chosen silver-brocaded blue satin from France and a velvet cap of the same shade adorned with black feathers, which set off the skilled pleating on his fine batiste shirt. The Earls of Moray and Huntly were clad in purple, while the ladies were dressed in ruby satin, richly coloured taffetas, diamond-patterned emerald velvet, gold-trimmed damask, and crepe fringed with bronzed silver.

For herself, just as she had opted for her marriage to the Dauphin, her mourning and her second marriage, Mary had chosen to wear white, her favourite colour, trimmed with silver braid and a white fur lining. A gold belt encrusted with diamonds accentuated the slenderness of her waist and her famous black pearl necklace was worn over her bodice of velvet and silver-embroidered damask.

Mary had sent for wall hangings and tapestries from Holyrood to adorn the chapel where the double doors had been left wide open to allow the procession to pass through. Near to the baptistry had been placed the solid gold font inlaid with precious stones gifted by the Queen of England. Archbishop Hamilton, the Primate of Scotland stood waiting, wearing a gold-embroidered cope. On either side of him stood three bishops, a prior and twelve priests.

As the little Prince made his entry, carried by the Earl of Bedford and accompanied by the Countess of Argyll, the voices of the royal choir rose in unison amid the blaze of candles and torches. James and Mary exchanged brief glances.

The Queen knew that Bothwell together with Moray and Huntly would remain outside the doors of the chapel. No amount of pleading or coaxing had managed to shake the Earl's determination not to attend the ceremony. Her own Catholic faith, with its ostentation, its gold, its music, the splendour of its sacred objects, the beauty of its statues, and the sweet fragrance of its incense, took her back to the time of her childhood. It reminded her of her family and her adoptive country, her upbringing and her individuality as Princess, Queen, and daughter of the Church. This heritage was the most precious thing she possessed and she wanted to pass it on to her son.

Inside the chapel the representatives of the Scottish Catholic nobility, each holding a candle, formed a guard of honour, and the candlelight made precious stones glitter and pearls shimmer, softening the appearance of fabrics and accentuating a glance, the contours of a mouth, or the rounded shape of a bodice.

The festivities lasted for two days and included banquets, balls and dancing displays. Bastien Pages, the Queen's head valet, who came from the Auvergne region of France, had organised a spectacle, which caused the only incident of the ceremony. Bursting into the room at the end of a feast, actors disguised as fauns had waggled their tails under the very noses of English dignitaries, who, interpreting it as an allusion to an old folk superstition attributing hairy appendages to the English as punishment for the murder of Thomas Becket had taken offence and threatened to leave the table. Thanks to the Queen's and the Earl of Bedford's intervention, the situation had been defused and the final act restored a more relaxed atmosphere. In the park near the cemetery, a tent had been erected to shelter the fireworks experts who were ready to light up the night and dazzle the spectators. Attacked from all sides by hundreds of demons, wild beasts, ogres and wizards, the defenders of a cardboard fort decided to blow up their bastion in a glorious fireworks finale, which left even the most blasé awestruck.

At no point had the King made an appearance.

'You must sign, Madam.'

After Bothwell, Moray and Maitland, it was the Earl of Bedford's turn to sign the amnesty. Mary had to forgive Rizzio's murderers and put the past behind her. Although no one had mentioned Darnley, everyone knew that allowing the Douglases to return to Scotland would signal his demise.

The Queen gave a heartfelt sigh. To put in danger the life of a man she had once loved and who was the father of her son seemed like cowardice to her; but what choice did she have? Darnley, who had now become her enemy, was still at Stirling. What was he plotting against her now? Only a few weeks ago at Craigmillar she had consented to having him apprehended and sentenced for treason. Would a few more dogs hunting in the pack make a difference to the fate of this twenty-year-old boy?

Bothwell kept silent.

'I am ready to forgive them all,' she said in a solemn voice, 'except Kerr of Fawdonside, and George Douglas, who offended against royal majesty by threatening me. But before I do so I wish to know the opinion of the French Ambassador.'

'Monsieur du Croc is in favour of an amnesty.'

'And you, my Lord Bothwell?'

'I too, Madam.'

James was aware that in order to get rid of Darnley a general truce was necessary; he could not disassociate himself from the others and should for a while at least assure himself of their neutrality. For as long as he was gaining power but without being fully in control, he would not consider acting independently. Once Darnley had been eliminated, he would be prepared to collaborate with Moray and Maitland concerning matters

of the realm. He hoped to make lasting allies of Morton and the powerful Douglas family.

The dry weather, which had graced the christening celebrations, had turned
to rain. The next day the Queen would leave Stirling to go to her friend
the Countess of Mar in her Castle of Tullibardine, while James would
spend the festive season with Jean at Crichton. At the beginning of
January, after meeting one last time, the lords would act on the decisions
upon which they had settled.

James did not manage to see Mary privately before his departure.
The extreme caution with which they had to proceed forbade them to
take the slightest risk or to enjoy intimate conversations, which could lead
to suspicion. Mary was torn apart by these restrictions. Her spontaneous
nature encouraged her to express her love and to rejoice in it but this joy
was denied to her. James, who was more in control of his feelings, would
reassure her with a glance, a few apparently innocent words, or the pressure of his hand.

At Crichton Jean asked her husband to join her in her bed and took
trouble to seek his company. Her attitude was changing, but this reversal
of affection, which only a few months earlier he would have welcomed,
now left him unmoved.

4I

My sweet love,

Having realised the likely consequences of the pardon granted to the Douglases, the King has departed in great haste to take refuge in Glasgow with the Earl of Lennox his father. Be at Stirling as quickly as possible. We will meet at Lady Reres' apartment. I can wait no longer for the joy of being yours, body and soul.

BOTHWELL CRUMPLED THE piece of paper and threw it into the fire. A short distance away Jean was leaning over her needlework, with her favourite water spaniels lying at her feet. On the previous night, he and his wife had shared the same bed. 'The King is in Glasgow,' he told Jean, who looked up. 'The Privy Council is soon to convene at Stirling.'

Darnley's flight was a disaster. The plan, which had been so carefully worked out, was now falling apart. The Earl of Lennox was not short of supporters, and if he involved them in his son's intrigues then the Queen, and particularly the young Prince, would be in danger. James realised that a decisive game of chess had begun and it was his and Mary's future that was at stake.

The Queen was waiting for him at Lady Reres' apartments. The dark circles under her eyes and her paleness and agitation betrayed a state of extreme anxiety, and it was well into the night before James managed to calm her down. He told her there was no use in tormenting herself but it was vital to find out what Darnley was plotting and make him come out into the open. These two objectives would not be easy but they were not impossible.

'You will have to go and see the King,' Bothwell urged her. 'Tell him you want to make up your differences, speak nicely to him and don't reproach him for anything. Reason like a spouse who is trying to make sense of a disconcerting situation. Darnley is conceited and eager to please. Don't underestimate your powers of persuasion.'

The Queen smiled at Bothwell. Only he knew how to restore her trust and awaken her fighting spirit. The year 1567 which had only just begun would be the year when her authority and her love life would both triumph. Before long the one who held her in his arms would be her husband. Together they would share the burden of power and the joys and worries of a husband and wife.

'I have just restored judicial powers to the Archbishop of St Andrews,' Mary announced suddenly. 'He will now be in a position to declare the dissolution of my marriage and of yours. If proof of the King's betrayal can be established, then the breakdown of our union will not result in my child's illegitimacy.'

James was lying on his stomach, with one arm wrapped round Mary. Knowing that he had made her happy, he wanted to enjoy this moment to the full and smell the intoxicating fragrance of her hair spread over the pillow beside him.

'Stay away from the Privy Council.' Mary warned him. 'No one at Stirling has seen you, and your appearance early in the morning on a fresh horse would arouse suspicions. At break of dawn go to the Setons' residence and I will send for you officially. We will convene another Privy Council meeting in a few days' time.'

Their lips brushed against each other.

'Do you have any other orders for me, Madam?'

Events were moving fast. The Earl of Bedford had left for London, ready to give a detailed report to Queen Elizabeth concerning the difficult situation in which Mary Stuart found herself, and informing her of the plots which he sensed were afoot in Glasgow as well as in Stirling.

Darnley had arrived at his father's residence stricken with a high fever and had immediately taken to his bed. Doctors were summoned to his bedside, and seeing him disfigured by pustules had diagnosed the pox. Purged and bled the King lay seriously ill. The Earl of Lennox, who suspected poison, was in a state of alert, and from a distance followed his daughter-in-law's every move. He had now come to detest her, and resolved that as soon as he recovered his health his son should strike quickly and forcefully by abducting their child and dictating terms.

On the day following the departure of the English emissary the Earl of Bedford, the Privy Council convened anew. All were present except for Maitland, who was on the eve of his marriage to Mary Fleming, the third of the Queen's Marys to be wed. Unanimously the Lords confirmed the necessity of getting the King back to Edinburgh as soon as possible.

As soon as the Council adjourned, the Queen decided to travel without delay to Glasgow, where she planned to persuade her husband to return with her. Despite the likely objections of the Earl of Lennox, she hoped the promise of resuming their conjugal relationship would be sufficient to sway him.

The lords had listened in silence to their Queen while she reaffirmed her will. She stipulated that nothing should be undertaken which might jeopardise her honour. She wanted only to obtain an annulment of her marriage without compromising the legitimacy of the baby Prince, and she wished no harm to Darnley, to whom she had just sent her doctor Monsieur Arnault. The dull tone of Mary's voice betrayed the effort she was making to overcome her nervous tension. Several times her eyes dwelt on her half-brother and then on Bothwell, as if she was looking for a sign or some kind of encouragement. However, Moray did not utter a word, and James was adamant he would not give the lords the satisfaction of noticing any sign of intimacy between him and the Queen. He was setting off the next day for the Borders and did not know whether he would manage to have a private conversation with her before he left.

As he was about to leave the Council chamber Bothwell was surprised to be stopped by Moray, who normally avoided him.

'Go to Whittingehame Castle tomorrow,' he said to him in muffled tones, 'Morton and Maitland will be waiting for you there.'

Maitland due to his recent marriage, and Morton because he had been temporarily banished from court after his pardon, had not taken part in the Council.

'Will I receive a formal invitation?' asked James in similar tones. 'Do you mean to say you don't trust me, my Lord Bothwell?'

The Bastard's scornful look exasperated James.

'The matter they wish to speak with you about concerns the King,' Moray explained. 'As soon as he is back in Edinburgh we will have to take action.'

'This is assuming Her Majesty succeeds in persuading him to leave Glasgow.'

'I am confident she will succeed,' Moray assured James. 'I am sure you will be able help her find the right words to persuade Darnley. You have influence over her do you not?'

The following day as James was about to mount his horse to ride to Whittingehame before continuing on to Hermitage, French Paris arrived bringing a letter for him. The Queen had personally asked James the favour of taking the young Frenchman into her service. She placed absolute trust in his discretion and only he could play the role of intermediary.

He handed over the letter with an artful smile on his lips.

'What a pity you were not here this morning to dry our sovereign's tears!'

Bothwell was on the verge of going up to Mary's antechamber to have a brief audience with her, but the words uttered by Moray the previous day had made him even more cautious and on his guard.

'Tell her that I kiss her hands and that I will be back as soon as I can.'

Having just passed through the archway that divided the curtain wall of the fortress, James broke the seal on Mary's letter. Behind him, the cobblestones resounded with the clattering hooves of the fifty horses of his mounted escort. He intended to stop only a few hours at Whittingehame, but he was pleased to know that Morton and Maitland were keen to share his points of view.

Stirling, this Saturday

Tomorrow, my Lord, I will leave for Craigmillar with the Prince. Believing these rumours of a plot to be well founded, I will leave him in safe hands before returning to Holyrood, where you will be able to join me. Write to me from the Borders, as not a single hour passes by without my thinking about you. Only the prospect of being relieved of my anxiety gives me the strength to keep going,

but I am so tormented that I am losing sleep. Without you, my dearest love, I have everything to fear from the future. Hurry back, as I need your advice concerning this difficult journey to Glasgow. However, I am determined to go. Lennox's plotting cannot be allowed to continue. Do not forget me while you are at Hermitage. When you were fighting for your life there, I spent the most anxious hours of my life. If there was any moment when I became fully conscious of my love for you, it was then. Your death would have caused my own...
Love me as I love you.

It was such a beautiful day that the Earl of Morton took his guests to the wooded park that surrounded the old Castle of Whittingehame. The sky was almost cloudless, and beyond the woods the rocky outcrops on the hills were clearly outlined. The three men walked along beside a small stream that meandered between clumps of bushes, flowing over boulders worn smooth by the current.

A little further on they came to an open space, where some bottles of wine and glasses had been placed on a wooden table surrounded by plain benches.

Morton raised his glass and gave the toast,

'Let us drink to the success of our enterprise!' His flaming red hair and beard accentuated his harsh features and wily expression. On his guard and watchful, Bothwell raised his glass.

'The die is cast!' Maitland exclaimed. 'What we decided at Craigmillar last November must be carried out. I have information from a reliable source that Darnley is in the process of passing himself off as a champion of Catholicism in order to obtain the support of the Pope and the King of Spain. The rumour that the Queen is planning a counter-attack is beginning to be spread among the courts of Europe. It would be a miracle if news of this had not yet reached the Lennoxes.'

'Her Majesty the Queen is about to travel to Glasgow,' said Bothwell. 'She will bring the King back to Craigmillar.'

Morton, who had listened with increasing interest, turned his gaze on Maitland.

'I understand, my Lords, that your intention is to arrest Darnley for treason and to divest him of his dignity of Kingship in order to bring him to trial. However, the Douglases will never be satisfied with a mere internment or banishment. Darnley has betrayed his own kind. In Scotland this sort of crime deserves its just punishment.'

Bothwell put his glass down.

'Do you mean to say, my Lord, that the King must die?'

Bothwell's thoughts were racing through his head. Would he and Mary not benefit from Darnley's death?

'I cannot take part in this plot,' he said in a non-committal tone, which left the door open for discussion.

'We only ask for your approval, my Lord. The Douglases do not need assistance from anyone else to take the law into their own hands.'

'What do you think, Maitland?' asked Bothwell.

'The interests of our country come before those of the Lennoxes,' was all that Maitland replied.

The table at which they were seated was situated in a meadow that sloped gently down to an enclosure where a small flock of black-faced sheep were grazing.

'Someone must persuade Darnley to refuse to stay at Craigmillar. He would be too well protected there.'

'Are you jesting?' interjected Bothwell. 'The King will be sure to suspect a trap.'

Morton chuckled.

'Not necessarily; what if he chooses another abode himself?'

'And who would be able to convince him to do that, my Lord?'

Taking small sips, Morton finished the contents of his glass. James saw on his face an expression of ferocious joy.

'Somebody whom Darnley trusts completely and who is also our ally. He could encourage this conceited youth to be the one to strike the first blow... all we would have to do then would be to retaliate.'

For the first time, James had a vision of Darnley being killed. His thoughts were confused and in turmoil.

'I thank you for your trust,' was all he managed to say, 'but remember that at Craigmillar we promised the Queen not to use violence against her spouse.'

'Would you consider yourself a virtuous knight of the true cause, my Lord?' mocked Morton in stinging tones.

42

My sweet love,

An informer has just broken the news to me that the King is preparing to seize the Isles of Scilly and the fortress of Scarborough, two strategic posts for the English. Such acts of hostility will totally undermine the future of the cordial relationship which I strive to maintain with my cousin Elizabeth, and would deprive me of any chance of one day succeeding her on the throne of England. As planned, I will set off for Glasgow the day after tomorrow, and I beg you to return to Holyrood as quickly as possible. Without your strength, your love, and the devotion you have always shown me, it would be very hard for me to undertake this tedious and difficult journey.

JAMES SET OFF FOR Edinburgh immediately. Since his conversation with Morton and Maitland, he had been overwhelmed by feelings of anxiety mingled with elation. It was obvious that the bond uniting him with Mary was partly out in the open, and he had not attempted to deny anything. Did the lords intend to support him or oppose him? For the time being they had a common cause, but once the jack was out of the box, would they be able to keep it under control?

During his long ride on horseback through the Borders, James had wondered about the identity of the double agent to whom Morton had alluded. Very soon, he had started to suspect James Balfour, a relative of Darnley known by the name of Balfour the Blasphemer. Starting out as a Catholic, he had become a Protestant and had taken part in the siege at St Andrews castle. After the murder of Cardinal Beaton, he had cleverly re-converted to Catholicism. He had made a good name for himself as a lawyer, and was also involved in very profitable religious matters, occasionally acting as a judge. Flexible, pleasant and cultured, he was friendly towards all, had no respect for keeping his word and no real attachments. His two brothers were not much better.

The moor was covered with a thin coat of frost, making the tough dry grass glisten and the horseshoes echo on the hard ground. The water in the peat bogs had frozen solid and the moss crunched underfoot. An eerie silence reigned over the hills, and high in the sky soared birds of prey. The Palace of Holyrood seemed a world away, yet James knew he could not dally long in the Borders. A kind of venom seemed to be coursing through his veins, relentlessly driving him on towards the Queen and the pursuit of power. As for the designs of those who wished to eliminate Darnley, he knew that although he would not become involved with them, neither would he oppose them.

James had only just arrived back at Holyrood when he had a premonition that by returning of his own accord he was inexorably sealing his destiny. The Queen, looking wan and feverish, received him immediately and as soon as Lady Reres left, threw herself into her lover's arms.

'This anguish is killing me,' she confessed in a broken voice.

She desperately wanted to be reassured and loved.

The intense pleasure of physical love calmed Mary, and she lay on the bed in a state of abandon and euphoria.

'Let us go to France, you and I,' she whispered to him. 'Let us flee this violence and escape the stench of death. As Queen Dowager, I would have a substantial income over there. Let us hide away in a chateau and lead a happy life together.'

The Queen did not expect any reply. The strength of a dream was enough to sustain her. With the passing of time France, which she had so cruelly missed, had become for her a symbol of a paradise lost.

'Let us fight,' James answered. 'You and I are the conquerors. You are the Queen. Give your orders and if they are not obeyed, be ruthless.'

'Write to me every day when I am in Glasgow.' Again Mary sought James's mouth to kiss him. James thought about Jean alone at Crichton, stiffened with this pride of hers, which after she distanced herself from him was now inciting her to demand her rights. Now she had lost him forever.

At the break of dawn, Mary was ready to leave. James would accompany her as far as Lord Livingstone's castle where she would spend the night, then he would ride on with all speed to Hermitage. He was confident Mary would play her part to perfection. Seductive, persuasive, tender or dominating, she would know how to give Darnley the illusion she still loved him and wanted to give him a second chance. Under her spell, the King would stand up to his father, who would without doubt try to keep him from leaving with Mary. Once Darnley was on his way things would happen very quickly. If the Douglases were out for revenge, there was no need for James to intervene. He had promised the Queen legal action; the rest did not concern him.

At Callander, the fief of the Livingstones, James with a heavy heart bade the Queen farewell in pouring rain. He watched the little procession as they vanished into the distance, seemingly engulfed in torrents of water.

Having arrived from Glasgow in a state of exhaustion, French Paris handed James Mary's first letter. She reproached him for not having sent her a message to reach her as she settled in. However, all was going well. Darnley was in a good mood, almost amorous, and she felt reassured. She needed his support, advice and encouragement, and begged him to write as soon as possible.

Bothwell's hand, which was about to commit the piece of paper to the flames, stopped in mid air. The Queen's letters might serve as surety in the future. Could it be that Lennox was planning some treachery? Or that the Douglases' revenge might be misrepresented as the royal will? So many people were working behind the scenes that it was difficult to distinguish between friend and foe.

James had in his chamber a precious silver casket bearing the initials of King François II, a recent gift to him from Mary. Without further hesitation, he opened the security lock and deposited the letter inside.

Almost every day a new message arrived from Glasgow for James. Mary was staying at the Palace of the Archbishop, her ambassador in London, and went daily to her husband's bedside. Gradually she was coaxing him into admitting that if he wanted to live by her side he should follow her to Edinburgh where affairs of the realm were being attended to. She could no longer remain in Glasgow and had arranged a litter for him so that he might travel comfortably all the way to Craigmillar Castle, where a pleasant apartment had been made ready for him. There in her care he could complete his convalescence. She was surprised by the young King's lack of resistance. She should have felt pity for him, but her heart was no longer capable of compassion. In fact, Jean and Darnley are quite alike, she thought. Both self-centred and lacking in imagination, they make use of those to whom they are attached with a childish egotism.

James was uncomfortable with Mary's criticism of Jean. Mary was jealous and possessive, and having at one time considered Jean to be a friend, now held nothing but contempt for her. A hundred times, he had had to reassure Mary that he no longer touched Jean, and a hundred times again, she had made him swear it. The very thought of them sleeping under the same roof together was unbearable to Mary. Being equally jealous of the over-familiar attitude the Queen adopted towards her male entourage, James protested. If Mary loved him as she claimed, she should always keep her distance from other men.

After deciphering the Queen's letters, which were often long and written in haste, James tried to understand the young King's motivations. He was perturbed by his docility as well as by the silence of his father, who kept to his room under the pretext of suffering nosebleeds. The Regent Marie de Guise had long ago warned him against Matthew Lennox, saying that he was a hypocrite and a traitor. How could Lennox be fooled by this revival of affection from a daughter-in-law in whom he had lost all trust?

French Paris had made several journeys back and forth between Glasgow and Edinburgh bearing letters and a few presents; a bracelet for her lover braided by the Queen with her own hair, and a stone pendant on which tears and bones had been painted, symbolising her death and everything that was not their love. The last time he had seen him the servant had reported that Darnley was ready to leave, but that Lennox was still nowhere to be seen. With greater verbosity, he had waxed lyrical over the forthcoming marriage of Bastien Pages, the Queen's page from the Auvergne, to Christina Hogg, her favourite chambermaid. The Queen had promised to attend their wedding celebrations, which were to be held at Holyrood. Paris added that despite the pain in her side from which she suffered the Queen looked well. Urged on by Bothwell who wanted to know more, the servant finally admitted the Queen was extremely nervous, and slept little and poorly. If I dared mention it, he hinted, I would say to your Lordship that she has left behind her raison d'être. James smiled.

Bothwell was counting the days. Mary should be leaving Glasgow, and together with Darnley be on her way to Linlithgow where they would spend the night. A mixture of sleet and snow was falling. The Earl had twice been to Craigmillar to make sure everything was ready to receive the King. The doctors had assured him that a week of treatment, especially the baths, would be sufficient for the patient to recover. The countdown had now begun.

'I have been looking for you since yesterday, my Lord.'

The mud-spattered messenger who had just joined James was tired out. He had just galloped all the way from Linlithgow to Edinburgh then on to Craigmillar, before heading down to the Borders. The message was creased and wet from the rain. Feverishly James broke the seal. Mary wrote that Darnley was refusing to settle in at Craigmillar. James Balfour had offered him a house belonging to his brother Robert at Kirk o'Field, close to the Hamiltons' residence. Abutting the town wall, the property was located in a quadrangle, at the centre of which stood the ruins of an old church. Some pleasant houses surrounded this well-situated, quiet and respectable square, which was not far from Holyrood. This proposal had appealed to the King and nothing now would change his mind. Mary was waiting impatiently for James's instructions, and insisted that he come to meet her. Burn this letter as soon as you have read it, she said. James had his horse saddled immediately and galloped northwards. As he rode, he tried to make sense of Darnley's choice, which no doubt had been suggested by Balfour. Did he have wind of the plot? If this were the case, he would have returned at once to Glasgow to place himself under his father's protection. Did he wish to be closer to Holyrood Palace, and if so for what reason?

Edinburgh was quiet. Servants were bustling about in the Queen's apartments where she would sleep the next night, unless she preferred to stay at Robert Balfour's house to be near her husband. The little Prince was in good health. His head seemed rather large in proportion to his body, but the baby was vigorous, smiling and inquisitive. Uncertain of the King's intentions James demanded that the child's door be guarded day and night.

Moray and Maitland were waiting for Bothwell to ride to meet the Queen. The day was dull with grey skies and a cold wind. The Bastard and the Secretary of State commented only briefly on Darnley's rejection of Craigmillar in favour of Kirk o' Field. Moray seemed to be waiting for something before giving his opinion. Only a short distance from Kirk o' Field, the Douglases were lying low in their town residence.

'You are looking rather despondent, my Lord!' Maitland commented in a voice in which Bothwell detected a hint of irony.

The two men were complete opposites. James's almost brutal honesty contrasted with Maitland's ambivalence and the former's impulsive nature clashed with the latter's subtlety and cunning, a trait that James considered unbecoming in a gentleman.

'Who could claim at this moment that we have an occasion to celebrate? You perhaps, my Lord Secretary?' replied Bothwell.

Moray held up his hand to calm the protagonists. His face was an expressionless mask and forbade any question or remark. Despite James's hostility towards the Queen's half-brother, he could not bring himself to feel contempt for him. Had he been a legitimate child Moray might have made a good King.

'In due course we will discuss the new situation in which we find ourselves,' he said in a calm and almost indifferent tone. 'Morton, Argyll and Huntly, will be informed.'

Moray pulled up the collar of his voluminous riding cloak against the fine but penetrating rain. Bushes and trees were being blown sideways by gusts of wind, bearing the scent of the wet earth. James, who was riding behind Moray, looked at his broad shoulders and head held high. Of whom should he be most wary; the King, or this formidable man? Suddenly The Bastard slowed his horse to let James catch up and ride beside him. With a faint smile he said,

'The Queen trusts us, you and I. Notwithstanding the differences which divide us, it is her interests as well as those of Scotland which concern us, do you not agree?'

43

JAMES GAZES AT the bundle of clean clothes they have just thrown onto his bed. For a long time now, they have neither dressed him nor talked to him. Each day he paces again and again round his room, ten steps to the right, ten steps to the left, on and on, or else he sleeps. He is like a caged wild animal. As he touches the coarse material James remembers the fine clothes he used to wear, the doublets of precious fabric, gold chains and embroidered baldrics. When he was at her court Mary wanted him to be as well dressed as the most elegant courtiers. In order to have clothes made for him she had given him sumptuous fabrics and antique vestments in which silk and gold thread were intertwined with intricate perfection. He, whose greatest pleasure was to ride his horse across the open moors in all weathers and feel the wind on his face, learned to appreciate shirts of fine linen with pleated collars, velvet slippers, deer-skin gloves and caps adorned with exotic feathers. When he fled from Scotland James remembers he had had a few trunks sent containing his most valuable possessions. The ship transporting them had been separated from the rest of the flotilla and had never reached Norway. What had happened to the ship? Did she sink in the storm? Was her cargo sold at auction? The prisoner does not care. His past stopped belonging to him long ago; he has no possessions, no friends, no lovers and no honours. His mother is dead, and only the Queen, his sister Janet, Janet Beaton his former mistress and perhaps Jean, will still remember him. Nevertheless, their memory of him is of an attractive man, a gentleman, who has ceased to exist.

James takes off his shirt made stiff by sweat and dirt, and puts on the fresh one they have given him. His muscles have wasted away, he likens his arms to dead branches, and his ribs protrude like those of an old horse led to the slaughterhouse. The one-time athlete has become a dried up cadaver. His fingers, crippled with arthritis, struggle to do up the wooden buttons. French Paris, Gabriel and his other servants used to dress him quickly and competently. While they busied themselves tying cords, pulling up stockings and fastening the often minuscule buttons of mother-of-pearl, silver, ebony or ivory, he would read his correspondence, dictate a letter, or listen to a visitor. A barber would come to shave him and trim his moustache. James thinks about French Paris. How did he die? James believes they subjected the young Frenchman to long-drawn-out torture. After his defeat at Carberry Hill, his faithful servant had followed him. Together they had landed in Norway and been transferred to Denmark. However, in Copenhagen Moray had had the Frenchman abducted and taken back to Scotland. James knows that beyond a certain degree of suffering a man will confess to almost anything. French Paris had given a positive answer to all the judge's questions. Moray had been satisfied and relieved. A dead man does not go back on his statements.

Most of those brave enough to defend James were tortured and executed.

He who always tried to avoid being a loser has now become a victim. His fate horrifies him. He will continue to fight back, to contest and confront until his very last breath. Here at Dragsholm they fear his violent temper. He still lives. Even if King Frederick ignores him he remains a thorn in his side, just as he disturbs those others who are still alive after the tragedy of Kirk o' Field: Morton and the Balfours... and they do know the truth of what happened there.

Bothwell puts on the breeches and lanoline-oiled woollen stockings. Since the previous day, his chest has been torn by a searing cough like the one he had thought he would die from two years ago. At that time, a servant told him they had even ordered an oak coffin to be made for him. This apparent act of consideration had only served to infuriate him. Is this how King Frederick intends to salve his conscience? Does he think that by spending a few pounds on his burial he will erase the shame of having held James prisoner for over a decade? Or excuse his cowardice in always refusing to receive him whom he used to consider a friend?

Had it not been for the personal intervention of the King of France he would have handed James over to Lennox.

Now the sun is rising higher in the sky, James knows that winter is coming to an end. Will he still be alive for the arrival of spring? In the Lothians near Crichton and Hailes, the meadows will become verdant again. Catkins and pussy willows will replace the first buds, tender new leaves will clothe the trees in green, and birdsong will fill the air. James clenches his fists. He does not want to think about Scotland. His memories torture him more than the cold, his solitude, or his illness. If only he could rest at Crichton...

The plaintive cries of seagulls herald a storm. James crouches beside the peat fire and stretches out his distorted fingers to the flames. He who believed himself to be brave cannot muster the courage to set his clothes alight, thereby regain his freedom through death, and finally go home forever.

44

IN ORDER TO accommodate the King, furnishings including a bed, some tapestries, carpets, counterpanes, curtains, furniture and toiletries were hastily transported from Holyrood. Before the arrival of the royal cortege, the Old Provost's Lodge where he would stay had become a hive of activity. In the kitchens, the cook Bonkil was preparing his cauldrons and pots and pans, harassing the kitchen assistants and turnspits, and upbraiding the kitchen maid. In the event that their Lordships wished to eat, they would have to start roasting poultry, blanching vegetables, whipping creams, stirring sauces and heating up a basin of oil for the apple doughnuts and fritters. A room on the ground floor had just been made ready for the Queen and another on the first floor for the King. Four servants toiled to carry upstairs the copper bath in which Darnley would be immersed each day in order to complete his treatment. Two apothecaries had been sent for to assist Mary Stuart's personal doctor Monsieur Arnault.

Darnley, wearing a taffeta mask to conceal the pustules on his face, dragged himself up the narrow staircase supported by Taylor, his valet. A welcoming fire crackled in the hearth of his chamber, his bed had been warmed and the lighted candles filled the room with a pleasant aroma of beeswax. A gallery, resting on the old town wall, and added at a later date to the house, extended but darkened the chamber. The other window faced east. A few chairs had been placed around the bed so that the Queen and some of her nobles could converse with the patient.

'I hate this bed!'

The King's sulky voice irritated Mary, who did her best to conceal her impatience.

'We will have your own bed brought over from Holyrood tomorrow,' she reassured him, 'as well as any other piece of furniture or anything else you may wish to have here with you.'

Bothwell observed with some contempt this twenty-year-old young man, who had spent his short existence demanding, criticising, whining and betraying. Adored and spoilt by his mother Margaret, niece of Henry VIII, Darnley had been brought up to believe that he was the most handsome and brilliant of men. Married at eighteen to the Queen of Scotland, who was also Queen Dowager of France and niece of Henri de Guise 'the Scarred', adulated by France, his ambitions had become insatiable. To the Lennox family, who were involved in a bitter dispute with the Hamiltons over their hereditary rights, obtaining the Crown Matrimonial was crucial. On no account would Darnley renounce it.

Bothwell could not dispel the uneasiness he had been feeling for the past few days. His instincts as a battle commander warned him of some hidden danger. Darnley had followed his wife without any show of resistance and was now here in Edinburgh, deprived of the Lennoxes' protection and vulnerable to his enemies' attacks. Did he not realise the Douglases had sworn to seek vengeance? Had the rumour of the conspiracy plotted by the Lords not reached him? Seemingly carefree and frivolous, he demanded mulled wine, an additional quilt and rosewater to wash his hands.

'Stay with me tonight,' he asked Mary suddenly, 'I want to have you near me.'

The Queen had had the ground floor chamber modestly furnished; a bed with green and primrose curtains, a table, an armchair and a walnut cabinet with carved reliefs of palms and cherubs. However, her maids had nowhere to stay the night except in the narrow vestibule.

'Maybe,' she acquiesced.

Mary refused to think of the serious events that were about to take place, but it had become vitally necessary to her that this dangerous man should be put out of action. All the same, she was still sometimes reminded by a fleeting expression or an attitude, of the suitor whom only eighteen months previously she had adored. From the time of their first encounters, she had deliberately ignored his self-conceit and vain pride, which she had mistaken for high-mindedness, and she had been smitten by her cousin. Tall, slender, elegant and witty, he seemed to possess all the right qualities, including that of being a close relative of the Queen of England. This beautiful house of glass had been shattered to pieces when James Hepburn returned from exile in France. James had always affected her emotions, but his brusqueness, aversion to compliments and courtly conversation, and easy success with women provoked her. All those around her seemed in agreement that he was an ambitious and crafty opportunist, and for a time she had abandoned him to his enemies.

George Gordon and James Hepburn had insisted on spending the night at Kirk o' Field. It was out of the question that the Queen should stay on her own only in the company of her maids, Darnley, and his five young and unarmed servants. Some guards would be sent there from Holyrood, but being right up against the city wall the house was vulnerable. Along the length of the wall ran narrow dark closes, potential havens for cut-throats, and in the vicinity stood humble cottages, which could serve as refuges for ruffians in the pay of the Lennoxes.

James was annoyed at being obliged to spend the night at Kirk o' Field, as he wanted to speak to Moray, Maitland and Argyll as soon as possible. There was little time for them to carry out their plan. The doctors had advocated another ten days of complementary medical treatment before the patient could be declared fully recovered. As early as the tenth or eleventh of February the King would be allowed to return to Holyrood where he would find the little Prince. This possibility was not to be entertained.

James paced back and forth. Between his frequent visits to the convalescent with the Queen's retinue, and Moray's continuing evasiveness about setting a time for a new meeting, James's anxiety intensified. He now had only five days left at his disposal. The baths administered to the King had healed his sores and the scabs were starting to drop off. Darnley now sometimes removed his mask when in the company of his close friends. Contrary to earlier statements diagnosing the pox, Darnley had probably contracted syphilis during his excesses in England and Scotland. Mary had escaped contagion only by reducing the frequency of her sexual relations with the King, and above all thanks to divine protection.

Jean had joined her husband at Holyrood and was maintaining her position with dignity. She had given up pretending to be in love and was sharing his bed with indifference. She no longer spoke to him in loving or reproachful terms, but enjoyed discussing projects she had in mind for making the best use of the estate revenues, and her enthusiasm brought colour to her cheeks.

Finally, on the fifth of February James received a message from Morton. He was awaiting him forthwith.

The head of the Douglases was patiently waiting for James in a study adjoining his chamber. With him were James Balfour, George Douglas, who was still supposed to be in exile in England, and Archibald Campbell, a close relative of the Earl of Argyll. The room was lit by feeble rays of sunshine piercing through the clouds.

'I will come straight to the point,' began Morton, looking at his guests one after the other. 'Sir James Balfour here has just given me some extremely important news. In a moment he will answer any questions you wish to ask him, but before that, you need to know that the King has decided to make the first move. As was unfortunately likely to happen, Lord Darnley has had intelligence of our intention to arrest him. Under his father's advice, he feigned docility by accepting to return to Edinburgh and only refusing to be installed at Craigmillar. He confided in Sir James, who offered to put at his disposal the Old Provost's Lodge, which he owns. The cellar there is packed full of gunpowder destined to kill the Queen together with those of us who never leave her side. Darnley is planning to leave Sir James's house before the explosion takes place, to go to Holyrood to abduct his son and then join the Earl of Lennox at Linlithgow, from where they will return to Glasgow. Being the Prince's governors, the King and his father the Earl of Lennox would rule Scotland until the Prince's majority. With the support of the Pope and the King of Spain Catholicism would then return and with it, civil war.'

The little group stood horrified and dumbstruck. Finally James Balfour spoke:

'Be assured my Lords, the decision to reveal the conspiracy of the King and his father was a difficult one to take. Nevertheless, His Majesty's intentions are so malevolent and detrimental to our country that my conscience dictated my present actions. I did indeed consent to large quantities of gunpowder being transferred during the course of last night into the cellar of my brother's house, which is next door to mine. I acted out of obedience to the King, but I realised that my loyalty to him is in fact a perverse emotion. Our Queen is not flawless, but she is our Queen.'

Bothwell, Douglas and Lord Archibald looked at each with amazement.

'The Queen must not set foot in Kirk o' Field again!' James said emphatically.

'On the contrary, my dear friend,' Morton declared, 'we must keep to our normal schedule. Her Majesty has already spent two nights in the same house as her husband. She has shown willing to stay with him, and this effort is sufficient to allow for her nocturnal absence from now on. However, during the day, she must visit Lord Darnley punctually. Besides on no account should the Queen be warned of her husband's intentions. She is easily upset and suffers from weak nerves, and she could awaken his suspicions.'

'Without a candle or coals, gunpowder is not dangerous,' George Douglas asserted, as though trying to put Bothwell's mind at rest concerning the risk incurred by Mary Stuart. 'It is not contained in barrels but is scattered in drainage trenches along the walls and in between the cracks of the stonework.'

The window of the small study looked onto an area of fallow land, and just visible beyond was the roof of a farmhouse from where chimney smoke curled skywards. There were few trees, and no animals grazed in the frost-covered meadows.

'We are going to smoke out the badger,' said Morton in a resolute voice. 'Darnley wants to keep her Majesty with him during his last night at Kirk o' Field. He is prepared to act like a child and plead, and we all know the Queen is kind-hearted. He plans to sneak out just before the explosion.'

'What do you want from me?' James asked abruptly.

'That you take part in our plan. We will need a key to the Queen's chamber. It should be easy for you to obtain a duplicate from French Paris. During the course of the evening of the ninth of February, when Her Majesty leaves Kirk o' Field for Holyrood to attend the wedding festivities of her head page Bastien Pages, one of your men will have to scatter gunpowder beneath the King's bed. As the King's bed is located exactly above the Queen's, we will thus be certain he does not escape the explosion. Your role, my friend, will be simply to provide a small quantity of explosives, obtain the key and deposit your powder horns under the ground floor bed.'

'The gunpowder is at Dunbar,' James replied, 'I would need two days to get it.'

'Is there not a small quantity at Edinburgh Castle or at Holyrood?'

Bothwell held Balfour's wily gaze. Where had this man found enough explosives to blow up his house?

'I will use the same source as you, Sir James'.

'Unfortunately my supplier has run out, but they assure me there are one or two small barrels left at Holyrood.'

'Probably,' James admitted.

It was not the time to quarrel with Balfour, but to free Scotland from the malicious Darnley.

'On fireworks night,' Morton continued, 'each one of us will send three or four reliable men to Kirk o' Field, in order to quell any outside interference if necessary.'

A servant entered carrying a carafe of wine and cups. A pair of ravens croaked above one of the towers on the city wall.

'Let us drink to our success, my Lords!' Morton toasted.

'What does Moray think about all this?' James asked.

'He will pretend to know nothing about it.'

James was thinking fast. Admittedly, this was an excellent way to get rid of the King, but it all sounded too easy. In his capacity as Sheriff of Edinburgh, it would be his responsibility to lead an enquiry. All the European courts would be shocked by this death, and the consequences could be grave.

'Why use such a spectacular means of eliminating Darnley?' he asked, taking a large sip of claret.

With eyes half-closed, Morton observed James as though he were a venomous snake.

'Because Darnley will be the author of his own death; a fire in the kitchen that was not properly quenched; an inquisitive servant who went down to the cellar with a candle.'

'We will also have to prove that the King had placed explosives in his own house.'

Balfour nodded.

'Anonymous letters, denunciations... everyone is mortal including gunpowder merchants. We will ensure everyone knows about the King's treason and we will rejoice in the intervention of Providence. If Lennox counter-attacks, we will find a way of keeping him away from Holyrood. No one in Scotland apart from his father will mourn Lord Darnley.'

Silence reigned once more. Although the fire was burning merrily in the hearth, the air was damp and icy. It seemed no one wanted to be the first to speak.

'Let us sign a bond to seal our agreement,' said Morton at last. 'Maitland will add his name to ours.'

Thus, we will be bound to each other, thought Bothwell. Although he was determined to go along with the decision that had just been taken, he was extremely worried.

Gabriel his page would ensure that two horses were held ready.

James would be the first to take the road back to Edinburgh.

From the window of Morton's study, George Douglas watched the Earl until he was out of sight.

'Two birds killed with one stone!' he exclaimed, satisfied.

Campbell and Balfour raised their cups.

'To the Earl of Moray!'

45

February, 1567

'I BESEECH YOU TO remain my friend. Tomorrow we will return to Holyrood together. I want to make my entrance by your side,' said Mary as she gently caressed her husband's hair. In a few days time he would be put under arrest, and a certain feeling of pity awoke a trace of tenderness within her. Once the dust had settled and the annulment of their marriage had been declared, she would obtain his extradition to England, where he would join his mother Lady Lennox, who adored him. Being a close relative of Queen Elizabeth and the father of a future King of Scots, he would no doubt one day recover his lost honour.

'I promised Bastien long ago that I would attend his masque, my darling.'

'Do you give preference to a servant over me?'

Only the Queen's eyes betrayed her annoyance. Darnley never failed to say things that riled her.

'He has served me for the past six years and is marrying my most loyal chambermaid.'

'Honour him with your presence for ten minutes, and then come back here. I will be waiting for you.'

Mary sighed. She did not know precisely when the plan hatched at Craigmillar would be set in motion, but she suspected she had little time left to spend with the King. In order to persuade him to come back to Edinburgh she had promised to let him share her bed again, but this possibility did not bear thinking about. From now on, she belonged to the Earl of Bothwell.

'I will do my best,' she whispered.

'You will come back. Give me a pledge that you will sleep beside me tonight.'

Mary removed a ring of enamelled gold from her finger and handed it to her husband.

In the King's chamber James Hepburn and George Gordon were finishing a game of dice, the Earl of Atholl was chatting to the Lords Sempill and Argyll, while lesser courtiers gathered in the large ground floor hall. Outside, the grooms were getting the horses ready, dogs were barking with excitement, and the Lords' servants were lighting the torches. In the kitchens, Bonkil the cook and his assistants had put out the fire, snuffed out the candles, and retired to their quarters for the night.

'I am leaving my guards with you,' the Queen told Darnley, kissing him softly on his forehead.

Her every word and gesture made her feel guilty. Had she not been madly in love with Bothwell she would never have been capable of such falseness.

'I have no need for them.'

'How can I leave you in such an isolated place with no other company but that of your valet and four servants?'

'Who have I to fear, Madam?'

Mary bit her lip. She looked to where the brightness of the torches cast a reddish glow on the windowpanes.

'Un roi ne reste pas seul chez lui comme un vilain.' A King should not stay on his own like a common peasant... In her confusion, Mary had spoken in French.

'What are you afraid of?' Darnley insisted in a cajoling voice.

Mary took the fur-lined cape which Mary Livingstone, Lady Sempill, handed to her.

'As you wish,' she conceded.

Her heart was beating fast. What kind of treachery was afoot? Did Darnley have wind of the plot hatched against him, and was he planning a counter-attack to which an armed guard would be a hindrance? Moreover, why had her half-brother Moray left Edinburgh that very morning, making the excuse of his wife's health? She was not convinced this was the true reason. Whatever conspiracy he might secretly be involved in, Moray was trying to keep his name in the clear, and she was suspicious of his motives.

Thin layers of snow were building up on the frozen ground. Valets and courtiers were thronging around the horses in the torchlight.

'Go now,' James ordered French Paris.

Without any difficulty the Frenchman had been able to have a duplicate made of the key to the Queen's chamber and had brought back two powder horns from Holyrood. All he needed was a moment to lock himself inside the ground floor chamber, open up the leather pouches and scatter their contents underneath the bed.

James was struggling to calm his nerves. Would Balfour be able to provide sufficient evidence of the King's guilt? If he betrayed them once more what kind of enquiry would James then have to lead? However, he had no choice. Such an opportunity to get rid of Darnley would most probably never arise again. The mere fact that the King had planned to murder Mary carried a death sentence with it.

Wrapped in her flowing cape lined with squirrel fur, the Queen was already on her horse. As soon as his servant appeared, James mounted his stallion.

'Mon Dieu!' exclaimed the Queen in cheerful surprise as she stared at French Paris. 'Have you looked at yourself? Where on earth have you been, you are as black as a charcoal-burner.'

As Mary left the ballroom at Holyrood, Bothwell walked up to her with Lord Traquair, the head of her guard. Her heart missed a beat when she saw James; he looked so handsome in his suit of black velvet, embroidered with silver thread.

'We have a matter to discuss with you of the gravest importance, Your Majesty,' said Lord Traquair. Without saying a word, she listened to her officer as he informed her that a conspiracy was being plotted at Kirk o' Field and that on no account should she go back there. For the moment, he was not in a position to give her more details, but he felt able to vouch for its source.

'Perhaps my Lord Bothwell would be kind enough to confirm these suspicions to Your Majesty,' Traquair suggested.

'I thank you,' the Queen managed to say. 'You may go now.'

Mary was in a state of panic.

'Come into my ante-chamber,' she asked James, 'we will have more peace there.'

Striving to appear as calm as possible, Bothwell told Mary that Darnley had hoped to do away with her that very night before abducting the little Prince and joining his father. The King had written some time ago to Lennox, who was waiting for him at Linlithgow.

Mary had to sit down. In what kind of monstrous world did she live? To think that all the while he was cajoling her, her husband had already decided on her death!

Two maidservants and a lady-in-waiting were observing them. She therefore had to maintain her regal composure in the presence of the man she adored.

'By what means did the King intend to eliminate me?' Mary asked in a faint voice.

'By an explosion, Madam, Kirk o' Field's cellar has been filled with gunpowder.'

The young woman put her hand to her chest. She could not breathe and felt she was suffocating.

'Then you would have died too?'

'Probably, along with your closest friends the Lords Huntly and Atholl.'

'And who was the person who warned you?'

'Sir James Balfour, a most despicable man but one to whom we owe a great deal, as he has saved our lives.'

It was now almost one o'clock in the morning. James knew that time was short.

'Go and take a rest, my darling,' he whispered to Mary.

As planned, he would send five of his men to Kirk o' Field as soon as possible to ensure that Darnley would not slip through their fingers. An informer had confirmed that the King had given orders for three of his best horses to be ready from five o'clock in the morning. At the scene, his men would find the men sent by the Douglases, Argyll, Balfour, and perhaps Maitland too. However, James mistrusted the Secretary of State, who hated committing himself to anything irrevocable. To satisfy their honour it had been decided that the Douglases should light the fuse.

James slowly walked back to his apartments where Jean was waiting for him. He would slip between the sheets but would not be able to sleep. When would the explosion take place?

The noise of the blast reverberated through the city and gave the inhabitants of Edinburgh the impression that twenty cannons had been fired simultaneously.

In an instant, the Palace of Holyrood was in turmoil. It took no more than ten minutes before two guards were hammering on Bothwell's door.

'The Old Provost's Lodge has been blown up and demolished,' one of them exclaimed. 'All have been led to believe that His Majesty the King has been slain in the explosion.'

James dressed in great haste. His hands were trembling, as he struggled to fasten the buttons of the doublet which he had taken at random from his wardrobe. He had hardly finished tying the laces of his breeches, when he again heard violent knocking on his door. One of his guards stood on the threshold.

'They are searching the rubble my Lord, and three bodies have been found. There is one survivor, but there is no trace of the King or of Taylor his valet,' he announced to a stunned James.

Mary was shaken by uncontrollable sobbing. Wrapped in her dressing gown, with her hair dishevelled, she paced up and down her chamber. James remembered with consternation that it was almost exactly a year since Rizzio's bloody corpse had been dragged to this very spot.

'Those who committed this barbarous deed thought I was with the King, didn't they? They wanted to kill us all, him, me, and you...'

James gritted his teeth. How could Darnley have fled, and where was he now?

'It is quite possible His Majesty is still alive, Madam. Try to calm down.'

Mary Seton came up to the Queen and took her arm. A maid returned with rosewater, vinegar and some fine linen. Mary dabbed at her cheeks. She was pale and had deep dark circles under her eyes.

'All this violence is destroying me,' she whispered, looking at James, 'I don't think I can bear it any more.'

They heard the sound of tramping boots coming from the main courtyard and echoing in the stairway. There was screaming and shouting, and the neighing of horses.

'You are going through tough ordeals Madam, but you will overcome them.'

The Queen was weeping. James felt that at this precise moment she had lost all hope of happiness. He too was at the end of his tether. This doomed night would remain the worst memory of his life. What were the Douglases and Maitland up to?

French Paris was waiting for his former master in the Queen's reception room. The young Frenchman, normally so cheerful, looked stricken with fear. The Earl hastily led him to a corner of the room where the ladies-in-waiting had gathered. Outside in the dark a fine flurry of snow continued to fall and seemed to dance in the glow of the torches.

'What has happened?' Bothwell urged him.

French Paris extracted a handkerchief from one of the pockets of his breeches, and mopped his brow. Despite the cold, he was sweating profusely.

'There were about fifteen of us standing guard, when George Douglas himself emerged with five of his gentlemen. They ordered us to go away. Their own men had just lighted the fuse, and we warned them of the imminent explosion; in five or six minutes' time everything would blow up. Lord Archibald scaled the city wall and slipped into the King's antechamber. He knocked on one of the panes and I think that Taylor came. Then very quickly, we saw the King in his nightgown rushing barefoot out of his chamber, jumping the wall and fleeing into the garden. After that, I know nothing, as we all ran away.'

'George Douglas...' murmured Bothwell.

Not content with an anonymous death, George wanted to be personally involved. The King's defection after Rizzio's murder could only be avenged face to face, man to man.

James leaned against the wall. How was he to get out of this situation? The King was no longer a murderer caught at his own game, but a victim, and James would have to lead an enquiry in order to find out whether he had been killed and if so, by whom. Some of his own men had been hanging around the house. Had they been identified by neighbours?

The only evidence against me, he thought, is my signature at the bottom of a document and it is alongside those of Morton, George Douglas, Argyll, Maitland and Balfour. The enquiry will come to nothing.

At sunrise James went to Kirk o' Field where he found a scene of total destruction and desolation. There was nothing left of the Old Provost's Lodge belonging to James Balfour. The three mutilated bodies of Darnley's servants were laid out on the ground. A fourth one who had been miraculously spared was waiting for him with a blanket wrapped round him.

'This way my Lord,' directed the Commander of the Watch.

James followed the man into the garden, passed through a small door set into the city wall and arrived in an orchard. On the ground lay the body of the King, with his gown rolled up to his chest, and a little further away the hunched body of Taylor his valet. The King was barefoot and Taylor wore only one slipper and his nightcap.

James stared for a long time at the man lying at his feet. His body bore no mark of injury. Had the Douglases strangled him or smothered him? Lying half-naked on the frozen ground, the dead man seemed young and vulnerable. Is one a man at twenty? Bothwell wondered.

'Take His Majesty's body away,' he ordered, 'and lay it out with dignity in a neighbouring house.'

A crowd began to gather round the Earl.

'Are there any witnesses?' asked Bothwell.

'Nelson the surviving servant, and a few women from the neighbourhood,' the Commander of the Watch replied.

The snow was now turning to rain. A few prowling dogs were chased away by the archers, who threw stones after them. Those people who had been allowed access to the perimeter of the ruins gathered round the large bonfire that had been lit.

Bothwell started by interrogating Nelson, but he had neither seen nor heard anything. He had been asleep and had suddenly woken to find himself astride the city wall, with his shirt torn from top to bottom. As he had been hoping to see the Queen, Lord Darnley had only gone to bed at around one o'clock in the morning, and had asked to be woken at half past four. Together they had sung a psalm. He knew nothing more.

After him, a few over-excited female neighbours had given statements. They had indeed heard a great noise, and had caught sight of numerous silhouettes draped in cloaks. They had all simultaneously been horrified by a heartrending cry: 'Pity me, kinsmen, for the sake of Jesus Christ, who pitied all the world...' then silence had returned. The most talkative of them, Barbara Martin, declared that just before the explosion had occurred she had seen with her own eyes several men running in all directions like rabbits. All James's senses were on the alert. Thus had the Douglases perverted the game. Who could now accuse the King of having filled his cellar with gunpowder in order to destroy his wife before being blown up himself, if he had died smothered or strangled some distance away while trying to escape from this very explosion? The two events were now inextricably linked. The former had been provoked in order that the latter could then be perpetrated.

One of the Douglases had thus been able to warn Darnley that the fuse had been lit, causing him to run for his life. As James was about to dismiss the women, one of them spoke up and said;

'There is something else I should like to tell your Lordship, if it is of any interest. There was a lit candle behind one of the windows of my Lord Hamilton's residence. It was snuffed out just a few minutes before the explosion.' A sign to the Douglases, Bothwell thought. Who else could have involved the Hamiltons in the plot other than Maitland, or even Moray?

James's throat felt dry. Despite his apprehension, he would have to appear calm.

He slowly walked past the fortifications again and entered the garden, where lay scattered mounds of rubble, which only a few hours earlier had been part of Balfour's house. Behind the church, they were already burying the remains of Darnley's three servants.

'Follow me, my Lord,' French Paris whispered in French, 'I have something interesting to show you.'

James pulled up the collar of his cloak. He felt frozen. Approaching the ruins near what used to be the entrance to the kitchen and the cellars, he saw a small barrel that was miraculously still intact.

'There is a marking,' French Paris pointed out.

The torches had been extinguished, and the early morning light was opaque. James leaned forward, and was astounded to see the stamp of Dunbar, of which he was governor.

'Bloody hell!' he cursed.

Whoever had planted this clue involving him in the crime was underestimating him. All trace of fear now left him. It was plain he had determined adversaries. All the better! He was already making plans to defend himself, to counter-attack, and keep the Queen from harm as far as possible. Even if he had to wait a year or more to marry her, nothing would prevent him from taking control of a country torn apart by dissensions.

46

EVERY MORNING JAMES went to Edinburgh Castle, where the Queen had taken refuge with her son. Apart from the four Marys and her two maid-servants, he was the only person to have been granted permission to cross the threshold of the royal chamber. Mary either lay prostrate on her bed or sat sobbing by the fireside, and only came to life when he took her in his arms, trying to reassure her and instil courage into her.

Darnley had just been buried at Holyrood Abbey alongside the other Kings of Scotland. The official enquiry was following its course, but the people of Edinburgh, outraged or shocked by the brutal murder of so young a king, were now beginning to change their attitude towards him. Originating from feelings of pity, sentimentality or rebellion, and in the face of such a premature death, each day that passed Darnley appeared to them more as a victim and a neglected husband. He who had been attempting to extend a hand of friendship to the Holy See was reborn as a young Protestant hero who had been sacrificed by a spouse and pres-surised by the Pope and the French. Several times, an armed force had to be called in to disperse the mob, which gathered at the foot of the castle rock to hurl abuse at the Queen. Had Her Majesty brought the King back from Glasgow only to take him to the slaughterhouse? they cried.

James was well aware of the rumours and accusations, but it was essential to maintain order in the city, and gossip he hoped would fade with the passing of time. With her eyes still filled with tears, Mary raised her head towards James and reached for his lips. He put his arms round her and returned her kiss.

'This is all my fault,' sobbed the young woman.

A hundred times she had blamed herself for being the instrument of

Darnley's death, and a hundred times James had reasoned with her. How could she possibly forget she had been condemned to death by Darnley, and only saved by providence?

He was certain that one day the whole truth would become known.

Mary allowed her lover's words to soothe her, but beneath the pain, James sensed a feeling of panic that she felt unable to put into words.

'An envoy from Queen Elizabeth, Lord Killingrew, has just arrived,' James told her.

'I shall not receive him.'

'You do not have to see him just now. I suspect his brother-in-law William Cecil has sent him here in order to find out who his friends are in Edinburgh.'

Mary's fragile mental state prevented James from explaining that England might well try to find ways to implicate the Catholic Queen of Scots in the murder of Darnley. While serving Marie de Guise he had learned a great deal about English hostility towards any form of Papist power. Queen Elizabeth wished for a united Protestant realm, and thus would never choose Mary as her successor. The Queen's future lay in Scotland. She needed to develop a love for this country, to defend it and be entirely devoted to it, and he was there to help her.

'I shall go to stay with Lord Seton tomorrow,' the Queen announced suddenly. 'I cannot stand it here any longer. I feel I am dying here.'

'I will come with you.'

'You must stay in Edinburgh to guard my son. I want to recover and regain my sense of purpose, so that I can face up to the future with the same courage as you. We need to set up a court of law as soon as possible, and I leave it to you to carry this out. The Earl of Lennox keeps sending me letters demanding that those who are guilty should be punished. I also need to write to my ambassadors, my brother-in-law King Charles IX, my dear Guise grandmother and my half-brother the Earl of Moray.'

'Beware of false friends!' warned James. Moray was diabolically clever. Without having signed anything, he had sneaked away from Edinburgh on the morning of the tragedy to avoid any suspicions concerning his involvement. Now he was probably devising a strategy that would enable him to remove any rivals from his path.

'Find those placards and destroy them!' Bothwell shouted furiously. Early in the morning, still wearing his nightgown, he had been informed that during the night notices had been nailed on the walls of certain public monuments and churches. They listed several names as being those of the King's murderers, and his name featured on most of them. Although James had hoped for lasting peace, the alliance forged with his enemies had already been breached.

'We are already doing so, my Lord.' One of James's cousins handed him a sheet of poor quality paper. Five names were listed on it: the Earl of Bothwell, James Balfour, the lawyer David Chalmers, a John Spens whom James could not remember, and Bastien Pages.

'How absurd!' James exclaimed. 'Bastien was getting married on the night of the murder; everybody saw him at Holyrood, where I was too. The inclusion of his name discredits the slanderer.'

Who was the instigator of this revolting smear campaign? Moray no doubt, the only one to hope to triumph from the disastrous situation in which many nobles now found themselves. Who could denounce whom? Apart from The Bastard, they were all bound by a contract bearing their signatures.

'Go and call on all the printing presses,' James demanded in a harsh voice, 'and interrogate the clerks. It is essential that we immediately put out of action the unsavoury perpetrator of such a calumny.'

The Queen and James wrote to each other daily. The company of the calm and understanding Lord Seton was beneficial to her, Mary assured him, although she was unable to suppress the anguish that tortured her daily. Every morning, she woke up anticipating some terrifying event that never took place. She must have been weeping while writing, because the ink was diluted in several spots.

James resisted the temptation of joining her and stayed in Edinburgh, where he lived in a state of unbearable tension.

A new letter from Mary arrived at the same time as an alarming report from French Paris. During the previous night, a man had run through the Cowgate, Blackfriars Wynd, the High Street, and on to the Netherbow, proclaiming the name of the King's murderer: James Hepburn, Earl of Bothwell.

They needed to double the number of watchmen and infiltrate spies, remunerating them generously. It was vital that scandalmongers should be located as quickly as possible, and compelled to give the name of the man for whom the nocturnal crier was working.

Gradually the suspicion took shape in James's mind that they were trying to bring down the Queen. If such was the case, the names of the sponsors were now becoming clear; Moray and Lennox; the former to grasp power and the latter to avenge himself against his daughter-in-law. In addition, Lennox would try to obtain the Regency until the majority of his grandson, while at the same time double-crossing Moray. The hyenas had been unleashed. To add to James's anxiety, Jean had retired to her bed and was ill with a high fever. Was she tormenting herself over the scandal besmirching their name? She said not a word about it, but the young woman seemed overcome by an immense sadness.

Come and see me at Lord Seton's house, the Queen wrote, *I can wait no longer for the happiness of seeing you. Without you, my enemies will soon get the better of me.*

Mary and James were able to spend one hour alone together in the royal chamber at Seton Castle. He was reunited with her slim, almost boyish, body, delighting in the softness of her skin, her lilac fragrance and the taste of her mouth. In their passion for each other, they barely exchanged a word.

A bright spring light filtered through the windows and the aromatic scent from bowls of sandalwood, dried orange peel and cinnamon sticks permeated the chamber.

'Let us hide away here and never go back out into the world,' Mary whispered, 'or let us leave together and cross the sea... I am sure we will find a place where we can both be happy, you and I.'

James touched Mary's face, and with his finger he wiped away her tears.

'We will be happy here in Scotland. We just need to ride out the storm with patience and steadfastness. Do you not trust your High Admiral?'

Mary forced a smile.

'You will never leave me Jamie, will you?'

Lord Seton's castle was in his image, peaceful and hospitable. Looking down on a small valley, it had a pleasant aspect across open country towards a small village grouped round its church, situated at the edge of the forest.

Two letters came for Mary, one from her Ambassador in London and the other from her father-in-law the Earl of Lennox.

'I have no secrets from you,' the young woman said, as she broke the seal of the letter from London.

Majesty,

I have just obtained an audience with the Comte Moretta during his sojourn in London. He was your guest just before the death of His Majesty the King, and was able to give his report to Sir William Cecil as follows:

I have the impression that the Earls of Moray and Lennox have formed an alliance to avenge the death of the King. The Earl of Moray plans to sway public opinion in order to eliminate the Earl of Bothwell, a very valiant man in whom the Queen places great trust. This is with a view to being in a better position to make an attempt on the life of Her Majesty. Due to the Earl of Lennox's inability to rule over the affairs of the country, he is probably hoping to be granted the charge of governing the Prince, and consequently the entire realm.

I believe it my duty, Madam, to relate to you the words of the Comte Moretta, even though they seem unpleasant to hear. I add that Sir William Cecil does not really credit the accusations naming the Earl of Bothwell as the murderer of His Majesty the King. The result of the enquiry ordered by Your Grace is awaited in London, and it is hoped that very soon, one or several culprits will appear before a court of law.

James and Lord Seton listened to the Queen without interruption as she read the letter out to them, but their faces betrayed their astonishment.

'This is what it has come to,' said Mary. 'A succession of lies, friends who betray me, and the name of my half-brother the Earl of Moray dragged through the mud.'

'Madam,' Bothwell exclaimed, 'I implore you not to protect anyone, not even me! If I must be tried, so be it. Do not cover your eyes. Lord Moray has already betrayed you once, have you forgotten that?'

'He did not like Lord Darnley even then, and he was the only one to advise me not to marry him.'

The young woman's hands were trembling, and Lord Seton feared another crisis of nerves. Several times during her stay, Mary had been overcome by sudden and violent emotions which had left her prostrate.

Despite Seton's presence, James seized Mary's hand and took it to his lips.

'I know you are brave, Madam,' he assured her. 'You must be prepared to fight, and I will always stand by your side.'

In the letter he addressed to Mary, the Earl of Lennox demanded the immediate trial of the man whom public opinion designated as the murderer of his son. Curiously he mentioned neither the Douglases nor the Balfours, but only one name, that of the Earl of Bothwell.

'Forget all this poison,' Seton advised,' and let us go hawking.'

Beyond the pastures, the moor stretched out with clumps of whins growing amongst the stretches of heather and russet-tinted grass. Seagulls blown by the wind were circling in the sky. Wearing her black velvet riding skirt beneath a cloak lined with fox fur, Mary led the way, with Seton and Bothwell on either side of her. The lovers compensated for the need they had to touch one another by letting their horses walk flank to flank. Mary, who had always previously considered herself a chaste woman now found herself overwhelmed with desire. In order to hold on to James she was prepared to sacrifice everything.

Behind them rode some of Lord Seton's friends, and the falconers at the rear completed the party.

'With all due respect, Madam,' Seton suggested, 'tell the Earl of Lennox that you are waiting in Edinburgh for him to appear before the court as plaintiff. This sordid smear campaign must be stopped as soon as possible by a bona fide trial, before your name is sullied.'

James sat up straight in his saddle. In his present state of nervous tension, any double entendre caused him extreme agitation.

'Are you trying to suggest, my Lord, that my name besmirches that of the Queen?'

'That is what the slanderers are implying. By denigrating her close friends, they are indeed trying to compromise Her Majesty,' answered Seton.

'Well then, I will not leave Edinburgh before they render their judgement on me and my name is cleared.'

Mary extended her hand, which James held briefly in his own.

'Your Queen is ordering you to stay by her side. Let us hunt,' the young woman continued, striving to seem cheerful. 'Are we not here to enjoy ourselves? Tomorrow we will play golf.'

No sooner had Bothwell returned to Edinburgh than he was shown a new notice, which had become the talk of the town. A bare-breasted mermaid, designated by the initials MR held a long-stemmed flower in her hand. Below this effigy of a seductress was a hare placed between the initials JH, running in a circle surrounded by dirks pointing outwards. At the base of the placard were written the words: 'Destruction awaits the immoral on whichever side they stand'.

'Good God!' Bothwell cried out. 'Find the author of this abomination, that I may wash my hands in his blood!'

Although none of his relatives or friends had dared refer to the degrading symbol of the hare, an animal always ready to mate, and the mermaid, a creature given to every form of lust, James knew that the whole city was mocking them.

Early the next morning, he would take the young Prince to the impregnable fortress of Stirling, where he would reside from now on under the authority of the Earl and Countess of Mar.

At the Setons' castle at Niddrie James had argued over the wisdom of this decision. Nevertheless, in the Queen's eyes, the child must be sheltered from any future troubles as she herself had been in her childhood days. Moreover, her trust in the Earl of Mar, who up until now had been the governor of Edinburgh Castle, was absolute.

The Queen was in regular correspondence with the Guises. James himself had written to François 'The Scarred' and the Cardinal de Lorraine to beg them to ignore the lies disseminated about their niece and himself. He told them the Queen was bearing with dignity the misfortune that had befallen them.

Preparations were well under way for the journey to Stirling, but James could not cast off the doubts that haunted him. If Mar defected to the enemy, Mary would be in grave danger. Whoever held the heir to the throne had a major asset in his possession. The Earl of Angus had once understood that well when he had held little James v hostage. Yet the Queen's arguments were acceptable. Life should proceed as normally as possible, and at nine months old, the young Prince should have his own house and governor. Furthermore, no one would be able to abduct him from Stirling. She still retained a few memories of her early childhood spent in the fortress. She remembered the steep rock face, the cannons that protected her, the high curtain wall patrolled day and night by guards, and the impressive portcullis blocking the entrance. She had never felt afraid up there.

'I have received numerous pieces of information which I need urgently to impart to you,' Mary whispered to James.

Their horses were walking along at a steady pace. Still very pale, wearing a dress of black serge, with a high collar bordered with silver interlacing fringe and a bonnet lengthened with a veil, Mary had spurred her horse on in order to get ahead of the rest of the cortege making its way to Holyrood.

'I saw that odious placard. Why did you not tell me about it?'

'There is no need to alarm you with obscenities.'

'Did those dirks not mean you would be untouchable under my protection?'

'My men are on the brink of arresting the culprit. Put your mind at rest.'

'My half-brother has told me that he will soon leave Edinburgh for Paris,' Mary continued. 'He plans to stop in London on his way to France.'

Where he will receive William Cecil's orders, thought Bothwell. Once again, Moray was slipping away in order to escape what could be an inextricable situation. In due course, he would reappear in Edinburgh blameless and as white as snow.

As they rode down the High Street, passers-by watched their Queen with unsmiling eyes and with no signs of pleasure. Some of them even openly averted their gaze.

'Could my brother be jealous of you?' Mary asked timidly.

Tears welled up in her eyes at her lover's reply,

'It is you, Madam of whom he is jealous!'

With the Queen once more settled at Holyrood, James immediately went to look for his informers. He was so enraged at Moray's departure that he felt he would have liked to strangle the troublemaker with his bare hands, had he found himself face to face with him. The silence he was forced to keep due to his involvement in the murder of Darnley was sapping his spirits. How could he denounce the Douglases when his own name featured at the bottom of the pact? They had all been sworn to secrecy, and the rottenness generated by this situation was now contaminating the Queen. From now on, he could not wait to be tried and to leave Edinburgh. Who could condemn him? It was a case of an eye for an eye; whoever put him in the pillory would not be far behind him.

'We have the culprit's name,' William Hepburn declared without further ado. 'The few lines he added to his placard gave him away. Do you remember? "Destruction awaits the degenerates, on whichever side they stand." That quotation comes from a book given to Lord Darnley by his uncle the Squire D'Aubigny. Whoever had access to this volume must be well acquainted with the Lennoxes. This certainly helped me narrow it down to just a few names then to only one, that of a talented sketcher and scholarly man; James Murray of Tullibardine.'

'By the Blood of Christ!' Bothwell shouted. 'Bring him here!'

'When we knocked on his door the bird had flown the nest.'

The colour drained from Bothwell's face. Murray of Tullibardine was the brother of the Countess of Mar, to whom the Queen had just handed over the little Prince. The noose around his neck had just tightened by a few more inches.

47

NOTES AND LETTERS were piling up on Bothwell's desk. Now that the date for his trial had been set, he felt somewhat relieved. However, the Queen's state of health did not allow her to leave her bed. Lady Reres had confided in him that she barely ate anything, and that whatever little she ate, she brought up. Under her doctor's orders, her door was closed to all including James.

Jean was feeling better and wished to continue convalescing at Crichton. Not once had she tried to comfort James, nor had she asked for an explanation concerning the odious placard. When they happened to walk past each other, she contented herself with exchanging pleasantries. James felt hurt. Jean had not been happy with him nor he with her, but he had grown to like and admire this young, intelligent and proud woman.

It was already dark when the Earl arrived back in Edinburgh, having escorted his wife to Crichton. The flames of the sparse lanterns illuminating the Canongate flickered in the cold wind. At the last minute, he had been overwhelmed by a desire to remain in the countryside, but eventually he had his horses saddled and set off on the return journey. As he rode away from Crichton, he cast a look back at the massive square tower, flanked by a rectangular crenellated building and pierced by the vaulted entrance archway. The riders descended the hill, passing through woods of larch and juniper and fording the waters of the Tyne, swollen and foam-laden after the rain. Softly contoured hills grazed by sheep stretched away into the distance.

In Edinburgh, a large number of his friends and relatives, both close and more distant, together with his vassals, had come to support Bothwell on the day of his judgement. Faced with those loyal and determined men, nobody would dare to intimidate him.

James, followed by his kith and kin, proceeded at a walk down the

Canongate. Ahead of him was the Palace of Holyrood with its backdrop of steep rocky hills. Torches illuminated the stones of its façade with a golden hue.

The Earl headed for his apartments. A few servants were passing back and forth along the corridors and several ladies-in-waiting sat chatting by the fireside in the small chamber on the south side. When she saw him, Lady Reres stood up immediately.

'The Queen is waiting for you,' she told him.

The chamber was in semi-darkness: the only light came from a candelabrum standing on the Flemish chest of red and silver tortoiseshell placed next to Mary's bed.

'I have not forgotten what you said to me at Niddrie. I am determined we will fight, Jamie.'

Mary's voice sounded resolute. James felt as though the woman of earlier days had returned; she who when six months pregnant had escaped from Holyrood after the murder of Rizzio; the Amazon who had not hesitated to ride sixty miles in bad weather in order to visit him at Hermitage when he was hovering between life and death. He approached Mary's bed. Propped up on pillows she looked at him tenderly.

'Sit beside me,' she demanded.

She extended her hand, which the Earl took in his.

'I have recovered control of myself,' Mary continued. 'I had forgotten who I was.'

Her grave undaunted expression disconcerted Bothwell. Why this meeting at so late an hour?

He sat up straight. It was time to reveal to the Queen the course of action, on which he believed it was most urgent to embark.

'After the ruling, which God willing should acquit me since I do not have the murder of the King on my conscience, I will leave Edinburgh for a while. This resolve has been difficult to make but it is the wisest strategy. Remember Queen Elizabeth accepted the departure of Robert Dudley when his wife was found dead in strange circumstances. With the passing of time, the rumours subsided, and Dudley was able to return to court with his head held high.'

'You are not to leave Edinburgh.'

There was no animosity or childishness in Mary's voice, which showed only great calmness and a royal determination.

'I must,' Bothwell insisted.

Mary leaned towards her lover and kissed his lips softly.

'I am pregnant, Jamie.'

At break of dawn James returned to his apartments. A cold determination had replaced his initial dismay. Mary and he should marry immediately, even at the risk of their honour. However, before this could happen he would have to take a series of urgent measures.

For a long time the Earl lay on his bed, his eyes wide open. This news, which should have been the happiest of his life, could in the circumstances in which he found himself, lead to his ruin. However, like the Queen he also would fight, and once again tempt fate.

The mob thronged the High Street and Canongate all the way to the Tolbooth where the Earl of Bothwell was to be tried that very morning. Already mounted on their horses, a large group of Hepburns waited in front of the Palace of Holyrood, ready to assist their leader. James had not yet appeared. Since the previous day, there had been a rumour that the plaintiff, the Earl of Lennox, would not show up. Several times he had asked for the trial to be adjourned so that he might finish compiling his case, but as he had persistently harassed her for justice to be done, the Queen had denied his request.

The weather alternated between sunlight and shade. Above the hills large clouds blown by the wind rolled across the blue sky; the cobblestones and rooftops still glistened from the rain that had fallen during the night. When the Earl emerged from the Palace, followed by Maitland and his relative James Ormiston, a muted clamour rose from the crowd. Looking dignified and soberly dressed James seemed indifferent to the curiosity he aroused. Without looking around him, he mounted a superb bay stallion, put on his gloves and adjusted his buff-coloured beret, set off by an onyx gemstone. The sunlight that pierced through the clouds lit up his dark eyes, reddish brown hair and elegant moustache. With the splendour of his sword sheath and the jewelled handle of his dirk, he conjured up a memory of ancient Scottish legends in which the hero rode out to vanquish the forces of evil.

As the cortege was about to move off, James turned round and saw the Queen standing at the window of her chamber giving him an affectionate wave. He touched his beret with a finger then spurred his horse into a trot.

He had no more lingering doubts. He knew where he was going and how he would get there. Neither the traps they would lay for him nor the war of attrition he would have to engage in daunted him. Once he became Prince Consort, he would be master of the field of battle.

The soldiers had to disperse the mob gathered in front of the Tolbooth in order to let the riders pass. Servants rushed to catch hold of the horses' bridles while Bothwell, together with his relatives and his friends dismounted. Immediately, his presence and his proud gaze halted the jibes of the crowd. Women stood on tiptoe, craning their necks to get a better view of this man, who was reputed to have bewitched the Queen before murdering her husband, in order to gain complete control over her.

The audience chamber was full to overflowing, and they had to close the doors to prevent curious bystanders from entering. Crushed together on benches within were the fifteen jurors, a great number of nobles and wealthy burghers, and the large group of James's relatives, together with a handful of the Earl of Lennox's friends. Rays of sunshine penetrated the chamber, illuminating the old stone wall, which was plain and unadorned. A few panic-stricken doves fluttered about on the wooden beams above.

'I move for the adjournment of this trial,' the Earl of Lennox's representative, Lord Cunningham, said in an aggressive voice. 'The plaintiff has not been able to collect all the testimonies he wishes to submit to the court.'

The Earl of Argyll who chaired the tribunal, smiled sardonically.

'And yet my Lord, the Earl insisted on the immediate convening of this court, considering it outrageous that so much time had elapsed between the murder of His Majesty and the indictment against his alleged murderer.'

'The Earl of Lennox is not free to act as he would wish,' protested Cunningham. 'The room is packed with relatives of the accused, while the offended party is only allowed ten people to escort him.'

'Such is the law, my Lord. Do you intend to alter it?'

On the previous day, Argyll had spoken to Maitland, who was in contact with the Earl of Moray. At that moment the Earl of Lennox's grievances were not of prime importance.

Cunningham sat down grumbling. For a brief moment silence reigned over the court.

'Please come forward, my Lord Bothwell.'

James managed to suppress his emotion. His trial was only the first hurdle; there would be others just as difficult to overcome.

First, the witnesses for the prosecution came in one by one, followed by those for the defence, the latter in great numbers. No one had seen the Earl around Kirk o'Field on the night of the explosion. The duty watchman stationed that night at the Netherbow Port had let five or six men through claiming to be 'friends of Lord Bothwell.' Would murderers openly have revealed their identity?

James stiffened. The blunder committed by those he had sent to keep watch on the vicinity of Balfour's house had worked in the end in his favour.

The day was getting late. The jurors had listened for hours to the witnesses and were now reading out documents, letters and statements from people who had not been able to travel. A verdict was close. The Earl of Argyll looked at each of the jurors in turn.

'Make your decision, gentlemen.'

James was seated between his cousin William and his lawyer David Chalmers, who had performed brilliantly for him at this trial. Despite tiredness and nervous tension, he appeared calm, and he had decided for the time being not to think about Darnley and his atrocious death. He needed to channel all his strength into the next two months.

'Not guilty, unanimously,' announced Lord Lindsay.

The room echoed with the sound of clapping and cheering from the hundred or so Hepburns who stood up and raised their fists as a sign of victory. As soon as the verdict was pronounced, Cunningham and his supporters slipped away.

According to custom, James faced the courtroom.

'And now, weapon in hand, I defy anyone who dares accuse me of being guilty of the King's death!'

With nightfall, the doves had gone to sleep, and the starkness of the stone walls was softened by the brightness of the torches, which cast flickering shadows over those present. All remained silent. With a telling gesture, James drew his sword out a few inches and replaced it in its sheath with a sharp click. He felt overwrought and had to make an effort to maintain his cool composure. In just a few minutes, he would cross the threshold of Holyrood victorious.

While Mary watched the progress of the cortege headed by her lover, she was handed a letter from her English cousin, and immediately broke the seal to read it. Elizabeth exhorted her to let justice be done and to spare no one, not even those dearest to her, in order to preserve her honour. She beseeched her to adjourn the trial for a few days in order to allow the Earl of Lennox to compile his case. The gentle words of friendship that followed were always the same ones. What did it cost the Queen of England to write these, when she obstinately refused ever to meet her?

Mary folded the letter before throwing it into a casket. There was no need to lecture her about honour. After all, who were the Boleyns compared with the Guises?

The Queen remained all day in her apartments. Every now and then, a messenger arrived to tell her what had happened at the court. The Earl of Bothwell was in control of the situation, he maintained. He had remained dignified and calm, had refuted one argument after another and had interrogated his witnesses. Had they not found him lying by his wife's side when they burst into his chamber in the minutes following the explosion? The colour drained from Mary's face when she heard those words. It was impossible for her to overcome the jealousy she felt towards Jean.

The announcement of his acquittal caused Mary to burst into tears. James was right. Their determination would bring about the defeat of their enemies. Together they were invulnerable.

48

'I CANNOT SAY I AM surprised by your request,' George Gordon admitted, 'but it is impossible for me to hide my displeasure. My sister has done nothing wrong and does not deserve this rejection.'

'Who is talking about rejection?' James said on the defensive. 'Jean wants this divorce just as much as I do. We were never happy together.'

Huntly was pacing up and down in the office of the substantial house granted to James in his capacity as Governor of Leith. The Earl had chosen this neutral ground to obtain the consent of his friend, who was chief of the Gordon clan.

Jean would not be at all surprised by the action on which he was embarking. The Countess of Bothwell was well aware of her husband's liaison with the Queen, just as she had known about his adultery with Bessie Crawford. The divorce would be settled in favour of Jean on the grounds of infidelity, without any mention of the Queen's name being necessary.

An odour of seaweed was borne in on the wind from the beach. Low clouds were scudding across the sky, and across the waters of the Firth of Forth the distant countryside appeared almost purple.

'The divorce must be pronounced as quickly as possible,' James insisted.

George drummed his fingers on the dark oak table with carved acanthus feet.

'And what benefit would the Gordons gain from bowing to such demands?'

'Considerable,' James assured him. 'You know I am a man of my word, and I guarantee that neither you nor any member of your family will live to regret this decision. Do you really think I would keep Maitland on as Secretary of State?'

'What will happen to my sister?'

'Jean will be allowed to keep any of my castles she chooses for as long as she lives. I believe she is fond of Crichton. She would also be granted the entire revenue of its lands.'

James had started to grow a narrow beard on his chin, which emphasised the virility of his features. Huntly could not help but admire him. Faced with a situation most men would consider untenable he still maintained his air of authority and confidence.

'I have little time to spare and wish for a decision to be reached within the next few days. Speak to Jean yourself; she is intelligent and determined and not given to sentimentality. She will see straightaway where her interests lie.'

'You have a need to control everything, don't you?'

Huntly's voice bore no trace of anger. He had known James far too long to reproach him for anything.

'Events beyond my power have decided things for me. I am trying to limit the harm they can bring about, or at any rate be the first to exploit them to my advantage. You must know that Edinburgh is like a seething vipers' nest.'

George nodded in affirmation. He knew James was taking a huge gamble. Only someone with his audacity would consider pressing on where others would not dare.

'My mother is still very devoted to the Catholic Church,' he said, observing from the window the path that led to the shores of the Firth of Forth. 'She will demand that your marriage be dissolved by an ecclesiastical tribunal. However, there are none left in Scotland.'

'A Catholic Consistory will be created in the next few days. Jean will get every annulment she wants, and she will be able to remarry before a Cardinal,' replied James. He laughed... the ways of men were full of make-believe, cruelty, and hypocrisy.

'Parliament will ratify my acquittal and will ask the Queen for the Protestant religion to be declared the official religion in Scotland. The people will rejoice over this news.'

'Will Her Majesty agree?'

'She is realistic. There is no gain without pain.'

Huntly kept quiet. Only someone like Bothwell could have the stomach for such unpalatable fare. However, he was not prepared to oppose it. Looking out of the window, he could see in the distance the masts of ships entering and leaving the harbour with their sails unfurling or being taken down, surrounded by flocks of seagulls. The tide was on the turn and the sea had taken on a steely shade of grey.

'After the closing of the Parliamentary sessions I will invite all my friends, and my enemies too, to join me at Ainslie's Tavern,' James declared suddenly. 'I cannot aspire to marry the Queen without the consent of the principal noble families of this country. Right now I am in a powerful position and need to use it to my advantage.'

George Gordon did not reply. Hepburn still had friends, and if he persuaded the Queen to bestow on Morton the magnificent castle of Tantallon, which he had long coveted, he might well prove to be a reliable ally. On the tightrope James was walking, any foothold, however temporary, was worth grasping.

'Are you not considering the possibility that Jean might refuse you a divorce?'

'Not for a moment,' James replied.

His determination was his best asset. As long as no one suspected that he was soon to become the master of Scotland, then they would rally to his cause.

'We have lived through difficult times, you and I,' said George, turning towards James, 'and even if I am soon to lose my title of brother-in-law I will still be your friend. But be careful, my family is my first priority, and if there are ever any conflicts of interests I have to tell you that I would not hesitate to abandon you.'

'Would you fight against me?'

'No,' Huntly admitted, 'but I would not come to your rescue either. I would return to Strathbogie, gather my people round me and content myself with praying to God for the Queen and for you.'

While Mary was on her way to the Setons' Castle at Niddrie where they were awaiting her arrival, James had arranged a meeting of the nobles whom he hoped would approve his marriage to the Queen. He had invited a number of prelates and lords, all still in town after the closing of Parliament that same day, to join him at Ainslie's Tavern, one of

Edinburgh's finest eating places. On the previous day, James Balfour had, under Bothwell's instructions, drafted the petition he would read out to them at the end of the meal. He was confident that most of the twenty-eight guests would sign the document.

James coolly observed his guests all gathered around the long table as they emptied their first carafes of Loire wine. Except for Moray, all the members of the Privy Council were present, as well as Morton, George Douglas and a few of the Hepburns who had been instructed to give him vociferous support when he read the petition at the end of dinner.

The room put at his disposal by the innkeeper had an intimate atmosphere, and the pleasant warmth had already encouraged some of the guests to unbutton their doublets. The air was filled with the aroma of grilled meat, spices and sauces prepared in the kitchen by a dozen scullions. They will sign, James told himself. Half of them are to a greater or lesser extent involved in the murder of the King, while the others will be pleased to seize the occasion to have a Scottish Protestant Prince. In other words, it is a case of give and take: if they approve my marriage then I will not forget them.

The Queen had left for Niddrie in an anxious but confident frame of mind, and James admired her composure and her fighting spirit. The perilous situation in which they both found themselves had banished for a time her physical ailments. From being passionate their love had now become intense and violent, as if the fusion of their bodies expressed their will to vanquish both enemies and doubtful friends, all waiting for them to make the slightest false move, before pouncing and tearing them to pieces. There were many peaceful and tender moments too; he loved to cover his mistress's stomach with kisses, speaking to his tiny child within, and pledging he would always love and protect it.

After the first dish, a mutton broth cooked with barley and herbs and sprinkled with cumin, saffron and cardamom, the guests began to raise their goblets to the Queen's health. They made a toast to the welcome decision she had just made declaring Calvinism to be the official religion of the state, and to those who had inspired her to do so. All eyes turned to Bothwell.

'To Her Majesty's health!' he exclaimed in a jovial voice.

The glow given out by the flames in the great fireplace spread round the room, imparting a rosy tint to the wood panelling which reached halfway up the partition walls. Hanging on the walls were engravings depicting rustic scenes, and in one corner stood the stone bust of a flute-playing satyr.

Leaning over their plates, the lords and bishops were now relishing portions of salmon basted in a lemon sauce, honey-glazed trout, legs of mutton resting on a bed of pickled beans and pears, quarters of beef marinated in sweet wine and onions, and chicken spiced with ginger.

It was getting dark, and servants came to light the torches and the candles in the copper candelabra in the centre of the table. The wine that flowed in abundance stimulated the guests, who started talking freely about their amorous exploits. They called out to the maidservants, and by chance as they walked past hands caressed buttocks and lingered for a moment on plump breasts held in by tightly laced bodices. The girls screamed with laughter and answered back with spirit. That devil French Paris has picked me whores, thought Bothwell. And after all, why not? He had asked for the more heady Burgundy to be served after the Loire wine. The sweet wines from Madeira and Greece, along with grain and grape spirits, would accompany the desserts. James expected to be compensated a hundred times over for his considerable expense.

Voices were now starting to become raised. Every now and then, a guest would with difficulty rise to his feet and break into song. This is the time now, thought Bothwell. If I leave it until later, they will be too drunk to sign. He rose to his feet, pulled out a document from his doublet and unrolled it.

'My Lords,' he said in a loud voice, 'I ask your attention for a minute.'

James cleared his throat and drank a sip of wine.

'I need to speak to you on a matter of the greatest importance for the future of Scotland... '

Sitting side by side at the far end of the table James thought he saw little smiles of complicity on the faces of Maitland and the Earl of Argyll. He looked away.

'Her Majesty is currently deprived of a husband, and the State cannot allow her to remain in such a lonely situation. Our Queen needs someone to support her, to lean on and defend her. There is every reason to believe this necessity coincides with her own desires. If this is indeed the case, there is no other spouse who could love, honour and serve her better than the Earl of Bothwell. On numerous occasions he has proven to her his absolute devotion... Her Majesty having agreed to lower herself in order to take a husband born in this country, rather than choose a prince who is foreign to our customs and laws, I am petitioning your Lordships for your approval to this union, and for the offer of your services, advice, and swords for its prompt achievement.'

James observed his guests. Certain faces were showing indifference and others contentment, but none displeasure.

The document was passed from hand to hand with an inkpot and quill, and James was surprised by the resoluteness with which most of the lords and bishops signed. Even Maitland and Argyll had not hesitated for an instant. If they think they can betray me he thought, they had better think again. He and Mary would act swiftly.

With the document back in his hands, James rolled it up and put it inside his doublet. Tomorrow he would go to Niddrie, show it to the Queen, and make a public proposal of marriage, which in accordance with their plan she would firmly reject. The die was cast.

Mary had only just arrived back in Edinburgh when she advised her entourage that she planned to leave the following day for Stirling to visit her child. It was to be a short visit as she wished to be back at Holyrood a few days later. She firmly refused the escort proposed by Maitland, of one hundred armed horsemen to accompany her, together with Huntly and Melville. She had insisted that thirty horsemen were more than sufficient for her needs.

James experienced feelings of anxiety as he watched the little group disappearing into the distance. The game he was about to play in three days time was hardly flattering to his pride, but he had been left with no alternative. The honour of a gentleman had to come after that of his sovereign. Mary had surpassed herself, pretending to take offence when he had proposed to her, so that everyone had been able to witness that she did not consider him as a potential husband. Nevertheless, James was under no illusions. Even if Mary and he had mastered the theory of their plan, the reality had yet to be played out. Everybody had his own game, but the winner would be either the one who was most astute, or the one who was most determined.

Left on his own James shut himself away in his apartments. He had already received a petition from James Balfour asking for the Lieutenancy of Edinburgh Castle, only recently entrusted to his relative Lord Ormiston. Balfour had wasted no time in claiming what he was owed. Others would follow. Mary had already shown herself to be generous with Morton, Moray and Huntly. Only Maitland refused all favours.

He should probably give in and offer the fortress to Balfour. Whoever held it controlled Edinburgh. It was a great risk to run, but he would have no other option. James wiped his hands over his face. He was weary and not yet at the end of his troubles. Without delay, he needed to compile the documents necessary for his Protestant divorce and Catholic annulment, and collect statements before handing the file over to David Chalmers, his lawyer and friend. The ecclesiastical tribunal would be ready within forty-eight hours to deliver its judgement. Jean had signed all the documents. She was filing for divorce on the grounds of adultery with Bessie Crawford. By way of thanks she would get Crichton and another residence gifted by Mary, whose revenue would allow her to live comfortably. As she was not the kind of woman to burden herself with futile regret James was certain she would soon find herself a new husband.

The Earl's quill ran over the paper. The following day at break of dawn, he would set off for the Borders where he would muster a troop large enough to justify the fear it was intended to inspire. Then the adventure would be under way.

'God spews out fornicators, adventurers and hypocrites!' ranted John Knox from behind his pulpit. 'He turns his back on whited sepulchres whose nauseating stench offends His nostrils… We are, my brethren, living in an era of abomination in which cowards and the weak have no place, because God loves warriors and those who defend His honour by denouncing the sinners without respite. Do not allow the wolves to devour the lambs, nor the depraved to pervert the righteous. In the eyes of the Lord no sins are rendered acceptable by the rank of those who commit them. On the contrary, the masters must constantly serve as examples to their servants by the purity of their deeds and the honesty of their characters.'

The voice of the preacher filled the Kirk, and roared as though declaiming the Last Judgement.

'A father cries out for vengeance,' Knox continued, 'and a mother weeps over her murdered son: your King and mine, my brethren, whose memory is being tarnished today. Pray that God may give you the strength to demand the punishment of the murderers and their accomplices, and to speak out loud and clear in the name of justice and of the importance you attach to the honour of your country.'

Knox's eyes seemed to be burning in his angular face with its ivory complexion and long white beard. From time to time, he raised his almost translucent hands in the air as if trying to raise his words up to heaven.

His terrified audience were reduced to silence.

'Amen,' was uttered finally, by a few of the men.

The rumour was spreading of the forthcoming wedding of the Queen to the Earl of Bothwell. It seemed that those people were speaking the truth, who maintained that the latter had killed the King with the complicity of the former, in order to indulge their lust openly. Knox had now sided with them and backed their claims.

Satisfied, the preacher gathered his notes and left the pulpit. He was not very close to the Earl of Moray, but he had adopted his cause wholeheartedly and was keeping him carefully informed of the state of mind of the Edinburgh populace. It was his opinion that no one but the Queen's half-brother was capable of ruling Scotland. With her weaknesses, her political incompetence and her passions, the Papist had disqualified herself, and with her downfall she was about to bring down with her a man whose pride, ambition and reckless temerity had forever severed the bond which united him to his Protestant brothers. He disowned him.

Some of the Lords had come to him, having regretted signing a document that was a carte blanche for James Hepburn to marry the Queen. He had reassured them. God worked in mysterious ways, and what they believed to be a mistake, would soon reveal itself to be a great blessing. Sooner or later, those who played with the fires of hell would be consumed by them.

49

KIRK O' FIELD! For three years now that name has been throbbing in his mind, torturing and destroying him. He signed a pact with the wolves and they ended up devouring him. As soon as Darnley's intentions became known they had used James as a scapegoat. Among all the signatures written at the bottom of the conspiracy document, his alone had been drawn in his own blood.

Disparate images float through James's mind, as he sits on the edge of the bed holding his head between his hands: a duplicate key, a barrel of powder, leather pouches, Huntly sitting opposite him holding a dice cup in his hands, Mary's tense smile and the tall silhouette of Darnley who has discarded his taffeta mask for the first time. His pimples have dried up and his skin is wan and pitted; he looks like a ghost. Everybody knows he did not have the pox, but was suffering from syphilis.

It is a carnival day and courtiers are dressed in festive clothes. Sounds of laughter, bagpipes and the rolling of drums are coming from the street. Some are drinking and dancing, while others are about to die.

A country dance proceeds before the prisoner's closed eyes. Hands stretch out towards him and he is swallowed up in the whirl. Those he had mistaken for merry revellers turn out to be ghosts, who are dragging him into their macabre dance.

James stands up and impotently smashes his fists against the walls. He now knows the identity of the master of the game, he who has always set its rules in collusion with the English. He calls out for Moray and challenges him, an imaginary sword in his hand. His ghost should be prowling around somewhere here. Just let him show himself and James will finish him off.

The prisoner laughs sarcastically. He has outlived nearly all his enemies; Moray, Maitland, Lennox, Knox, Kirkaldy of Grange and Argyll. Morton is the only one left; he is a traitor of the same ilk as the others, a repugnant character, who sooner or later will die an ignominious death.

James is still laughing as he clings to the bars. People in the courtyard hear him and look up to watch the madman, now imprisoned in the tower for almost five years. The men raise their eyebrows and the women smile sadly.

Kirk o' Field, the church in the field, is a field of devastation, where stones from the Old Provost's Lodge are scattered all over the derelict sanctuary. Who wanted to save Darnley? No one, not even Mary. She had demanded only that no act should be committed which might compromise her honour. She wanted Darnley to disappear from her life, and as for the rest, she turned a blind eye.

Still clinging to the bars James yells out the name 'Mary!' Will his voice carry all the way to England? He is weeping now, shaken and torn with tearless sobs. He has difficulty in breathing. The air he inhales burns his lungs, and he is so weakened by dysentery that even the short distance from the window to the bed is an exhausting walk.

When did Moray find out the Queen was pregnant? Most probably at the end of March before the trial. It could have been merely the indiscretion of a chambermaid, or possibly a confession made by Mary to the Countess of Mar, whom she considered a close friend. Already the trap was slowly closing in on them.

Beams of late winter light cut across the darkened room. James examines the shadows. Are they friend or foe? He has little faith left in the quality of human tenderness. Perhaps even Mary has now forgotten him.

Only one door, the one leading from his room, separates him from the rest of the world. The courtyard gate is always open. Perhaps he could drag himself all the way to the sea and slip into a fisherman's boat. Then with the help of the wind, he would reach Scotland, where his Borderers are waiting for him. Moray massacred hundreds of them, both Reivers and simple chicken thieves: they were hanged, drowned and decapitated. Who holds Hermitage today? Who owns the heart of his dearest sweetheart? James rides over the moor along the path leading to the fortress and recognises every feature of the countryside, the long undulations of the hills and the twists and bends of the river; the earth echoes beneath his horse's hooves. He approaches a shadow; it is a black fog... it is himself.

Hermitage is empty and abandoned. He sees a section of wall, the remains of the formidable square tower, plunged into darkness by low-lying clouds. There is no sign of man or beast. He is alone with himself, as he was at Dunbar after Carberry hill. How much time has he left to live? A week, or a month? The wind groans in the chimney. Why was Darnley not blown to pieces by the explosion? Who terrorised him so much that he jumped out of the window barefoot, wearing only his nightgown? Who was waiting for him in the orchard? Was it George Douglas and his men?

James desperately searches his memory; the accomplices were Morton and Moray, Balfour was the double traitor who advised Darnley before selling him... it had been the kiss of Judas. He had not realised before that treachery could reach such depths.

Darnley looks at him but James does not want to see him nor hear his long drawn-out cry of terror: Pity me, my kinsmen! They cram the sleeve of his gown into his mouth; he struggles and takes a long time to die. Only two months ago, he had celebrated his twentieth birthday. As for James, he is the Queen's lover, the lover of Darnley's wife.

He had suspected at the time of the King's funeral that Moray was pulling the strings in England, and that the agreement signed at Craigmillar was a trap, but he was not able to draw back nor go over to the enemy. He had never lowered himself to beg like Darnley, was never submissive. Hatred lives on within him and consumes him like a flame. He has laughed and gloated each time on hearing news of the death of his enemies, and has drunk a whole bottle of spirit to their eternal damnation.

James struggles to make his way back to his bed. The dead haunt him, and he is the accomplice of ghosts.

50

ACCOMPANIED BY SOME hundred horsemen, Bothwell had been waiting for almost two hours near the bridge spanning the River Almond. On the previous day after leaving Stirling, the Queen had suffered a sharp pain in her side, and had stopped to rest at a humble farm along the way. Since her youth, anxiety had caused her serious ailments, which caused James concern. If the Queen doubted the success of their venture even for an instant, they would be lost. Nobody would believe Darnley could be the father of the child she was now carrying. Everyone knew the royal couple had not shared the same bed since the previous spring. Even at Kirk o' Field, Mary had never been alone with her husband.

At the distant sound of horses' hooves James sat upright in his saddle. He signalled to his men to hold themselves ready. Mary was certain there would be no resistance, but Maitland needed to be kept under close watch. The grass along the riverbanks was growing green again and wild shrubs were in bloom. Newborn lambs capered around their mothers in the grassy meadows, which rose gently to join the slopes of the nearby hills; the sound of hooves clattering on the ground drew closer.

'Let us move,' he ordered.

His troops followed him. James had no qualms; he needed to carry out scrupulously what had been agreed upon, and make sure no unforeseen circumstances came to delay or thwart his plans.

The previous day he had asked his mother not to believe the fabricated lies which were about to smear his name. She would soon understand the reasons for his actions, and would realise not a single one was dishonourable. Lady Agnes had listened to him without interruption. The tenderness she felt for her son was unshaken by all the accusations.

She knew that like his father, James loved women, but her son had never ventured into that quagmire in which 'The Fair Earl' Patrick had become bogged down, with his life of flattery, vanity and treason. The Lady of Morham knew that the Queen loved her Jamie. Although she barely knew her, she admired this young woman who at eighteen years of age had the spirit and courage to take on the task of ruling a country, whose never-ending troubles had sapped the life from her own mother. With God's help she believed her son would be worthy of the trust Mary Stuart placed in him and of the love she bore him… together they would restore the realm of Scotland to greatness.

Mary was riding in front. James could clearly distinguish her tall silhouette, the outline of her black cloak, and the veil wrapped around her headdress. The closer he came, the more certain he was that this was a moment of destiny.

'Stop!' he ordered, seizing the bridle of the dappled gelding ridden by the Queen.

Just as Melville looked as though he was about to put his hand on his sword, Mary stopped him.

'What pressing news do you have for me, my Lord Bothwell?'

James, who had taken off his hat, bowed to her.

'Edinburgh is in a state of unrest, Madam, rebellious groups have formed, and they pose a threat to you. I have sent some troops there, but would prefer Your Majesty to follow me to Dunbar, where you will be in complete safety.'

The Queen turned round to consult those escorting her. Maitland shrugged his shoulders as if to indicate this sham was not worthy of any comment. Huntly nodded his head in approval, while Melville remained impassive.

'I trust you, my Lord,' Mary said calmly, 'but I wish to send one of my men to Edinburgh so that he may report back to me on the situation prevailing there.'

James bowed in acknowledgement.

'Let us proceed,' the Queen ordered.

She looked pale, but her voice remained firm.

'We will reach Dunbar before nightfall,' James assured her.

Maitland had gradually ridden his horse up level with the Queen.

'Does Your Majesty permit me to return to Edinburgh? '

Mary's face expressed genuine surprise.

'Would you abandon me Maitland, now that I find myself in real danger?'

At Dunbar the wind blew in gusts, and waves crashed against the rocky shores where the formidable military fortress stood. Darkness was falling when, warmly wrapped in their travelling cloaks, the riders crossed the wooden bridge spanning the outer moat before passing through the port-cullis, which safeguarded the entry through the curtain wall.

Curls of hair, dislodged from her headdress by the wind, swept over the Queen's face. James could see only the longish profile of her fine nose, and her gloved hand trying to tame her hair. He was certain now that his mistress would not back away from their decision. The struggle had roused within her the combative spirit of the Guises and the unshakeable resolution of the Stuarts. She was ready to defy her people and rid herself of her adversaries, thereby giving a name to their child and creating him a Scottish prince.

The Queen had three plainly but comfortably furnished chambers at her disposal, as well as a water closet and a garderobe. The view from the windows looked out over the grey, often foam-crested, open sea, where ships in full sail could be seen making their way towards the Firth of Forth.

'Here we are back at Dunbar,' the Queen said to James, as they walked towards the great hall in which a large fire had been lit. 'This is the first time we have been here together since my flight from Holyrood a little over a year ago.'

Mary lowered her voice until it was just a whisper:

'It was here that I realised just how much you meant to me.'

The fortress was under the control of James's men, and both Maitland and Melville seemed to adjust easily to their situation as prisoners. They were not at all surprised by Bothwell's audacious execution of his plan. Who else could have abducted their Queen without her protesting?

Despite the Earl of Moray's innuendoes, Maitland had been sceptical about the Queen's alleged wish and intention to marry her lover. However, he was now fully aware of the true situation. The law was crystal clear; any man who abducted an unmarried woman and dishonoured her was obliged to marry her under pain of punishment, varying from ten years imprisonment to a death sentence. It was plain to see that Bothwell was sacrificing his honour at the altar of his ambitions. As for Mary's protests and the coldness she had shown towards the one who had ravished her, this was nothing but the pretence of a willing and loving accomplice.

'The die is cast,' said Bothwell with finality.

Mary was nestling up to him. As they listened to the roar of the waves and the whistling of the wind outside, they made passionate love together. Dawn was about to break and the sky would soon turn from black to leaden-grey.

'I have never looked back,' Mary said softly. 'You are my future.' She paused while drawing James closer to her, 'You are mine... you are the light of my life that will shine for ever.'

In silence, he lovingly caressed Mary's hair.

At Dunbar, he had arranged a chamber for himself adjoining the Queen's apartments, and could thus enter in secret. During the four or five days spent at the fortress, they had been able to enjoy a degree of intimacy in the daytime which would not so easily be accorded them in future unless they were alone or with friends. Once married, etiquette and their duties and activities, with the constant attendance of courtiers and guards, would restrict and keep them in their reciprocal roles.

'Before meeting you, I knew nothing of love,' Mary whispered in French.

James turned to kiss her lips. He loved her as his Queen, who commanded obedience and respect, but also as a wonderfully sympathetic and sensitive lover.

'I will always make you happy, I promise,' he said, kissing her again.

Most of their obstacles had now been overcome. All that remained was the formalisation of his divorce from Jean, then the publication of the marriage banns between Mary and himself.

The plan devised with Mary had worked without a hitch. His acquittal of any complicity in the murder of Darnley; Mary's honour remaining untarnished; the lords' signature at the bottom of the deed stipulating a union between the Queen and himself; Mary's obstinate and public rebuttal of his marriage proposal; the abduction and supposed rape.

'Do you know how much I am in the mood to ravish you?' he whispered.

Mary's body, soft, warm, vibrant and alive, belonged to him. 'My body is yours,' she had said. His spirit and his very existence found fulfilment in his undying love for her.

'I am your shadow, and am yours for ever,' she swore to him. 'You are my sun which warms and sustains me, and I cannot live now without your love. You are my happiness, my dearest Jamie, and the love of my life.'

Locked together in a passionate embrace, they made love... she felt such power and excitement with James, and was filled with feelings of euphoria.

The following morning Huntly had such a violent quarrel with Maitland that he threatened to kill him. Melville was restless, begging the Queen to let him return to Edinburgh, and Mary consented. Apart from the few days of freedom she was enjoying with James, nothing else seemed to matter to her at this moment. The situation was so new to her, to be free now of routine commitments, that any everyday gesture or object she saw seemed unique and of the greatest interest. Had the sea, the light and the rocks always looked so spectacular? Even James had lost his usual rough and slightly abrupt manner. In the early morning, she had seen him climb the rocks to watch ships tacking into the wind, bound for North Berwick and the Firth of Forth. Sheltering his eyes from the sun with his hands and wearing a simple grey linen jacket and soldier's breeches, he resembled a young man on some light-hearted escapade, she thought. The thin band of beard he had grown covered his chin but left exposed the dent above his chin.

Her lover possessed none of the feebleness of her first husband François, nor was he gifted with the blond charm displayed by Darnley. James could be abrupt and could curse or swear like a sailor, but the courage he had shown during the tragedy they were living through, and his determination to sacrifice his honour for her, placed him in her eyes above all other men, whether they be courtiers or princes.

At Dunbar, life had become almost normal. James asked his sister Janet as well as Lady Reres to come and assist the Queen with the necessities of normal life. Mary appreciated their company and knew she could count on their total discretion. Part of the guard had been dismissed, and in the spring sunshine the fortress took on almost a welcoming appearance.

'Let us all ride over to Hailes if that would please you, and we can stay the night there,' James suggested to Mary. 'Hailes Castle is a cradle of the Hepburns where I spent my early childhood. We will ride by Waughton and Smeaton where my cousins live. We can stop for refreshments and they will accommodate some of our party for the night, as there is not enough room at Hailes.'

Followed by ten armed men, the horses proceeded at a walk along a road bordered by thickets of bare-stemmed bushes ready to burst into leaf, continuing past sharp rocky outcrops and pastures turning green with new spring growth. They passed by peasants who barely glanced at these travellers, whom they took to be guests from Dunbar, or Tantallon Castle, the Douglas stronghold.

The feverish unrest in Edinburgh had not spread to the Lothians villages, and peasant farmers were busy preparing for the spring sowing season, lambing, and the planting of peas, beans and other vegetables in the strips behind their cottages. It was the time of traditional May festivities when villagers played their viols and fifes, with skills and melodies passed down through the generations. The old castle of Waughton stood as a lone fortress amidst the farmland. In a nearby field grew a yew tree of great antiquity. James related the more than two-hundred-year old story, which told that it was to this tree that the horse belonging to Patrick de Dunbar the Earl of March had been tied, when Adam Hepburn of Waughton had rescued him after a fall. Thereafter the yew tree with a grey horse tethered to it became the Hepburn crest, and the castle with its lands were granted by the Earl to Adam Hepburn... in later years the titles of Lord Hailes and the Earldom of Bothwell were granted by the King for brave and outstanding services to the Crown and the Stuarts.

A group of villagers riding bareback on stocky horses passed the travellers, and their dogs followed them a little way before turning back. Hens and ducks ran across the road squawking and flapping their wings. They stopped at Smeaton where James was welcomed by his cousins, who paid courtly homage to Mary and warmly greeted her and her companions.

As they rode through the spring countryside Mary gazed at the hawthorns just coming into bloom.

'How lovely the May blossom is!' she exclaimed with delight. Close to their path, sheltered from the wind by a cowshed, stood a clump of small trees bearing masses of white flowers, some of whose petals had already fallen and were scattered over the small stone troughs beneath. James was pleased to see her in such relaxed and happy mood away from all the royal pomp, taking spontaneous pleasure in her surroundings. She, who had been the jewel of the Valois Court, who had married at Notre Dame in Paris amid a display of priceless luxury, was filled with delight and wonder at the sight of wild flowering trees in the spring countryside. Excitedly she pointed out to James a brood of young chicks, following the mother hen down a narrow lane leading to a thatched cottage.

'I sent a messenger to Hailes,' he told her, 'there will be a meal ready for us when we arrive.'

Months had passed since he had last seen the old castle, a large stone building devoid of military defences. It stood close to the River Tyne, which flowed beneath low-hanging branches of trees and was the haunt of herons. Beyond the castle stretched fields, some bordered by dry stone walls and others enclosed by stockproof fences of intertwined cut and laid branches. Here and there were ponds where cows came to drink, and where in summer they stood keeping cool in the water.

Mary knew that her father King James v had loved to travel through-out Scotland, often speaking to peasants and other country folk. He had taken great pleasure in their music and local dances, and had sometimes even joined in with the villagers.

In the royal progresses she had made in Scotland, she had not dared mingle in the same way with her people, having contented herself with smiling and waving, and having small coins distributed to them.

When I have stopped fighting to survive I will have time to show I am a good and conscientious Queen who cares for all the people of Scotland, she said to herself.

James, sensing her thoughts, ironically asked her, 'Will you make me King?'

'No, that would bring you bad luck. François and Darnley both suf-fered terrible fates. I want to keep you by my side for the rest of my life.'

James looked away. What did he care about the title of King? The Queen would be his wife, and would be relieved to hand over to him the reins of government. She would give birth to their children, a large family, which would provide him with the joy and affection he had never known.

'We are approaching Hailes,' he announced.

Every feature of the surrounding countryside, each copse and stone wall was familiar to him. He knew the farms where his mother's servants had gone to fetch milk, eggs, butter and cheese... the bonesetter's shack, the smithy, and the lowly dwelling of the Dodds, who had five sons with whom he would go birds nesting, catch fish, and occasionally indulge in fisticuffs.

The path skirted the Tyne, and the riders let their horses drink from its waters and graze for a few moments on the greener grass growing on its banks. The water swirled past on the bends of the river, lapping against the banks where thistles, nettles and fresh grass were starting to grow. Small flies started to torment the horses, so they moved on, dismounting and handing their horses to the grooms before entering the castle.

After their repast, they explored the old castle, which was plainly furnished since no one except occasionally Janet resided there any longer. The kitchen, used by the five servants who maintained Hailes, was the only place which still held real signs of life. However, the charm of this great dwelling had not diminished and it still held a distinct fascination. Its vaulted rooms, narrow windows, huge fireplaces and faded scents of the past all conjured up wonderful memories, with visions of happy child-hoods and summers spent roaming the fields and woods, and swimming or fishing in the river. The castle had been made ready in some haste to receive the royal visitors. The apartments assigned to Mary were fur-nished simply and pleasantly, with private access for James.

Mary slipped her hand into James's and together they walked along-side the banks of the Tyne. In life they had chosen a difficult path, but with total mutual trust, they believed their futures to be forever intertwined. Basking in each other's presence, they shared a silent communion of happiness. As the sun started to go down, they followed the narrow path used by cattle and wild animals, which led them back to the castle. Mary exclaimed in delight at the gossamer threads shimmering in the rays of the sun, of the many spiders' webs spun between the stems of the long grasses.

James's thoughts were elsewhere. 'We must sign a promise of mar-riage,' he suddenly said. 'It would bind us together, and if I were to die our child would not be illegitimate.'

Mary's cheeks reddened slightly. She is blushing now as Queen; these are words she does not wish to hear me speak, James thought to himself.

'It is something we must do,' he insisted.

Mary looked at him, then making up her mind, she said, 'We will do it tonight.'

She was filled with emotion, and could not look at James. He took her hand gently and sat her down on a flat boulder by the riverbank from where as a boy he used to catch fish with the Dodds.

'We will get married in the weeks to come... by the fifteenth of May at the latest. David Chalmers is taking care of the divorce and the annulment by the Catholic tribunal of my marriage to Jean.'

'On what grounds?'

'Consanguinity. Jean and I are cousins to the fourth degree.'

'There was a dispensation, was there not?'

'We will not mention that. Jean also wants to re-marry. She knows what is in her best interests.'

'I am aware of that,' replied Mary sharply.

She was still jealous of the one she considered a rival, and who still bore the title of Countess of Bothwell.

'Jean will move away from Edinburgh and it is unlikely you will see her again,' James reassured her.

Sitting close to Mary, he placed his arm round her shoulders and held her tightly against him. He would conceal from her his concern about Morton, Argyll and Mar, who must have been waiting with impatience for the return of Maitland. They were plotting to take advantage of the unfavourable situation in which James found himself, that of a dishonoured man forced to marry his Queen, having sexually assaulted her. The signatures at the bottom of the deed signed by the Lords at Ainslie's Tavern, stipulating and agreeing a union between them both, would protect him for a while... but for how long?

He knew from his informers that Morton and Argyll were in Stirling, and did not like the sound of this news. As soon as Mary and he were married, he would need to form a small regular fighting force to protect them both and ensure his orders were obeyed. They would find the money somewhere... he would melt down the gold font gifted by Queen Elizabeth on the occasion of her godson's baptism.

'I do not wish to see Jean again, nor any other woman around you,' Mary said to him in a determined voice.

James smiled and held her closer. 'We are so alike,' he whispered. 'Demanding and jealous. We take what we want, if necessary by force, and both of us are stubborn and proud.'

James thought about the obstacles they still had to overcome, the

Protestant divorce, the Catholic annulment, and the signature of the marriage contract.

Would his friends continue to remain steadfast, and would they out-number his enemies? Would he have the nerve to carry it all through for his and Mary's sakes?

The sun was now low in the sky and the air becoming cool. It was time to return to the castle for the evening meal that the servants had prepared for them. Mary wished to retire early, being tired after the long ride.

At dawn next morning, they set out to ride back to Dunbar. A ren-dezvous with those who had stayed at Smeaton had been arranged at the foot of Traprain Law. From the lower slopes of this hill steeped in ancient history, Mary was able to enjoy a distant view of the coast of Fife, and the Bass Rock in the Firth of Forth.

In the evening following their return to Dunbar, Mary tried to appear cheerful and talked about a game of golf, which she suggested they might play the following day. Lady Reres had sent to Edinburgh for a casket of feather-stuffed leather balls and club sticks. Few women practiced this sport, but it was a game at which the Queen excelled. James was only an average player and she took pride in challenging him. He was in his element when mounted on a horse, and was a brilliant rider who won many contests and races.

Sitting in their private chamber they discussed their recent expedition to Hailes, and James pensively reminisced, 'When I last stayed at Hailes you had just dismissed me like a dog. I felt humiliated and in despair.'

'I was probably more upset than you were,' said Mary, 'but you have to remember I was not brought up like other women. So many barriers were erected all around me which I used to believe were insurmountable. I had constantly to be on my guard, and was never able to forget who I was.'

'What about Rizzio?' Bothwell asked her.

'He was a friend who made me laugh and enchanted me with his music. In killing him, it was me they were trying to wound to death, me the Queen, a Catholic, a woman and a Papist. Being a friend of France I was seen as an enemy and potential traitor. However, you were there waiting for me as my saviour, to prove that I was not alone. It was during our first sojourn at Dunbar that I accepted the attraction you exercised over me and realised there was something special between us. It was for those reasons I urged you to marry Jean soon... I was frightened of what the consequences might be for us. I wanted you to be near me but physically inaccessible; it was crazy of me to think that way... '

James said seriously, 'You were being sensible then. Today maybe we are crazy, but destiny and love have played their part in bringing us together, and by God's grace will never part us.'

5 1

BAREHEADED AND LEADING the Queen's horse by the bridle, James walked up the High Street followed by his troop of Borderers. Bystanders observed them from either side of the street as they passed by.

The week spent by the Queen at Dunbar in the power of the Earl of Bothwell had given rise to all sorts of contradictory rumours. Some maintained she had been held against her will, while others were outraged by this sham intended to fool the people and justify a shameful marriage. The Earl of Bothwell had made a decisive move. The Queen's husband had been slain; he was now engaged in the dissolution of his own marriage and was bringing the affair to a swift conclusion.

It was said that in three days time the marriage banns would be published on the doors of St Giles Cathedral and at Holyrood Chapel.

The road rose steeply towards the castle, where Mary planned to reside for a few days. Before returning to Holyrood she needed to make sure the city was under her control.

There were few nobles to welcome her. The Queen was not unduly alarmed; she was now sufficiently acquainted with the rebellious temperament of the Scots, and was prepared to wait patiently for them to relent and come back to her. However, James was vexed and uneasy. The closer he came to realising his ambition, the more he felt his enemies would attempt to lay traps to obstruct him and make his victory a hollow one. John Craig, who had become John Knox's right hand man, had been reprimanded for publishing the banns, and Mary had been forced to confirm in a note written in her own hand that she freely consented to marrying the Earl of Bothwell. With the stress imposed upon her the young Queen's resistance was beginning to falter. Anxiety knotted her throat and caused her heart to race. Meanwhile James's divorce had been ratified and he was now a free man.

Feeling ill at ease at Edinburgh Castle, the Queen suddenly decided to move back to Holyrood. Once again, the long procession stretched down the High Street and Canongate. The weather was mild with hazy sunshine and Arthur's Seat was shrouded in a thin veil of mist. Mary remembered her arrival in Edinburgh six years earlier when the crowd had cheered the young Queen enthusiastically after she landed at Leith. On every street corner, little girls had offered her flowers, and groups had sung and serenaded her as she rode to Holyrood.

Despite the sadness she felt over leaving France, she had been happy to be greeted as Queen and had contemplated her future with serenity, certain she would be loved by all her subjects and that in time Elizabeth would choose her as her successor to the throne of England.

With her illusions now shattered, James had become her sole reason to live. He was a strength on which she could always lean, and at twenty-four years old, she knew she loved him with all her heart and that he loved her in return.

She felt her subjects were deserting her and judging her harshly. Should she confront and reason with them, and accept that some might hate her?

James, like Mary, had been born in Scotland. He was one of them, and with her blessing and authority he governed with a moderate but firm hand. His main concern was the future of his country, and in order to further his aims of an independent and prosperous Scotland he was considering the implementation of a series of laws. They were designed to promote commerce, stabilise the currency and reinforce authority in local communities throughout the land, giving better protection to the country people. He planned to rid the country of bands of brigands, and send foreign mendicants back to their countries of origin.

At Holyrood, the peace of mind the Queen sought continued to prove elusive. Nobles and courtiers seemed all to be playing some sort of pre-ordained role. Why did those closest to her speak to her in such guarded tones, and what had changed their outlook? Mary felt persecuted, conspired against and scorned. Of her four Marys, only Mary Seton remained loyally by her side. The others had left Holyrood to join their husbands.

'James Balfour is to take over the command of the castle.'

From his detached tone of voice, Mary sensed James's exasperation and anxiety. Had he not promised this key post, on which the safety of the capital depended, to one of his trusted relatives?

'Why him?' she asked. 'All he has done is exploit every situation in which he has been placed to his own advantage, and in so doing abandon his friends.'

He is a useful intermediary between ourselves and our friends,' James replied. 'He will not betray those from whom he gains honours and benefits.'

However, Balfour's increasingly urgent demands for the defence and supplies for the castle worried James. At present, he could not be sure whether he had won him over to his side in granting him this post, or whether given the least excuse he would turn the castle's cannons against him. The man was untrustworthy and as venomous as a snake. If he made an enemy of him there was no doubt Balfour would delight in creating trouble for them.

'I trust your decision,' Mary assured him. 'Are you ready for the ceremony this evening?'

After the sounding of trumpets, the banner-bearers and standard-bearers entered the great hall. The walls had been adorned with tapestries and pieces of velvet or silk cloth embroidered in gold and silver thread. In between hung garlands of flowers and leafy boughs. At the end of the long room linking James v's tower to the Abbey, Mary's throne with its royal canopy was flanked by two candelabra of gilded silver, each bearing nine waxed scented candles.

For the first time since her return to Edinburgh, the Queen was happy. She had overseen in great detail the order of the ceremony, in which she would honour the man she loved, by making him a Duke. To him she had dedicated each feature of the ceremony, each musical composition and each dish of the feast that would follow.

Retrieved from the royal treasury, the ducal crown rested beside her on a velvet cushion. This symbol of power and dignity, which she would place on James's head, had been worn by Stuart Princes in the past, and she was gratified at the thought of performing this investiture for her loved one.

Behind the standard-bearers walked Bothwell and the four relatives he had selected to be dubbed knights, followed by the pages of the Queen's household dressed in red and yellow and wearing white plumed hats.

Then followed the ladies-in-waiting in ceremonial robes, the city of Edinburgh's civic officials, and finally Mary Stuart's own personal guard, with their short pelerine capes bearing the Arms of Scotland.

James kneeled bareheaded before his sovereign. He knew the audience had their eyes fixed upon him, some looking at him with an expression of bitter jealousy, while others such as his mother and his sister watched him with pride and tenderness. Once again, the sound of trumpets echoed through the hall, and James felt as though his ancestors and even his father were there with him to share in the honour being bestowed upon their house. Like the first Earl of Bothwell, he owed his crown to his unshakeable loyalty, his courage and his fervent desire to transcend others in the service of the Crown.

'I, Mary Queen of Scots,' she boldly proclaimed, keeping her eyes fixed on James, 'grant you the Duchy of the Orkney Islands, which is yours and for you to bequeath to your son, so that you may give proof, as you already have done, of your zeal for justice and fairness of judgement. Be righteous and firm in the duties to which this crown binds you. May Christ the mediator between God and men find in you a faithful servant for the greater good of His people.'

Slowly she placed the golden circle of the crown inlaid with six sapphires upon her lover's head.

'James Hepburn, Earl of Bothwell, Lord of Hailes, Crichton, and Liddesdale, I proclaim you Duke of Orkney and Lord of the Shetland Isles.'

After the fanfare of trumpets, the choir began to sing a psalm:
'Be strong and firm, do not shudder, do not tremble.
Yes God, my God, is with you,
He will not let you weaken, He will not abandon you.'

James kept his head lowered. He was so overcome by emotion that he was oblivious of those surrounding him and did not hear the voices acclaiming him.

The terrible moments he had endured had been vanquished and were behind him now. His eldest son would be a Prince of Scotland, Duke of Orkney and Earl of Bothwell, and would be an equal of members of the royal families of Europe.

Standing, he listened to the speech addressed by the Queen to those assembled.

Mary was careful to avoid paying too ardent a tribute to the new Duke, and focused on praising the dignity and courage of the members of the Scottish nobility. She was to dub four Knights, who according to custom had been nominated by the Duke. They would be assigned honours as well as duties, and she was keen to emphasise the latter. Her words resounded beneath the splendid hammer-beamed ceiling of the great hall. Its stone walls and large flagstones on the floor gave off a fresh odour of dampness.

The Queen fell silent. Lord Seton handed her the sword that she would lay on the shoulders of the men kneeling before her, creating them Knights of the realm.

Bothwell was aware of the silence filling the hall. The grim resentful looks and unsmiling pursed lips of some of the guests made a striking contrast to Mary's happy face and the sweetness and authority of her voice.

Since Dunbar, he had not held her in his arms, and he had been waiting impatiently for the day of their marriage, and for his official installation at Holyrood in the apartments formerly occupied by Lord Darnley. He would sleep in the bed of the great-nephew of Henry VIII, the cousin of Queen Elizabeth. His own clothes would hang in the wardrobe of the late King, and he would be free to possess the one who had once been the spouse of the King of France. He knew that Mary loved him not only for his physical attractiveness, but because he offered her calmness of mind and total constancy.

A procession of servants brought in dishes of venison, followed by poultry, geese, capons, ducks, pigeons stuffed with honey-glazed almonds and finally fish served in a green herb sauce. Sitting beside the Queen, Bothwell knew they did not need words in order to savour the intensity of this moment of triumph. In two days' time they would sign their marriage contract, and on the fifteenth of May at break of dawn, they would become husband and wife. It was not a time to worry, even if he had to give way to James Balfour's intimidation by entrusting him with the Lieutenancy of Edinburgh Castle.

As a compliment to the patriotism of her future husband, the Queen had sent for the best bagpipe players from the Highlands, a famous viol player from Inverness, and singers from the Borders who knew the long and ancient ballads passed down from generation to generation, celebrating lovers, cattle thieves, heroes and assassins. On this evening of celebration, the guests were relaxed, and some had begun to join in the chorus when they knew the words of well-known tunes.

Even the stern Maitland seemed cheerful; Morton was courting his neighbour, the eldest daughter of Lord Oliphant; Maxwell, who knew every Border ballad, had stood up, goblet in hand, to join in the singing. An enjoyable feeling of rapport united all present, be they from the north, south, east or west... they were here to celebrate their country with its moors, lochs, mountains, firths and rivers, its mists, hills scattered with rocks and heather, and its fortified castles and keeps, erected like sentinels against time and the folly of men. So many in Scotland were cousins, distantly related or connected by marriage, and many families were affiliated to the Stuarts through the numerous illegitimate children conceived or sired by them. Regardless of these close or distant kinships, the Scots never ceased tearing each other apart and betraying one another, seemingly unable to resist the fiendish appeal that incited them to fight each other. The people of Scotland were wild, rebellious and proud, dedicated to protecting the independence and honour of their own clan or family, and all attached to their country as to their own flesh.

James was not deluded by the apparent friendliness displayed by the nobles and courtiers. Although united around their sovereign today, tomorrow they would be ready to oppose her mercilessly. They would scheme and plot to punish her for the unpardonable crime he was about to commit with her benediction of aspiring to govern them. How did Kirk o' Field compare with such intolerable arrogance? If James had been content with running his estates, pacifying the Borders and going hunting with the Queen, the murder of the hapless Darnley would have become a matter of little importance. However, with the prospect of his marriage with the Queen, many had signed the Ainslie's document only to be in a better position to ruin him.

Alone in his room James could not sleep. Beyond his windows the moon lit up the nearby hill, the gardens and the elegant outline of the abbey. It cast iridescent shadows over the hills and rocks while salty air was blown in on the wind from the Firth of Forth. Was Mary resting? He should not, could not join her before the day of her marriage. In the space of a just a few months, with the spur of necessity and honour, he had fulfilled his dream. With firm resolution, he had overcome all opposition, and the child Mary carried, his child, would have a legitimate father and mother.

Bothwell had obtained Mary's consent to have a Protestant marriage ceremony. He fully understood the magnitude of her sacrifice, the only one he had asked of her since the tragedy of Kirk o' Field and the announcement of her pregnancy. In contrast to James, her infant son and future King, their child would be Protestant. He secretly hoped Mary might one day convert to the religion most widely practised by her people, if not out of conviction then out of a sense of national awareness.

The moon was veiled by thin clouds. In the Borders beyond the Lammermuir Hills Reivers would be saddling their horses and donning leather jacks and helmets, before taking off on a raid to settle a family feud by stealing cattle and setting fire to dwellings. Jock o' the Park who had nearly killed him had fully recovered. Did the saying not go 'As tough as a Borderer'?

James retired to his bed; he would try to rest, and for a while forget his anxiety over the future, and the certain knowledge that Moray was writing in secret to Argyll, Morton and Mar. It had been a grave mistake to entrust the young Prince to the safekeeping of the Earl and Countess of Mar. Mary was very fond of them, but James realised they would not hesitate to join their enemies.

Wearily, the new Duke of Orkney allowed French Paris to undress him. Out of affection for his former master, he was happy to serve him long after other servants were asleep. The young Frenchman had lost some of his zest for life. In his contacts with other valets and their masters, he had heard alarming talk circulating concerning the Queen and her future husband.

'What rumours have you heard?' Bothwell asked him.

'Always the same gossip, my Lord: your Lordship is said to be holding the Queen prisoner and forcing her to marry you.'

James smiled and replied, 'Her Majesty has repeatedly proclaimed she is free, and that she has taken the decision to marry me entirely of her own volition.'

'If your Lordship permits me to say so the enemies of the Queen and yourself are not interested in the truth; they are sick with jealousy!'

Silently French Paris handed him his nightshirt, left a carafe of wine and a goblet by the side of his bed and snuffed out the candles. The Frenchman could not stop thinking about Lord Darnley's last night at Kirk o'Field, and about his bed placed above the gunpowder he himself had spread there.

Yet everyone maintained that the quantity of explosives contained in the cellar had been sufficient to destroy the house completely. Why then had they wanted to involve the Earl of Bothwell in such a well-organised attack? The more he pondered the more French Paris was seized with alarm. If they were out to get the Earl, he was certain they would come for him at the same time... and he had no sovereign to come to his defence.

52

15 May 1567

THE SUN WAS RISING over Edinburgh, and in the cool air of dawn cocks were crowing, echoing each other from house to house. Stars were fading and disappearing one by one as the sky lightened.

The Queen was plainly dressed for her third wedding. There was to be none of the pageantry of her union with the Dauphin at Notre Dame in Paris, nor even of her marriage with Lord Darnley. Money was scarce and she was aware that in current times her dowry could be put to better use than by renewing her wardrobe or purchasing the Parisian frills and baubles she had raved over in her youth.

When she arose on her wedding morning, the women of her wardrobe presented her with a skirt of yellow taffeta overlaid with a black dress trimmed with silk braid. For her headdress Mary had chosen a cap descending to a point on her forehead with a long black veil attached at the back.

James had risen before dawn to get himself dressed. This day, which would see him at the height of his power, did not bring him the feelings of joy that he had the right to expect. Not many nobles would be present, and the French Ambassador Philibert du Croc had told him the previous evening that in the absence of his King's orders to attend he was unable to support the Queen's marriage with his presence.

Without speaking a word, James allowed himself to be shaved. In this situation he would now have to act as if he were at war; position the troops who still remained loyal to him, manoeuvre them with skill and foil the enemy's plans. The time for negotiations was past.

'Who is present?' he asked Huntly who had come to fetch him.

'Rather let us talk of those who are not present, my friend. There is no sign of Maitland, Morton, Argyll, Mar or Atholl.'

Bothwell clenched his fists in frustration. He would soon be in a position to make them swallow their pride.

'I have to tell you that the Lords of this realm will not rejoice at seeing power transferred into your hands, as they will soon be dependent on you for their lands, wealth and honours,' added Huntly.

'They will be dependent on Her Majesty the Queen,' corrected Bothwell.

Apart from his cousin William Hepburn of Gilmerton, there was no one who knew him as well as his former brother-in-law and friend the Earl of Huntly.

Adam Hepburn, together with the Bishop of Orkney, waited patiently in the hall, and the general atmosphere was more melancholy than joyful.

Although those attending the ceremony were well dressed and turned out and tried their best to be cheerful, the tension was palpable and it made Huntly anxious. The Queen would be devastated by this poor attendance, which included only a single bishop. Mary was a proud woman. How would she react?

In the antechamber, James was pleased to see a great number of his relatives, who all greeted him enthusiastically. Their jubilant smiles and laughter put him at ease and raised his spirits.

Let us go, he thought, and let us not croak with those despicable crows outside.

When Mary entered the great hall, James was already standing in front of the Bishop. The newly risen sun was still too low in the sky to light up the room, and torches remained lit. Silence reigned while the ladies curtsied deeply and the men bowed. As she walked towards her husband the Queen noted and counted those who should have been there but were absent, and her face took on a stern expression.

Hand in hand, the couple repeated the words which would unite them. In marrying the man she adored, Mary knew she was committing an act of folly.

Queens were no ordinary mortals, and by binding her fate to James she was acting as a subject, not as a sovereign. Yet she knew she had the courage neither to live alone nor to marry an unknown prince for political reasons. James, she felt, was her better half, her strength and her joy, and she carried his child proudly. Why should she care about the opinions of others? A Stuart or a Guise did not need to be answerable to anyone.

Bothwell slipped a gold braided wedding ring inlaid with small diamonds onto her third finger. Mary suddenly felt the urge to flee from the room, abandoning the Protestant Bishop and departing with her Jamie to the ends of the earth.

The Prelate was delivering his sermon, exhorting the spouses to repent of their sins in order to live according to the laws of the Lord. His moralising and patriarchal tone exasperated James. He would hasten the meal that was to follow, with all its inevitable speeches and tributes. Then he would lock himself away with his wife, hold her in his arms and reassure her. He would implore her to lean on him, and find in the pleasure of love some compensation for all the humiliation she had had to endure.

The people of Edinburgh had been invited to come and witness the wedding banquet, and one by one they filed past the table headed by Mary and Bothwell. She barely noticed these friendly, derisive or hostile faces, and felt at the end of her tether. Her joy at being united to James was mixed with fear of the future combined with a feeling of guilt and isolation. Then her spirits rose, and she thought, how dare her subjects defy her? And she wondered which families were engaged in running a deliberate smear campaign designed to undermine her authority and happiness.

With sorrow, she thought about the respect she had received in France, and the adoration she had enjoyed in those earlier days. Wherever she went, the crowds welcomed her, poets celebrated her and men courted her. She heard the bells of Notre Dame pealing out on the day of her marriage, she saw the brightly-coloured crowd gathered around the dais erected in front of the cathedral, and stretching all the way down to the banks of the Seine where the royal standards of France and Scotland were flying. 'Largesse, largesse!' the pages shouted as they threw small coins into the crowd. They had released flocks of white doves and turtledoves; the horses, caparisoned with precious fabrics, champed at their bits, and were ridden by princes, gentlemen, ladies and demoiselles of the noblest families. In the evening, during the banquet held at the Louvre by torchlight and to the sound of the orchestra playing, the guests had been offered exquisite dishes to eat, and they had all danced late into the night. This had been followed by six days of merry-making, punctuated by tournaments, warlike displays, parades and concerts. François her young husband had inaugurated them, dressed in velvet and brocaded satin, and wearing a plumed hat. She recalled his wan face and his beautiful smile.

At the end of the table, James was talking to his neighbours, the Lords Oliphant and Huntly. Mary listened to the sound of his voice and laughter. He was her husband now, and she hoped to live with him to the end of her days.

When he entered the Queen's small chamber, James found the French Ambassador, who stood up at once, gave him a frosty greeting, and walked out.

'Monsieur du Croc came to reproach me for getting married without waiting for King Charles ix's assent,' Mary revealed in a distraught voice.

Bothwell banged his fist angrily on the table where Mary stored her boxes of needlework.

'And why not the King of Poland, or a Red Indian Chief from America as well? Pay no attention to such humiliating remarks about your sovereignty!'

James knew he should not have lost his temper, but the tension that had weighed so heavily on his shoulders during the entire day had suddenly become impossible to bear any longer.

'It seems we have few friends left,' cried Mary tearfully.

James picked up a silver-gilt goblet and poured himself some Loire wine. He was exhausted.

'How much do you care about the friendship of your subjects? It is true we should have waited for the storm to pass before getting married, but we could not. I did everything in my power to preserve your honour.'

'I wish I were dead!' Mary sobbed. 'How can I live amid such hatred, nastiness and suspicion? Only this morning a new placard appeared in the Canongate. On it, people can read a phrase from Ovid—"Wantons marry in the month of May".'

James roared with laughter, dumbfounding Mary.

'Let pigs roll in their own dirt! You should be able to rise above them and show what a Stuart is made of.'

He went up to her, leaned over and forced her to look up.

'Neither you nor I are about to die my love. We have better things to do. Tomorrow we will write to the King of France, the Queen Mother,

Queen Elizabeth, the Pope and the King of Spain to make an official announcement of our marriage, and give reassurance that Scottish policy concerning them is not going to change. Everyone must be convinced you have a firm grip over your country, that I am behind you to support and defend you, and that you intend to govern in a conciliatory manner. Do not look back to the past, forget France, no longer look towards the throne of England, but develop your sense of belonging here in Scotland.'

Tenderly James caressed his wife's face. He needed to convey his strength to her, not his anxiety. For the second time in her married life, she was carrying a child in trying circumstances, and he knew there would be other ordeals for them to face.

'Come,' he whispered, 'let us go to bed. Is this not our wedding night?'

'You must write to William Cecil as well,' Huntly insisted. 'The Secretary of State of her Majesty Queen Elizabeth of England fears you might become a despot and cut off all English connections. If this is the rumour spreading throughout London, I am sure it will be the same in Edinburgh and Paris.'

'How is Jean?' enquired the new Duke.

He felt a touch of guilt over his former wife, and retained some affectionate concern for her. Jean did not deserve to be spurned within so short a time.

'She is in complete control of the situation,' her brother George assured him, 'She even invited Janet and little Francis to Crichton. Your nephew seems to love it there. I also think Jean feels sorry for you, having got yourself into such a predicament.'

It caused James heartache to hear of the peaceful lifestyle of Crichton. He who had advised the Queen not to look back could not help but mourn a kind of lost happiness. He had to forget Hermitage, the long rides on horseback across the moors, and springtime at Hailes.

'The Privy Council will meet tomorrow,' he said in a matter of fact voice. 'I know I can count on you, as I intend to announce the changes which I consider making to the way it is run.'

Three council meetings had taken place in the space of a few days. So far, James had not encountered any particular opposition. His proposals to control the money originating from Flanders, hitherto contaminated by forgers who were to be severely punished, and to confirm the decree signed a few weeks earlier by the Queen, establishing Protestantism as the State's religion while tolerating the private practice of Catholicism, had all been approved unanimously.

In order to entertain Mary, and prove to the citizens of Edinburgh that life had returned to normal, he had organised maritime festivities in Leith, which had attracted large crowds. Some of the crowd applauded when the Queen arrived escorted by James, bareheaded as was his wont. Laughingly she had grabbed the hat he was holding and placed it on his head. She seemed to have recovered once again from her nervous anxiety. Her waist was expanding and her stomach getting rounder, and both of them were emotionally moved by the first tangible signs of their child's existence. If she had a son, Mary wanted to name him Robert after her second brother, who had died as an infant at the same time as her elder brother James. Marie de Guise and James V had been devastated by the loss of their two boys, and the King had never recovered from it.

The two of them often talked about Marie de Guise. James waxed lyrical quoting examples of her courage and her indomitable will to preserve Scotland from the covetous greed of Henry VIII. He praised her air of composure when faced with the treason of those on whom she had relied for support. James remembered her at Holyrood, very weary but remaining upright and determined, writing and reading reports, despatching emissaries and summoning her Lieutenants to make plans for a forthcoming battle. She had become so attached to her country that she had not even taught her child to speak French. Mary listened to him with avid enthusiasm. James reconnected her to her beloved mother, from whom she had been separated far too early in life. He brought back to life for her a woman who had devoted her life to serving a crown belonging to her daughter. He told her about many small details, including her tastes, her behaviour and the books she read. Mary drew great inspiration and strength from these conversations. She would show herself worthy of this admirable woman, her own mother, who inspired her to stand up for herself.

It was a mild spring. Buds had burst into leaf and the first flowers were in bloom around Holyrood. The warmth of the spring sunshine gave the Queen a feeling of rebirth. Why be alarmed? James was capable and strong, and no one would ever get the better of him.

'I have bad news, my Lord!'

One of James's old friends Lord Borthwick had just arrived at Holyrood. It was he who had given him refuge when he was being hunted for having stolen the English gold at the time of the Regency of Marie de Guise. Dust stains on his coat betrayed the haste in which he had travelled.

'Atholl, Argyll, Home, Morton, the Douglases, Kirkaldy of Grange and some other lords are about to march on Edinburgh at the head of their men.'

The Duke, who had just sat down to eat, pushed his plate away and abruptly stood up. With a wave of his hand, he dismissed all his servants.

'They are crazy!' he cried out. 'I shall take the Queen to the castle at once and we will control the city from there.'

'Do not do so, my Lord! The governor James Balfour has betrayed you. He is about to sign an agreement with the rebels, who in return will remove his name from the list of the King's alleged murders'

James was agitatedly pacing up and down. He believed Borthwick and had little time to make plans.

'Then let us retreat to the safety of Dunbar. If necessary, I will not hesitate to face them in battle. This corruption sickens me; it is putrefying Scotland, and before this wound can heal it needs to be cleansed with a knife. On the way to Dunbar, we will stop at your castle. I will leave the Queen in your safe hands and ride to Melrose to round up my Borderers.'

Mary resolutely accepted the arrangements made by James. She was ready; it was no longer a time to be tolerant, and she showed the same determination as her husband to crush the rebels. Hastily she gave orders for a few of her belongings and small items to be packed along with some boxes containing coded correspondence. Looking gloomy, Maitland was filing important documents for her. Mary was pleased with the loyalty of her Secretary of State, husband of her beloved Mary Fleming. She knew that James intended to replace him with the Earl of Huntly but she was determined to stand up for him. Maitland was a clever man, experienced in diplomacy and close to William Cecil, who respected his judgement. They had not always seen eye to eye but she was now mature enough to overlook opinions on which they had differed.

When James entered the room, Mary smiled at him confidently. The previous night they had discussed at length this type of situation. The rebellion was not the first they had dealt with; in the past they had easily triumphed over the conspirators after the murder of Rizzio, and before that Mary had rallied her subjects without difficulty after her half-brother's rebellion.

From Dunbar at the head of a powerful army they would march on Edinburgh. James had not given up on the idea of bribing Balfour. The promise of a comfortable revenue and an honorary title might persuade him to change sides once more. He had sent David Chalmers, who was a good negotiator, to see him. If the promises failed to have the desired effect, there were still threats that could be used. Although it was impossible for him to produce the contract signed before the explosion because both their names featured on it, he could still denounce his collusion with Darnley. The merchant who had sold him the gunpowder would testify by fair means or foul. Once Morton, Home and Argyll had been brought to heel, he would deal with them with the utmost severity.

Mary was impressed by her husband's calmness. She believed everything would happen as he foretold. Before July, they would be settled back at Holyrood, where she would be able to prepare in peace for the birth of their child.

'Madam,' James said in an icy tone, 'I do not like to think of you alone in the presence of another man.'

'Do you doubt the uprightness of our Secretary of State, my Lord?'

Maitland stood before James wearing a hostile expression. With horror Mary sensed an altercation was about to ensue.

'I am filing letters, my Lord,' he snapped in a caustic tone, 'and have no evil thoughts on my conscience. Should not those who are jealous examine their own actions? It is said your Lordship is still in regular correspondence with Lady Jean.'

James was caught off guard. How did this man know that he sometimes wrote friendly letters to his former wife, to which she replied in equally amicable terms. Divorced and living at a distance from each other they enjoyed communicating.

'I forbid you to speak of personal matters!'

Maitland did not lower his eyes. Once and for all the Secretary of State wanted to have his say with this arrogant man who behaved as though he were the King of France.

'I also know, my Lord, that you wish to see me resign from the post to which Her Majesty has entrusted me, but in the absence of any direct order from her I will not comply.'

'I implore you to refrain from further comment,' Mary pleaded. 'Maitland, please leave us alone, we will talk later on.'

James was surprised by the abruptness of her tone.

'Your anger is absurd,' she reproached him. 'We are going to lose a precious ally.'

'Madam, the Secretary of State is in league with your half-brother, and he, since your return from France, has thought of nothing else but taking power away from you! Do you refuse to admit it? Before long you will see that I am right!'

53

HASTENING FROM THE Borders back to Edinburgh, James had to change horses three times, having ridden them to exhaustion galloping over the Lammermuir Hills in difficult conditions through squalls of rain, which had caused the slopes to become dangerous and slippery and the country roads to be boggy in parts.

He was concerned over the limited number of Borderers who had responded to his appeal to rally to his support. Had his message not been passed round? Had something delayed the men he had relied on to join him? Leaving a few of his men behind in Melrose to go from farm to farm and persuade those who were still hesitating, he had ridden speedily to Borthwick Castle where the Queen was waiting for him. The solid and well-defended fortified building stood at the edge of a forest and towered over the plain stretching out in before it. A few years earlier, watching from the main tower, Bothwell had witnessed the sacking of Crichton, which fortunately he had later been able to restore.

No sooner had he passed through the main gates of the castle than the guards pointed out the movement of troops on the plain below. From the wall walk, the royal couple could see a considerable number of horsemen approaching from the west.

Sheltering her eyes with one hand in order to see them better, Mary's heart turned to stone, as apprehensively she sensed further danger.

'Here are your friends, Madam!' announced James in a grim voice. He was struggling to contain his anger. The news that had reached him in the Borders was now being confirmed; Home, Morton and Kerr of

Cessford were leading an army with the intention of killing him and taking the Queen as their prisoner. Moray would then appear as saviour and reap what he had always coveted… the Regency.

'I shall send a message to Huntly asking him to muster his men immediately and come to our assistance.'

The Queen made no reply. The hem of her skirt flapped in the wind, which lifted the short veil attached to her headdress and disturbed the curls carefully arranged on her temples. She was reliving the moments of anguish and fear but also the feverish tension that had followed Rizzio's murder.

'What should I do?' she asked eventually.

'Stay here, Madam. I am going to try to negotiate to see if it is at all possible to bring these people to their senses.'

Beneath the grey overcast sky, they could see the multitude of horsemen coming nearer and could hear the muffled tread of hundreds of horses trotting. They began to recognise individual silhouettes, and Mary, mesmerised, could see in the front ranks those who had dined and danced with her, loyal members of her Privy Council, and men whose ancestors had always been allies of hers through mutual interest and blood ties, many being illegitimate relatives.

Behind her, the soft green leaves of the beech trees dripped with rain. A horseman detached himself from the foremost group and galloped towards them; Mary recognised him as Morton's standard-bearer.

'My Lord Morton wishes to parley with his Lordship the Duke of Orkney,' he shouted to them.

James was pacing up and down on the ramparts like a caged lion.

'Tell Lord Morton that under these circumstances we have nothing to say to him,' the Queen retorted. 'Let him lay down his arms and submit, then we will receive him.'

She saw an ironic smile cross the messenger's face as he gathered up the reins and turned his horse to leave.

'Go back to your apartment, Madam,' James pleaded. 'I do not want to see you exposing yourself to these stinking rats.'

Mary shook her head. She was determined to stand her ground. After what seemed an interminable time the front ranks of the enemy approached as far as the moat, and whether out of mockery, contempt, or in an effort to intimidate them, the soldiers fired their muskets at the walls of the castle.

Finally, Home appeared below the ramparts and cupped his hands to shout,

'We only want the traitor, murderer and butcher who is hiding away here!'

Instinctively James drew his sword from its sheath.

'Come and get me,' he yelled, 'and tell your friends I spit in their faces!'

'We will come when you stop hiding behind the Queen's skirts, my Lord Bothwell.'

James was livid with fury.

'Come down,' Home continued, 'and one of us will challenge you to single combat, man to man.'

It took six men to hold James back and prevent him running down the castle stairs.

'They want to murder you! I order you to stay here,' cried Mary.

The corners of James's mouth were trembling, and his right hand was tightly clutching the pommel of his sword.

Walking towards the crenellated wall, Mary called out to them,

'Withdraw!' in a tone that permitted no reply. 'It is an order from your Queen!'

Home touched his large deerskin cap.

'We are at your service, Madam, and only wish to protect you from a traitor who is using you.'

'I have no need for your help when choosing my personal friends. Disarm your men and I will receive you,' Mary rebuked him.

'Not as long as Lord Bothwell is holding you captive,' Home declared.

'I am free,' Mary yelled at him. 'Take care, my Lords; you will soon live to regret your treachery.'

Home touched his cap once more and withdrew on his horse.

'They are going to besiege us,' said James.

He was slowly beginning to calm down. If he were to master the situation, he would have to remain in control of himself. Yet he knew that as long as he lived he would want to seek revenge for this public affront.

'Borthwick has a well-fortified position and is difficult to take,' his host reassured them. 'Their siege is unlikely to last long.'

'Huntly's reinforcements will arrive at the same time as the Borderers,' Mary said softly. 'Let us go inside, there is no need to expose ourselves to those vermin or to the rain.'

It was late afternoon, and the assailants seemed to have decided to remain in their existing positions. Refusing to give in to fear, Mary had retained her composure, and had dined before continuing her needlework with Mary Seton and Margaret Carwood, who had followed her to Borthwick. Bastien Pages, her loyal valet from the Auvergne had taken up his lute, and the Queen had sung some French songs without interrupting her work.

Before nightfall, she asked James to follow her into their chamber.

'What are your plans?' she asked James as soon as the door had closed behind them.

'To leave Borthwick during the night and go to Dunbar. It is for me the rebels have come. They will respect you. Besides, as you are well aware, I like to act on my own.'

'There are two of us now!' the Queen said with some feeling.

She put her arms around James and tried to kiss him, but he only brushed his lips across her mouth.

'My duty is to ensure your safety and your realm's domestic peace. I will come back for you as soon as possible,' James reassured her.

Mary showed her concern. 'I will not leave you,' she insisted.

James held his wife tightly against him. Never had their fragile union felt as strong as it did now. Mary was not mistaken in considering their fates to be inextricably linked. If James was ever taken or killed, the rebels would certainly turn against their Queen.

'Well then, let me be the first to go,' James urged her. 'When you are ready to join me send a messenger, and I will come and wait for you at a place of my choosing, then we will ride on to Dunbar.'

'How will you escape from here?' she asked.

'There is a postern gate facing the forest. Once through it I am familiar with all the tracks, and Crichton is not far away. I will assemble some men there and wait to hear from you.'

'Mar and Maitland have betrayed me,' Mary murmured with dismay.

James replied, 'Mar holds your son, and he hates me because I have never been fooled by his false show of friendship. As governor of the

Prince, he is sure to occupy a key position in Scotland. If they succeed in removing you from the throne, Moray is sure to include him on the Regency Council.'

'He will have to kill me first,' Mary asserted, 'because I shall never abdicate.' The vehemence of her tone warned James that he must stop alarming her. However, he too was struggling to recover a semblance of calm. Two narrow windows were set in a ten feet thick wall, and clusters of elongated clouds, tinted pink by the setting sun, could be seen through the opening which narrowed towards the outside. Down below all seemed quiet. It had stopped raining and the solid mass of the large tower stood out in the twilight. Swifts and swallows flitted past at lightning speed swooping for insects.

James led Mary towards the bed. He needed to reassure himself that she belonged to him body and soul.

The Duke was ready to leave before midnight. Morton, Kerr and Home's troops were camping some distance away on an area of pastureland. The soldiers had lit campfires, which gave off sparks in the darkness. Light from the crescent moon faintly illuminated the hazy contours of distant hills.

James and Mary remained for a long while wrapped in each other's arms.

'It is time,' he said softly to her. 'Have no fear for me. Life has taught me more than one trick. Lord Crookston's son is waiting for me with a good horse about one league from here. I will be at Crichton before break of dawn.'

Cheerfully he added, 'Don't worry; Jean is at Strathbogie with her mother.'

Mary forced a smile, 'May God go with you!' she said.

In the morning, Mary was woken by her companion Mary Seton.

'The troop has not moved, Madam. Lord Home had a message sent to Lord Borthwick reiterating that they want only his Lordship's surrender. They will withdraw as soon as they get their hands on him in order to put him on trial.'

Mary let herself be dressed in haste and had her hair coiffed, then she went to a table on which some paper, a quill and ink were laid out.

'You will give them this note,' she ordered.

My Lords,

Your insulting claims are senseless, as the Duke of Orkney, my husband, is no longer at Borthwick. I entreat and command you to lay down your arms, dismiss the rebel soldiers accompanying you, and return to your estates to await my orders.

Briskly the Queen folded the sheet of paper, melted a little wax and sealed it.

'Give it to a messenger as quickly as possible. I am now going to write to Huntly. He must make haste.'

The morning seemed to be interminable. The Lords had not responded to her message and the troops seemed entrenched in their positions. At least James must be safe at Crichton by now, Mary thought.

At noon when the sun had reached its high point Mary, accompanied by Lord Borthwick and a few other gentlemen, insisted on climbing up onto the wall walk again. A servant from the castle had succeeded in slipping past the rebel troops. He was able to inform the Queen that Bothwell was safe but that Lord Crookston, whose son had met James with a good horse, had been captured not far away. He had heard also that Home and Morton were asking for the reinforcements of five hundred men promised by the Earl of Mar.

Catching sight of the Queen on the wall walk surrounding the massive square tower, Morton and Home were tempted to call out to her one last time before breaking camp.

When Mary saw them approaching she called out to them in an imperious voice, 'So you are refusing to obey my orders!'

'We can only obey orders which are acceptable Madam. We came here to protect you. '

'Look after yourselves, my Lords, for your situation is extremely precarious. Go away and enjoy your properties… they might not be yours for much longer.'

The Queen's cheeks were flushed with anger. If she had had a cannon at her disposal, she would have threatened them with that.

Sitting up straight in their saddles Morton and Home were unmoved.

In the bright sunlight, Mary could see the flaming red beard and hair of the chief of the Douglases.

'Since when Madam, have Scottish sovereigns become tyrants?'

Home's voice though weakened by the strong wind, still struck the Queen like an insulting whiplash.

'It is the judges who will condemn you to the block, my Lord!'

'Come,' whispered Lord Borthwick in her ear, 'there is no use wasting your time on these rebels. Morton would betray even his own mother for power, and Alexander Home is one of those men who are both cowardly and opportunistic; he also has an ugly type of arrogance.'

The oblique rays of the sun cast shadows over the meadows where the troops were bivouacking. At the edge of the forest, dead leaves swirled and eddied in the wind. Mary was determined to leave Borthwick that same night to join James. The servant who had managed to pass the guards unchallenged had forewarned her that James would wait for her in the forest, with a horse ready saddled to ride astride. Mary was able to borrow stockings, breeches, a riding cloak, and boots and spurs from Lord Borthwick, who was almost the same size as her. She was determined that nothing must impede her course of action as she galloped and leapt over walls and hedges on her way to wherever James would lead her.

By ten o'clock that night the Queen was ready, wearing her boots and spurs. The cloak concealed her slightly swelling stomach, while the breeches hugged her thighs. She wore a close-fitting cap, which concealed the mass of her hair gathered on top of her head.

The rebels had departed, leaving only ashes and pieces of charred wood to betray the sites of their bivouacs. Without hesitation, Mary went through the same postern gate James had used and stepped out into the forest. Mary Seton handed the Queen her gloves, a purse containing some gold coins and a handkerchief.

'Everything will be fine,' Mary assured her. 'I will send you news as soon as I can.'

Her childhood friend was weeping, and the Queen kissed her on the cheek, saying, 'God protects just causes!'

The path she had to follow wound its way through the forest. Less than a league further on it linked up with two other woodland tracks at a junction where once a cross had marked the spot. There James would be waiting for her with the horses.

The path through the trees was lined with bushes and young saplings stretching up towards the light. The scents of wild plants, humus and rotting tree trunks intermingled in the night air. Mary had been walking for only a short time when in the darkness she felt a strong hand taking hold of hers.

James led her to the clearing in the forest where two of his finest horses from the stables at Crichton were tethered, attended by a groom.

'We shall head straight for Dunbar,' the Duke explained. 'When we get there we will decide on a plan of action; either to wait until we have assembled a sizeable army, or make do with the troops we have at present, and march on Edinburgh.'

They rode by the light of the moon, and dawn was rising when Mary smelt the sea. Everything reminded her of her flight after the death of Rizzio, the wild ride through the night and James's comforting presence at her side.

'I am ready to cook an omelette!' she said as they arrived at Dunbar.

In this impregnable fortress together with the husband she loved, the situation they were now enduring would surely take its place as one of the most difficult moments in her life.

Before the year was over she would give birth at the Palace of Holyrood, and she would always keep the child close by her side. She should never have parted with her little James, and she felt devastated by the thought that he was taking his first steps and speaking his first words not to his own mother, but to Lady Mar.

The fortress was coming to life. Maids were carrying water while servants brought in armfuls of firewood for the kitchens. The sea was grey and so were the skies.

Nothing had been made ready to welcome the royal couple. The princely chambers had not been aired, and were dank with humidity. The cook had only fish, dried beef, oatmeal and peas, the ordinary fare of the soldiers at the castle.

None of the female maidservants were in any manner trained to assist the Queen.

Mary undressed herself and lay down on the bare bed. She felt stimulated by this rough style of life; the Guises were all good soldiers who did not baulk at discomfort or hardships. Nevertheless, at Joinville her family had lived as luxuriously as the King of France. Mary thought about her brother-in-law King Charles IX. Had he received the letters James had sent to him? She was hoping for his tacit support. Did he not also have a secret relationship with Marie Touchet? Behind his royal mask, he was said to be tender and hungry for love. Catherine de Medicis had always preferred his younger brother Henri.

James lay down beside his wife and placed two pistols under his pillow. 'Let us sleep for a few hours, 'he said, 'then we will make a plan.'

54

May it please Your Majesty not to listen to the wicked rumours spreading about me. The most contradictory news is circulating in Edinburgh at the moment and I beg you Madam to keep a cool head. Despite numerous exhortations to take up arms, the population remains calm. My Lords Morton and Home are no longer certain of being able to keep up their accusations for much longer. Your Grace's entry into Edinburgh at the head of her troops would wipe out any resistance. Our friends Lord Huntly and some of the Hamiltons have taken refuge at the castle... they are at my side.

I am, Your Grace, your humble and obedient servant

James Balfour

PERPLEXED, MARY READ the letter twice through. What was the meaning of this extended hand? She had barely awoken from a few hours of light sleep when she had been handed the note.

'Read this,' she said to James.

The Duke, who was about to review his troops, took the letter hurriedly.

'Huntly and Hamilton are at the castle,' he exclaimed. 'Has Balfour turned his coat once more? If this is the case we must hurry back to Edinburgh as soon as we can.'

A kitchen maid had lent Mary a skirt of red linen and a laced bodice which had sleeves that were gathered with ribbons below the elbow. The skirt was too short and only reached halfway down her legs, while the oversized bodice gaped in unsightly folds. Dressed like this, Mary looked as though she was wearing a typical peasant girl costume.

James was walking back and forth holding the letter in his hand. Had Balfour pretended to be on the rebels' side? If the people refused to rise up, the Lords' rebellion was doomed to fail, and perhaps sensing this Balfour had become a loyalist.

'I do not want a civil war,' Mary said in a worried tone.

Bothwell, thinking aloud, answered her worry.

'We will fight if necessary. It is not a matter of starting a civil war, but of crushing factions which want to ruin us. Lord Morton can send me all the peace messengers he wishes, but I no longer trust his word. Has he forgotten that it was I who persuaded you to pardon him?'

'By allowing Rizzio's murderers to return to Scotland, we unleashed the forces of evil,' Mary said in a forlorn voice. 'First Darnley, now it is you and I.'

Bothwell and Mary discussed what to do until noon. Should they march immediately on Edinburgh, or wait at Dunbar for additional troops and leave the rebel Lords to get bogged down in conflicting arguments? Mary felt certain that some of them like Maitland and Atholl would come back to her. The Borderers would rally to their Prince and the Highlanders would regroup under Huntly and Argyll.

The heat intensified the odours of fish and seaweed, and behind the ramparts the sea sparkled and small clouds stretched out on the horizon.

'Let us march on Edinburgh,' Bothwell eventually decided.

Incapable of making up her mind, Mary nodded her head, also influenced by the grim situation at Dunbar where she had no convivial company, no personal belongings and no competent maid.

'We will take four light cannons with us,' Bothwell went on, 'as our opponents have no artillery available to them.'

As dawn broke the following morning early signs foretold a hot day, and the light seemed to quiver on the horizon. Soon a heat haze developed over the sea, and over all the countryside beyond Dunbar where hawthorns, rowans and brambles flourished on the slopes of the hills and round the edges of the fields.

James and Mary emerged from the fortress riding side by side. James was mounted on a powerfully built black horse, and Mary rode the same dappled grey gelding that she had ridden from Borthwick to Dunbar. Behind the Duke rode his two valets carrying his armour and double-edged sword. Then came four cannons drawn by strong workhorses, the ammunition stacked in carts, the infantrymen and lastly the harquebusiers.

James had been able to muster around a thousand men, mostly from the Borders, but he was hoping shortly to link up with further troops that Huntly was bringing with him in all haste from Strathbogie.

On the previous day Mary had heard that the French Ambassador, Philibert du Croc, was attempting to calm the situation in Edinburgh and start negotiations between the rebel lords and the royal couple. Had they not already signed the document approving the Queen's marriage?

James and Mary halted their troops at noon for refreshments. Hailes was only two miles away and sudden nostalgia gripped James. He remembered all the carefree times he had spent in the old ancestral castle; yet since his father's death all he had done was fight, flee, and put his sword at the service of the Stuarts.

'Where are Lord Huntly's troops and those of my cousins the Hamiltons?' asked Mary anxiously.

'They will probably join us at Haddington,' James told her.

The sight of Mary's rustic attire drew a smile from James. When the Queen was seated the red skirt revealed her round knees, and a little of the milk-white skin of her legs was visible just above her boots.

Without saying a word Mary ate the oat bread and cold chicken she had been served.

'We will spend the night with Lord Seton,' James said and then paused. 'You will be in great need of a good night's rest.'

Quietly Mary held her husband's hand. Ever since they had left Holyrood, James had never ceased to worry about her and to do everything in his power to make the tragic times they were enduring together more bearable.

'I love you,' she whispered. 'Do not ever leave me.'

James pointed his finger at her stomach,

'Part of me is right there,' he replied.

Towards the end of the afternoon, the royal troops arrived at Lord Seton's castle. Both men and animals had suffered from the heat, and all were eager to drink and refresh themselves in the cool waters of the small river which flowed through the pastures to the sea.

No trace of the enemy was to be seen.

Lord Seton had a lavish dinner prepared and opened his best bottles of wine, but having neither spouse nor daughter at home, he was unable to offer clothes better suited to Mary. She however, did not seem to care, and with a clear and by now vindictive mind revealed the measures she would take as soon as she returned to Holyrood; this time there would be no pardons for the rebels, only exile and sequestration.

James barely uttered a word. Seton guessed that his silence betrayed his anxiety. As a man of action, he must have been thinking about the possible battle that might lie ahead of them, and the organisation and placement of his troops.

The royal couple retired early with the setting sun. The bell was to be rung the following morning for a dawn departure.

In their room, Mary immediately sought refuge in her husband's arms. All they wanted was to be together and to savour the intense pleasure of holding each other close.

The night was warm and there was not a breath of wind blowing through the wide-open windows.

Outside, insects buzzed, night birds called out to each other, and a few dogs, excited by the presence of nocturnal creatures, barked incessantly. A half moon had risen in the star-studded sky.

All night long James had held his young wife tightly against him, and finally she had fallen asleep. In the dim light, he could just make out the oval shape of her face, her heavy eyelids, and the curling mass of her hair spread over the pillow.

Of all the women he had loved, she was the one who placed the greatest trust in him. She had the unshakeable faith of a young girl who had never known her father, and who had witnessed the brutal deaths of those who had replaced him in her affections. Since the tragic accidental death of Henri ii and the murder of her uncle François de Guise, she had sought a father figure. She had hoped that men like Moray and Maitland would fulfil that role, but they had proved to be nothing but a disappointment to her. Now she had total confidence that James would protect her until his last breath.

Mary donned the creased skirt and dusty bodice without complaint. Dawn had not yet broken but the castle's surroundings resounded with the whinnying of horses being harnessed, soldiers shouting orders, and the general clamour of several hundred men preparing to strike camp.

Although they had no appetite Mary and James drank some soup and ate some white bread with sesame, a precious seed which Lord Seton kept carefully locked away with other spices. He was ready too and equipped for battle, determined to defend his sovereign with his life. Apart from his sister Mary, who remained at Holyrood, the rest of his family was safely ensconced in France.

The columns set off as the sun rose. Earlier the Queen had hastily drafted a proclamation, which she asked to be read out to the soldiers:

A *number of rebels, under the pretext of rescuing the little Prince, notwithstanding the fact that he happens to be under their own guard, have clearly demonstrated their wish to cause harm. Their sole aim being to dethrone their legitimate sovereign in order to take the rule of law into their own hands and so be free to do as they please. Sheer necessity has forced me to take up arms against them, and my hopes rest with you, my loyal subjects, who will be rewarded with the lands and possessions of the rebels, each according to their merit.*

The horses were being tormented by midges. There was not a breath of wind to help keep the men cool as heat from the sun beat down upon their helmets, thick leather jacks and protective coats of mail. The small hills and banks were steep and hard to climb and the hooves of the straining horses raised clouds of acrid dust, which caught at the backs of their throats. Scouts had returned bringing news: the enemy army was progressing rapidly towards them and had already passed through Musselburgh. They had a large body of cavalry but no cannons.

'We will meet in battle at Carberry Hill,' James predicted. 'If we are the first to arrive we will be able to choose the best position, which will give us the advantage. We must quicken our pace.'

Having made a swift reconnaissance at noon, James expressed his preference for ground which gave him a clear strategic advantage. Carberry Hill towered over a plain through which flowed a small river, an obstacle that could potentially slow the approach of the enemy cavalry. From the knoll on which he stood, he could see that the lords' army would be in range of his four cannons and exposed to their bombardment.

From the top of the hill, the Duke could see the enemy vanguard at a distance of about a mile, with a large contingent of cavalry and infantrymen armed with pikes. The prospect of combat instilled in him a desperate desire to inflict an overwhelming defeat on all those who had betrayed him and the Queen.

His troops took up their positions in good order. The standard-bearers unfurled the flag displaying the Red Lion Rampant of Scotland and the banners bearing the St Andrews Cross. The air was muggy, and the pale blue sky above was cloudless. A faint odour of fresh water and decaying vegetation rose from the river.

The Queen's cavalry dismounted from their horses while the foot soldiers, exhausted from their long walk in the heat of the sun, collapsed onto the ground and prepared to eat the meagre provisions they had brought with them from Dunbar. Some reinforcements, coming mainly from the Lothians where the Hepburns held sway, arrived at Carberry to swell the ranks of their small army, which now numbered over a thousand fighting men.

The Queen removed her velvet cap, letting her sweat-soaked hair cascade onto her shoulders. She had had barely three hours of sleep, but nervousness banished all trace of tiredness, and stressed her mind to the point of dizziness. Thirstily she emptied a flask of water and poured a few drops over her hands and face. Some distance away she could see James walking back and forth as he inspected the defences of the ground they occupied. To his Hepburn cousins who had hastened to join him, he showed the position of his troops from whence he was intending to launch his first attack, their first and second lines and the right and left wings. The cavalry would be positioned at the rear, ready to charge and complete the defeat of the enemy.

Suddenly James stopped in his tracks. A few rebels had forded the river on horseback and were trotting towards them. A short, slim and elegantly dressed man whom James immediately recognised led them. Respectfully Philibert du Croc, the French Ambassador, kissed the Queen's hand and greeted her husband. The Borderers gazed in amazement and admiration at the magnificent harness of the French Ambassador's handsome palomino horse, the brow band and noseband of whose bridle were inlaid with gold, with mouthpiece rings of solid silver. Never in their lives had they seen the like.

'Madam, I have come to negotiate a truce, not as an agent of the lords attacking you,' he explained at once, 'but purely in my own name.'

Philibert du Croc took a deep breath, as his task was awkward.

'The lords who are present here,' he continued, 'are not seeking to ill-treat you, Madam; on the contrary, they are prepared to bend before you on their knees. They all claim to be your loyal subjects.'

'They have a very poor way of showing it,' Mary replied interrupting him, 'and furthermore, I am shocked by their intemperate behaviour. Did they not acquit the Earl of Bothwell? Did they not sign the deed approving my marriage? Did they in any way try to prevent my marriage taking place? Tell them, Monsieur du Croc, that if they surrender now I am prepared to forgive them.'

'Madam, they make a condition for their surrender; it is your separation from the Duke of Orkney,' the Ambassador uttered in a deadpan voice.

Mary stood up straight, her eyes shining. Even wearing this poor peasant girl's outfit, the Frenchman recognised the stature and bearing of a Queen.

'Madam, I fear then there may be no possible compromise. They are all mortal enemies of the Duke.'

James had approached silently.

'Do you know, Monsieur du Croc, why they hate me? It is because they are all filled with envy. I have never harmed nor humiliated any of them. On the contrary, I have always shown myself to be conciliatory and ready to listen to any of their proposals. There is not one among them, who does not wish to be in my place, but destiny favoured me and I accepted her offer.'

The Ambassador remained silent. Even if he did not much like Bothwell, he respected his courage and his frankness.

'My role is not to pass judgement, Monsieur le Duc, but to try to prevent civil war which would ruin this country once more.'

The Queen wept. James was deeply distressed to see the tears shed by one who up until now had shown such courage, and who had placed all her trust in him.

'I am very upset by the Queen's distress', he said resolutely. 'We can indeed do something to stop Scotsmen from killing each other. I am ready to fight in single combat against a willing opponent who must be of equal standing and birth to me. God will rule in my favour as I have nothing on my conscience.'

Mary was listening, and with a tremor in her voice she interrupted him, saying,

'I refuse to let you expose yourself to this danger. To have to watch you risk your life would kill me. Your cause is mine too, so let us fight.'

'Enough of parleying,' James agreed. 'Go back and tell those rebel nobles that we are ready for combat. There is no more room for mediation than there was between Hannibal and Scipio. Please remain, Monsieur du Croc, you are about to witness a great battle.'

'There is nothing admirable about civil war, Monsieur le Duc.' replied the Ambassador, and so saying he hoisted himself into the saddle, saluted the Queen and rode away.

The Frenchman having departed, James at once moved to place his first line of troops at the bottom of the hill. The enemy had not altered their deployment.

James became alarmed as he realised that overcome by heat and lack of action, part of his rearguard had scattered into the countryside to search for water and food. To his further dismay, he saw the morale of his troops was rapidly declining. It was now getting late in the day, and soon the advantage James had tried to secure of having the sun at his back and in the enemies' eyes would be lost. This stalemate had to be ended at all costs.

'Let me fight in single combat,' he pleaded with Mary. 'In that way our cause will emerge triumphant, and we will avoid a battle which now we are now unlikely to win. Our men are thirsty and exhausted; they have lost their vitality and have started to disperse.'

The Queen hid her face in her hands. She had reached the limit of her strength.

'I shall send a herald over to our enemies and request them to choose the one they wish to confront me,' announced James.

The royal standards fluttered in the gentle breeze. At the side of the enemy ranks they had unfurled a banner depicting the little Prince kneeling beside his dead father's body and demanding revenge from God.

The emissary sent by James descended the hill on horseback, raising a cloud of dust as he went.

'Sir James Murray of Purdovis is ready to confront you, my Lord,' the herald declared.

Immediately James asked for his armour. He wanted to fight without further ado.

'Not Purdovis,' Mary intervened. 'He is a traitor devoid of any nobility! The husband of the Queen of Scots should not even condescend to speak to him.'

'Morton then!' demanded James. 'If his courage equals his treason, he will accept my challenge.'

The herald galloped back again. James watched the horse's hooves splashing through the river. Without haste he finished donning his armour. He thought of nothing except the duel he was about to fight, which he had to win at all costs. Seeing Morton struck down, Home would waver and wish to negotiate. Moreover by now half his troops had deserted from Carberry Hill, and James was no longer in a position to fight a battle.

Sitting on the slopes of the hill, Mary watched him and was filled with despair. She thought of the prestige she had once enjoyed with the crowds that had adored her; she thought of the fatal mistake she had made in trusting her half-brother, and of her threatened happiness. Her tears had washed away the dust on her face, and her pitiful bodice laced with ribbons was now stained and grey.

In the distance, Morton was parleying at length with the herald, who finally took off at a gallop. James had had enough of waiting. What other excuse were they going to give him to prolong this waiting, which was getting on his nerves?

'My Lord Morton is letting Lord Lindsay fight in his place,' the herald reported. 'Lord Lindsay says he is ready to fight in a man-to-man duel, or six against six, or even ten against ten, as you wish. Your Lordship may also choose whether he wishes to fight on foot or on horseback, and with or without armour.'

'One to one, on foot and without armour,' James replied sharply, struggling to conceal his irritation.

Time was passing, and there was still no sign of Lindsay. James paced up and down the ground chosen for the duel, soaked in sweat and with nerves on edge. For the first time since leaving Edinburgh at the Queen's side, he feared events might take a turn for the worse. His enemies were clearly taunting him. Why had he not launched his troops against them at the very beginning that morning? By trying to help, du Croc had unwittingly played a disastrous role.

Soft rays of sunshine now lit up the slopes and stretches of fields beyond. On the hilltop the horses, pestered by swarms of flies, were shaking their heads and stamping their feet on the parched ground. Nobody is going to appear, James thought to himself. The cowardice of his enemies was breaking his heart. Now his forces were reduced to a few hundred men, the enemy vultures watching closely for the death throes of the wounded animal were about to pounce. The Duke rejoined the ranks of his soldiers, now thinned out by desertions.

'We can no longer fight a battle,' James admitted. 'It would be certain defeat.'

'What can we do?' Mary asked in despair.

James thought for a moment,

'We could ask for another parley, and you could let them know you are willing to receive another emissary in person.'

Finally, Kirkaldy of Grange made an appearance. He was the person amongst the rebel lords whom the Queen most trusted. He was a righteous and valiant man and a proven leader of men in combat. She felt she could talk to him, listen to his proposals and arguments and at the same time prepare her own. A shadow of hope returned to her. An agreement might be possible...

During what seemed like an eternity James watched the meeting from afar. He saw Mary's intense concentration and the telltale signs of worry when she constantly bit her lips and joined her hands over her red skirt as if she were praying. Kirkaldy of Grange was listening to her with deference.

As soon as his enemy had left, James went over to his wife. Suddenly a desperate tiredness descended on him like a lead weight. He had not slept for two days.

Mary gently began to speak,

'Kirkaldy swore to me I would be treated with respect if I accepted the proposals he brought, and joined them now. He also assured me that you would be allowed to withdraw to wherever you wish, and will not be troubled.'

Her voice was trembling with emotion and hope.

'Liar!' the Duke exclaimed. 'The rebels are going to deprive you of your freedom just as they tried to do after the murder of Rizzio. Once they have you at their mercy they will turn their attention to me, knowing I will never cease trying to rescue you.'

'Kirkaldy is a man of honour,' Mary sighed, 'who cannot be intending to betray me.'

James wearily replied,

'A man of honour Madam, who rebels against his legitimate sovereign? I beg you not to allow yourself to be deceived yet again!'

'We have no more choices,' Mary murmured sadly.

'We do,' insisted James, 'let us return to Dunbar, where we will wait for Huntly and Hamilton's troops to arrive. In the meantime, your subjects will come to their senses and support you. The people are fickle, Madam. Today they may growl, stirred up by dishonourable men spreading their venom, but tomorrow they will lie at your feet. Those lords disloyal to you have done nothing but denigrate and insult you; how can you expect the people not to be poisoned by those lies?'

Mary, thinking of Kirkaldy's reassurances, replied,

'We will lose an opportunity for peace. Once I am back in Edinburgh holding the reins of government, I will negotiate your return. A certain number of the rebel lords will accede to my demands.'

'You do not know them well, Madam. I am certain you will become nothing more than a hostage in their hands,' James warned her in desperation.

'We have to try, James.'

Bothwell closed his eyes. When would this nightmare end?

The brightness of the evening was veiled in a heat haze, and in the distance the village of Carberry looked almost as though covered with a fine layer of ash. Mary summoned the herald.

'Tell Lord Kirkaldy of Grange that I will surrender to him on the faith of his word of honour, on the condition my husband is free to go, and that no one seeks to molest him in the future.'

When the herald had left Mary finally looked at James. An occasional tear rolled down her face as though the source of her weeping had dried up. Bothwell expressed no word of criticism; his concern was for the Queen, his deeply loved wife who had taken this decision as the only way she hoped would safeguard them both and in the future reunite them.

A small group of horsemen forded the river. Traumatised, Mary could not take her eyes off them.

'Here comes Kirkaldy of Grange,' she whispered. 'Let them fetch my horse.'

Suddenly she threw herself into James's arms. He embraced her and their lips met in a loving kiss.

'We have to say goodbye,' Mary said softly.

'Goodbye my dearest love. I am going back to Dunbar to raise a new army. When you are at Holyrood, be conciliatory and friendly, we will need as much time as we can get.'

Kirkaldy had dismounted and stood respectfully a few steps away, his hat in his hand.

Mary moved away from James, then went back to him and kissed him one more time.

'Stay faithful to me,' he whispered in her ear.

Mary was sobbing too much to reply, but she closed her eyes by way of a promise, and making a tremendous effort to regain her composure, she walked towards Kirkaldy with her head held high.

Feeling awkward and uncomfortable, the soldiers watched Bothwell, standing tense and overcome with emotion, and their Queen, distraught but proud, riding towards an uncertain future.

With intense emotion, James watched Mary mount her horse and ride away. He then mounted his own horse, turned round and galloped in the direction of Dunbar, followed by a dozen horsemen.

Mary looked back sadly, seeing nothing but the lengthening shadows drawn out by the setting sun.

55

AT DUNBAR JAMES was so busy completing preparations for his counter-attack that the first few days went by without anger or sorrow engulfing him. The Queen's absence was still an abstract concept. At night, he collapsed on his bed worn out. During the day, he filled his time sending out messages, debating various strategies with his supporters, ensuring his arms were in good order, checking the large quantity of stores laid up in case of siege and finding solutions for his woeful lack of money. All the while he was going about his business a single thought occupied his mind: to avenge himself, crush the lords and make them pay dearly for their treason.

Sometimes James became deeply absorbed while contemplating the foam-crested waves, as if drawn to this silent expanse which submerged men's sorrows and obliterated everything. Then once again, his energy was restored. Nothing except death was beyond repair. He had successfully overcome many obstacles in his life and he would surmount this one too.

One morning as he was being shaved, French Paris handed him a letter brought by a stranger from Edinburgh. The paper was rough and the note was not sealed.

My sweet love,

They stole my first message, and I am trying again to write a few words. I am in the depths of misery and despair. After exposing me to a crowd they had stirred up, which condemned me to hellfire for being an adulteress and a witch, the lords locked me up at the courthouse without any food, nor any way of washing myself, and without any female company. I thought I would lose my mind.

No one, not even Maitland, whom I saw walking beneath my windows, came to comfort me.

This morning, they took me to Holyrood, and I was beginning to regain some hope. But they are coming to fetch me again. I must follow Lindsay and Ruthven to Lochleven to stay with the Countess of Douglas, where I will be held prisoner. My women are putting together a few things, but I do not know whether I will be allowed to take them with me. Only the faith I have in God and in you, my true friend, enables me to keep going. You were right; Kirkaldy's friendly words were nothing but lies. Beware of everyone, my love. I do not know when, nor how I will be able to write to you, but be certain that I will. I shall then let you know how to get your letters to me. Let us hope for a compassionate soul on this island.

Your forever faithful spouse, Marie R

James pushed the shaving dish away from him, threw the towel to the ground and jumped to his feet. Consternation and anger flooded into his mind. So he had been right: the Queen had been taken prisoner! It no longer made sense to continue waiting at Dunbar. He needed to approach his potential allies and persuade them to march on Lochleven to free her. It was also vital to recover the documents concealed in his apartments at Edinburgh Castle as soon as possible, his jewellery, his clothes, and above all the silver casket given him by Mary in which he kept some of her letters and poems. That same day he would entrust Geordie Dalgleish, his tailor, with the mission of bringing them back to Dunbar.

A few days later James had regained his confidence. Argyll and Boyd, two men in whom he had no great faith, had voluntarily agreed to support his plans. The Duke requisitioned a large fishing boat. At nightfall, he would sail up the Firth of Forth all the way to Blackness where a groom would be waiting with horses. From there he would ride to Linlithgow where Lord Claude Hamilton, the second son of the Duke of Châtelherault, resided. He would also meet Lord Fleming whose support he had so grievously missed at Carberry Hill. Not for one moment did he doubt the loyalty of Huntly and Seton; he knew they would be there for him when the time came.

Pushed by the rising tide the boat glided along the Forth. From Dunbar James had chosen to navigate along an arm of the sea in order to avoid the area around Edinburgh, which was likely to be in the hands of the rebels. Off Queensferry, the Duke could see the bluish hue of the coast beneath the rising sun. Here and there, a few burghs and square towers became visible, shrouded in a thin veil of mist. Wrapped up in a blanket on the deck and soothed by the sound of water lapping against the hull and the faint whistling of the breeze in the rigging, James managed to get some rest.

'If this tail wind continues we will be there by tonight,' the captain assured him.

At Linlithgow, Hamilton and Fleming both pledged their support to James in his campaign to liberate Mary from the rebel lords, and at dusk the following night, James set off from Blackness on the return voyage to Dunbar, impatient to resume command of his loyal forces gathering there.

In the half-light, as they sailed closer to the shore, he could see seabirds circling above their nests on the cliffs, and in a meadow near the sea, a small flock of sheep guarded by large grey sheepdogs had lain down for the night beside a copse of rowans, alders and pine trees. James thought sadly about his hunting dogs and Skye terriers, left in Jean's care at Crichton. Among them was the bitch presented to him by Anna, to which he had given the French name of Bagatelle, either out of derision or mockery. Generous and loving, his mistress's greatest shortcoming was not to have known when to disappear. Nowadays, he thought, she probably reigned over a wealthy Jutland farm, and held a child in her arms.

As for his own child, he tried to think about it as little as possible. The thought of not being by Mary's side on the day of its birth caused him unbearable frustration. His son or daughter was due to come into the world at the end of November. Where would he be then?

James drank a large mouthful of wine from the flask French Paris handed him, which helped to clear his thoughts. He must have no doubts concerning his future. Some of his allies would arrive from Stirling, whilst others would join him at Dunbar, from where they would converge on Lochleven to rescue Mary. Thereafter they would return to Edinburgh.

'Lord Seton is waiting for you,' announced Sir James Whitelaw, a close friend of the Duke. Back at the fortress of Dunbar James was baffled by this surprise visit. He had exchanged a few messages with Seton, without having had reason to suspect anything.

He hastily climbed the steps leading to the surrounding wall and hurried towards the part of the castle where he had his apartments. Seton was anxiously waiting for him, while turning the pages of a book on the art of sieges.

In a distraught voice, the head of the Queen's house informed him that reprisals against him had already begun. In Edinburgh, William Blackadder, a vassal of the Hepburns, had been tortured and hanged. His brother Jock and some other friends were in gaol, including William Powrie, Bastien Pages and some valuable informers.

'But the news you are going to dislike most,' Seton continued, staring straight into the Duke's eyes, 'is without a doubt the arrest of your tailor Geordie Dalgleish, who was carrying papers and items belonging to you.'

The colour drained from James's face. The Queen's letters were now in Morton's hands!

'Your man will probably be tortured,' Seton went on. 'Everything which he had salvaged from the castle is now in the possession of the Douglases.'

'We will have to act even faster,' Bothwell said in a listless voice. 'Go back to our friends, my Lord, and tell them to hold themselves ready. I will ride to the Borders today to round up as many men as possible and bring them back to Dunbar. Most of the local lairds will follow me.'

Seton was concerned by the tone of apathy in the Duke's voice. Being the brother of one of Mary's childhood friends, he was not particularly fond of the Duke, whom he considered authoritarian, brusque and ambitious, but he admired his courage and total integrity, and above all, he respected the love which the Queen bore him.

'John Knox,' Seton felt obliged to add, 'is unleashing all the demons of hell in his sermons against you and Her Majesty the Queen. Our enemies have realised that they must have complete control over the people's minds. The weight of an accusation is as powerful as an army.'

'Could we not get rid of...?'

'John Knox? Do not even think about it my Lord. His death would initiate the destruction of everything that is sympathetic to Her Majesty. There would be a downpour of the vilest denunciations.'

James kept quiet. The very thought of Morton reading Mary's letters filled him with a terrible rage. His enemies would be able to find material to incriminate the Queen in the murder of Darnley even though her confessions referred to projects that had never materialised. However, there was no time to agonise over it.

Seton hesitated to administer the cruellest blow to the Duke, preferring to keep quiet. He would write him a letter which would find him at Hermitage.

The Borders did not bring James the peace he was hoping to find. The moors stretching out as far as the eye could see were still the same; coarse sharp tufted grass still grew around the bogs and the bare hills still showed their stark outlines against the sky, but the feeling of unlimited freedom he had always relished at Hermitage was absent. His enemies had captured his spirit if not his body.

James had secured the support of five minor local lairds who had each committed themselves to recruiting a hundred soldiers. This detachment added to the four hundred men who had gathered at Dunbar after Carberry Hill, and to the troops his allies would send him, would constitute an army of about five thousand men. Morton could hardly improve on that. They would confront each other on equal terms.

Since his marriage, James had known he could count neither on England, where there was no sympathy for him, or on France, embroiled in her own religious wars and outraged at having been informed of his union with Mary Stuart after the event. He had even less hope of support from Spain or the Pope, who were appalled by Mary's decision to declare Protestantism the official religion in Scotland. The only defenders the Queen had left were himself and a handful of loyal subjects.

Lord Seton's letter arrived as he was sharing a meal with soldiers in the inner courtyard of the fortress. To keep their spirits up beer was served freely together with mutton quarters, a stodgy pea mash and oatmeal cakes. These moments of bragging and crude jokes were the only ones during which he managed to relax. After their meal, some of the men would start to sing ballads, the rest joining in the chorus, hitting their mess tins and pewter goblets.

James, who was sitting on a bench, a piece of meat between his fingers, stood up to receive the note. As soon as he broke the seal, suppressed anguish replaced the pleasure of the meal. Seton had written in French:

My Lord Duke and friend,

A terrible decision has been made in Edinburgh, which it breaks my

*heart to have to tell you. You are to be summoned to appear here
before judges in two weeks time, failing which you will be outlawed,
and stripped of your property and titles. It goes without saying that
the tribunal convened by Morton, Maitland, and from a distance
by Moray, will be made up of men who want your demise. Coming
to Edinburgh would amount to signing your own death warrant.*

*However, as an outlaw, you will no longer be able to count on the
assistance of the lords who have adopted your cause up until now,
as being the accomplices of a fugitive they would all risk losing
their property, estates and honours.*

*I myself am devastated to have to abandon the Queen for a while.
We must play for time. Hide away from your enemies, who will
not take long to set off in your pursuit.*

James looked up. Through the studded gate in the archway of the surrounding wall, he saw the barren moor devoid of trees, paths, or dwellings,
unfolding towards an invisible horizon. He thought about his future, and
his throat knotted with an acute feeling of helplessness.

From the east coast harbour of Peterhead, James, accompanied by French
Paris and about fifty loyal men, rode in the direction of Strathbogie and
the Gordons' castle. He was turning to his friend and former brother-in-
law Huntly as a last resort for an armed rebellion. Not long after he had
received Seton's letter the summons had arrived for him to appear before
the Provost of Edinburgh to answer for his 'crimes': the murder of the King,
the abduction of the Queen and a marriage he had obtained by threats and
violence. The lords, having received no reply from him within the set
deadline, declared him an outlaw, and a reward of one thousand crowns
had been offered to whoever would bring him back dead or alive.

To remain at Dunbar where he risked being besieged was impossible,
and Bothwell had taken to the sea to travel up to the North.

The ancient fortress of the Gordons was a massive square building,
flanked by four towers and roofed with slates, which stood at the foot
of a line of softly contoured hills. Pillaged at the beginning of Mary
Stuart's reign after the demise of the old Earl of Huntly, the castle had
since recovered all its former glory. On either side of the path leading to

the heavy door of the main entrance, George Gordon had ordered the planting of pinewoods, which had now grown up and towered over the ancient holly bushes. Behind the castle stretched a vast expanse of grass-land, grazed by flocks of sheep, and beyond lay a large mixed forest, with leaves in every shade of green.

From the outset James detected a certain amount of reserve in his for-mer brother-in-law's expression of friendship. This courteous man, who welcomed him as his host, was very different from his old friend with whom he had shared dangerous as well as happy times. There was no doubt about it; Huntly was in a state of fear.

After the evening meal, James revealed his plans in detail. Nothing had yet been lost, and many a noble stripped of his property and honours had later recovered them. The Gordons were in a position to acknowledge this from their own past experience. With two thousand soldiers, he could march on Lochleven, keep potential enemies at bay and free the Queen. Once they were within the safety of Dunbar, they could turn the situa-tion around. If fate continued to be hostile and thwart their plans, they would sail for France and persuade King Charles IX to help them.

Huntly listened to him without interruption, but from the expression on his face, James could see he was not convinced.

'Your plans are fanciful,' George wearily replied. 'Reality is cruel, but one must have the necessary courage to face it: Morton, Argyll and Mait-land now hold power in Edinburgh, and Moray is on his way back to Scotland to claim the Regency which he believes is his due. The minds of the people are being continuously poisoned; there are false rumours and reports, placards, and disclosures by spies in all the public places in the city. Believe me, I remain completely loyal to my sovereign but now is not a propitious time to act. I suggest you leave for France on your own, seek refuge, and wait for Moray to make a mistake or for the Scottish people to lose faith in the new government, which can only impose itself by force.'

'You are abandoning me!' James accused him angrily.

George only shrugged his shoulders. He was tired of intrigues, aborted plans and fruitless violence. Without a popular uprising, he knew that a takeover by force was doomed to instant failure.

'Are you aware of the consequences of your cowardice?' James up-braided him. 'In her isolation the Queen will be persuaded to hand over the crown to her son. A long Regency under iron rule will follow.'

'An abdication obtained under duress is worthless,' responded Huntly.

James placed his face between his hands. He was exhausted.

'Let us get some rest,' George suggested. 'We will talk about all this again tomorrow.'

The night was mild and moonless. James woke French Paris, who occupied a closet adjoining his room, and asked him to saddle their two horses at once and warn the men sleeping in the barn. They were leaving Strathbogie. George would not help them and he did not want to inconvenience him any longer with his presence. By the time his old friend awoke in the morning, he would be on his way to Spynie where he would be certain of a welcome from the Bishop of Moray, his old uncle who had raised him, and whom he had not seen for fifteen years.

Their road led them through forests and alongside rivers, where the clear waters flowed over beds of smooth stones, polished over the ages by the current. They were on Moray's lands, and James brooded over his hatred towards the man, who from the very moment Mary had landed in Scotland, had never ceased conspiring against his own half-sister. Why had he not seen more clearly, long ago, through his game? If William Cecil, Queen Elizabeth's cunning and forbearing minister supported The Bastard, it was not for his love of Protestantism. It was in order to rid England of a Catholic neighbour, who as legitimate pretender to the throne of England represented a permanent danger.

The rising dawn caught the band of fugitives as they were about to enter a forest. The valley in front of them took on a golden tint and a light breeze ruffled the grass. The pastures were strewn with wild flowers and clumps of tall thistles, which the horses stepped over with care. Caressed by the morning mist the distant hills were hyacinth blue. The little group of men were stimulated and reinvigorated by the clear light and the scent of the air and earth. James inhaled deeply. Was it really true he had been outlawed, expunged from the land of the living in his own country?

His great-uncle would help him to see things more clearly. At Spynie, in the large diocese he knew so well, he would catch his breath, find a way out and throw himself into it wholeheartedly. We must play for time, Huntly had said with a sigh. James did not have the patience to let time go by.

56

'I NEVER THOUGHT to see you again before I die, Jamie.'

The Bishop of Moray hugged the fugitive. His great-nephew's sudden reappearance at Spynie brought back many old memories from fifteen years ago when James had taken leave of him to finish his studies in Paris. He had missed the young man with his strong personality and headstrong ways, hearty infectious laughter, daring exploits and ability as a horseman, as well as his taste for drinking and pretty girls, the last of which they both shared. After his departure, not one of his own illegitimate children had been able to replace James in the special affection he felt for him, and he was overjoyed at their reunion. He showed him to the room he had formerly occupied and sent for a bottle of good Chinon wine, some pheasant pâté and a Chester cheese.

'Even if the night seems long, the dawn always rises again,' he said cheerfully. 'Make yourself at home and we will chat after supper.'

The Episcopal palace of Spynie was situated close to the sea, separated from it only by low hills from which the clouds seemed to burst out and scatter across the sky. James opened the windows of his room and recognised the same scents he remembered from long ago... the salty tang of the sea and seaweed, the aromatic scent of pine trees and of plants dried by wind and sun.

In this place where he had spent so many happy years, the recent traumatic events appeared unreal to him. How was it possible to visualise the Queen as a prisoner, the rebels in power and himself declared an outlaw, when barely a month earlier it had been he who had issued the orders as absolute master? He thought ceaselessly about Mary, imprisoned at Lochleven Castle and hoping to be rescued. Since receiving the letter she had sent to him from Holyrood during the few hours she had passed there, after the dreadful night spent under the jurisdiction of the Provost, he had heard nothing more from her. As her husband who loved her with all his heart, he felt tortured and humiliated by their anguished parting at Carberry Hill, when he had been forced to flee, unable to defend her against her enemies.

His mind often became absorbed with thoughts of his mother. Whilst growing up at Spynie he had frequently mourned her absence, and now he was not sure if he would ever see her again. She must have been devastated by the wicked lies spread about her son and by the dire peril of his present situation.

Seated at the dinner table, James was reunited with his numerous illegitimate cousins, who had grown from lanky and sly adolescents to stubborn and dour young men who showed him little friendliness. Their jealousy had been exacerbated by his success, and James realised that his fall was their revenge. His great-uncle tried hard to liven up the conversation but with little success, and the atmosphere round the table remained oppressive.

'To hell with those grumblers and whiners!' the prelate exclaimed as he swallowed a mouthful of whisky. 'Instead of reading my prayers, I should have learned not to beget children! I try to give them a decent start in life but they never stop begrudging me the fact that I caused them to be born illegitimate.'

'Her Majesty the Queen is pregnant,' James told the Bishop after his cousins had left. 'Our child is due to be born at the end of November.'

'And you were married in May? If we do not produce illegitimate children, we Hepburns give birth to premature babies. What else can we do... that is the way God made us!'

'Amen,' replied James, half smiling.

Sitting beside his great-uncle, he watched the sun going down over the Moray Firth. Far away, he could just make out a square spire and some cattle grazing. He could hear the twittering of small birds as they gathered for the night to roost amongst the branches of the beech trees beside the palace.

'You can stay here as long as you like my child,' said the Bishop, as he helped himself to another goblet of whisky. 'I do not care whether there are any retaliations from those gentlemen from Edinburgh. They may publish their decrees forbidding my flock from providing me with meat, grain and vegetables as their Christian duty compels them to do, but they will not prevent me from surviving. My granaries are overflowing, my cellars are well stocked, and I have a great quantity of supplies in my storerooms.'

'Do not worry uncle; I don't intend to abuse your hospitality. Before winter comes, I will go to France to ask for assistance… unless I decide to stay in Scotland in order to harass Moray and his men. But first of all I will take refuge in the Orkneys at Kirkwall Castle, which belongs to me.'

The Bishop was pondering. Even when in a solemn mood his round face and fleshy lips gave him a jovial appearance.

'There are quite a number of men in the North who live for danger and love taking risks, such as mercenaries, pirates and other adventurers,' he said to James after a while. 'If you are able to pay them and charter a small fleet you would then have an itinerant force at your command, and you could intimidate the lords by making surprise attacks on them. It would be almost impossible for them to capture you, and brigands by contrast do possess a sense of honour.'

James was pacing nervously up and down. His great-uncle had just come up with an interesting idea. If he were able to transform the Orkney and Shetland islands into a lawless area, then he would be able to hold out for quite a long time. Their inhabitants were mainly tough sailors who cared little about orders coming from Edinburgh, and they would remain loyal to their Duke who was a more undisputed leader than the Earl of Moray. Besides, from there he would be able to negotiate with the King of Sweden, who had always supported his differences with Frederick II of Denmark. He would try to obtain additional soldiers and ships to make a landing in Leith and then storm Edinburgh.

'The idea appeals to me,' he said.

The principal island of the Orkneys archipelago stretched as far as the eye could see and contained pastures, moors, small villages of granite-built houses and steep rocky cliffs battered by crashing waves. James immediately perceived a kind of harmony between the harshness of the scenery and the straits of his own situation. There he would be able to draw the strength needed to live as an outcast, and acquire the toughness necessary for his revenge. Strong gusts of wind swept over the shingle beaches and bent the tufts of bleached grass in the meadows.

Accompanied by about ten of his men, James travelled around the island inspecting the harbours and talking to the locals, who upon hearing his name took off their hats and bowed. Here he would find loyal support, and could with peace of mind leave his vessels tied up in the shelter of well-defended harbours or anchored in coves which were so remote that no enemy ship would dare venture into them.

James felt all his vigour returning at the prospect of going back on the offensive. He would soon make his presence known to Gilbert, the younger brother of James Balfour, who by misfortune commanded the fortified castle of Kirkwall, and would order him to hand the fortress over to him. He was furious at finding a member of this family of vultures once again standing in his way, but Gilbert Balfour would probably be too isolated to put up more than token resistance.

After a week of exploration, James returned to Spynie strengthened in his resolve. He was already considering the purchase of three ships. On his next voyage, he would make contact with some Hanseatic merchants, who owned high-tonnage vessels that could be fitted with cannons of which he knew there to be some at Dunbar. He would send a boat to sail to the fortress, which was still in the hands of the Hepburns, without delay, and it would return with the cannons together with supplies of gunpowder, muskets and pistols. In his excitement, the Duke barely noticed the scathing remarks and hostile looks of his cousins. When his great-uncle warned him against his own children, James did not take it seriously and merely shrugged his shoulders. Were they not related? No one in Scotland betrayed one of his own who had fallen on hard times.

A second voyage to the Orkneys enabled James to bring together the first vessels of his fleet and to take on around a hundred men who were eager to share in the adventure. He waited impatiently for the return of the ship he had sent to Dunbar and hoped that a letter from Mary would have reached the fortress where she still believed him to be hiding. With immense satisfaction, James gave a last round of inspections to the two fishing boats... a large narrow-sterned Dutch cargo boat, and a big-bellied merchant vessel, which could take around fifty of his men. In the harbour of St Margaret's Hope, he had already noticed the *Pelican,* a solid two-master fitted with some artillery pieces, belonging to a Hanseatic merchant. Negotiations had just been initiated, and James was hopeful of an agreement.

Back at Spynie and engrossed in his preparations, James was like a caged lion and even his uncle's geniality was no longer sufficient to relax him.

He was so embittered by news of the arrest of his crew on their way to Dunbar, that he almost came to blows over some trivial matter with Will, the eldest of his great-uncle's illegitimate children. The ship had been well within sight of the fortress when it had been boarded by two vessels armed with cannons. Although the sailors had been lucky to have their lives spared, her captain John Hepburn of Bolton was to follow those of his relatives who had already been executed to the scaffold.

One evening after supper, the old Bishop held James back. Standing in front of the fireplace, the Duke was brooding over his disappointment. Even in these friendly surroundings, the dark curtains, brown leather seats and dark wood furniture were stifling him. The pastures and rush-bordered ponds near the palace were bathed in the soft light of dusk. The last rays of the setting sun suffused with a copper hue the stones on the exposed and windy path to the sea and the outcrops of rocks emerging here and there in the meadows.

'I would love to keep you here with me for a long time,' the old man began, 'but I fear my children may be planning to betray you. The thousand crowns reward on your head is a large sum of money. Do not forget that Judas sold Christ for thirty pieces of silver.'

'I was about to bid you farewell, my uncle,' James confessed. 'I cannot wait to put my plans into action.'

Patrick Hepburn sighed. As a child, James would never accept a compromise; even in a fight he would only let go when forced to do so. To make him come to his senses he had to be dragged away, even if his adversary was taller and stronger. If even one of his sons had been like his great-nephew, the Bishop would have considered himself a lucky man.

'This is your home,' he said. 'Come back whenever you want.'

'I know,' James said softly.

Once again, he would have to enter a new stage in his life and bury a happy episode of his past.

'Everything will be all right,' he continued. 'By tomorrow evening I shall be in the Orkneys and will order Balfour to hand the fortress of Kirkwall over to me.'

'So you have become a pirate,' the old Bishop sighed. 'Prince, Duke, Earl and now pirate!'

'Freedom fighter,' James corrected him. 'A soldier on his way to re-conquer Scotland!'

He gave a bitter laugh, which broke his great-uncle's heart.

At break of dawn, James was woken by the sound of footsteps approaching. French Paris was already up and dressing in haste.

'This commotion doesn't sound too good to me,' the Frenchman said anxiously. 'I think someone is trying to pick a quarrel with us.'

'Slip through the door of the garderobe and alert our men sleeping in the stables. Tell them to bring their weapons and join me.'

Since the previous day, he had been expecting his cousins to make an attempt to stab him in the back. Having been warned of his impending departure, they wanted to take him prisoner in order to pocket the thousand crowns.

'You will have to work for your money, my friends,' he said in a low voice.

How did these miserable characters believe they could catch him by surprise and get the better of him? Throughout their childhood he had thrashed them on numerous occasions; now he was about to hammer the final nail in their coffin.

Resolutely James unbolted and opened the door. He held his sword in his right hand and his pistol in his left.

Some men were climbing the stairs. The Duke estimated there were about six of them. He would have no trouble keeping them at bay while awaiting reinforcements.

The confrontation that ensued was brief and violent. While James was fighting off his assailants, the ten men alerted by French Paris had rushed to the staircase to attack the little group from the rear. The Duke was surprised to recognise amongst his attackers an English spy held on parole in Elgin, a town near Spynie. His presence there was no doubt linked to English orders to eliminate him.

The soldiers stopped at the sight of a body pierced through with a sword. Will, the eldest of James's cousins, lay dead in a pool of blood.

When he went to say goodbye to his great-uncle, the Duke found him praying in the chapel. Tears were rolling down his cheeks.

'God did not intend that His creatures should be happy,' he said. 'All at the same time, I am losing a son to whom I had become accustomed, and a nephew whom I love. I will never find consolation for these sorrows.'

James extended his hand and the old man held it in his own.

'However, I would like to live to see the day when you are back at Holyrood with Her Majesty the Queen.'

'If such is God's will, my uncle.'

'God's will…' the Bishop murmured. 'Is it not rather the desire of men?'

'Well then, I will soon be back in Edinburgh.'

Patrick Hepburn held James in his arms for a long time. James's grandfather had been his brother and he had seen him die at the battle of Flodden before burying his only son Patrick, James's father. He did not want to live long enough to see the grandson die too.

James was about to leave when his uncle called him back.

'I almost forgot to give you this.'

He extracted from his cassock a sheet of paper tied with a cord.

'This letter could well be from the Queen,' he added with a knowing smile.

The woman bearing this letter, Mary wrote, *is a midwife who came to take care of me after my miscarriage. I have lost our children, two boys born too soon to survive. I lack the time to express the pain that I feel, my despair at being separated from you, and my anger at having been coerced to abdicate in favour of my son by a brother whose true colours I can finally see, the ones you so often depicted to me. Do not forget me; I am only surviving in the hope of seeing you, and of getting my revenge.*

James had to lean against the wall of the chapel. He was choked with tearless sobs. Why were these unbearable ordeals inflicted upon him? Whose faults was he redeeming? Everything he loved and touched was turned to ashes. At thirty-two years old, the age of ambitions, nothing was left for him.

'My Lord Duke,' said French Paris, who was standing next to him, 'we are ready to raise anchor, it is high tide and the wind is favourable. We must make haste.'

57

GILBERT BALFOUR HAD STUBBORNLY refused to open the doors of the fortress of Kirkwall. James was powerless to make him yield. Demoralised by the loss of his infant sons he had resigned himself to the situation. Besides, he had now accumulated six vessels including the two-master, the *Pelican*.

More and more often, the fugitive considered leaving Scotland. As long as Mary was held prisoner he could not undertake an audacious surprise attack without endangering her life. Moray would baulk at nothing to stay in power. James thought to himself, why not go to Sweden and then to France, and ask the King to support him with a fleet and soldiers? The Regent had no professional army, and with three thousand hardened men, victory would be assured.

Towards the middle of August, satisfied with his squadron and the hundred men he had taken on, James set sail for the Shetland Islands, fief of his mother's family the Sinclairs, who were certain to give him a warm welcome.

At the end of summer the temperature was already dropping and westerly winds gaining in strength. The season of storms began in September... he would have to spend the winter in the Shetlands and go back to sea in early spring.

However, maintaining and feeding his men for all those months on islands where the only resources were fishing and sheep rearing would be costly.

Admittedly, he still owned some jewellery and clothes made from precious fabrics, but would these luxury items attract any interest among the Swedish or Danish merchants who had come to buy fish or wool?

No sooner had he landed at Lerwick than James was taken to meet one of his mother's cousins, Olaf Sinclair, the Lord of these remote islands, a fine well-built man, his face weathered by sea and wind.

'My Lord and cousin, let me welcome you to the Shetland Islands!' he said, bowing to James who embraced him. Every friendly face was now of vital importance to him.

'Any news from Edinburgh?'

Olaf Sinclair sighed. Just a few days earlier one of Moray's messengers had landed, charged with publishing the decree declaring James Hepburn an outlaw.

However, the population had no time for orders coming from the alleged Regent, and in the few taverns frequented by fishermen The Bastard's claims were openly derided. James was most welcome there.

Feeling relieved, the Duke accepted the invitation to stay at his cousin's house. Half fortress, half keep, the large stone rectangular building was lime-washed and roofed with slates. The room in which he was lodged looked out over the sea, a wide grey expanse where the horizon merged imperceptibly into the sky. A winding path led from the castle down to the sea where fishing boats had been hauled up onto the shingle beach.

James slept for a full twelve hours, waking to the sound of baaing from a large flock of sheep that had approached the castle. Two black dogs chained to a kennel barked furiously. Down by the seashore a group of wild geese waded in the mud at low tide, and oystercatchers pecked about among the seashells. It took Bothwell a few moments to pick up in his mind the threads of his journey and arrival the previous night in the Shetland Islands. Although he felt rested and safe, a vague feeling of apprehension remained. As an outlaw, he would need to be constantly on his guard.

Olaf Sinclair succinctly summed up the situation for James. It would be possible for them to spend the winter in the Shetlands, but he would have to hide his squadron at the far end of the sound of Stuis on the west coast, where boats with a deep draught could not venture. As for his men, if they wanted to make themselves understood by the locals, they would do well to learn to speak Norn, an ancient Norwegian dialect.

Sinclair had not received any recent news from Edinburgh, but he knew the Earl of Moray would stop at nothing and was ready to act with brutality against those who still held out against him. It was inevitable that those lords still loyal to the Queen would soon submit.

'Be patient too,' Sinclair advised him. 'The European courts cannot fail to react against the crime of incarcerating a legitimate sovereign. Her Majesty has a powerful family in France which has her interests at heart.'

James, who knew Catherine de Medicis, was not convinced she would lift a finger to help her former daughter-in-law, but King Charles IX had always had affection for Mary and surely he would not remain indifferent to her plight.

His cousin's calmness and common sense restored James's confidence. He decided he would careen those of his ships that did not require repairs, accommodate his men as best he could and take care of their provisions. Then he would go and inspect hidden anchorages on the west coast and send his fleet there.

A warm breeze blew in from the south, giving the stern landscape a softer, more friendly appearance, emphasised by a blue sky and a calm sea.

Sinclair had had tables set up on the meadow facing the shore.

To honour the Duke of Orkney and Lord of Shetland, he had invited all the great landowners of the islands, ruddy-faced men who were partial to drinking grain spirit. They arrived riding sturdy horses and accompanied by their large dogs. With great interest they observed the Queen's seducer, who seemed to them a somewhat rough fellow with his crooked nose, cropped hair and broad shoulders, but they agreed he was worthy of the Sinclairs. It was said that his father had been as pretty as a girl, but that the son was his mother's child. A fine spread had been prepared for the guests. There was a profusion of oysters, fried crabs, several varieties of fish served in aromatic sauces, and roasted mutton quarters with side dishes of cranberries and peas. Beer and strong spirit flowed abundantly and the guests' already ruddy complexions soon became even more flushed. Children and dogs, excited by the occasion, ran up and down the beach, while buxom serving wenches bustled round the tables.

'My God!' swore Sinclair suddenly, looking out to sea.

He pointed at four ships in full sail emerging on the horizon.

'Royal vessels!' he exclaimed in a horrified voice.

The large sails on one of them indicated it was a warship, probably the *Unicorn*, which was armed with twenty cannons. Was Kirkaldy of Grange commanding this fleet? wondered James.

'Where are your men?' asked Sinclair.

'On land, but the sailors are all aboard my ships,' replied James anxiously.

The guests rushed onto the beach, jostling each other to get a better view of the four approaching vessels, and loudly voicing their indignation over this interference by Edinburgh into their own island affairs. James was aghast. Moray had wasted no time at all, and the bloodhounds were already on his trail.

By now, they could make out the outline of the hulls. Apart from the *Unicorn*, James had no difficulty identifying the *Primrose*, the *James*, and the *Robert*. What chance did his squadron have against these ships? Even if he galloped all the way there, he would not reach them in time.

The guests were in a state of shock, and lost for words they stood on the beach as if frozen, their dogs lying at their feet.

When James reached the Sound of Bressay, he discovered his fleet had already taken to the open sea, having saved time by severing their anchor cables. Some fishermen told him they had sailed northwards with the wind behind them, hotly pursued by four large vessels which were at great risk of going aground in the shallow waters of the channel.

'Your men will be all right; they have pilots with them,' explained the cooper who was translating Norn into Scots. 'They will sail through without any problem.'

'Where do you think they are making for?' asked James.

'Yell or Unst, my Lord. Wait until nightfall. Two boats took to sea to follow your enemies and they will return with news at high tide.'

At twilight, James was able to see two small craft approaching the harbour, tacking with difficulty into the wind. In haste, he sent French Paris on a mission to gather all his men together in the north of the island. As soon as possible they would embark for Yell, and if need be for Unst.

The Frenchman had lost his cheerful disposition, and was dismayed by this mad flight to remote regions. He would gladly have given up the little nest egg of savings he had accumulated whilst in the service of the Earl of Bothwell and the Queen just to be able to find himself back on the banks of the Seine.

'The *Unicorn* hit some submerged rocks and sank,' announced one of the fishermen with satisfaction. 'The other ships have interrupted the chase to rescue the survivors and transfer the cannons. A small party of men have landed, consisting of a Lord and about ten soldiers.'

'Describe their leader to me,' urged Bothwell.

'A tall thin man, with a very pale complexion.'

The Duke remembered the deferential expression on Kirkaldy of Grange's face at Carberry Hill. He was a liar and a traitor of the worst kind. He had succeeded in gaining the Queen's trust which he had immediately betrayed, and had let her be thrown into prison.

'There was a man of the cloth on board the *Pelican*,' added another fisherman. 'It took several men to hoist him aboard the *Primrose*. He was squealing and kicking like a pig.' That will be the Bishop of Orkney, who officiated at my wedding, James thought straightaway. It seems the dogs are hunting in a pack...

If Kirkaldy had decided to disembark, it could only be with a view to capturing him. He must make haste towards the North to join his mercenaries. From there he would send one of his ships to Scalloway on the west side of the main island to pick up the men who had remained with his cousin.

He wrote a hurried note to Sinclair, explaining the situation and the necessity of moving north immediately, adding his hope that after the loss of the *Unicorn* the enemy fleet would abandon their pursuit. He warned him of the presence of Kirkaldy of Grange in Shetland, accompanied by a small armed group.

The little craft that James boarded made good speed sailing north. They passed the furthermost point of the main island, and in the distance in the fading light of dusk, they could just make out the coast of Yell. Standing at the stern of the frail boat the fugitive felt neither the spray nor the cold. He was tormented with anxiety that Kirkaldy of Grange might succeed in capturing some of his men. If he did, torture and death would await them in Edinburgh; it would be an ignominious end in recompense for the loyalty they had shown him.

The wind was rising, creating troughs between the waves. Sudden gusts caused the small boat to heel over but the sailor at the helm seemed confident and in control, even taking pleasure in playing around with the sails in the wind. Following them were several other small boats into which were crammed James's small troop who had succeeded in embarking near Hannavoe.

When they reached Yell, James decided to set up camp for the night near the seashore. The following day they would walk across the island from south to north. The sailors had told them they would have no trouble in finding ferrymen to take them to the isle of Unst. At low tide and in fine weather it was even possible to dispense with boats as long as one did not mind getting a little wet.

The fugitives lit a bonfire with driftwood and wrapped their cloaks around themselves. Some girls appeared from a nearby village, bringing with them smoked herrings, oatcakes and bottles of berry spirit that they all drank thirstily. James could not sleep, and sat awake for a long time lost in thought, his hands stretched out towards the flames.

The wind was laden with iodine and the odours of fish and seaweed. James found it hard to believe that only two months ago he had been living at Holyrood dressed in velvet and silk, with stables full of the finest horses in Scotland. He had eaten off silver dishes, and worn baldrics and belts inlaid with gold and precious stones. Now, clad in thick leather boots and coarse woollen clothing, he was lucky to be able to dine on a kipper washed down with a harsh spirit that burned his stomach.

At break of dawn, the troop set off to cross the island. The wind was continuous with squalls of rain at intervals. Clumps of soft tufted grass gave way beneath their feet, the moss was saturated, and the path indistinct, boggy in places and hard to follow. Few carts or horsemen could have travelled that way, and the only clear tracks over the moor were those made by sheep that quickly scattered as the men approached.

Driven by the strong winds large clouds swept across the sky, casting shadows in billowing waves across the moor. A light mist hovered over the coastal pastures and faded into the grey horizon.

Around noon they reached the north coast of Yell where the tide was low. The channel separating the island from Unst was indeed narrow and local children were scattered on the beach in search of seashells.

In a poor village sheltered by dunes from the worst of the gales, James was able to buy a supply of oatmeal, dried apples and small barrels of light-coloured ale. Fishermen were busy near the shore mending nets or careening their boats. By the time his men had finished their meal the tide was coming in, and James decided to hire a few small boats to make the crossing to Unst. By then the sun was already setting.

'Five foreign vessels are anchored at Norwick,' a little man dressed in black had emerged from a small thatched cottage and addressed James. 'Are they perhaps yours?'

Without waiting for a reply, he extended a calloused hand.

'I am the minister of Yell, catcher of souls and of fish, and at times I go out to sea. I have been told that a fugitive of high quality is trying to escape by sea. Would that be you my Lord?'

James stared straight into the minister's eyes. Did he think he was naïve enough to reveal his identity to a complete stranger?

'I am indeed looking for my ships,' he muttered. 'They were at Lerwick and were forced by the wind to raise anchor in all haste.'

'That is where a vessel has just sunk they say. You are right to find a safe haven for your ships as there is a storm brewing.'

The minister looked up at the sky adding,

'The wind will soon veer to the west. Dropping anchor here will be safe enough.'

James touched his hat and walked away but the little man raised his voice:

'Your Lordship has nothing to fear here. The locals are not inclined to be talkative and they dislike busybodies. Those gentlemen from Edinburgh will find closed mouths and doors slammed in their faces.'

The sailors enthusiastically told James about their escape, the shipwreck of the *Unicorn* and their arrival at Norwick where the small number of fishermen who lived there had given them a warm welcome. Any day now they were expecting the arrival of the *Margaret,* which following the Duke's orders had set sail for the west to collect the trunks and other effects put together by Sinclair.

'I think I managed to identify the other two commanders,' the captain of the *Pelican* whispered in James's ear, 'and I am almost certain they were Murray of Tullibardine and the Bishop of Orkney.'

'Tullibardine!' repeated the Duke with incredulity.

Once again, this agent of the devil was obstructing him. What madness possessed the brother of the Countess of Mar to try to exterminate him? As for the Bishop, he held him in too much contempt to waste a single thought on him.

'What are our orders?' asked the captain.

'The troop will rest for a day or two, and then I shall decide.'

In reality, James's options were limited. If his pursuers decided to abandon their prey, they could then consider spending the winter in Unst; otherwise, they would have to fight.

The evening passed without further incident. The men were all on board and had fallen asleep, having had to content themselves with a meal of sour milk and oatcakes. Neither moon nor stars were visible and the sky was as black as ink.

Wrapped in a blanket, James surrendered to sleep. He no longer had the strength to make plans nor even think about the day when he would free Mary and take her back to Holyrood.

At break of dawn, the three enemy vessels were so close that they could see the men busying themselves in the shrouds. James woke up and rose immediately.

'Prepare for combat!' he shouted.

They sailed out to sea to form a squadron, with the two ships armed with cannons providing cover for the others. James took command of the *Pelican*, and took on board French Paris and most of his men.

The gales reached a peak strength of thirty knots, and were succeeded by a steady westerly wind of eighteen knots. In the intermittent sunlight, the choppy foam-crested sea took on a greenish reflection.

Soon the little fleet reached the high seas, rocked by a regular swell. Two miles distant at most, they could see their enemies heading straight towards them.

With his nerves on edge, James had gone to stand at the prow of the *Pelican*. The first volley from the *Primrose* took them by surprise. They had insufficient gunpowder to retaliate, and needed to bide their time and avoid acts of rash bravado. If they were boarded and there was hand-to-hand fighting, he would take great pleasure in tackling Tullibardine himself. Being easier to manoeuvre his ships managed to dodge most of the missiles aimed at them, but some ships had been damaged and one had been obliged to turn back.

Suddenly James heard yells from his crew. Severed by a cannon ball, one of the *Pelican*'s masts crashed heavily onto the deck.

'Cut off the rigging,' the captain screamed. 'We must disengage the vessel from the mast.'

Another volley narrowly missed them, and James realised defeat was close.

'Signal to the other crews to escape with their ships,' he ordered the captain.

The westerly gale continued to gain in strength, pushing the *Pelican* forward at a speed of more than ten knots. Plunging through the swell and sailing off the wind the ship managed to maintain her speed, gradually putting distance between her and her pursuers. James and many of his men became seasick and some of them collapsed onto the deck. French Paris was as pale as a ghost.

The storm showed no signs of abating. Now alone amid the waves the *Pelican* had cast out a line trailing a sea anchor behind her. Large waves broke over the deck and in the darkness of night the men clung to the rigging to avoid being swept overboard.

'What course are we taking?' James asked the captain, who was clutching the helm.

Soaked to the skin Bothwell was shivering, and his stomach was contracting intolerably.

'We are racing due east with the wind behind us,' shouted the helmsman. 'The wind is going to abate; in about an hour it will become calmer and we should be able to see the Norwegian coast.'

By dawn, the *Pelican* was borne along on a regular swell. The brutal shocks and foaming breakers had ceased. One after another, the men got to their feet, wringing out their drenched clothes, and exchanging a few pleasantries as they tried to forget the terrible night that they had just endured.

Suddenly a shaft of pale sunlight pierced through the thin layer of clouds. The tide was turning and the leaden water took on a greenish hue.

'Look over there!' the captain said, pointing to the horizon.

James shielded his eyes with his hand. He could see a line that was a darker grey than the sea.

'Land?' asked the Duke.

'Bergen,' answered the captain.

58

IN THE EARLY MORNING the *Pelican* sighted a merchant vessel approaching flying the Hamburg flag. The Scottish ship was in a sorry state with a broken mast and torn sails.

'Do you need some help?' the Captain called out in German, having brought his vessel alongside.

'We need a pilot,' James shouted back.

'Follow me; we are on our way to Bergen.'

The men watched with interest as they drew nearer the coast, seeing in the morning light the bluish outline of hills and unusual irregular-shaped crags and rocks on the shoreline. Small houses huddled close to each other around the harbour, and here and there the tip of a spire was visible above the rooftops. In the distance was a range of mountains.

James took heart once more. In Bergen he would have the sails mended, a new mast erected and the hull caulked. Then he would decide where to head for next, Sweden or France. Far behind and still only a speck on the horizon, a light vessel was following them, probably the second of his fleet to have managed to escape. Two ships and around a hundred men would be enough to start on his long campaign of winning back Scotland.

While sailing past the harbour mole the Duke immediately noticed the *Bear*, a warship flying the Danish flag. Norway allowed armed vessels under Denmark's authority to patrol her coast in order to repel the numerous pirates attempting to unload clandestine cargoes or capture isolated boats.

'Salute the *Bear*!' he ordered the captain.

Immediately the sailors hauled down the topsail and fired a blank volley. The *Bear* replied to this signal forthwith by hauling down then raising the topsail of her mizzenmast, while two men put to sea in a longboat.

'Who are you?' asked a man cupping his hands around his mouth.

One of the *Pelican's* sailors who spoke a little Danish explained they had come from Scotland, and had been caught in the storm.

'What is your destination?'

James hesitated to mention Sweden, which was an enemy of Denmark so might cause difficulties.

'Tell them we are gentlemen ready to serve their King,' he whispered to the sailor.

It was not wise to identify himself. Who would believe a dishevelled man in tatters who claimed to be the husband of the Queen of Scots, Duke of Orkney and Earl of Bothwell?

'Admiral Aalborg requests to see the captain of the *Pelican*,' a sailor shouted back. 'He wants to see your documents and the ship's log.'

'Go on,' James said to his captain. 'Explain to the admiral that as the Queen is being held prisoner the authorities were very disorganised in Scotland, hence we were unable to have our navigational documents stamped.'

The captain returned a moment later, crestfallen. The Danish admiral would not accept his explanation and wanted to speak to the owner of the ship. He had invited James as owner to come aboard the *Bear*, along with some twenty of his men.

James hesitated. Dividing his troops would leave him in a weak position. There were no more than two dozen Danes on board the *Bear*. If he so wanted, he could easily ignore the orders he had been given, and could set sail for Sweden. Although damaged, his *Pelican* was still seaworthy enough to manoeuvre at sea. However, for the second time he would become an outlaw. It was better to negotiate and obtain legal permission to refit in Bergen. He decided to speak to the admiral and to take fifteen of his men with him.

'I request your authorisation for my men to go ashore and get supplies from the ships' chandlers and merchants in Bergen,' he asked the Danish admiral.

The Dane spoke English fairly well, and listened without emotion to what James had to say. He reflected awhile, then suddenly announced he would keep on board those men who had accompanied James. There were so many pirates around the coasts that he could not afford to take risks, and James would have to understand his position. As soon as he received orders from Copenhagen, he would act in accordance with them. Apart from two men who were allowed to disembark into a longboat to get supplies, the rest of the *Pelican*'s crew were meanwhile to remain confined. James realised he needed to make a quick decision in order to avoid having his plans thwarted, the *Pelican* impounded and his men and himself held as prisoners.

'May I speak with you in private, My Lord Admiral?' he asked.

With amazement Aalborg listened to this visibly exhausted man with unkempt beard demanding to be set free, telling him he was the husband of the Queen of Scots and a ruler of Scotland.

'You have to understand, my Lord,' the Admiral uttered finally, 'that I am not totally convinced. The Governor of Bergen, Earl Erik Rosencrantz, will receive you and you can tell him your story.'

With a heavy heart and weary step, James trudged up the road, which rose steeply from the harbour and led to the fortified castle. Just like the *Pelican,* he felt as though his own body had been broken and battered by the wind and the waves. On either side of the road stood brightly painted cottages with small front gardens in which autumn flowers bloomed, together with a few vegetables. The peaceful life these dwellings evoked and the glorious sunshine gave James a feeling of irresistible wellbeing and raised his spirits.

The next hour would influence the course of his destiny. If the governor gave him his freedom, he would regain some faith in his future, but otherwise he would have to write to King Frederick II. He had got to know him quite well on his way to France when Marie de Guise had sent him as an emissary twelve years earlier.

Halfway up the hill James paused to regain his breath. Below where he stood, he could see the harbour and town spread out, with its German quarter separated by a barricade. There merchants drove hard bargains over the purchase of fish, oil and whalebone, in exchange for canvas, grain, and in particular schnapps, which the Bergen sailors consumed in great quantity. The sharp spikes on the barricades protecting the German district of the town clearly indicated that its inhabitants were not well liked by the other residents.

James was surprised to be received by the Bishop of Bergen, who was the judge of the maritime tribunal, and some of his colleagues. At this stage in their enquiry, Rosencrantz had not deemed it necessary to put in an appearance.

Calmly James recounted the details of his voyage and confirmed his identity. He said he intended to stay only a few days in Norway before setting sail for Denmark, where he wished to meet the King. Thereafter he would head for France, his final destination, where the Guises were awaiting him.

'We believe you my Lord,' the Bishop replied in perfect English. 'Some merchants have already recognised you. However, you have no documents in your name, no passport, and no evidence whatsoever to prove that the two ships you claim to be the master of actually belong to you.'

'And who would sign my documents my Lord?' James exclaimed. 'Whose authorisation am I supposed to request, since I am a leader of my country?'

His voice was shaking and his tone so proud that the Bishop raised his hands in a placatory gesture.

'Indeed my Lord, indeed so,' he admitted.

The spacious room in which the Duke stood was furnished with chairs upholstered in purple velvet and a large walnut table. The torches and chandeliers were not of silver nor even of copper, but of plain wrought iron. There were no curtains hanging at the windows, nor any tapestry to soften the austerity of the stone walls.

'I ask your Lordships,' Bothwell continued, 'for permission to hire a room in one of the inns of Bergen. If you want me to appear before a court I am prepared to justify my actions and those of my men too.'

Flies were buzzing in the windows, which looked out over the sea. James longed to return to the *Pelican* to get some sleep and particularly to get some nourishment. Since his last meal at the house of his Sinclair cousin, he had eaten virtually nothing.

'Permission granted,' the judge agreed peremptorily. Then as James bowed before taking his leave, the judge added, 'Would you by any chance have any jewellery, silverware or personal documents on board the *Pelican*?'

'I have nothing left,' Bothwell replied firmly.

In fact, he had carefully hidden on board the documents signed by the Queen making him Duke of Orkney and Lord of Shetland, together with a copy of the 'wanted' poster issued by Moray with the confirmation of a thousand crowns reward to whomever caught him dead or alive. He was aware it would not be wise to let these items fall into the hands of men he was not sure he could trust.

'What about the *Pelican,* my Lord?' queried the judge. 'Some German merchants said they recognised your ship, which they claim belongs to one of them.'

'It was properly chartered,' James quickly replied. 'You can carry out your own investigation.'

He felt at the end of his tether, but his nightmare seemed now to be coming to an end. Having found lodgings at an inn, he would ensure the careening of the hull was completed rapidly, and then set sail for the south as quickly as possible.

The inn with its half-timbered walls and thatched rush roof was a hub of activity by day and night. The innkeeper, a tall strong man, controlled the serving maids, kept an eye on the kitchens and gladly sat down to talk with his customers in the dining-room, which was warmed by a smoking peat fire that brought tears to one's eyes. James had rented the best room, which included a garderobe and a cubbyhole where French Paris slept. The two crossbar windows looked out over the harbour and hills visible beyond the surrounding town walls. The investigation into the *Pelican's* documents would last two weeks at most, and James was not at all concerned about the result. The hire transaction was all above board and the agreed sum had been paid. He would without question pay for the repairs out of his own pocket and he was ready to charter the two-master for several more months.

The men were lodged throughout the town and were enjoying themselves and not complaining about their idleness. French Paris's humour had returned and he was teasing everyone, mimicking the residents speaking to one another, and imitating the poses of the local girls who regarded them with considerable interest. For the first time in ages, James found himself laughing heartily. Being well fed, sleeping soundly and feeling more confident about the future, he felt at ease in these moments of respite when only minor considerations mattered such as a flask of grain spirit, which he could take pleasure drinking while sitting outside in the sun. He enjoyed taking a stroll along the main street, having a conversation with a merchant or returning the smile of a young girl who reminded him of Mary.

At present, he was not in the least angry or resentful about the actions taken by the Danish authorities, and felt completely at ease in his surroundings. The two letters written by the Queen since their separation at

Carberry Hill he carried safely inside his doublet. Whenever he felt lonely and was missing her, he would read them over again. In the evenings he would sit at a table with the innkeeper, or some local notable who was curious, and pleased, to meet the 'King of Scots,' as he had become known.

Finally, James received the summons to appear at the court in Bergen. The judge quickly accepted the legality of the charter of the *Pelican*. The Hanseatic merchant had produced the documents, all signed according to legal requirements. However, the legality of the purchase of the second boat belonging to the Duke of Orkney was less clear. The owner, a German not known for his honesty, had acquired it from an individual suspected of piracy. The prosecution had found three merchants whom this pirate had robbed of part of their cargoes, and who were willing to testify against him in court.

The lawyer whom Bothwell had engaged strongly defended his client. How was his Lordship to know that the former owner was was a free-booter and pirate who did not have the right to sell his ship? The Duke did not even know his name. Although James did not understand the judges' spoken deliberations or the witnesses' testimonies, he remained confident of the outcome. These good merchants, who formed the jury for his case, were likely to be in a hurry to return to their businesses, and would speed up his acquittal verdict. The sunny weather continued, despite the mist which shrouded the harbour each night, leaving the lighthouse looking like a luminous dot surrounded by a spectral halo.

The deliberations of the judge were drawing to a close, and in good French his lawyer confirmed his optimism to James. He had already started to file away his documents in a thick leather briefcase, when from out-side the court came the sound of cart wheels and horses being pulled up sharply, followed by a dog barking furiously. The next litigants were talking together in the hallway outside the courtroom.

The judge had seated himself in his high-backed chair with its thread-bare green velvet padding. He was anxious to bring the proceedings to a swift close, and with hands folded and an ingratiating look, he interrup-ted the translator who was conveying in Danish the defence statements of Bothwell's two men, deeming them no longer necessary.

Suddenly the door of the tribunal hall burst open and a short thin man approached the judge in great haste, carrying under his arm a bundle of documents tied with a strap.

'I petition your Honour for the indictment of his Lordship, the Duke of Orkney here present, on behalf of my client Anna Throndsen, a subject of the King of Denmark, who accuses the said Duke of having robbed her a few years ago of sizeable sums of money'.

James, in shock, felt the blood drain from his veins. Could Anna really be appearing out of his past at this very moment? What twist of fate would allow a vindictive former mistress to throw herself in his path at the very moment he was being granted his freedom?

The judge, who hitherto had been favourable toward him, now spoke in stern tones, 'Your Lordship is kindly requested not to leave this town before the preparation of a new trial.'

The hammer crashed down on the light-coloured wooden table. James started. He felt as though it was he who had been struck a deadly blow.

59

THE LEGAL PROCEEDINGS instituted by Anna had been going on for several days. In cold terms his former mistress's lawyer listed the successive sums of money lent by Madame Throndsen, to which had to be added the value of the jewellery she had had to sell to satisfy the personal needs of the man who had made a promise of marriage to her. Perniciously, the little man had mentioned to the judges that Madame Throndsen was not the only one to have been used by the Duke, adding that he was notorious in Scotland for his debauchery.

Mortified, and with nerves at breaking point, James listened to his lawyer translating the accusations. How could he accept that mere fish merchants were to judge his love affairs, he who was the spouse of the Queen of Scots? How could he tolerate this malicious gossip of the lowest order, smugly paraded by Anna's lawyer?

His former mistress's demands were precise, and there was to be no negotiating.

Suddenly James capitulated. He could not stand any more talk about Bergen, about judges, or about Anna Throndsen. He desperately wanted to leave, and be able to think about his future and about Mary.

'Tell Madame Throndsen's man of law,' he said in French to his advocate, 'that she can have my smaller ship with all its rigging. When I return to Scotland she will receive an annual allowance until my debt has been completely paid off.'

The negotiations seemed to go on forever. It was getting dark and a clerk lit some crude lamps, which gave off an odour of whale oil that caught at the back of his throat. James felt nauseated by the smell.

'We accept your proposal,' whispered the lawyer. 'You should consider yourself fortunate, as Madame Throndsen is a cousin of the Earl of Rosencrantz and it is within his power to keep you here or to release you.'

'I am sure your Lordship appreciates my position,' the Viceroy said in a clear voice. 'It is not that I doubt the legality of the documents relating to your ship, but since you have decided to leave it to my dear cousin Anna I wish to verify their authenticity scrupulously. I am told you have applied for a Danish passport. I must consult with my sovereign before granting it to you. I believe you have armed men in your retinue?'

'I would indeed be grateful to obtain an audience with the King,' said Bothwell briskly. 'I am certain he will be prepared to help me free the Queen of Scots my spouse... she is also his cousin.'

'Well then, my Lord Duke, let us go to Copenhagen. I am happy to offer you the hospitality and protection of one of His Majesty's war ships.'

The next day Aalborg returned from his visit on board the *Pelican* carrying a casket, the contents of which were examined by three commissioners. They consisted of a sheet of parchment listing the titles and privileges granted to the Earl of Bothwell by Mary Stuart shortly before their marriage, and various documents including the warrant on his head issued by the Regency Council in Edinburgh and the order to track him down throughout Scottish territory by land or by sea. Finally, there was the copy of the letter from the Queen addressed to the Regency Council, in which she expressed her indignation over her imprisonment and over the accusations made against her and her husband.

'Your Lordship,' Admiral Aalborg began, 'seems to have left his country to save his head. Our Viceroy will be pleased that he has made the decision to take you to Copenhagen. The *Bear* will set sail at daybreak the day after tomorrow. His Grace requests that you take with you only four or five men. The rest will be free to go wherever they wish. Moreover, the Earl of Rosencrantz is holding a banquet tonight in honour of your Lordship and requests the privilege of your presence.'

These words, spoken with a deference he had not heard for a long time, gave James a sense of personal satisfaction, which made up for some of the recent humiliation he had undergone. He would employ the afternoon in searching out a doublet, cap and shoes, for himself and French Paris, who would escort him.

The apartment in the austere Bergen Castle occupied by Erik Rosencrantz was comfortable and even cosy. The furniture came from France, the tapestries from Flanders, the carpets from Turkey, and the gleaming silver from England. Wearing a ruff and dressed in velvet with a heavy gold chain around his neck, the Earl welcomed James warmly, insisting on pouring him a goblet of grain spirit.

Gradually the Duke of Orkney felt himself relaxing. The refinement of the objects that surrounded him, the discreet efficiency of the servants and the spicy fragrance of the cedar wood shavings thrown onto the hearth took him back to the time when he had enjoyed such luxuries every day. He recovered his sense of self-esteem, resumed his elegant manners and recalled the way he had been taught in France to conduct a conversation. Mary naturally possessed this gift. She knew how to launch a subject, revive it, find paradoxes, change course, and spiritedly deny that which she had passionately asserted just a moment before, tease, lie, and play the coquette or the wise woman with equal talent. The four walls of Lochleven Castle must seem to her like a tomb.

The guests lent an attentive ear to James's story: his flight and his struggle against the storm. The ladies listened excitedly and the men with interest. Everyone expressed their indignation at the insolence of the Scottish nobles who had dared to imprison their Queen. European powers would intervene, the Duke could rest assured, and their monarch Frederick II would be the first to act.

James was intoxicated by their words as much as by the abundance of wine. Everything he had hoped for since his flight had been confirmed. They would help him, grant him troops and money to win back power and restore Mary to the Scottish throne. He was not as alone as he had feared. A heady rose fragrance emanated from the bodice of the lady sitting beside him. He remembered how at Crichton in early summer the air was filled with the scent of roses. Had Jean altered the arrangement of the rooms or made any improvements or embellishments to the castle? He was pleased his property had not been abandoned. His nephew little Francis enjoyed staying there, Jean had told him. It was a year since he had last seen the little boy and he could barely remember his small face, dark eyes and the straight hair that his mother tried to tame. Would his own sons have looked like him?

James emptied his glass in one draught. If he wanted to move forward, it was best to suppress certain memories.

The guests had become light-headed with the wine and conversations began to flag. Once more they toasted the King's health, and then each asked for his cloak and his horse. James was about to take leave of his host when Rosencrantz held him back.

'Please understand, my Lord, that your situation is a little delicate,' he said, taking his guest's arm in a friendly gesture. 'You may be the spouse of a sovereign, who has blood ties with all the royal families of Europe, but there is a price on your head, and your enemies are tenacious. Be patient and do not take personally delays that may seem unbearable. Once Her Majesty the Queen your wife recovers her throne you will have the means to make yourself heard, and to negotiate or inflict punishments.'

'My Lord,' James answered dryly, 'I must act now, not languish and wait patiently. If I may say so, you are not up to date with Scottish politics. My enemies, who know I will fight until the end for justice to be done will not spare me. Do you want me to expose my jugular to them? Resignation is not one of my strong points.'

Rosencrantz nodded. With his eyes half-closed, he observed his guest with sympathy.

'Life does not always give us a choice my friend. Wisdom is the prudent man's companion.'

'Wisdom leads to the grave. I am thirty-two my Lord, and am not ready to let those men, all of whom have blood on their hands, sacrifice me like a sheep. The forced abdication of the Queen of Scotland is a crime which no sovereign in Europe should allow to go unpunished.'

French Paris handed James his cloak and cap.

'When do you want me to go aboard the *Bear*?'

'The day after tomorrow at dawn. Although my cousin Anna Throndsen has suffered a breach of trust on your part, I am not your enemy, do believe me, and if I am sending you to Copenhagen it is for your own good.'

James bit his lip. It mattered little to him whether Rosencrantz considered him a friend or not. In Copenhagen, he would count only on himself to persuade the King.

'His Majesty is in the north of Jutland just now,' Peter Oxe, Frederick II's chamberlain announced respectfully, 'but your apartments are ready my Lord, and I have been instructed to ensure you have everything you need.'

'I thank you, Sir,' said Bothwell in appreciation.

After ten days at sea, James had returned to the city where he had stayed several years earlier. From the coach taking him to the royal palace he had seen canals, numerous churches, shops bustling with activity, pretty girls dressed mostly in red, fine looking horses and prosperous houses.

During the interminable voyage, he had alternated between hope and darkest dread. Separated from his ships and his men he was now powerless to impose his will by force, and could rely only on his powers of persuasion. The vessel loaded with his personal items, silverware and jewellery had not gone with him, and he had been obliged to embark for Copenhagen destitute and deprived of all his belongings. What fate awaited his men? He had failed to persuade them not to set foot in Scotland again. On their native soil, death was all they would find.

Oxe spoke excellent French, and James was happy to be able to communicate with him for as long as the King remained absent from his capital.

James was pleased to find a spacious and bright chamber with two windows, a garderobe, and a cubbyhole where French Paris could settle. The furnishings were lavish, the walls adorned with paintings and tapestries, and the two hearths gave out a pleasant heat.

'I have received orders,' Peter Oxe explained with some embarrassment, 'to advise his Lordship not to leave his apartments.'

'So I am a prisoner.'

James wanted to avoid raising his voice. He wanted to gain a reputation for impeccable conduct before meeting the King.

'Not exactly my Lord,' Oxe stammered, 'more like a protégé. His Majesty cannot let anything happen to you.'

James did not reply. From his windows, he saw small boats sailing down the canal, and the sails of larger vessels arriving at the harbour.

'Is there anything at all you wish for?' Oxe asked affably.

'I would like to speak as quickly as possible to the French Ambassador.'

Ambassador Dancey, a venerable gentleman, had spent so many years in Denmark that he now spoke his mother tongue with a trace of an accent. Although he had not so far received any instructions from King Charles

IX, he knew how to proceed with the greatest circumspection without appearing hostile towards a personage as important as the Duke of Orkney. No one yet knew in which direction the wind would blow. Mary Stuart might escape or be rescued by her supporters and return in triumph to Edinburgh. Her husband would then regain his place by her side and he would not forget those who had shown sympathy towards him during his exile.

Dancey found James reading by the fireside, comfortably dressed in a fur-lined house robe. The King of Denmark was obviously treating his guest with generosity and with his clean-shaven face and moustache with finely tapered points the Duke cut a splendid figure.

'Were you reading, My Lord Duke?'

'Ronsard, Monsieur L'Ambassadeur. I am curious to discover a poet who composes such beautiful verses to celebrate the Queen, my wife.'

James laid down the book, which was bound in crimson leather and stamped with the arms of the King of Denmark. Frederick II had given him free access to his library and reading helped him to bear the monotony of the day.

Despite the warmth of his greeting, Dancey sensed the state of tension within the Duke.

'Let me remember,' he said, trying to keep the conversation on a pleasant topic:

'Though still the sea's broad barrier lies between
us two, yet still the light of the bright sun
of your matchless eyes, equalled by none,
is never far from where my sad heart has been.'

James remained pensive, and Dancey feared that by trying to help he had reopened his wounds.

'I was very impatient to meet you, Monsieur L'Ambassadeur.' The Duke's tone had changed and the man who now stood in front of the old diplomat was unsmiling and contentious.

'My situation in Denmark is unacceptable at all levels. I am a Scot and I do not have to account to anyone but my sovereign. I believe you are aware that I have always sought out and obtained the friendship of the French, to whom I am linked both by my education and by the commitment

I made since my earliest youth to serve our late Regent the Queen Dowager Marie de Guise. There is therefore no need to beat about the bush when I tell you that I am impatient to receive the assistance of His Majesty the King of France.'

Dancey cleared his throat. Bothwell was a warrior more than a diplomat and he was not ready to go to war.

'His Majesty my King is indeed aware of your misfortune, and was greatly astonished to hear that the Queen's subjects had imprisoned their sovereign. However, the atrocious death of the previous King has also profoundly disturbed His Majesty as well as his mother, brothers and other princes of Europe.'

'If you are insinuating that I might be guilty of the death of the late King, I have to remind you that I was tried and acquitted by a tribunal whose verdict was ratified by the Scottish Parliament.'

James's tone was aggressive and almost threatening.

'I do hear you My Lord Duke,' protested Dancey, 'but the Earl of Moray, who spent several months in Paris, had the opportunity to convey his version of those events. His Majesty is currently deliberating and needs a little more time.'

Bothwell's fist crashed down onto the little table on which he had put Ronsard's book.

'Time, Monsieur L'Ambassadeur is in short supply when the Queen my wife is in prison and under threat. Do you know that she was forced to abdicate on the same day she miscarried my sons?'

'I know, I know, My Lord Duke,' Dancey commiserated, 'it is abominable and it calls for sanctions.'

'So what is your King waiting for? I am prepared to go to France to tell him the truth and beg for his assistance. My wife was once his sister-in-law and he cannot abandon her to the hands of traitors who have shown not the least regard for her.'

'Indeed,' the Ambassador repeated, 'when the King acts he will not spare his enemies. Nevertheless, France is in great turmoil just now due to the expansion of the Protestant faith. People are volatile and intolerant and we all fear bloody confrontation.'

'That did not happen in Scotland, as the Queen managed to introduce freedom of religious practice.'

'At the expense of Catholicism My Lord Duke, do not forget that.

Protestantism was recognised as the state religion in your country. His Holiness the Pope as well as the King of Spain strongly repudiated this decision, for which they possibly quite wrongly hold you responsible.'

'So,' James murmured, 'politics come before ties of friendship or of blood.'

'Provisionally My Lord Duke, but I suggest that you yourself write to His Majesty. The King and I give you my word of honour that your letter will leave for Paris tonight. Personal bonds are worth more than any messenger's words or ambassador's reports.'

James had managed to calm down. However, Frederick II's absence, the prohibition on leaving the castle and the lack of news from Mary was all very hard for him to bear.

'You will get this letter before nightfall, Monsieur L'Ambassadeur. A copy will be made for His Majesty King Frederick II.'

'If I may give you some advice,' Dancey interrupted, 'send one of your servants to the King of Denmark. His Majesty will then be able to make known his decision or intention.'

The old gentleman was forcibly struck by Bothwell's determined expression when he asserted,

'If his intention is to keep me against my will Monsieur, I will then consider myself free to do as I please.'

The letter left for Paris, and at the same time one of the five men still in Bothwell's service was on his way to Elsinore where the King was staying. Peter Oxe had added a message of his own to the one written by the prisoner. He had conversed at length with James and could not decide whether he was innocent or guilty. Yet whatever the case might be, a doubt had been cast on the messages that had come from Edinburgh accusing him of treason and all kinds of villainies. At the end of his own letter, Oxe added that the temperament of the Duke of Orkney did not suit house arrest, and given the man's courage and intelligence, he feared that eventually he would succeed in regaining his freedom. A transfer to the fortress of Malmö would perhaps be wise. There he would be well treated and they could keep a close eye on him.

Frederick II's two replies arrived simultaneously. To Bothwell in a letter dictated to his secretary he spoke of his sympathy for him, and of his wish for him to stay in Denmark for a while so that he might protect and help him. To Oxe in a letter written in his own hand, he gave the authorisation to transport the Duke by boat to the castle of Malmö. At the bottom of the letter, the King's secretary had added as a postscript:

The Duke's apartments will be on the first floor below those of His Majesty. Make sure that our guest enjoys all conveniences, but also see that the bars of the windows are in good order and indestructible, in order to render any escape impossible.

60

BEFORE LEAVING COPENHAGEN for the fortress in Malmö, Bothwell had written a long account in French to the King of France, explaining the reasons for his journey as well as his relationship with those in Scotland who had declared themselves his mortal enemies.

In the detailed chronicle he told him about the death of Darnley, his own marriage to the Queen, and the treason committed by those whom she had honoured yet forgiven, and to whom she had shown the greatest clemency. Some fifty pages long, the narrative had been dictated to a secretary and corrected in his own hand. He had received no reply from the King of France.

In Malmö James's new apartments faced south, and comprised a large vaulted chamber, a smaller one adjacent to it, a garderobe, and the beginnings of a corridor which had been walled up. He had been forced to part with the five loyal servants who had previously accompanied him, and now had only French Paris and a Scot named William Murray to look after his needs and remind him of the past.

The Frenchman was free to go outside, and he had given his master a detailed report on the size of the garrison and the presence of a guard-room next to their accommodation. Everything combined to make escape difficult if not impossible.

'Well then I must try some other means to obtain my freedom,' James mused aloud to himself. 'The King of Denmark will not be allowed to forget me, as I shall write to him today to protest once more against being unlawfully detained. They will have to cut my hands off in order to silence me. Every bargain must be mutually satisfactory, so in return for my freedom I shall propose to His Majesty the restitution of the islands of Orkney and Shetland to Denmark.'

Listening to him French Paris commented, 'Moray will oppose it.'

'He may, but the Queen will sign and secure my release.'

Just before leaving Copenhagen, an anonymous agent delivered to him a letter from Mary, who had started to feel more hopeful again about their future.

The youngest son of her gaoler Lady Douglas had shown affection for her, thus enabling the Queen to receive news from outside Lochleven Castle. She hoped that with his help she would be able to correspond regularly with her husband. In her recent letter, she entreated him to try by every means possible to obtain his own freedom, assuring him that she would approve any political proposal he might make to achieve this. She insisted that her abdication was worthless, having been gained under duress, and that the Queen's signature still bore the weight of the law.

Although only seven months had elapsed since their separation at Carberry Hill, James felt as though he had been parted from Mary for an eternity. Often as he tried to conjure up the elegant woman with her spirited eyes and bewitching smile, the image of the fallen Queen clad in a peasant girl's stained red dress and bodice, her face marked with tears and dust, came back into his mind. Was he to blame for her downfall and captivity? James refused to believe it. Mary's ruin had been decided between Moray and Cecil soon after her return to Scotland. One out of ambition; the other to protect England from the threat of a Catholic rebellion, and to silence an heir apparent who was too arrogant. James had arrived on the scene too late in Mary Stuart's life. Had they been married soon after her investiture on the throne of Scotland, their destiny might well have turned out differently.

James noticed bitterly that he spent more and more time reliving the past. Did he consider he had come to the end of the road? His anxiety gave way to anger.

He was well treated at Malmö, where they supplied him with plenty of firewood, wine and good meals. He dressed in velvet and fine linen and had his own barber, tailor, apothecary, and the company of French Paris, who had become a friend more than a servant. However, the thick bars sealing the windows and the walled-in corridor reminded him constantly of his status as prisoner.

French Paris would return to the fortress with the latest news circulating in the town of Malmö. Sometimes by chance, he would meet a merchant or Scottish mercenary who told him the latest news about his country. The Regent was tightening his grip, the Borders were being ruthlessly cleansed, Parliament was subdued and the Queen's supporters silenced.

James, in bewilderment at the news, placed his face between his hands, and closing his eyes let his mind wander over the sunlit moors, the firths and lochs of his beloved Scotland. He saw the fleeting shadows of his dreams, then the darkness of the night, leading to oblivion and death. Opening his eyes again, he saw the grey light of the courtyard, the low cloud ceiling, and a still landscape with neither horizon nor future.

At the end of January Dancey paid another visit to James. The short crossing from Copenhagen had been rough, and the old man was not feeling well. After warming himself at the hearth and drinking a glass of schnapps, the French Ambassador handed Bothwell a letter bearing the Danish royal seal. Frederick II was interested in the Duke's offer of the restitution of the islands of Orkney and Shetland, and would find a way of sending the documents to Lochleven for the Queen's perusal and ratification. In his letter the King made a polite enquiry about the Duke's health, and hoped that according to his instructions his needs were being satisfied. However, there was never a mention of any future meeting.

James carefully folded the letter, which had now given him a glimmer of hope. Backed into a corner, Moray would have no alternative but to give in and return those islands to the Danes, or risk instigating a conflict over them. Bothwell's reward would be his freedom.

Dancey lingered for a while longer, delighted to converse with this cultivated man who spoke such impeccable French. Unfortunately, he had to confess that he had not yet received a reply from the French King to the letter the Duke had sent him some ten weeks earlier. He was however hopeful that Christmas festivities might have delayed the royal correspondence. On the other hand, he had received confirmation that Charles IX would never consent to his extradition to Scotland. The King of Spain had adopted a similar stance, but Queen Elizabeth was still insisting that her cousin's husband be delivered to her, maintaining he would be given a fair trial.

'If you want my opinion,' the old Ambassador ventured to comment, 'you are better off here than in London.'

From news gleaned from his letters from Paris Dancey enthusiastically told James of various happenings and events in the French capital. The pleasures of court life had been affected by persistent religious conflicts. A Scotsman named Stuart had killed Constable Anne de Montmorency during the battle of the Saint-Denis plain. Montmorency had belonged to the royal family, hence a Mass for him had been celebrated with great pomp at Notre Dame in Paris. The body of the Constable had been interred at Montmorency, and his heart placed next to that of Henri II in the Church of the Celestins. The general lieutenancy of the realm had been entrusted to the Duc d'Anjou, the future King Henri III, who was likely to clash very soon with the Prince de Condé.

James listened eagerly to Dancey's tales. Protestants and Catholics were coming to blows, stirred up by their priests, pastors or grands seigneurs, who were keen to settle old quarrels and put an end to tenacious and long held ambitions. He himself had always shown great religious tolerance, and would never contribute to the intrigues of the agitators.

The Ambassador left at nightfall. Left alone James grew depressed. Outside the castle, the wind blew in gusts, driving the rain against his windowpanes and blowing smoke from the hearth back into his room. Supper would soon be served, then to avoid brooding on the past he would empty a carafe of cherry spirit.

Until the arrival of spring, the Earl's life revolved around the news he received from Scotland. Moray was insisting on his extradition, and alternatively suggested that he be executed at Malmö without trial. Frederick II refused categorically, protesting that his honour forbade him to execute a nobleman under his protection. For the first time France officially expressed her wish for the Duke of Orkney not to be sent back to Scotland.

James alternated between losing and regaining hope. Gradually his drive and impulses became numbed. He stayed in bed longer in the mornings and had himself shaved and dressed just before eleven o'clock, when the first main meal of the day was served. From time to time he had a few visitors, some of whom were Frenchmen and Scotsmen passing through Malmö, eager to meet the famous husband of Mary Queen of Scots. Some merchants visited as well, selling lace, buttons and doublet frills. Others were pastors whom he dismissed summarily without giving them a chance to lecture him, but the librarians who came he received with real interest.

In May, James found pleasure in gazing at the cherry blossom flowering on the only tree he could see from his windows. In the spring weather, the sky was a cloudless pale blue, and down in the courtyard of the castle, maids sang as they went about their tasks. Children laughed with excitement as they played ball while soldiers sat and basked in the sunshine.

The arrival of a horseman attracted the Duke's attention. His mount was a spirited fine-boned thoroughbred with broad chest and gleaming coat. James would have given anything to ride such an animal and gallop away into the distance. He longed for the flowing movement of a horse between his legs and the feel of the wind on his face.

The horseman dismounted and talked for a long time to the captain of the guard, a tall fair-haired soldier who exercised a strong discipline over his men. Finally, he indicated the door that led to the King's and James's apartments. Could it be that Frederick II was coming to Malmö?

The horseman inclined his head, 'I have come from Scotland, my Lord, with a letter for you.'

The man spoke with a Lothians accent. James was seized with a strange emotion, and when he looked at him questioningly, the horseman smiled and nodded his head.

'Let your Lordship read the letter for himself,' he urged.

James unfolded the piece of paper, and at once recognised Mary's handwriting.

I have managed to escape from Lochleven Castle, my sweet love.
I am free! Friends are arriving from all directions to join me,
and I am hopeful to be able to make my entry into Edinburgh
before long. I will send for you immediately. I have too little time
to pour out all the feelings of my heart. Be sure that I think of
nothing except victory and you, whose loving and faithful wife
I remain forever.

Upon reading her letter, James was so overwhelmed with emotion that he had to sit down, his head spinning. He was suddenly filled with enormous joy. Soon he would leave this fortress with his head held high. He would embark on a ship bound for Scotland and be reunited with Mary, his mother and his sister. Once again, he would see Hermitage, Hailes and his own people; everything he loved, and from which he could not bear to be separated, even if for the sake of his sanity he had forbidden himself to think about them.

At that moment, the bolts on the door to his past were gradually giving way.

'When did you leave Scotland?' he asked the messenger.

'Ten days ago, my Lord. The Queen was on her way to the castle of the Hamiltons who came to meet her, together with the Earl of Argyll, the Setons, Livingstone, Huntly, and your cousin Alexander Hepburn of Riccarton, who was entrusted with recapturing the fortress of Dunbar for Her Majesty. Her Majesty may well be at Holyrood right now.'

Every day James waited impatiently for the announcement of his liberation, and he was ready to leave at a moment's notice. French Paris and William Murray had packed his belongings, and he had filed his correspondence before locking it away in a leather case. Now even the grey weather seemed glorious to him, and the dismal outlook over the courtyard of the fortress almost pleasing. The cherry tree had now come into full leaf and birds were nesting in its branches.

One day Dancey entered James's chamber, his ivory complexion unusually flushed. The little man was so agitated that he lost his stick, and bumped into the backrest of a chair when trying to pick it up.

'My Lord,' he exclaimed in an anguished voice, 'I have come with all speed from Copenhagen, where I received some very distressing news.'

The old Ambassador's sudden arrival had put James on the alert. He had had to deal with so many ordeals in his life that he had learned to anticipate fate's nasty blows.

What had he come to say to him? Had Mary been recaptured?

'What have you come to tell me?' he asked apprehensively. 'Have you brought bad news?'

Dancey collapsed into a chair and took off his hat, which he continued to hold in his hands.

'All is lost, my Lord Duke,' he said at once. 'The army of Her Majesty the Queen of Scots was heavily defeated at Langside by the Earl of Moray's army commanded by Kirkaldy of Grange.'

James once more felt the blood draining from his veins, and no coherent thought came into his mind.

'Defeated,' he repeated to himself mechanically. He could not believe it.

'Crushed, my Lord, despite having superiority of both men and arms. They lacked a general, and the Queen's troops were badly led, and routed in disorder. The Earl of Argyll was taken ill during the combat, and, deprived of their Chief, his clansmen left the field of battle. Lord Seton and the Bishop of Leslie were both captured, but your friend Sir David Chalmers managed to escape.'

'And the Queen?' Bothwell interrupted him.

'The Queen fled to Dumfries with the Lords Herries, Maxwell, Fleming, Livingstone and about twelve other loyal men. She wishes to go to England.'

'That's impossible!' exclaimed Bothwell in horror.

'My Lord, her supporters begged her to sail to France, but according to the most recent news I have received from Monsieur du Croc the Queen has indeed crossed the Solway Firth and is now in Carlisle Castle.'

James paced up and down his room like a wild animal.

'At the mercy of her enemies! Good Lord, has the Queen lost her mind?'

Was what he had just heard part of some terrible nightmare?

Gradually his thoughts cleared and Dancey's words took shape in his mind. Argyll seemed once again to have acted like a man who would not risk his future by being on the losing side. Yet what about her other supporters? Claude Hamilton, the Lords Fleming, Livingstone, Seton and Herries? How could they have allowed their greater military strength to be overcome without a real battle? Was there not one amongst them with red blood in his veins?

'I am distraught at bringing you this terrible news,' Dancey said in an agonised voice.

James was no longer listening. His thoughts were filled with Mary, and her catastrophic decision to throw herself into the arms of her cousin Elizabeth and her enemies in England, when she could have sailed to France and lived there in comfort and safely on her prosperous estates, where the Guise family would always support her.

Had she not for one second considered that her presence in England would infuriate Cecil and annoy Queen Elizabeth? A hundred times he had stressed to her that her half-brother Moray walked hand in hand with the English. Had she never believed him? Had she forgotten that when she was Queen of France she had added the arms of England to her blazon? It was an aggressive decision, which had acutely offended the daughter of Anne Boleyn, whose legitimacy it thereby contested. How could she ever have conceived that a Protestant sovereign would impose a Catholic sovereign on a nation that had fully espoused the Reformation?

In his despair, Bothwell also felt a passionate desire to shatter the bolts sealing his apartments, break free, strike down anyone in his way and find a ship on which to embark for England. If he could reach Carlisle, all would not yet be lost. He would rescue Mary and make for Dumbarton Castle, where they would barricade themselves in and reorganise a strong supporters' army.

'By the blood of Christ!' he shouted. 'Give me a sword, a horse and a ship, and I will restore the throne to my wife.'

'Alas, alas!' was all Dancey could find to say.

The old gentleman was appalled. In the aftermath of defeat and fleeing the enemy, Mary Stuart's decision had been all too hastily made and lacked any reflection.

Through diplomatic channels, he knew that if the Queen had chosen to go to back to France, Catherine de Medicis, once over the shock, would not have turned her back on Mary who had been her daughter-in-law, and all the Guises would have been ready to help her.

'Her Majesty gave in to panic,' he felt obliged to offer as explanation. 'A battle lost does not mean the end of the struggle. For the Queen this is only the beginning. '

'The Queen,' James said bitterly, 'has fought non-stop since her arrival in Scotland. No other sovereign has had to face a more difficult situation. If only Moray had been executed after his first rebellion, events in Scotland would have taken a different course.'

'One cannot so easily do away with a close relative, my Lord.'

James was not in the mood to argue.

'A Queen sometimes needs to make decisions which are contrary to her own feelings! If she had listened to me, Maitland too would have been done away with. '

'Her Secretary of State is on excellent terms with William Cecil,' Dancey replied.

With a violent gesture, James swept away the glasses and the carafe of Cyprus wine placed on the table.

'Those two wretches have done nothing but fuel discord between the two Queens. I consider them the prime instigators of the tragedy which now faces us.'

Standing in front of one of the windows, James was trying to shake loose one of the solid bars, but to no avail. Dancey felt nothing but pity for this passionate and intelligent man, who was condemned to solitary imprisonment, and soon to oblivion.

If the Queen of England, instead of helping her cousin recover her throne, kept her in England against her will, who would remember her husband the Duke of Orkney? He believed King Frederick II was sufficiently humane not to hand him over to the Scottish axe. Nevertheless, having lost all political value the prisoner would now become more and more neglected, and the walls of his prison would become a tomb.

'Allow me to take my leave, my Lord Duke,' he said gently, 'as I must return to Copenhagen today, but I will come back to see you as soon as possible.'

Still standing in front of the window James did not move. Probably he had not heard a single word.

'Farewell my Lord Duke,' the old Ambassador said as he left the room.

The prisoner did not turn round.

61

JAMES OBSTINATELY REFUSED to allow himself to be discouraged. Every day before seeing the barber, he summoned his secretary to dictate correspondence, which most of the time did not leave Malmö. Then he read and ate his meal served by French Paris or William Murray, before preparing to receive any visitors who might come to call on him, such as the governor, the commander of the garrison, or some other local notable. After that, he studied maps, pored over battle strategies and tried to exercise his intellect by thinking up different tactics. He frequently relived that fatal day at Carberry Hill, and in his mind positioned his soldiers ready to launch the attack, with the firing of the cannons, followed by a charge from the right wing supported by light cavalry. Had things gone according to plan, they would have won the day, and Kirkaldy would have had no chance with his battalion of badly trained mercenaries and militia hastily recruited in Edinburgh. Then he folded his maps away, waited for his supper to be served and drank himself into oblivion, collapsing onto his bed in a drunken stupor.

With the return of spring, James had a sudden desire to acquire new books and certain maps that he lacked. He also looked forward to a delivery at Malmö about which French Paris had told him, of a consignment of whisky, oatmeal biscuits, and honey, sent all the way from Scotland.

It promised to be a beautiful day. James could see gulls and terns circling in the cloudless blue sky. Through his window, borne on the light breeze, wafted the scents of spring, of apple blossom, fresh thyme and seaweed newly washed up on the shore by the latest tide. In May two years ago, he and Mary had been married in the great hall of the Palace of Holyrood. At that moment his head had been brimming with projects and desires, and plans for the future of Scotland. He loved the Queen, and she was deeply in love and had totally given herself to him, body and soul. She was pregnant with his child, who would come second after little James in the order of succession to the throne of Scotland. His friends were gathering round him in support, while his enemies bided their time and remained silent. Over the past year, events had moved fast, their luck had run out and their enemies had gained the upper hand. Mary's escape from Lochleven had given him new hope, and in his mind he had already slammed the doors of Malmö behind him. Now his last remaining hope was for a trial in Denmark before an impartial jury with credible witnesses. However, the preliminary negotiations concerning the islands of Orkney and Shetland had come to an abrupt end, and the King could not make up his mind whether or not to hold a trial. Some days Peter Oxe would assure him he was seriously considering it, and other days that the King had no right to judge a subject of the Queen of Scots for a crime that had not been committed in his realm.

Despite repeated requests from Regent Moray, the King was not contemplating Bothwell's extradition to Scotland. He was inclined to listen to his close German relatives, who had advised him not to take any action for the time being but to be patient and await the turn of events. Now he refused even to answer the Regent's pressing letters.

'I will see you later, my Lord,' called out French Paris as he firmly fixed a red satin beret onto his head, 'I will be back before nightfall with a large flask of whisky, a box of biscuits, and the books you ordered from Mr Petersen.'

'Go,' James told him, 'and if you go chasing after the girls, don't spend my money.'

He would use the first half of his afternoon to write to Mary. The Earl of Shrewsbury and his redoubtable thrice-widowed wife Bess of Hardwick now had charge of the Queen at Sheffield Castle. Mary was waiting for a final judgement to be pronounced in the action brought against her by the Scottish lords.

James knew that the Duke of Norfolk had written to Mary as a prospective suitor, and that she had not rejected him outright. His help was so precious, she had explained, that she could not alienate him in anyway. When she wrote back to him, the terms of affection she used were only a lure to attain her own ends, she assured James. Once she had regained her freedom, she would not offer him anything beyond friendship.

As the months passed by the words of passion that Mary used in her letters were becoming less frequent. She still swore she would love her husband until her dying day, but the memory of their embraces must have been fading, as she mentioned them less often and in more modest terms. Little by little, James sensed he was becoming no more to her than a precious memory and an image which helped her bear her imprisonment. His physical presence in her mind and his power to make her dream were fading. She too sometimes seemed so remote to him that he struggled to remember the little peculiarities he loved about her body: a beauty spot, a red mark, fine blond downy hair. Only the light in her eyes and the charm of her smile were unforgettable.

As usual, French Paris slammed the door noisily behind him. William Murray was already waiting in the courtyard and James heard the Frenchman's hurried footsteps running down the staircase. He was grateful to his two servants for remaining loyal to him. There was no pleasure for them in life at Malmö, but both had sworn not to leave him for as long as he remained a prisoner there. James sat down at his desk.

What was the likelihood that he would stay in Denmark for as long as Moray lived?

He wrote on, and told Mary again about his hope that a trial would soon take place. He was not in any doubt about the verdict. Once free, he would go to France and find the Guises. The convictions which he had formulated and gone over in his mind countless times were beginning now to lose their power. Did he still believe implicitly in them or was he merely playing with words? Yet without something to hope for what else could stop him from going mad? His body was deteriorating, his muscles were wasting away, his skin, normally tanned from exposure to the open air, had now become pale, and a few grey hairs had appeared on his temples and in his thin beard. His quill hesitated over the page when he tried to express his tenderness. How could he say to a woman that he was missing her, and admit that he had not made the most of his love for her while living with her?

Having finished the letter James sealed it carefully. Young George Douglas, who had followed Mary to England from Lochleven, was a safe means of communication between them. Nevertheless, for how much longer would their letters escape the vigilance of their gaolers and Moray and Queen Elizabeth's spies?

It was well into the afternoon, but his servants had still not returned. They were most likely trifling their time away in the port, and he could not hold it against them. If they took too long, all he had to do was knock on his door and Danish servants would come running to do his bidding.

James was careful to conceal the letter in a hiding place between two stones at the base of the wall. Tomorrow French Paris or William would take it to a Scottish merchant who twice a month added the Malmö correspondence to his cargo sailing for Ipswich.

Although he had tried every means to put it out of his mind, the reality of the correspondence between his wife and the Duke of Norfolk brought back an acute feeling of powerlessness, and he felt consumed by jealousy. Any woman who belonged to him must neither trifle with another man nor even look at him too intently. The weakness of passionate and impulsive beings like Mary was their need to please. Perhaps it was just because Jean was independent and matter of fact that he had grown fond of her.

By nightfall, James had started to worry over the non-appearance of his servants. It was almost time for the evening meal, and never before had French Paris failed to serve him his supper in person.

The Danish valet he summoned was unable to tell him anything. All he knew was that the two Scotsmen, as he called them, had not reappeared at the fortress.

'Call the governor,' the prisoner ordered him curtly.

It took two days of enquiries to find out that French Paris had been abducted in the quiet part of the city by two strangers. William Murray had managed to escape, and must have been hiding out somewhere.

James was devastated to hear of the fate of the one who had served him for so many years, in times of fine living as well as of hardship and adversity. He knew they would take the unfortunate Frenchman back to Scotland and torture him barbarously, just to make him confess anything and everything, truth and lies, the plausible and the absurd.

For several days, incapable of accepting his powerlessness to take any action, James alternated between rage and apathy. Up until then he had continued to have faith in himself, in his resilience and his fighting spirit. As a child he had seen his mother leave, later he had known exile, been separated from friends and mistresses, and finally his wife had been torn from him. Now the loss of a mere servant affected him profoundly and brought down the tower he had thought was indestructible. With the loss of French Paris, he felt the whole of his past had disappeared, and he was now a man without links or heritage, existing in a kind of living death.

Time elapsed and James gave up counting the passing of the days. He was served by Danish valets, read books, and spent long periods of time standing in front of his windows watching the comings and goings of servants, soldiers and visitors in the courtyard of the castle. It was only when he received news from outside, conveyed to him by a Scottish mercenary in the service of the King of Denmark, that he became roused from his state of indifference. Once again, Moray had attacked the Borders. With his customary brutality, he had ordered the hanging, drowning, or life imprisonment in filthy dungeons of many of those familiar to James. Their crimes were insubordination and a taste for plunder, but also courage and an unquenchable thirst for freedom.

At the end of August, he was informed of the execution of French Paris without trial. They had dragged the wretched man straight from the torture chamber to the scaffold where he had been hanged, no doubt to prevent him from retracting confessions extracted at the cost of the most horrible suffering.

James wept. His courage was failing him and he was haunted by the unbearable prospect of remaining a prisoner for the rest of his life.

One day when it was snowing heavily and the sky was so low it seemed almost to wrap itself round the walls of the castle, James heard a tapping at his door. The Scottish mercenary entered with a broad smile on his face.

'The Regent has been murdered my Lord! It is rumoured that it was the Hamiltons who armed the murderer.'

James let out a wild cry of triumph. So Moray had finally met his punishment. He dressed immediately and asked for paper and ink. He would write to his cousins and to the Queen, make new plans, and revive his faith in the future. From now on, the mercenary would take care of his mail; God was helping him, and his light had not been totally extinguished.

The governor was able to provide him with more details: Moray had been stabbed by a cousin of the Hamiltons, to whom Mary Stuart had granted a pension for life as a token of her gratitude. The Earls of

Northumberland and Westmoreland had tried to raise a rebellion in support of Mary Queen of Scots, but it had been brutally crushed; the former had fled and the latter had been captured, but Westmoreland's wife, who had sought refuge in Scotland, had been taken in by the Kerrs.

'I fear, my Lord,' the governor concluded coldly, 'that it is England that is in charge of the situation in Scotland, and it is said the Earl of Lennox is to be elected Regent.'

The months passed, and James more often than not wore his house robe all day long. News of Lennox's murder barely provoked any reaction from him, neither did the peaceful death of John Knox, who in the past had stirred up so many souls against him in the name of God and justice.

He no longer received any letters from Mary. Was she under close watch, had she forgotten him, or worse, did she now regret ever having loved and married him?

Spring had come round again. What spring? Feeling no emotion, James opened his windows protected by the thick metal bars, and let the sun stream onto him like a warm caress.

When the governor suddenly burst into his room, James knew at once that he had come to break bad news.

'Tell me the worst, governor,' he demanded immediately. 'There is little now that can make much difference to me.'

The Dane seemed ill at ease.

'News has come that your mother Lady Sinclair is dead, my Lord Duke.' For a long time James remained motionless as if frozen, then suddenly as though animated by an uncontrollable force, a terrible rage took over his body and mind and he went berserk. He threw the furniture around, turned over the table and chairs, smashed the china jars, hurled the pewter plates against the walls and ransacked the library. When the governor tried to calm him down James leapt on him and tried to strangle him. It took the strength of five men to overpower him.

The announcement of the surrender of Kirkaldy of Grange and Maitland, who had been holding Edinburgh Castle for the past month on behalf of Mary Stuart, left James totally unmoved. Kirkaldy had been beheaded and Maitland had taken poison. 'The rats are devouring each other,' was all he would say to the Scottish mercenary, who observed the Duke with pity. The violence he had demonstrated the previous week had now classed him as dangerous. He would soon be transferred to Dragsholm, a fortress lost in the north of Jutland, where it was said to be on the edge of the world. Once there, he would never leave that grim place, and would be forever erased from the world of the living.

62

Early April 1578

JAMES HAS A burning fever and is failing. He calls for his mother, for Janet and for Mary. Cold damp air seeps in underneath the window. James has thrown the soiled sheets onto the ground and wrapped himself in a blanket. His teeth are chattering with cold. Someone is trying to make him swallow a few drops of greasy broth. It trickles down his beard, which no one now takes the trouble to trim. He struggles and screams, resisting the efforts of a man trying to turn him over. They leave him to his own devices.

He tries to smile, as he is going to be alone when those he has dreamed of come to fetch him. They are coming to get him out of this putrid hole where he has been rotting for five years and will take him away for good from the shackles, soiled straw, fetid water and decaying food. They will give him back the light, the open spaces, the smells, the sounds, the rain, the wind, the flowers on the banks of the Tyne. They will take him back to where his loved ones are all waiting for him; his mother, his uncle Patrick Hepburn of Spynie, his cousins and his friends, French Paris too with his cheeky humour and sudden impulses, and Ormiston, who always kept a flask of whisky for him when he went to visit him at his estates, which lay between Hermitage and Langholm in the Borders.

James manages to straighten himself and stares at the door, which he knows will soon be opened. He will stand up and go through. There will be no guard and no spy. He will be allowed to proceed peacefully towards the courtyard and pass through the entrance gate, which is always open during the day. Then he will make his way down to the sunlit sea where a ship is waiting for him with sails unfurled, ready to raise anchor to set sail for Scotland, his country and the land of his ancestors, which he has always defended and cherished. Then finally, he will be free.

Postscript

TO THIS DAY, the numerous requests made by the head of the Hepburn family and various associations to obtain the return of the body of James Hepburn, Earl of Bothwell, to Scotland, have remained unanswered by the Danish authorities. The prisoner's body still rests in the little church of Faarevejle in the vicinity of Dragsholm Castle.

Sir Alastair Buchan-Hepburn's proposal for a DNA test in order to formally identify the remains of his ancestor has also been ignored.

The fervent patriot who was James, Earl of Bothwell, can therefore not rest in his own country, which he never ceased to love and defend.

Addendum to Postscript

November 2010

WHAT WAS WRITTEN by the author, Catherine Hermary-Vieille, in her postscript in January 2006, was completely accurate at that time.

The Danish Government has since then stipulated that the request for the return of the remains of James Hepburn, fourth Earl of Bothwell for Christian burial in Scotland is a matter of national importance and not a family matter, due to his significance in history. They therefore require a direct approach from the Scottish Government, requesting them to consider returning the remains, if and when their specified conditions were met.

The Hepburn family and their associations, the Bothwell Society, the Stuart societies, Members of the Scottish Parliament, also individuals from around the world including France, Germany, Austria, Italy, Spain, Denmark, Sweden, Norway, United States, Canada, Australia, New Zealand, Tasmania, India, Egypt, South Africa, Kenya, Brazil and Mexico have written to two successive Scottish Governments. They have asked them to take this preliminary action to rescue this Scottish hero and patriot from Denmark where he still rests, after having been betrayed and condemned to a terrible end in a dungeon, without trial and without being guilty of any crime. The responsibility for this cruel death, and for the imprisonment and execution of Mary Queen of Scots, lies with those governing Scotland at that time. Let not further guilt lie with the present-day Scottish Government for doing nothing, by not answering the calls for Bothwell's return to Scotland and a Christian burial, thus assuaging at least in part the guilt of the Government and Regent in power at that time.

Today, those families whose ancestors were involved in those acts also wish to see James Hepburn's remains returned to Scotland and buried as a Scottish hero and patriot, the last Consort and husband of the last Queen of Scotland.

It is hoped that this book, now translated into English, will awaken the Scottish Government and their advisers Historic Scotland to the world-wide support for Bothwell's remains to be returned to Scotland, and to the simple but fundamental request of the Danish Government to make direct contact about it with them.

The Hepburn family are poised and ready to fulfil the other requests asked of it by the Danish Government, once the Scottish government meets the primary demand they make concerning the return of James Hepburn, the fourth Earl of Bothwell's remains to Scotland.

Sir Alastair Buchan-Hepburn

Luath Press Limited

committed to publishing well written books worth reading

LUATH PRESS takes its name from Robert Burns, whose little collie Luath (*Gael.*, swift or nimble) tripped up Jean Armour at a wedding and gave him the chance to speak to the woman who was to be his wife and the abiding love of his life. Burns called one of 'The Twa Dogs' Luath after Cuchullin's hunting dog in Ossian's *Fingal*. Luath Press was established in 1981 in the heart of Burns country, and now resides a few steps up the road from Burns' first lodgings on Edinburgh's Royal Mile.

Luath offers you distinctive writing with a hint of unexpected pleasures.

Most bookshops in the UK, the US, Canada, Australia, New Zealand and parts of Europe either carry our books in stock or can order them for you. To order direct from us, please send a £sterling cheque, postal order, international money order or your credit card details (number, address of cardholder and expiry date) to us at the address below. Please add post and packing as follows: UK – £1.00 per delivery address; overseas surface mail – £2.50 per delivery address; overseas airmail – £3.50 for the first book to each delivery address, plus £1.00 for each additional book by airmail to the same address. If your order is a gift, we will happily enclose your card or message at no extra charge.

Luath Press Limited
543/2 Castlehill
The Royal Mile
Edinburgh EH1 2ND
Scotland
Telephone: 0131 225 4326 (24 hours)
Fax: 0131 225 4324
email: sales@luath.co.uk
Website: www.luath.co.uk